NIGHT GAME

Praise for *Shell Games,* the first John Marquez crime novel

"Russell drops readers directly into the action on the craggy North Coast, carving a new niche in crime writing with an environmental edge. . . . Once hooked by *Shell Games,* readers may find themselves wanting to buy this guy Marquez a drink just to keep him talking."

—*San Francisco Chronicle*

"A large part of the considerable strength of Kirk Russell's first mystery novel (along with his clear and pungent writing, especially about the primal weirdness of life along the Mendocino coast) comes from the way he makes us quickly believe in Marquez and his cause . . ."

—*Chicago Tribune*

"Loaded with atmosphere . . . The bad guys are as colorful as Elmore Leonard's cast of wise guys."

—*Kirkus Reviews*

"The prose is clean and smooth, the setting fresh and appealing, and Marquez . . . is a solid protagonist who could easily carry a series."

—*The Denver Post*

"Excellent . . . a compelling plot, fully realized characters, white-knuckle suspense, and unusual yet accessible settings. What truly sets it apart, though, is Kirk Russell's vigorous, lovely, unadorned prose. *Shell Games* marks the debut of a substantial new talent in crime fiction."

—John Lescroart

"*Shell Games* integrates spellbinding suspense into a wonderfully unpredictable plot that holds the reader hostage to the very last page."

—Ridley Pearson

"Compelling characters, unrelenting suspense, and vivid settings all add up to a great read. Kirk Russell's *Shell Games* is so well-crafted, it's hard to believe it's a first novel."

—Jan Burke

"You know as you read this one that you are on to something good. Kirk Russell comes out of the gate with a story brimming with fresh characters and artful prose. *Shell Games* announces the start of what I think will be a great career."

—Michael Connelly

A JOHN MARQUEZ CRIME NOVEL

NIGHTGAME

KIRK RUSSELL

CHRONICLE BOOKS

SAN FRANCISCO

First Chronicle Books LLC paperback edition, published in 2005.

This is a work of fiction. Names, places, characters, and incidents are products of the author's imagination or are used fictionally. Any resemblance to actual people, places, or events is entirely coincidental.

ISBN 0-8118-5044-7

The Library of Congress has cataloged the previous edition as follows:
Russell, Kirk, 1954–
  Night game : a John Marquez crime novel / Kirk Russell.
    p. cm.
  ISBN 0-8118-4112-X
1. California. Dept. of Fish and Game–Fiction. 2. Government investigators–Fiction. 3. Bear hunting–Fiction. 4. California–Fiction. 5. Poaching–Fiction. 6. Poachers–Fiction. I. Title.
  PS3618.U76N54 2004
  813'.6–dc22
                              2004012040

Manufactured in the United States of America

Designed by tom & john: a design collaborative
Composition by Kristen Wurz
Cover photo by Getty Images

Distributed in Canada by Raincoast Books
9050 Shaughnessy Street
Vancouver, British Columbia V6P 6E5

10 9 8 7 6 5 4 3 2 1

Chronicle Books LLC
85 Second Street
San Francisco, California 94105
www.chroniclebooks.com

In memory of my father, James Kirkendall Russell

1

Beneath the trees the light faded and wind cut through his coat. He climbed the steep trail, hiked through another long switchbacking turn, then saw them standing near an outcrop, silhouetted by red-orange sky. Both men turned to watch him. Even from here he could tell it was the same pair.

When he reached them, Marquez looked first at the bearded man, then at the bullet-headed kid. "Tell me again, why it is we can't do these deals in a warm bar?"

"Let's just get it done," the beard said and clicked on a small flashlight.

Earlier this afternoon their seller, the man Marquez's under-cover team couldn't seem to get close to, had lingered on the line, a voice changer mechanically flattening his tone as he bragged about being better than the Chinese at bear farming, though the Chinese had been at it for more than a thousand years. Marquez had seen photos of bears living out their lives in cramped cages. He'd watched videos on the Internet of bears banging their heads against cage bars, catheters running from their abdomens to milk bile juices. The traditional method was a knife gash to open the bear's abdomen. Bile dripped through cage bars onto collection plates. Ounce for ounce, the bile on the plates was worth more than cocaine. But until this seller Marquez had never heard of bear farming in California or anywhere in the States.

The beard produced a couple of small, dark glass bottles and sprinkled bile powder onto Marquez's palm. The thin flashlight beam caught the powder sifting. The fiber-optic line feeding the camcorder sewn into Marquez's coat recorded everything.

"I need to meet the man you're working for," Marquez said. "I want to see these bear farms."

The beard shook his head. "Come on, man, let's not do this tonight."

Bullet-head said, "This is bullshit."

Marquez turned to him. "Look, I've got clients with cancer." "It matters that these farms are clean. I've got to know it's not coming out of some backwoods rat hole."

The beard answered for him. "He means we don't know where he keeps the bears. Like we told you last time."

Marquez got the money roll out, snapped the rubber bands off. He'd done five deals with this pair and believed them when they claimed they'd never seen the man they worked for. He recorded the beard pocketing the cash, then pulling a CD from the same pocket.

"What's this?"

"Supposed to give it to you."

"Yeah, but what is it?"

Neither answered.

Bullet-head started drifting away and the beard followed him. Marquez put the CD in his coat and cut back to the main trail. After rounding the first bend he called Carol Shauf, one of the wardens on his Fish and Game undercover team. She was hidden near the gravel road running over Barker Pass, positioned to cover his exit.

"I'm dropping down the trail."

"Hold up," she said. "I've got movement on the slope up off to your right."

"I'm less than a hundred yards from the car. I'll be there in under two minutes."

"I see you, but hang on, Lieutenant. There's someone up on the slope in the trees to your right. Wait until I get another look."

"Probably a hiker."

Her voice tensed. "It's not."

"Okay, I'm moving into the trees and I'll come down through them."

"I've got him again and he's looking your direction."

The "show car" used for buys, a Ford Taurus, sat in a dusty clearing near the trailhead sign, its white paint ghostly in the dusk.

"All right," he said, "how about you go to your van and come back over the pass with your brights on. That'll get his attention, and I'll drop down to the car and follow you out."

He waited. There were dark clouds stacked over Lake Tahoe, purple an hour ago, almost black in the dusk. First snow wasn't far away. When Shauf was seconds from cresting the pass, her headlights touching high in trees swaying in wind gusts, he came down across the exposed face to the car. He started the engine and bounced through the ruts toward the gravel road, glanced up the treed slope and then at a red laser dot on the dashboard. It danced across under the windshield, skipped over the face of the radio, and started crawling up his arm like an insect. He jerked the wheel left, scraping the underbody as he hit the road at a bad angle, bottomed out, and then kicked up gravel as he accelerated away. His tires squealed through the first turn. His heart hammered. He had the feeling if he could hear across the distance the sound would be laughter.

Now Shauf's taillights were visible ahead, and he wound down the steep canyon behind her, ran the seven miles out to the lake road thinking about what had just happened. In Tahoe City the rest of the Special Operations Unit was waiting. Brad Alvarez and Melinda Roberts had picked up Chinese food, and the team met up near recycling bins outside a Raley's supermarket. Sean Cairo pulled in alongside Marquez's car. They opened the doors of Shauf's van, and Marquez went through the sequence of events while they ate. When he finished, Alvarez spoke for the others.

"This changes everything, Lieutenant. It's going to make it harder to trip with this guy."

Going without backup, staying with the suspect, "tripping with him," was all they'd been able to pull off. Marquez looked around at the faces of the SOU. For over a decade before coming to California Fish and Game, he'd worked undercover for the DEA, making drug buys where guns were flashed routinely. Sometimes a seller would run a test before a big buy. That could be what was happening here. Might be the sign they were getting close to the takedown, but no way to know tonight. They talked it over some more, then broke up. Most of the team would finish the night at the safehouse outside Placerville, roughly eighty miles away.

Marquez sat in the dark car talking with Shauf after Roberts, Alvarez, and Cairo had left. He pulled on latex gloves, took the CD case out of the evidence bag, and cut the tape with a razor.

"Let's see what we've got."

"You sure you want to handle it?"

"I think we need to know."

He slid it in the CD deck, and there was loud crackling, then abruptly a toneless filtered voice. He reached, turned the volume up.

"I've downloaded all Fish and Game personnel records. I know about the SOU. I've got names, addresses, and phone numbers for every single one of your undercover team. Lieutenant Matt Fong, 23 Yolando Road, Sacramento, California, wife, Lisa Fong, home phone number as follows." He read Matt's home number and then a cell number. "Lieutenant John Marquez, patrol lieutenant heading Special Operations, lives off Ridge Road on Mount Tamalpais in Mill Valley. A couple of phone numbers, here." He read the numbers off. A sound like a chair sliding, some words lost, then much louder, "Marquez has a wife named Katherine, stepdaughter, Maria, age sixteen. If that's you, better disappear, better lose yourself before I kill you."

The CD ended abruptly, and Marquez stared at his right hand, pale latex reflecting the dash lights. His family, his wife and stepdaughter, were often home without him. From time to time his team got tailed by poachers trying to discover where they lived, and threats got made in the field or left anonymously on the CalTIP anti-poaching line. Most were vague, and SOU records were supposed to be bombproof, though, of course, they weren't. Still, he'd never worried too much.

Fong was no longer with the SOU team. He'd made captain, was behind a desk, but their seller didn't seem aware of that, so that was a clue to the timing of whatever computer hacking or bribing had been done to get the information. He heard Shauf sigh and looked at her profile in the darkness as she stared at the CD player.

"Let's hear it again," he said. He pushed play and the voice filled the car.

2

The next morning when Marquez walked into headquarters in Sacramento, Chief Bell was waiting. He took a seat, glanced at the chief's new nameplate, a heavy brass plaque mounted on a dark-stained piece of oak. The nameplate reflected another bureaucratic change, reading assistant chief rather than deputy chief, as the department aligned its ranking system with the California Highway Patrol. For a while a rumor had circulated that the CHP would take them over, despite having little in common with them other than an interest in roadkill.

"They want everything we have on him and that isn't much, is it?" Bell asked.

"Who's the 'they' we're talking about?"

"The CD will ship to an FBI lab this afternoon and they're going to do everything they can, but they're also asking me about our procedures, specifically your training. They want to know why you opened and listened to it, why you didn't wait."

"Because we'll hear from our seller before we have lab results."

Bell shook his head, let him know that answer didn't come close. But they weren't going there yet. Bell's priority this morning was the breach of computer files.

"I want the whole operation," Bell said, "everything. Start at the beginning when we first heard from this seller, brief me on all of it."

Marquez talked for two hours.

When he finished, Bell said, "We're going to take this up again this afternoon." He gestured toward his office door. "There's an El Dorado County detective in the conference room who's been waiting to see you about a homicide in the Crystal Basin. He's hoping you can help him."

"Is this about the body found up behind Barrett Lake?"

"Yes."

The detective was standing near the windows, hands on his hips, surveying the buildings below like a guy trying to decide what to do with his property. He was gangly, balding, and middle-aged, wearing elkskin cowboy boots and a tan corduroy coat that pulled tight under his arms when he reached to shake hands.

"Jack Kendall," he said, and Marquez realized Kendall's skin had the tinged quality of a chemical tanning agent, an unusual vanity in a homicide detective.

"We had a similar murder a couple of years ago near Placerville," Kendall said. "That case is still open, it's how I got in on this one. But I'm not saying there's any connection, though both victims were killed by rifle shots. In this recent killing the victim was a geology student doing research for a thesis out along the boundary between the Crystal Basin and Desolation Wilderness areas. Your warden up there, Bill Petroni, tells me your undercover team has been in the Crystal Basin on and off all summer."

"We have."

Kendall walked to the table, sat down, and got his briefcase, saying he had photos. Marquez took a chair beside him, and

Kendall pulled out a college graduation photo of the victim, Jed Vandemere, a brown-haired young man with a cheerful face, then a second photo, this one of Vandemere's truck, a '99 Chevy with a camper shell.

"The truck was stolen," Kendall said. "Theft is a possible motive."

He ticked off a list of other missing items—laptop, telescope, the latest backpacking equipment—things that could be easily fenced. Then he handed Marquez the missing persons report Vandemere's parents had filed in August.

"Who found him?" Marquez asked.

"His father."

Marquez read the strong handwriting, then the father's physical description of his boy, his love unmistakable even on this police form. Marquez knew what it felt like, knew from his first wife's murder about the anguish and long emptiness that came after.

"For the first month the parents called me every day," Kendall said, "but there wasn't much we could do. We don't have the resources to chase missing persons reports. You know that."

"Sure."

"For all we knew he met a girl and left. How long can you pick at rocks when you're that age?"

Kendall seemed to need a response, but Marquez couldn't assuage his guilt. He understood the dilemma though, knew Kendall was telling the truth about available resources.

"Do you recognize him?" Kendall asked.

"No."

"These are more recent."

He slid over photos of the body, Vandemere's ribcage partially wrapped in a blue shell, a North Face logo visible. Other photos, black-and-whites of scattered bones. From the thin bright line of sky Marquez figured he'd been found near a ridge.

"We know he had an altercation with some hunters up there in July. They were running hounds, and he got in a shoving match with one of them. I have witnesses to that." He paused, added, "There's this—his parents tell me he was into environmental issues. In high school he worked for something called the Bear Initiative in Idaho. He used his own money to take a bus to Idaho and help gather signatures."

"I remember the Bear Initiative."

"Tells you something about how he thought."

"How he thought when he was a teenager, you mean."

"Probably still spoke his views. The more years I put in, the more convinced I am that people don't change fundamentally." Kendall surprised him now, rising partway out of his chair and leaning toward him. He pressed his fingers into the middle of Marquez's spine. "We found a slug right about here, a .30-30 lodged between vertebrae. He also took an insurance slug from a .22 in the head at close range. Do you know the ridge back up behind Barrett Lake?"

"I've hiked through there."

"There's a gnarled stand of pine down the slope on the backside. But from there it would have taken a good shooter, someone skilled."

Kendall paused too long now, and Marquez got the feeling he was heading somewhere with this conversation.

"Has your team been in the Barrett Lake area in the last few months?"

"No."

"Your chief thought you had."

"That's why he's chief."

Kendall smiled. "I've been questioning bear hunters. Everyone says the .30-06 is the caliber of choice and that a .30-30 is unusual, but what do you think?"

"The aught-six used to be more of a standard than it is now, but anything .30 caliber or bigger will do the job. Bear aren't hard to kill, and an aught-six will break the shoulder and punch through the chest cavity into the lung. A broken shoulder will bring a bear down, and with a pierced lung they drown in their own blood. Smaller caliber guns are popular for shooting a bear out of a tree or bait hunting. That's where a .30-30 comes in. It shoots flat and is easier to handle."

"Your chief says you got a threat on a CD last night."

"Yeah, it's a first, a technological breakthrough."

"You can understand why I wonder if there's some overlap with my case. I'd appreciate anything you can tell me about your operation."

Marquez explained what the Special Operations Unit was doing in the Crystal Basin. "We're looking for a bear parts dealer we think is working out of El Dorado County."

He gave Kendall a quick rundown on bile products and then related a claim their seller had made, that he'd killed a female Virginia game warden a decade ago, adding that the only Virginia warden murder case they'd found so far was a case where an estranged husband had been tried, found guilty, and was serving time.

"This guy sounds like a nut," Kendall said.

"He's paranoid."

"Or worse. I'm confused why Warden Petroni doesn't seem to know much about your operation. If he's the warden out of Georgetown, doesn't that make him the main guy in the area?"

"We cross a lot of jurisdictional lines and tend to keep to ourselves until we have something. We don't always talk to the local wardens straightaway." He added, as much for himself as for Kendall, "I'll see Petroni tomorrow."

That morning Marquez had talked to Petroni for the first time in a long while. A backpacker had called CalTIP, the Fish and

Game hotline, and reported a dead sow black bear and two cubs in a canyon in the Crystal Basin Wilderness. Petroni would hike up there with him tomorrow, and Marquez planned to brief him during the hike. He hoped to talk some other things out with Petroni and get beyond some of the acrimony of their past.

"We're looking for a sow and cubs, but all we have is an anonymous tip."

"And you're involved because of this seller you're looking for? Otherwise, it would be Petroni's to deal with?"

"It would, but you're not here to make sure Petroni does his job."

"No, I'm not. But I am here to talk to you about him. Not in here though. What do you say we get lunch together?"

They rode the elevator down and walked out into a hazy fall afternoon. Marquez led Kendall across one of the capitol lawns toward a Vietnamese restaurant he liked, and halfway across the lawn Kendall stopped and fished out a pack of cigarettes and a lighter. He lit a cigarette and blew smoke toward the capitol dome.

"I'm ninety-nine percent certain Petroni lied to me. He told me he never had any contact with Vandemere, but I've got witnesses who saw Vandemere get into Petroni's Fish and Game truck in the Ice House Resort parking lot in early August. I also have a statement from a fisherman out at Loon Lake who saw Petroni give Vandemere a real hard time one afternoon and not over a fishing regulation."

"What kind of hard time?"

"A lot of finger wagging and getting in his face."

"Are you telling me Petroni is a suspect?"

"Nothing like that. What I'm telling you is he lied to me and I want to know why."

"I'm sure you've told him this."

"I have and it hasn't got me anywhere."

Kendall flicked his cigarette out into the grass. It bounced and sank.

"One reason I bailed out of LA homicide was to get away from the bureaucracy. It was like the bad air down there, I couldn't take another day of it. Your Chief Bell might be the greatest goddamned chief in the world, but if I told him what I just told you, he'd have an internal investigation going before nightfall, and I don't want to have to deal with that. But I am going to make Petroni's life miserable. I'm going to make it real miserable if he keeps stonewalling me, and I don't give a shit how many dead bear are on his schedule. I'm going to give him forty-eight hours. You're going to see him tomorrow, you tell him that."

"I'll tell him you're looking for him, but you can handle your own threats." Marquez smiled. "Send him a CD."

"He may hear someone in his department more easily than he hears me."

"I wouldn't be the guy."

"No?"

Kendall's smile was cruel. He pointed out across the lawn vaguely indicating the direction of the mountains.

"You don't want to stick up for him, do you?" he asked. He turned to face Marquez directly. "Nobody seems to want to. I wonder why?"

3

High clouds curled and colored like burning paper in the dawn sky as Marquez waited for Bill Petroni in the Crystal Basin Wilderness. Most of the cabins along the lake were already shuttered, and except for hunters the basin was emptying. The reflection off the lake quieted to a silver-blue, and sunlight touched the high granite peaks across the water before Petroni drove up.

When he pulled into the lot it was in the same red Honda he'd had a decade ago, its color faded to a tired orange, roof streaked with rust, the car testimony to the frugality a warden's salary demanded. Petroni walked over, breath steaming in the cold, hair silver at the temples, face fuller, but the same long stride as if hurrying to get somewhere. Marquez wondered if Petroni had ever figured out where that place was.

"Can't go with you," Petroni said, before anything else. "I got a call ten minutes ago, got a problem with a couple of deer poachers."

"Then let me ask some directions before you take off."

"Ask."

Marquez unfolded a topo map and flattened it on the hood of his truck.

"Show me where I leave the trail to get to Coldwater Canyon."

Petroni touched a spot on the map with his car key. "Head left of these rocks. You'll see where the creek comes down. Follow it. You'll have to do a little climbing near the top."

"And if I find something up there, how do I get a hold of you this afternoon?"

"Call my cell."

"On our hike up this morning I'd planned to brief you on our operation."

"Better late than never, I guess."

"I should have gotten to you before now."

"Right, and I'm sure you were trying to." He stared into Marquez's eyes, said, "I don't miss it. You don't need to worry about that. I'm over it and all the bullshit that comes with it. I remember undercover operations where I sat in a van for twenty hours and peed in the cup I drank soda from hours earlier, and driving all over the state because I had an 'operation' going. Tell you something, Marquez, the way you find poachers is living in an area. That's how you get to know the people and figure out who belongs and who doesn't. They're your real backup, not some slimebag tipster."

He and Petroni had been called to headquarters in Sacramento one summer morning eight years ago and told the department was cutting back to a single SOU team. Petroni's team was shut down. Petroni had been offered a role working under Marquez, but pride wouldn't let him do that. He'd gone back into uniform instead, asked for a transfer to Georgetown, and eventually gotten it.

For years afterward Marquez answered questions about what had happened between them. And meanwhile Petroni kept badmouthing him. Then in Placerville one afternoon Petroni had trailed him as he would a suspect. He'd confronted Marquez in a parking lot, accused him of things he should have known better about and other things he knew nothing about, such as why Marquez had left the DEA and come to Fish and Game. That finished whatever chance they'd had of remaking their friendship.

"You have any problem finding the canyon, give me a call," Petroni said and started walking away. "Your phone will work up there."

"I had a visit from a Detective Kendall."

Petroni turned back. "Let me tell you something about Kendall. He's a reformed drunk LAPD sold the county sheriff. Worst hire they ever made."

"He came to see me about the homicide up here, said you told him to talk to me. He also said you're dodging him now."

"Listen, I already told him what I know, and Kendall's problem is he's lazy. We've got all kinds of lowlifes up here now, meth cooks, pot farmers, cycle gang members doing drug deliveries, you name it. Hydroponics has made it so the pot farmers don't even have a down season anymore. You can bet some scuzzbags scouted Vandemere's gear and his truck, then decided to take it. Tell Kendall he ought to move his office out of his favorite bar."

"He's thinks you're stonewalling him."

"Fuck him." Petroni started to point a finger, stopped himself, said as he turned away, "Not your problem or your business, Marquez."

He was looking at Petroni's back now, watching him climb into his car. When Petroni's door slammed, Marquez began refolding the topo map and decided he'd drive over to the wilderness lot, walk from there. He heard Petroni's engine start and without turning around to face him lifted a hand to wave good-bye, a gesture to the conversation he'd hoped they'd have. But now he was glad to be hiking up alone.

4

Marquez slipped a day pack on, crossed the road, and picked up the Rockbound Trail. He liked the early cold, the fall bite to the air, the light, almost weightless feel of the pack. Within an hour he was on open granite in sunlight looking up at the V-shaped pass and the dark blue sky above. He stopped and studied the rock up ahead, figured out it was where Petroni said to break from the trail.

A jumble of dark-stained granite marked where the stream running from Coldwater Canyon tumbled down in the runoff months. He climbed alongside the stained rock, brown and orange lichen powdering under his fingers. He free-climbed the final forty feet where the stream cascaded as falls in late May, slipping once near the top, thick fingers gripping hard as his legs dangled. Then he pulled himself over the lip and rested. It was the kind of short climb he wouldn't have thought twice about twenty years ago.

He ate a candy bar and drank from a water bottle. Below, the forests of the Crystal Basin were dark blue-green in late morning light. Toward the southwest, the sky had whitened with high cirrus; the afternoon would cool down. He thought about Katherine and Maria, missing them this morning.

When he put the pack on again and turned he saw a tiny lake gleaming like a polished stone beneath the granite face at the far end of the canyon. More a pond than a lake and probably no real fish in it, the type of lake fishermen bragged about because it showed they knew the hard-to-get-to places. He hiked toward it, following the rocky, dry streambed. Juniper trees grew sporadically along both sides of the narrow canyon, pine in scraggly bunches near the stream. There was little here that would attract bear, and it was difficult to believe a sow with cubs would forage this high late in the season when elderberry, gooseberry, acorns, and apples were all at a lower elevation.

As a crow flies he wasn't far from where Jed Vandemere's body had been found, and he decided when he finished here he'd hike out that direction. Kendall's speculating that Vandemere's murder might be connected to the man they were looking for had gotten his attention. He hiked on into the canyon, caught the odor of something dead, and knew as he did that the backpacker who'd called CalTIP had been genuine. It made him melancholy, took away the brightness of the early morning.

People trafficking in animal parts preferred to do so quietly. With bear there was a steady flow of gallbladders and paws to the markets. Thousand-pound adult grizzlies got slaughtered in Siberia solely for their gallbladders. He'd seen similar abuse here too many times to accept the rationalizations and calls for patience, for more time to allow for cultural change. The last wild animals had their backs to the abyss. It was really that simple.

He found the sow bear at the base of a pine and guessed that she'd been killed within the last four or five days. Wasn't skinned but her paws were missing, abdomen cut open, gallbladder no doubt gone. He moved her and looked for bullet wounds and found one he could chase. Then working a circle outward from her carcass he found what was left of two cubs, fur and small pieces of bone.

He returned to the sow, took off his pack, brushed flies away from the camcorder lens, and videotaped the dead bear. He picked up a piece of dental floss lying between two rocks and knew it likely was used to tie off the bile ducts after the gallbladder had been removed. Then he pulled a tool from his pack, a piece of heavy-gauge wire with a blunt end that he pushed into the wound to try to establish the direction of the bullet track before cutting into her.

After slicing through several inches of putrefying fat he had to back away from the smell, his eyes watering, drawing several deep breaths of clean piney air before continuing. Had she been killed near a road her carcass could have been transported to the Fish and Game facility in Rancho Cordova where X-ray equipment would locate the bullet. Instead, he forced himself to overcome the smell and dig for it as flies swarmed around him. He cut deeper and then got luckier than it was fair to hope for, felt metal scrape metal and dug out a bullet lodged against a rib. He turned it in his palm before bagging it. It wasn't badly deformed, and he would call his friend at the DOJ lab in Sacramento when he got back to his truck. He'd drop off the bullet tomorrow before meeting with Bell.

He wiped the knife and probe clean, dropped them in a plastic bag, peeled off the latex gloves, then wrote his notes. Estimated the bear's weight at two-fifty, her age at four years, the cubs born last spring. He packed up and started toward the lake, still searching for what had drawn the bears here. Not far from the water he found his answer. Partially hidden by bushes was a bait pile composed of what looked like restaurant garbage. On a nearby rock he found oats mixed with honey. He gathered what clues he could, a fragment of brown paper bag with the letter R in red, crusts of bread that had fallen between rocks.

Now, climbing out the back of the canyon he looked down across a long slide of talus at Barrett Lake, small and windblown. He followed the directions Kendall had given him, hiked over a secondary ridge out of view of the lake, and spotted the fluorescent orange spray paint marking the boulder where Vandemere's remains were found.

He stood on the rock near a black-red bloodstain, keeping his boots away from it. Kendall had told him Forest Service rangers would clean the rock next week, removing both paint and blood. He studied a dark stand of pine well down the slope, trees corresponding to Kendall's photos. Kendall was right, took a marksman from there, not an easy shot, and he understood Kendall zeroing in on hunters. Vandemere up here working on his geology thesis— standing on this rock when the bullet hit him, did he even realize what had happened? Marquez knelt, touched the bloodstain, and remembered Kendall's mincing, almost angry acknowledgment that Vandemere's father had gone to his son's grad school adviser and gotten enough information to create a map of where Jed had been exploring. He'd made a grid to search and worked it with volunteers, friends of Jed's and family.

By the time he walked back toward Barrett Lake the sky had milked over completely and the granite peaks had dulled to flat gray. He took out binoculars and scanned the vehicles in the camping area at the far end of the lake below, saw a CJ5 jeep, yellow and tired looking; a Ford Explorer; and a third truck, an ancient Dodge pickup he recognized.

"Bobby, are you here?" he asked and swept the binoculars along the campsites.

Bobby Broussard's presence might explain the bait piles, and Marquez knew he'd have to get a hold of Petroni after he hiked out. He scanned the campsites, spotted a man sitting on a log near a small campfire, head tipped down as he poked at coals and laid meat on the grill, face hidden by the brim of a hat. When he finally looked up, Marquez recognized the leathered features of Troy Broussard, patriarch of the local poacher. Wisps of blue smoke rose from the fire and Troy looked his way again. The last time Marquez had seen him was in court four years ago when Troy had been sentenced to eighteen months for commercial trafficking in bear.

Marquez had given his testimony in the judge's chambers and listened to the trial from the judge's door. In court, Troy had acted as his own lawyer, making a statement to the jury that animals had been put here by God for the benefit of man. He'd stared into the eyes of the jurors until they'd had to look away. After he'd gone to prison there had been a spurt of anonymous threats against Fish and Game, messages left on the hotline, and naturally Troy's name had come up after the recent CD.

But it surprised Marquez how much seeing Troy affected him. He read the coarse white hair on his forearms, the Jim Beam label on the bottle near the log, watched him cut his steak with a Bowie knife and chew with his eyes closed. Pretty good bet he knew all about the bait pile and poached bears in Coldwater Canyon. Petroni would have to question him; the team couldn't.

You could drink all winter on one gallbladder sale, pay your mortgage with hide and paws if you were smart about it, and Troy was that. He'd lost his right to ever hunt again in California when he was sentenced, but Marquez doubted that had stopped him. Why else would he be up here? He studied Troy another few minutes before putting the binoculars away. Bobby might be here with him, but Troy seemed to be alone this afternoon. Marquez wondered if Bobby had been up on the rock watching him find the poached bears in Coldwater.

Marquez slid the pack straps on and circled the lake, staying high before dropping down through a finger of trees and working his way toward a meadow and then the jeep trail. The afternoon darkened as he walked, and in the last mile the forest became gloomy. He climbed a rise and had started down the other side when he saw movement up ahead, off the road in the trees. Not long after, he heard a branch snap.

He reached the paved road and walked down past Dark Lake to where he'd parked in the wilderness lot. Then, pulling out of the lot, perhaps feeling a presence there, he took a look in his rearview mirror. Standing just inside the trees was the silhouette of Troy Broussard. He stepped out onto the road as Marquez pulled away. There were many reasons why Troy might follow a man coming down from above Barrett Lake, and they were all disturbing. Marquez drove the slow winding road out to the highway, trying to decide which fit best.

5

Petroni didn't answer his cell phone. Marquez tried him twice more before heading to Georgetown in his pickup. In Georgetown it took a few trips down the wrong streets before he found Petroni's house. The pine in the front yard had grown much taller, the cedar-shingled house beneath looking like a summer cottage. Neither the Fish and Game truck nor the old Honda Civic were out front, though light glowed from inside. He rang the buzzer, heard shuffling footsteps, watched a lace curtain flutter. Bill's wife, Stella, looked out at him, eyes narrowing as she recognized him, a wary smile forming as she opened the door, as if perhaps he were here to sell her vacuums or religion.

"You're a surprise," she said.

"How are you, Stella?"

"I'm all right, but if you're looking for Bill, he doesn't live here anymore. We're divorcing. Try the Creekview Saloon in Placerville.

Suddenly he can afford to eat out all the time, and he has a girl-friend who works there."

"I'm sorry," Marquez said before walking away, heard her quiet, "Well, I'm not."

Leaving Georgetown, he called Shauf because she knew one of the other wardens who worked regularly with Petroni. Petroni must have a house or an apartment somewhere, and Marquez figured that warden would know the address.

Shauf called back ten minutes later. "Okay, the story is he's living with his new girlfriend and looking for a house to rent in Placerville. They're house-sitting somewhere in Pollock Pines. It's been a big scandal up here."

"I guessed we missed it. No address on him?"

"No, he said Petroni keeps to himself."

"What about the other wardens?"

"He asked and all they know is the house is in Pollock Pines. Petroni doesn't talk to anyone."

"Okay, well, Stella said there's a bar in town where the girl-friend works. I'll go by, and if he's not there, I'll head to Sacra-mento."

"Will you need me tonight?"

"Not at all."

She was quiet, and he knew what was coming and was sorry she felt she had to ask. Her only sister had had a hysterectomy three weeks ago and been diagnosed with ovarian cancer. Debbie lived in Folsom, a half-hour's drive from Placerville, so Shauf was spending as much time as she could with her.

"I'll be at my sister's house if you need me."

"Tell her I hope she's feeling better."

When Marquez looked in the door of the Creekview a few guys were at the bar. A pair of women sat at a table in a big empty room. It smelled like stale beer, and he didn't see Petroni, so let the door fall shut. Before leaving town he stopped at a taqueria he used to frequent. New owners had glassed in the outdoor area and tiled over the concrete with Mexican pavers. A large paddle fan circulated humid air smelling of fry grease and beans. He ordered two chicken tacos, a quesadilla, coffee, everything to go, and then gassed up at the Shell station before getting on the highway.

Driving westbound on the highway, falling out of the foothills, he unwrapped one of the tacos. Food smells filled the cab. He ate slowly, bagged the trash, then sipped coffee occasionally checking his rearview mirror because a pickup had been pacing him since Placerville. Not that big a deal, yet the truck had his attention. He called home and when no one answered, left a message saying where he was and that he'd call back later. Laying the phone down, he checked his rearview mirror again.

The pickup's headlights had started to close on him, though that didn't necessarily mean anything. Still, he cut his speed and as the highway climbed a grade, fell in behind a slow-moving semi, passed it at the crest, and then slid over in front of it. The big semi's lights lit up the cab, and he accelerated away, running with a long downgrade, watching to see how the pickup would react. What it did was come around the semi and start closing the gap. Ten miles later he called Shauf.

"I'm twenty minutes from Sacramento and I've got a pickup tailing me. He's not shy and I'm not sure what he's up to. He's either real bad at tailing or doesn't care that I know." Marquez heard children in the background and hated pulling Shauf from her sister's house. "How long would it take you to get out to the freeway?"

"Five minutes."

"I think you ought to roll. He's coming up alongside me, and I'm going to play dumb."

The truck, a modified Toyota SR5, silver-gray, a 2002 model, sat high off the ground, the driver looking down at him, his face unreadable through tinted glass. Marquez took his foot off the accelerator, letting the speed drift down. The Toyota stayed with him, the driver's head just an outline, the truck running with him, crowding him a little.

The phone rang. "I'm on the highway," Shauf said. "What's he doing?"

"Messing with me. I'm driving fifty miles an hour and he's staying with me. He's got a stainless-steel platform welded on the back bed."

"Bear hunter."

"Or the truck belongs to one."

Marquez kept the line open with her. The Toyota driver started riding the reflectors, easing closer to him, before braking hard and swinging in tight behind him. Their bumpers clicked hard, and Marquez fishtailed out into the fast lane. He fought for control, his truck going sideways, then a full tires-squealing spin, and he slid onto the center median, racked through oleander bushes, and clicked off the guardrail. He bounced back into the fast lane, and a big semi bore down on him, horn blaring as it swung right, just missing him.

He let a wave of traffic go past, then cut straight across two lanes and backed up along the shoulder until he could climb the off-ramp the Toyota had taken. He was still shaking when he talked to Shauf again.

"I heard your tires," Shauf said.

"He tapped me, sent me spinning."

"He could have killed you."

He told her the off-ramp, then swung right at the stop sign and drove toward the lights of a subdivision. Beyond the stucco houses was a strip mall, beyond that, dark farmland. He saw headlights way out there, told Shauf he was going after them, but by the time he'd passed the houses they were gone. Still, he continued miles into the darkness and finally pulled over, parked on the shoulder, and was standing outside his truck when Shauf pulled up.

"You okay?" she asked.

"I'm fine."

"Your truck took a hit."

Metal brackets on the median guardrail had raked the driver's side of the truck. He'd have to change vehicles in Sacramento early tomorrow.

"Troy must have made a phone call after he followed me out this afternoon."

"So he made you."

"Yeah, good chance he recognized me, though he may not remember where he last saw me."

Marquez looked out across the darkness, the fields, the long sweep of stars, Mars still bright in the southwestern sky. The Toyota driver was telling him, I know who you are and you don't scare me. A thick neck and shoulders, a face disguised by the glass. He felt angry at himself for not having gotten the plates. He looked at Shauf.

"It was a close call," he said.

"Where do you want to go from here?"

"I want to find that truck." He turned toward her. "Think it over tonight. If Troy made a phone call, where did this guy pick me up?"

"It's a little weird that Troy followed you all the way out, even for him."

"That's what I'm thinking too."

He didn't want to say what he was really wondering. Instead, he said good night and watched her drive away.

6

Early the next morning Marquez met his DOJ crime lab friend, Leon, at a coffee stand in Sacramento. Leon's body language said he didn't get what the big deal was over a bullet with no gun to match it to. He dumped sugar into a latte, mixed it slowly with a wooden stir stick, took a seat on a concrete planter box, and angled his face toward the sun, listening with his eyes shut as Marquez told him what he knew about the Vandemere killing.

"But this murder you're talking about was months ago, and you're saying these bears were poached this past week."

"Yeah, but the bears weren't far from where Vandemere was killed, and the bullet I pulled looks like it could be a .30-30."

"Common enough bullet for bear, isn't it?"

"Yeah."

Leon opened his eyes. "Besides, why bring it to me if you think it might be from the same gun? Why not turn it over to the detective?"

"Because if it doesn't turn out to be a .30-30, it stays with us."

"You don't trust this detective?"

"I don't know him, and we've got our own problem. We're trying to find someone who's treating the black bear population like a private herd."

Leon was a big backpacker and fisherman with a real interest in saving wildlife. He might play devil's advocate this morning, but he'd take it seriously later. Marquez handed him one of Kendall's cards and left him nursing his latte, enjoying a few moments of quiet sunlight before entering the fluorescent blandness of the lab and a day of concentration.

Twenty minutes later Marquez threaded through a power breakfast crowd at Rex's, the new hangout for the political set. The floor was highly polished black and white marble tile. Morning sunlight slanted through dark-stained windows. The chief sat at a round table in a corner, alone and out of uniform, dressed in neatly creased white chinos, a yellow linen shirt, and soft black loafers that probably had cost four hundred dollars. Other than the short trimmed hair, the faint hint of law enforcement there, you'd never guess looking at him that he had anything to do with Fish and Game.

"Have you eaten, Lieutenant?"

"I had coffee with a friend at Justice after I called you."

"Take a chair and have breakfast. The chef here is something else."

The SOU ate on the road all the time and way too much fast food, though they'd had a couple of dinners lately at safehouses that were pretty good, owing to Cairo's new interest in cooking. Marquez took a chair and watched Bell eat poached eggs on thick toast.

"We got another call from our seller this morning," Marquez said. "He wants to do a deal tonight."

"What did you tell him?"

"I said we're on."

Marquez waited. He knew Bell was close to saying they weren't going forward.

"It's worse than I told you earlier," Bell said. "Most of the department personnel files have been hacked. These hackers install a backdoor in files that then get transferred around the department. Eventually, it gives them access to everything."

Marquez knew Bell didn't know anymore than he did about how a backdoor was set up. Neither of them knew much about computer programming, but Bell sounded like he'd picked up some new jargon.

"This may be the time to pull back and re-evaluate," Bell said. He leaned forward, spoke quietly. "Let's put aside our jobs for a moment. How old is your stepdaughter?"

"Sixteen."

"Captain Fong's twins are eight. His girls walk to school every day. That CD made very specific reference to yours and Captain Fong's families. The computer experts say that there's a high likelihood the names, addresses, everything about the Special Operations Unit is in the hands of this person or persons."

"I heard he didn't get any photos of anyone on my team."

"He has enough."

"I think we stay with him a little longer. I told him today he sent the CD to the wrong person and he can have it back."

"I'm talking about reasonable caution." It occurred to Marquez that somewhere along the line Bell must have attended a seminar where they taught that good managers get those under them to agree to major decisions before they're made. "Other tips haven't been followed through on, other cases pushed aside," Bell said. "And we never had enough going into this one. You told me last week you were going back to our original source. Where are we at with that?"

"I'll see him in the next couple of days."

Their source on the bear farmer was a thirty-seven-year-old San Francisco resident named Kim Ungar. Ungar claimed a cousin had given him the phone number he'd passed on to the Department of Fish and Game. Ungar was Asian American and had told Marquez that his cousin was full Korean and only distantly related to him. The market his cousin was selling bear parts to was Korean. After that the story got hazy.

Bell dabbed at a sticky spot of yolk, then examined the napkin. Marquez rubbed the back of his neck and looked away. Nothing was said for a moment, and Bell laid his hand on the table. His nails were neatly cut, the skin smooth. Marquez glanced at his own big hand and wrist, the rough palm, scars along the back.

When he looked up Bell said, "We can take down the pair who've been selling to you."

"That's our last resort."

"I'm not sure you're hearing me, but excuse me a minute. I've got to use the rest room."

When Bell returned he said he was out of time. As they walked out, Bell added that he wasn't sure he could even get the buy money together, and that they'd have to talk later.

"And I'm not just saying that to stop you from going through with this tonight. I should also tell you that I sat in on a budget meeting yesterday that was very bad. Your whole team may be in jeopardy next year, John. The governor is asking for huge concessions."

Blame it on whatever you wanted, the collapse of the economy, a state running on vapors, or even as one exasperated state senator had told Marquez during closed-door hearings, "Compassion exhaustion. People are sick of saving the goddamned animals, and California is broke. The money we have has got to go other places."

Marquez changed vehicles, dropping off the damaged truck, and then drove to Placerville. He met Shauf at the office in town they'd rented for the operation, a second-floor space in a brick building with a couple of windows that looked down on the old water tower and hardware store. Cairo, Roberts, and Alvarez were back up in Humboldt County following up on a bear case that was going to court next month. They'd get back to Placerville this afternoon, barely in time to get ready for tonight's buy, if it happened, if they could gather the money to do the deal.

He sat across from Shauf. A stack of business cards with his alias, the name John Croft, rested on the desk corner, and he had a driver's license to go with the cards. Any officer running the license would get transferred from the Department of Motor Vehicles to the SOU officer at Fish and Game, keeping his cover intact.

"What do you think?" he asked her. "Is our operation blown, Troy tied in with him and they all know who we are?"

"I say we keep pushing."

The rented office had a business name they'd concocted, TreeSearch, stenciled in white script on a smoky glass door. The heart of their cover was that they had a federal grant to study the effects of global warming on native red and white fir.

"We may have to put up personal money if we do this buy today," he said.

"How long before we'd get reimbursed?"

"Could be a whole month."

Each SOU member had an account, but all five were currently depleted, and he had the strong feeling he wouldn't hear from Bell in time.

"I'm okay with that," she said. "I've got five or six thousand in a savings account. How much do we need?"

"Ten grand."

"I'm good for half."

"I've got the rest."

"Let's make the call."

She crossed the room, locked the door, and threw a dark grin at him as he punched in the numbers. He lifted one finger, then two, then three, letting Shauf know how many rings. After the fifth ring there was a pause, then the mechanical rasp.

"Identify yourself."

"John Croft. I need directions for tonight."

"Copy this down."

When he finished the line went dead, and Marquez laid the phone gently on the desk.

"On foot out a fire service road off 49 south of here," he said. "I'm supposed to walk up a dirt road alongside a creek tonight at 8:00 with a flashlight."

"So, we're on?"

"Yeah. What do you say we go scout this fire road?"

7

Kendall called as they drove toward the buy location, but the reception was poor and Marquez had to get Shauf to run her window up.

"Something to show you," Kendall said, and then the call got dropped.

"He's asking us to meet him," Marquez told her, and waited for Kendall to call back. "He's got something he wants to show us."

"Everything except respect," Shauf said.

"He called you?"

"Last night, and was all over Petroni."

Marquez had told each of the team they were likely to hear from Kendall, explaining that the detective was investigating the Vandemere murder.

"What did he ask?"

"Whether I knew Petroni, how well, and what did I think of his character. You know, what dirt have I heard about him, like he's writing a gossip column, not investigating a murder. He said there are conflicts with Petroni's statements regarding Vandemere."

Kendall called back while she was still talking, and Marquez copied directions. It took half an hour to retrace their route from Placerville. They got on the highway westbound and exited a few miles later.

"Down that gravel road," Marquez said, as they passed the tall windbreak of Lombardy trees Kendall had said watch for.

The road was dotted with yellow leaves. Shauf's van rattled through ruts, and two county cruisers came into view, parked alongside an old pickup. Behind the vehicles was a yard seeded with engine parts and a house clad in unpainted cedar. Marquez saw a converted Volkswagen bug with a plywood dog platform built over the trunk space in front.

"Who's the fat guy?" Shauf asked.

"Kendall's partner, Hawse. I don't remember his first name."

"Let's hope he's different than Kendall."

Kendall walked out of the house and blew snot onto the ground out of one nostril. He saw them, and turned his head, held a wad of napkin against his nose when he faced them again.

"There, he's showing some respect," Marquez said.

"What's going on with his hair and skin?"

"Let it be."

"Last night when I told Kendall I may have seen Jed Vandemere once in July but had never spoken to him, he started asking what Vandemere was like, and I think, oh, okay, he didn't hear me. So I explained again that I might have seen him—nothing more than that. About ten sentences later he's back at it, kind of slick like suggesting I'd talked to him and probably remembered him because he was a handsome guy. He said maybe I'd remember a conversation if I kept thinking about it."

"Trying to jog your memory."

"No, much greasier than that."

Kendall walked up to them, and Marquez watched him size up Shauf, her solid in-your-face build, shoulders that said she pumped a little iron, her short blonde hair. He nodded at her as if they had already met and said everything they'd ever need to say, then directed his conversation toward Marquez, turning his back on Shauf as he gestured toward the dog runs.

"Let's take a look," he said.

"At what?" Shauf asked. Kendall was already walking toward galvanized chain-link fence enclosing concrete dog runs. The dogs, black-and-tan hounds, lay on the concrete, and Marquez knew immediately they weren't sleeping. He heard Shauf murmur, "Oh, no," as Kendall started explaining.

"The owner here called 911 at 11:14 this morning, told the dispatcher his dogs had been poisoned and two rifles stolen out of his house while he was asleep last night. He found the dogs earlier but was too shocked to make the call." Kendall's eyebrows arched slightly as he said that. "Or maybe he has a problem calling the government. He's one of your crackpot survivalist types. You'll see the literature from his favorite think tanks on the table inside, if you're okay with going in. I understand if you don't want to risk blowing your cover, and I can also move him to a back room."

"What do you need from us?" Marquez asked.

"You know a lot more about bear hunters than I do. I want to know what you see here and whether you recognize him, if you're willing to meet him."

"What's his name?" Marquez asked.

"Eli Smith." He swept his hand at the yard. "This is his castle. It's all his, even the junkyard. He says he works as a roofer and does other odd jobs. He ought to do some of them at home."

"Does he have any idea who killed his dogs?"

"If you ask me, yes, but he's too 'heartbroken' to tell me what he knows."

"Have you got a dog, Kendall?" Shauf asked.

Kendall stared back at her, said, "My ex-wife had ugly little terriers she fussed over all the time." He blew his nose. "She didn't give our son as much time as she gave those dogs." He looked up at Marquez again. "Smith says the dogs were alive at 3:30. He went out then to stop them from barking at what he thought was a mountain lion. Somewhere between the time he went back to bed and 7:30 the dogs ate the hamburger balls and croaked."

"Yeah, we'd like to take a look inside," Marquez said, "but we'll want to get a look at him before he sees us."

Marquez stepped aside with Shauf and talked it over. Smith had survivalist literature, so she'd go in first and make sure he wasn't one of the two Marquez had dealt with on the buys. A deputy led her in, and Marquez was left standing with Kendall.

"What kinds of guns were stolen?" he asked.

"A .30-06 and a .30-30. I'm wondering if there's a bear angle I don't know about? The dogs, for instance."

"Could be. Bear hunters sell pups from the good strike hounds. Those pups can bring five thousand each, and the market supports only so many breeders, so there's competition and squabbles about bloodlines. Everybody is selling the best strike hound ever born. Ask him about his enemies in the hound world."

Shauf came out and said Smith wasn't either of the pair they'd been buying from, so now they worked out a crude cover story with Kendall. A vehicle leaving here had sideswiped their truck last night and broken the mirror, but they hadn't reported it until this morning. They'd say they were dropping off a friend after coming back from a party, and they'd confide to Smith they hadn't called the police earlier because they were drunk.

When they walked into the kitchen what caught Marquez's eye was an old Westinghouse freezer alongside the refrigerator. A black power cord supplying it ran under a door and out to the garage. He nodded at Eli Smith.

"This kitchen looks just like mine. I mostly quail hunt nowadays, but I used to bear hunt with my dad when I was a kid." He paused. "I'm sorry about your dogs. We're trying to help out the deputies, but I don't know what we saw, just taillights really." He leaned closer to Smith, out of Kendall's earshot. "We were pretty lit up or we would have called last night."

Marquez took in the rest of the kitchen, the old sink, metal stripping lining counters built from what might have been the first piece of Formica ever sold. They stepped into a tiny living room. Smelling dogs, he saw the folded blankets on the floor. Smith pointed at the paneled gun case where the two rifles had been. He described them, then added that at least they were insured. Marquez caught Kendall's skeptical look. You couldn't stand here without wondering how the guy paid his mortgage every month, and here he was saying his hunting rifles were insured.

"They're collector's pieces," Smith said, talking about the scope on the stolen .30-06. "9X scope, inlay silver on the gun," keeping an eye on Kendall as he talked. "I had them appraised. They come out to do that before they insure you."

"What's that cost a year?" Marquez asked.

"It just adds onto the policy."

Right, just adds onto the policy, and Marquez nodded he understood, then took the conversation to bear hunting, naming places in Virginia and Canada he said he'd been with his dad. He got a little interest from Smith, but not much.

"Ever hunt off bait piles?" Marquez asked.

"They're not legal out here."

"Not legal a lot of places." Marquez nodded toward Kendall. "If he wasn't around, I'd tell you a story."

Smith pulled back at that, wariness showing, and Marquez knew he'd pushed a little too far. Smith moved to his dining table now, rested a hand on it, then lifted the hand after a few seconds and rubbed his cheek. A small nervous man with bad teeth and worse breath. He wasn't their seller. Marquez took a last look around. He put a hand on Smith's shoulder, said he was sorry again and maybe he'd see him in town.

"I'd almost rather they killed me."

"Maybe next time," Kendall said and wiped his nose again.

Outside, Kendall said, "Not telling the truth, is he?"

"Not all of it."

"And you don't recognize him?"

"No, but Bill Petroni might."

Kendall cleared his throat. "Petroni is coming in tomorrow morning, says he'll clear things up."

"Coming into the sheriff's office?"

"That's right."

It surprised Marquez how much relief he felt hearing that. They got back in Shauf's van, and Marquez lowered his window as Kendall came around and thanked them for coming. Shauf let the van start rolling while he was still talking.

When they hit the main road she said, "Kendall doesn't like women in law enforcement."

"You get that from him?"

She turned and stared hard at him. "He's an asshole."

8

Shauf's phone rang just after they reached the main road. She eased off the accelerator, and the van slowed, though he didn't think she was aware of it. The car behind veered around them, driver honking as Marquez listened to a different Shauf, quieting, comforting, gentle as she tried to calm her younger sister. When they neared the eastbound on-ramp that would take them back to Placerville he reached and touched her hand, then pointed toward the opposite on-ramp and said, "We have time."

They'd be at her sister's house in twenty minutes and still have hours to check out where the buy would go down. He heard Shauf tell her sister she'd be there soon. After she hung up, she backhanded tears off her cheeks as though angry at herself for crying.

"What's happened?" Marquez asked.

"It may have metastasized after all. There's something in her lungs. They were hoping—" She shook her head, her voice choked off. "Now she's talking about something crazy, some surgeon in Houston—tries to cut them out." She glanced over as if bewildered. "This is my little sister. She's thirty-six."

Marquez talked with the team, briefing them during the hour Shauf was with Debbie. Then they drove the winding roads to where the buy was supposed to go down.

Ten miles from Placerville, in a creek canyon thick with brush and trees, they found what was left of an old fire service road. They crossed a wooden bridge over the creek, and below, visible off one side of the bridge, was the dirt track running up the right side of the canyon. Shaded and dark with bay, oak, and pine, the road followed the dark green ribbon of creek as it wound back into the hills. *You had to be from around here to know about this place,* he thought.

He studied the ridgeline, noted places where the team could take positions, and sketched a plan with Shauf. Two could go in early, Cairo and Alvarez, and find a location near the rock he'd been told to walk to. He locked in GPS coordinates, and they drove on, talking routes out, contingencies, whether to ask for any help from the Placerville or county police. They went on another couple of miles before turning around, coming back across the bridge slowly, talking again about who else they could rely on tonight. That brought up Petroni's name.

"What's the deal between you and Petroni?" she asked. Another time he might have said less, but understood she was grasping for something to take her mind off her sister, and she couldn't quite do it yet with the buy.

"When I came over from the DEA I didn't know anyone, and Petroni was a pretty good friend to me. A lot of wardens wanted onto the two SOU teams, and it was hard for them to accept someone walking in from outside without wildlife experience."

"I'd have trouble with you walking in and stealing a glamour job."

"You here for the glamour?"

She smiled and then said something that surprised him, "I did it to get out of a relationship."

He thought at first she was teasing but realized she wasn't, and in some way it made sense. She could brace a suspect and make an arrest without any hesitation, or back someone off, but he'd just watched her kneel and force her hand through the link fence of the dog kennel to stroke the ear of a dead hound. There was a gentleness about her mixed in with the rest, and he could see her having trouble letting go of a failing relationship.

"This team is the best thing that ever happened to me," she said, "but we're talking about you and Petroni."

"Petroni taught me how the department works, and we hit it off. We were working the coast, mostly abalone. I taught Petroni some things about undercover work, and he taught me about poachers, boats, the coastal towns."

"What happened if you were such good friends?"

"All I know is when things changed. My team made a bust up the north coast in Albion. In the last few days before the takedown we were on the suspects every minute. Petroni was down south, and I was out of communication with him before and then during the bust. He found out we'd made it by talking to our chief, and after that he was a lot less friendly."

"Why would it matter to him like that?"

"I got the feeling he thought he was running both teams, and he should have been told. Not long after that we both got called to Sacramento, and Petroni's team got shut down."

"Bam, shut down just like that?"

"Yeah. The chief wanted both of us there at 9:00 that morning. At 9:10 Petroni's team was over with."

"Who gave you the word?"

"Chief Keeler, so you can picture it. Petroni thought I'd kept this other operation secret from him as a way of making my team look better, and that somehow I knew it was all going to go down. He threw that theory at me in a parking lot in Placerville a year later."

"He was hurt."

"Yeah, and it didn't make any sense to him. He was the one with the wildlife experience."

He told her a little more but not the whole story as they drove back to Placerville. When they reached the safehouse Marquez called Bell and told him the team was kicking in the money and would wait to get reimbursed. They were going forward with the buy. Alvarez and Cairo were getting their gear ready, everything spread on the dining table. Roberts and Shauf stood in the kitchen talking.

"I don't like how you've done this," Bell said. "I feel like you went around me."

The conversation ended badly, and he felt lousy after hanging up. The team had all grouped into the kitchen, Roberts and Cairo laughing at some joke they'd shared.

"We're on," Marquez said, as he walked in.

"We were going either way, Lieutenant," Alvarez said, his face lit up, the energy building now.

Marquez stood among them, taking up the last space, larger than the rest. They were all from different walks of life, coming from different places, more than twenty years between him and Melinda Roberts. Roberts's hands flew over a keyboard while he still pecked out his reports. She was also a rated sharpshooter. Alvarez came out of East Palo Alto, had worked at his dad's auto shop, and had planned to be a mechanic. He was the guy who could adapt to any problem, the type you read about surviving an avalanche, somehow reacting quickly enough. Cairo had gone to a year of law school before going through the Fish and Game academy. He was an easy-going surfer type. Even the people he busted didn't get pissed off at him, and some apologized.

"Okay," Marquez said, "let's go over it again before everyone takes off."

They moved out to the dining room table, and Marquez spread the map. Alvarez and Cairo would leave first, get dropped off near the creek bridge by Roberts, and would hike in until they found the rock.

"The rock has white spray paint on it," Marquez said. "That's what he told me to look for. I'm supposed to start up the road at 8:00." He glanced at Alvarez, then looked at Cairo. "You need to find positions up the slope where you can see the rock. Time yourself going in this afternoon, and that'll tell you roughly how long it should take for me to get there."

"How about whistling as you come up the road?" Cairo said.

"Yeah, or I'll sing."

The team's laughter was a nervous kind, and Marquez could feel the change since the CD. The address in Roberts's file was her parent's peach orchard outside Colfax. She'd talked to him about the orchard's isolation, the vulnerability. They were all a little worried.

Marquez watched Alvarez and Cairo load gear, then climb into Roberts's van. Shauf left ten minutes later, and he was alone at the safehouse. He got his gear together and put on the Kevlar vest, but it didn't feel right. He sat and held the vest in his hand for a while and then picked up the coat with the fiber optic sewn into it, the camcorder, and it just didn't feel like the right move. *He's not through checking us out, and he gave us too much time to prepare today.* Marquez picked up his phone and called Roberts.

"I'm not going to wear anything," he told her. "Tell Alvarez and Cairo they have to get as close as they can. They've got to be able to move fast."

She chuckled. "You found a new way to cowboy it, Lieutenant."

"No, I'm running with my gut. He's giving us too much time to prepare."

She was quiet then said, "Okay, I'll let them know."

He hung up and took a call from Kendall. "How about meeting me in Placerville for a beer?" Kendall asked. "I want to compare notes and talk, and I met with your warden today."

Marquez got the name of the bar. An hour later when he walked in he found Kendall at a table with a thin red-haired woman he introduced as Sadie. Her freckled face was evenly tanned, hair heavily dyed, her smile shy and friendly. Marquez figured her tan explained Kendall's using an applied tanning product. Sadie smoothed her thin dress as she stood, and she brushed away Kendall's hand as he patted her rear.

"I won't be long," Kendall told her, then motioned for Marquez sit down.

On the table a bottle of Sierra Nevada Pale Ale and a half-eaten order of fried zucchini rested on a copy of the *Mountain Democrat*. Marquez watched Sadie take a seat at the end of the bar. She looked unhappy to be alone, and Kendall nodded toward her.

"Good woman," he said, as though talking about a reliable old car. "I drove down and picked the bullet up from your friend at DOJ. Thanks for having him call me, but the bullet is not a match. I'll get it back to you. That said, if you find your Coldwater Canyon hunters, I'd like to interview them."

"How'd it go with Petroni?"

"He bullshitted us again." Kendall leaned back, belched softly, covering his mouth. "I've got another witness tying him to Vande-mere, and we're going to have to kick it up a notch. I'm notifying your chief tomorrow unless you want to take a final run at convincing Petroni."

"I don't."

"Then it gets rough for him now."

"You're running on rumors."

Kendall looked at Sadie, then back at Marquez. "I don't have to tell you anything about rumors. You live off tips, don't you?"

Marquez left Kendall sipping a Jack Daniels. After he was in his truck and rolling toward the buy site, he checked in with Shauf.

"We're all in position," she said. "You're going to drive past Melinda right at four miles out."

"Have you seen anyone?"

"No, though we heard motorcycles."

"Dirt bikes?"

"That's what Brad and Cairo think."

Their map showed the road alongside the creek ending a couple of miles in, but that didn't mean there weren't unmarked trails.

"So maybe there is another way in," he said.

"That's what we're guessing."

"Okay, well, I just drove past Roberts."

He felt his gut tighten the way it had years ago when he'd gone out on the first drug buys. He didn't feel like himself.

"They say it's going to take you twenty minutes to walk up to the rock. It has the names Chloe and Ed spray-painted in white on it."

"Got it."

Twelve minutes later Marquez started up the creek road, smelling the moss and oak leaves, feeling the cold night. The flashlight shone on dark earth. He heard the trickle of water in the creek off to his left, and the night seemed unnaturally dark. On the phone their seller had warned him to keep the flashlight pointed down at the road, and he kept it angled just ahead and walked slowly, listening, expecting from what Shauf had told him that it might be a dirt bike that would round the corner and coast down toward him with its engine off. Half a mile in, a light flashed on and off ahead.

A deep voice he wasn't sure he recognized said, "Shine the light at your face and keep it there."

Marquez shone the light on his neck and stared into the darkness trying to see who was there. Holding the light on himself made him feel like a target. Two men walked down the road toward him, and he knew he'd done the right thing leaving the Kevlar vest and digital camcorder behind. One was big but light on his feet, fading to the side while his pale companion came forward with a garbage bag and a powerful flashlight. He dropped the bag on the ground and shone the light on it.

"Take a look," he said, and when Marquez didn't, "what are you waiting for?"

"You open it."

"What are you afraid of?"

The background man moved in and showed a gun.

"We want you to take off your coat," the pale man said.

"I don't really want to."

"Take it off anyway, but do it slowly."

Marquez unzipped his coat, hoping Alvarez and Cairo had a clear view. They'd have to come out fast with their guns drawn. He handed over his coat and watched the pale man check the pockets, knead the sleeves and every inch of the coat before dropping it on the ground. The big helper moved around behind.

"Your shirt."

"Right."

Marquez took his shirt off and tossed it on the garbage bag, let the guy bend and pick it up. He guessed they'd been hired to come check him out and who knows what else if they found what they were looking for. It changed everything again. He ignored the urgency in the next order that he spread his legs, did it slowly, asking, "If you're looking for a wire, it means you think I'm a warden. Why is this happening?"

The pale man squatted now, taking little time with the shirt, handing it up to Marquez while his partner carefully checked the rest of Marquez's body. The garbage bag got opened, exposing dried bear galls.

"Get dressed. Take your bag with you," the pale man said, then talking big, "You would have taken a walk with us if you'd been wearing anything." He pointed behind him. "Up the road."

Marquez put his shirt on, picked his coat up, and found the money was gone.

"Where's my money? I'm not interested in doing business tonight."

"You already did it. Take the bag and haul ass."

"Not going to happen."

"You leave it here, that's your problem."

"You tell him I want my money back."

Marquez put his coat on and walked away. His legs felt stiff, awkward, and he knew it was possible he'd get shot. But each step took him farther into darkness, and when he looked back they were gone.

9

After they'd returned to the safehouse and debriefed, Marquez felt too edgy to call it a night.

"I'm going to take a ride into town," he said. "Anybody want to come along?"

"I'll go with you," Shauf said. "I could use a drink."

They drove past the Creekview Saloon and spotted Petroni's orange Honda parked not far away. After a moment's hesitation Marquez pulled over and parked.

"You sure you want to do this tonight?" Shauf asked.

"Yeah, he owes us some answers."

The bar at the Creekview had been built to look like a big horseshoe, and they took a position along one side. Marquez leaned in to get the bartender's attention. Three bartenders stood talking to each other, wearing black shirts carrying a gold emblem in the shape of a prospector on the pocket. Gold rush branding was a change he'd seen start in Placerville a few years ago. The original town name, Hangtown, appeared more and more on store windows.

He ordered drinks and then spotted Petroni sitting with a young black-haired woman at a table in front of a bandstand where a country singer was tuning up her guitar and bantering with the crowd. A waitress wearing cowboy boots, red tights, a short black skirt, and a red bandana around her neck leaned over Petroni's table.

Marquez chatted with Shauf while waiting for their drinks. It was too noisy to unwind here, and after they had their drinks he wished they'd gone somewhere else. This wasn't going to be the place to sit with Petroni. He clicked his glass against hers, and she asked, "Who are these guys across the bar?"

"The one with the thin blond mustache is Bobby Broussard, one of the cousins. He lives out there with Troy. I don't know the other guy."

The other man was also young but much tougher looking, powerfully built. On this cold night he wore a tight T-shirt under a loose leather jacket open wide enough to show off his pecs. His hair was short, gelled, bleached, his face flat, cheekbone planes too sharp, as if someone had screwed up a wood carving but kept going at it anyway. He became aware of them now. He leaned and said something that brought a leering smile to Bobby's face.

Marquez took a sip of rum and said, "That's Troy Broussard's daughter, Sophie, sitting with Bill." He turned, got the bartender's attention, and asked, "Is Sophie working tonight?"

"She's over by the bandstand with her boyfriend."

"Oh, yeah, I see her now, thanks."

Marquez lifted the rum again, and the bartender lingered, did he want another? Marquez did, but rum wouldn't work for him tonight. He'd thought coming into town and cooling down would help, but the buy had been too disturbing. He glanced over, caught an arrogant expression on Bobby's companion's face.

Shauf turned her back to them and spoke softly. "They're focused on Petroni's table, aren't they?"

"Yeah."

"Why is that?"

Maybe it was the novelty of a Broussard going out with a game warden, or maybe these two at the bar didn't have anything else to occupy themselves with, Bobby like a schoolboy giving his girl cousin shit. Petroni's head shifted just slightly, perhaps sensing the conversation out of his view at the bar, then he finished his drink and stood heavily. He gave Sophie a grim smile before heading for the bathroom.

"Arguing with her," Shauf said. "Doesn't anybody in this town get along?"

Petroni moved awkwardly around a young couple, the new jeans he wore too tight for his middle-aged gut, the wide leather belt more fitting in a western bar than here.

As soon as Petroni disappeared into the bathroom, Bobby Broussard started weaving his way to Sophie, his thin frame sliding between tables, a geeky, sleazy smile offered to women he brushed into, his thigh and crotch rubbing against them as he squeezed his way through.

Watching him, Marquez remembered a much younger Bobby working as a spotter on bear hunts, keeping an eye out for the law, a thin kid with bad skin and always running his tongue over his upper lip in a way that made you glad you didn't know what he was thinking. When Bobby reached Sophie he tapped her on the shoulder and used his beer bottle to point at the bar where his friend stood smiling. Sophie turned, looked at the man at the bar, then raised her hand, and flipped him off as though there were no one else in the room. Shauf chuckled.

But then something more got said, and Sophie came out of her seat and stuck the same finger in Bobby's face. Even the singer looked over as Bobby grinned, backing up like this was all good fun, and Sophie's gaze returned to the other man, who toasted her with his beer and crooked a finger motioning her to come to him. A couple of women yelled at his gesture as if it offended them personally. Marquez heard the word "asshole."

"I'm ready to go," Shauf said. "Who needs this? You don't, I don't. Let Petroni have his midlife crisis. I'm fried, you must be too."

"Let's hang for a couple."

Petroni came back from the bathroom, and by then Sophie had turned her chair so her back was to the bar. Petroni sat down and looked around at the nearby tables, but what he needed to see was Bobby Broussard's companion crossing the room behind him. Within a few strides the man was there, and he jerked Petroni's right shoulder from behind. Petroni just managed to get on his feet as his chair went over, his drink skittering.

"Watch my drink for me," Marquez said, and started across just as Petroni and the man came to blows. He saw Petroni take hard jabs to the gut and one to the chin. Petroni went down on one knee, then fell to the floor. The man reached down, wadded Petroni's shirt, started to lift him, was swearing at him, calling him a cocksucker when Marquez got there and forced him to lower Petroni back to the floor.

"This is the part where the lowlifes haul ass," Marquez said. "That's you."

"Let go of my wrist, fucker, before I kick the shit out of you."

A moment later he threw his weight sideways, trying to knock Marquez off balance. A table upended but Marquez kept his feet, blocked a hard punch that hurt. He waited for the man to come at him again, but surprisingly, he didn't.

"Kick his ass, Nyland, kick his ass!" But Nyland had changed his mind, and the same voice egging Nyland on called to Marquez, "She's his girlfriend, asshole."

Two Placerville officers pushed through the bar doors. Nyland tried to back away, but the police closed on him and looked as though they recognized and didn't like him. Petroni got to his feet, wiped blood from his nose. Sophie handed him a napkin. Marquez didn't take his eyes off Nyland. If Nyland was local, he had to know Petroni was the warden out of Georgetown, and not many people come after law enforcement officers, at least not in a crowded bar.

"Take him in," Petroni told the officers.

But they didn't work for Fish and Game and went about it their own way. They stopped Nyland from walking away and asked Marquez and Petroni to come outside as well. Marquez waited near the bar entrance away from the patrol cars. But Petroni got close enough to Nyland to where one of the cops put a hand on Petroni's chest and pushed him down the sidewalk. Nyland swore as one officer clicked on cuffs and the other read him his rights. He yelled over at Marquez.

"I'm watching for you."

Marquez ignored him, instead watched Bobby Broussard, who stood in front of one of the cops and kept pointing down the street. Nyland's keys got handed over to Bobby, and Marquez realized that must have been what the conversation was about. After Nyland was in the back of the patrol car, Marquez moved close to Petroni. One of the cops walked over. He asked Petroni, "Are you going to press charges?"

Petroni shook his head. "I'll take care of it."

"What do you mean, warden?"

"I mean, I'll deal with it."

The officer looked to Marquez. "And who are you?"

"A friend of Bill's. I was at the bar and saw Nyland or whatever his name is cross the room and start the fight."

"And how did he do that?" The cop started writing.

"He came up from behind and yanked Bill off his chair."

Marquez gave terse answers and then his alias as a name. The police cruiser pulled away.

Petroni's voice was thicker, his nose clogged with mucus and blood as he explained. "Nyland used to be her boyfriend. They lived together for years."

"Is that his truck Bobby's driving?"

A Toyota pickup went past on Main Street, and Petroni nodded, touched his lip, and looked at the blood on his fingers.

"He's got dogs in the truck. That's why they let him take it," Petroni said. "Nyland's close with the Broussards, and he used to go out with Sophie. That's what that was about."

"How long have you been going out with her?"

"She's not one of them if that's what you're thinking. She left home when she was sixteen."

Petroni turned to face him, his nose still bleeding, teeth streaked with blood, the tissue paper in his hand saturated. He forced a strange pained smile, and Marquez didn't think it was the pain of the blows.

"This isn't over," Petroni said.

Marquez left it alone. Petroni was angry, humiliated, and he needed to cool down. He ought to go down to the station and press charges, let Nyland sit in a cell for a month.

"Want me to run you by the clinic and get your nose looked at?"

"No."

"Where does Nyland live?"

"I'll deal with him."

"I've got a different problem with him."

Marquez got directions to Nyland's place before Petroni went back inside to Sophie. Shauf was waiting for Marquez near his truck. As they got in he told her.

"Nyland was at the wheel the other night. That's the truck that followed me."

10

The next morning Marquez took an early run with Shauf, then sat at the kitchen table in the safehouse, cooling down, talking with Roberts and Cairo while Shauf showered. Shauf came back out, and her wet hair dripped onto the Crystal Basin Wilderness map as they talked about the day ahead. Marquez would make his first trip home in over a week, combining that with a reinterview of Kim Ungar at Ungar's apartment in San Francisco today. While he was gone, Shauf would start the team on a systematic sweep of the fire and logging roads in the Crystal Basin. Get the keys to all the gates and look for any signs of bait piles. He didn't yet know how he wanted to deal with last night's buy, but after finding the poached sow and cubs it made sense to look for other bait piles.

An hour later he grabbed his gear and left for the Bay Area. Traffic bled slowly across the Central Valley, and every year it seemed there were more strip malls and stucco houses alongside the freeway. The orchards were all but gone. He drove past Vacaville and Fairfield, climbed the dry rounded hills before Vallejo, making phone calls, still juggling thirty cases or leads, one in particular that sounded promising, a sturgeon poaching tip coming from a bait shop owner in the delta. Then Kendall called.

"I heard you ran into Eric Nyland last night," Kendall said. "We've got a file on Nyland you might want to take a look at, and I've got a story for you, if you want to hear it."

"I'd like to see the file, and, yeah, anything you know about Nyland I'd like to hear."

"Petroni could tell you all about his girlfriend."

"Tell me what you know."

"This happened about five years ago, just after I started here. A Tuolumne County sheriff's deputy showed up looking for help locating Nyland—this was in the fall, September the year I was hired. This Tuolumne deputy had traced Nyland through a partial license plate after a road rage incident in Yosemite where a camper went off the road and an older fellow was killed. The old boy's wife survived. She got a partial license plate and gave a description of the truck and driver. She and her husband had been on their way home to Lee Vining after staying in Yosemite Valley, so they were climbing toward Tioga Pass. I'm sure you know Yosemite."

"Yeah."

"A pickup came up behind them and got aggressive about passing, and the old boy got angry, started swinging wide when the truck tried to go around him. Eventually, Nyland, and I'm sure it was Nyland, got around him or rather, came alongside, lowered his passenger window, and shot a hole through the camper's windshield. The old boy swerved, lost control, hit a tree, and was DOA. So this Tuolumne deputy comes into the sheriff's office, tells us this story, and we all drove out to where Nyland still lives at the end of Six Mile Road. There's a meadow where a subdivision project went bust. Do you know where that is?"

"I know the road."

"Then you know where it ends. Do you know the story with the Miwoks?"

"No, but let's stay on Nyland."

"Remind me to tell you the local legend sometime about the Miwoks who got slaughtered out there. People claim their ghosts still haunt the area. There are three house foundations in that meadow that never got built on, and out past that are trailers the construction crews lived in. Nyland worked on the subdivision briefly as a carpenter, and the bank let him stay on because the bank officer was a friend of his dad's. Deal was he'd trade rent to watch the property, and believe it or not, his dad was respected around here, a lawyer that even the cops liked."

"Where's his dad now?"

"Heart attack when Nyland was nineteen. Probably having a kid like Nyland killed him. Okay, so we go out there in a couple of patrol cars and drive up to the first trailer, the one he lives in, and she answers the door, not Nyland."

"Sophie?"

"See, you know where this story is going. You know her better than you let on. Anyway, Nyland is standing behind her, and she's wearing a thin T-shirt, and I mean thin and tight, a pair of ragged jeans and is barefoot. Looked like she'd just pulled the clothes on as we drove up. She got right in my face, said she'd been in the sack with Nyland all night and they'd had sex, and we could swab her right there in the doorway if we wanted. I'm not kidding. She started unzipping her jeans, and there weren't any panties underneath. Then she told me I could be the one to do it."

Kendall paused, waiting for his reaction, the image of her opening her jeans, the place to make a comment. But what caught Marquez was not her body exposed, and she had a nice one, but rather, the aggressiveness, same thing he'd seen at the Creekview.

"Nyland came in for questioning and we worked on her separately, but she never wavered on the alibi. I believe Nyland was

the pickup driver in Yosemite, and I can promise you she's damaged goods. That's who your warden is head over heels about.
We've also suspected Nyland's involvement in meth manufacture
and a burglary ring, but never been able to pin anything on him.
He may look like a pinup for the steroid crowd, but he's a schemer
and smart. Knows what he can get away with. Did Petroni tell you
Nyland works for a hunting guide business?"

"No."

"Sierra Guides out of Placerville—they've got an office off
Main Street."

"I know where it is."

"That's where Nyland's truck came from. The owner there
loaned him the money to buy it."

"Have you ever met the owner?"

"Never seen his face, don't even know his name."

Marquez didn't say his team had already checked out the
owner, a Joe Durham, who lived in Sacramento and worked as a
lobbyist and consultant. As near as they could tell the guide business didn't do much trade. They'd looked at all the local guide
businesses, but they would backtrack now on Sierra.

When he hung up with Kendall he drove across lower Marin
and into Mill Valley, up Mount Tamalpais and home. His house
had been built by his grandfather in 1915 on a flank of Mount Tam
when land was still cheap. It had a stone fireplace, redwood case-
ment windows that had lasted seventy years, floors of quarter-
sawn white plank oak pegged with mahogany dowels cut from
wood his grandfather found on Muir Beach after a cargo ship had
foundered. The house looked down along a forested ridge to the
ocean. It was where his paternal grandparents had raised him and
his sister, Dara.

When he unlocked the door and walked in he smelled the
lime tang of the shampoo Katherine used and saw some of Maria's
schoolbooks stacked on the dining table. Both were comforting,

though the house felt empty without their presence. He pulled the clothes he needed from the bedroom, switched his gear into the old two-tone Explorer, and left.

He crossed the Golden Gate and went out Nineteenth Avenue through the park. Kim Ungar lived down this direction. Ungar drove a late model Lexus and lived in a drab white stucco apartment out in the avenues near the ocean in San Francisco. The apartment units had small decks with Spanish-style iron railings painted black, and Marquez drove past, checking for the Lexus or an open door on the apartment deck before parking around the corner. He didn't see the car, and when Ungar didn't answer a knock on his door he figured Ungar had blown him off, which wasn't surprising. Ungar's game was agreeing to meet, then not showing.

For a couple of weeks in the early summer they'd put Ungar under surveillance, despite his being the referring party and their informant. From watching him they'd learned his routine, so after Ungar didn't answer his door, Marquez decided to run some of the route they'd followed him on when they'd had him under surveillance. He checked a video arcade, a mall, and then in a parking lot next to the In-N-Out Burger where they'd seen him eat several times, he spotted Ungar in his car.

He parked and punched in Ungar's cell phone number as he crossed the street, watched him pick the phone up, stare at the screen, and lower it again. That's my guy, Marquez thought. He came up the passenger side, rapped on the window. Ungar's startled eyes brightened, then flattened. His hand went reflexively to his mustache and the window lowered.

"Hey, I forgot, I'm sorry."

"No sweat. Good to see you." Marquez reached through the open window to shake hands, Ungar's grip light, his fingers wet. "Why don't we talk here?"

"How'd you know I was here?"

"Remembered you talking about the burgers and was hungry. Lucky, huh?"

Of course, it wasn't, and he watched Ungar's face tighten. When the lock released Marquez swung the passenger door open, and the smells of fast food, cigarette, incense, and dope sucked out into the salt breeze. Ungar moved wrappers off the passenger seat.

"I just spaced it out," Ungar said. "Worked all night for a client. I've been sitting here listening to music, cools my mind down."

"Busy."

"Real busy. You ever work for yourself?"

"Only once and not for long."

"Used to getting fed by the government."

"Yeah, eating up your tax dollars."

Ungar had a computer business that as near as they could tell he ran from his apartment and the trunk of his car, building computers for clients out of generic parts or problem solving, pretty vague about how he got his clients. But they had confirmed that he'd worked in Silicon Valley for years. He was a bright guy, he knew people, his cell phone ringing often when Marquez had sat with him. He was pushing through his thirties with no family. Both parents had died in a car accident. Ungar carried a newspaper clipping of their deaths folded up in his wallet. He'd showed it to Marquez.

Informants generally wanted money or revenge or to eliminate competition, but Ungar had told them his motive was concern for the environment. He'd had a cathartic moment while watching the Discovery Channel, where they'd run a show on bear poaching. It so disturbed him that he'd called Fish and Game to rat out his cousin's connection, though not his cousin. That was the catch; he wouldn't give them the cousin's name. He'd spun a story for them about not being very connected with the Korean end of his family, but this third cousin and he had partied together when they were younger, and family was family. He couldn't give his cousin up.

So they'd figured there wasn't any cousin and Ungar was worried about getting caught for something he'd done. Or maybe there was a cousin. What he'd given them was a phone number to leave a message for a man selling bear parts and bile products. In June they'd made their first buy after using that number. Marquez had continued to tell Ungar they'd never reached the bear farmer, but then, he knew Ungar was lying to them too.

"How's that burger?" Marquez asked.

"Go get one. You don't need to order fries if you don't mind eating after me. You can have mine." Marquez looked at the fries, saw a stubbed-out cigarette in them. "Oh, yeah, forgot about that," Ungar said and pulled the cigarette out. "Guess you'll want to order after all."

"You don't mind waiting?"

"No problem."

Marquez looked back at him as he got out of the car, a clean-featured guy, a pleasant if bland face, black hair, small nose, gray sifting in, but keeping himself in shape, a single guy cruising toward forty with a pretty good idea of himself. They'd allowed him to smoke in the interview room because he'd insisted he had to if he was going to talk. He was that kind of nervous underneath. Ungar would watch him order now, watch him through the glass, watch everything he did.

Today Ungar wore jeans and sandals, a wrinkled white shirt rolled up to his elbows, a beaded belt. It was another thing about him, some days dressed hippie nostalgic, smoking a joint, chilling with the music, a computer type working best at night; other times they'd seen him dressed in a suit, tie knotted close to his throat, getting out of his Lexus wearing Armani. None of which figured with the fogbound, middle-income apartment complex, yet it was something Marquez had seen before, both with Fish and Game and the DEA, a guy showing just enough flash to enjoy the money he was taking in, but not so much as to get people really looking closely at him.

"Talked to your cousin lately?" Marquez asked when he got back with the burger, drink, and fries.

"You want to do the cousin questions right away?" His hand went to the mustache again, stroking it. "I talked to him yesterday. He's been selling stolen cell phone chips, taking a break from bear parts, I guess, but he's gotten a hold of enough weed he wants to sell me as much as I'll buy."

"Where's he living now?"

"Somewhere out in the valley, Stockton, Sacramento, maybe one of those foothill towns like Placerville. I don't ask."

"You mentioned a woman once in Placerville."

"You here about her?"

"Just wondering what you remember."

"You've come across her."

"Maybe."

"You hoping to get laid or bust her?"

"You said her boyfriend was a bear hunter."

"That's on the tape?"

"Yeah."

"I don't remember saying it."

Marquez took another bite and remembered Ungar racing down Highway 1 earlier in the summer. After he'd come to them with the tip they'd put him under surveillance for a week. He'd shaken them by passing cars, which had only added to the idea that he was the "cousin." Even now Ungar was checking his mirrors, probably looking for the rest of the team. Marquez ate some fries, another bite of burger, let the silence work.

"Let's say we grant your cousin immunity." Marquez pulled his phone out and laid it on the dash. "I mean, let's say I make an offer."

"Let's fast-forward this conversation. Next comes the part where I say I don't have his number. Then you ask, why not? I say I don't want you to bust my cousin and then you insinuate I am the cousin. Okay with you if we just skip to the end, because I'm a little wired this morning. I've been staring at a computer screen all night, and now I'm watching you use my car as a kitchen table. It depresses me. Why don't we deal with the rest of the predictable questions, then say good-bye?"

"What I'm saying is we won't bust your cousin."

Ungar smiled a tight-lipped private smile, kept his gaze through the windshield.

"That's for sure, and you say it every time. It's still not going to happen."

"We want to sit down with him, but it could be over the phone. He could give me information that makes it easy to get him immunity. Why don't we call him?"

Ungar started fiddling with the CD deck, and Marquez ate the rest of the burger, leaned back in the leather seat, wondering as he had each time if the expensive car had been bought with profits made selling bear parts. He still harbored the thought that Ungar could be their bear farmer. String it together a particular way, factor in his computer skills, trips to the mountains, the house he owned in Placerville that was rented to a family. You could get there, though Ungar didn't even have a speeding ticket on his record.

"Still can't help you," Ungar said, breaking the silence.

The CD changer clicked, and "Pass the Courvoisier" started playing. Ungar reached to turn it off and then withdrew his finger.

"What do you like more, Jay-Z or Busta Rhymes?" Ungar asked, then said, "Music has all gone past us, it's all about money and making a lifestyle for people like you and me. You got any kids?"

"Yeah."

"I never wanted any, but it's lonely at night. Now I want the money, build myself a lifestyle."

"You've got the car, maybe you move somewhere nicer." Marquez paused. "I think you did a really good thing when you called us the first time. That was a stand-up move."

"A cop knocked out my cousin's two front teeth. Hit him with the baton." He took his hand off the wheel and play-swung like a baton coming at Marquez's face. "Real cops too, not fish cops, and no reason for it. Just didn't like his Asian face. What do you think of my face?"

"I see tension."

"I'm tense because this is getting old."

"You told us you went to parties in Placerville with your cousin. You mentioned a woman with black hair."

"Already answered that."

Marquez tried a few more questions, then crumpled the paper trash from the burger, pushed open his door, and said, "Thanks for seeing me today."

"Anytime."

A couple of hours later, after he was home, Marquez got a call from their seller, the mechanized rasp coming through his cell. "They carried it too far," the voice said. "A mistake, humiliating for you, it shouldn't have happened that way. I'm delivering the galls. I'll tell you where to find them."

"This isn't working for me. You make it too hard."

"I can get you as much as you want."

"Why don't you personally bring me what I bought the other night?"

The line clicked, and he was gone.

11

That night Marquez walked with Katherine along Stinson Beach. Blue starlight reflected off the waves and surf foamed over their bare feet. He loved the salt smell, the long crescent of sand empty in front of them, walking with his hand on the smooth skin of her upper hip, feeling the rhythmic flow of her muscles, the warm heat. They caught up on things, talking about Maria first. More tales about Maria's driving too fast, having close calls, inches from one accident, and Kath feeling that he needed to have a serious discussion with her. Then talking about the bedroom they were going to add onto the house and a deal Kath had found on the Internet for a week's stay in a Kauai condo on a website called CondoBob.com. It was so cheap she wondered if they couldn't go at Thanksgiving.

She was making pretty good money with her two coffee bars in San Francisco, not great money but better money than they'd seen, though they both knew it was going to take everything they had and then some to do the bedroom addition. A lot of the work he'd have to do himself, and they wouldn't be able to afford to travel, but tonight it was nice to talk and dream.

They left Hawaii and talked about the house addition in more detail. Driving around Sausalito she'd seen the work of an architect named Barbara Brown and thought it was great. She wasn't saying change architects but wanted to show their architect some of the details she was interested in.

Marquez had hired Josh, a young architect whose plans the county bureaucrats kept sending back for revisions. Though both he and Kath had been enthusiastic about Josh at the start, Katherine had started to talk like she wasn't directly involved with him. But he knew Josh would get it done, and even if they had a permit now they couldn't start building.

All this second-guessing Josh made Marquez think of his grandfather and the patience his grandfather had shown him when he'd been an unhappy kid with a lot of nervous habits, an unintentional loner uncomfortable at school and distrustful of adults. Alongside his grandfather he'd learned the little bit of construction he knew, principles he hoped would help him build this bedroom addition. With his grandfather he'd built a dry rock wall along a dip in the driveway, the deck off the dining room, and a number of other small projects. His grandfather had shown him how doing something well shaped your whole life. Marquez figured his ghost would look over his shoulder as he worked out how to do this addition. He knew also that the architect would eventually deliver an approved set of plans, and the timing would be fine.

As they left the beach and walked to the truck the conversation turned toward the bear operation. He'd already told her the FBI crime lab hadn't pulled any fingerprints and had only trace DNA that came off the CD jewel box, probably a combination of the man who'd transported it and himself. Either way, the DNA would only serve to corroborate.

"Someone hacked into Fish and Game personnel files more than a year ago," he said.

"That long ago?"

"Yeah."

"What's being done about it?"

"We're getting emergency funding for new firewalls."

"Things are that tight?"

"They are."

She was quiet a moment, then said, "So they're not going to catch him by tracing who hacked in."

"The two things might not even connect. Could be some hacker was in and out for a while just because it was a fun challenge. May have read something about the Special Operations Unit and hacked into that for cheap thrills."

"The CD scares me."

She was voicing her feelings but also asking him a question. He was the one who did this for a living: how worried was he? He hadn't told her about this last buy, this shakedown, stripping his shirt on the empty creek road, or the call this afternoon propelling it all forward again.

"The guy we're dealing with is a little bit of a psycho, but he's also very connected, which means he's not too far out there. He can talk to people, and he's built a network. One thing, though, it feels like his problem with law enforcement goes beyond business. Still, I'm betting business comes first."

"Could he have anything to do with the murder of that student? Has anything more come of that? What's that detective's name again?"

"Kendall."

"Has he told you anything new?"

"Not really, and I'll probably go see Vandemere's father. I called him today and introduced myself, told him we were working a bear operation and that I was very sorry and wanted to do anything I could to help find who killed his son."

"You're kidding, you really called him?"

"He calls Kendall once a week. He wants to know where things are at."

"But it must be very hard for him to talk about. What did you ask him?"

"I introduced myself, told him what my Fish and Game team does, and then asked if Jed had ever mentioned anything in conversation or emails about bear poachers."

"Because you don't trust Kendall?"

"How do you get there from what I said?"

"I know you."

"In a way you're right. I asked to read the emails his son sent him this summer."

"Oh, my God—I could never ask someone to do that."

"I think he was glad to get the call, Kath. His twelve-year-old daughter is taking it very hard, and I get the feeling his wife is hurting too much to talk. He said over the years he did a lot of backpacking and fishing with Jed. He blames himself in some ways for Jed being up there in the Crystal Basin alone."

Marquez could understand feeling that way and thought briefly about Julie, his first wife. A terrible image came back to him as they returned to the sandy parking area and got in the truck. He and Julie had gone to Africa after the wedding, planning to travel and live on the cheap, camp wherever they could. She'd been abducted from their campsite, and for days he'd ridden around with a constable looking for her. They'd found her by watching the vultures, her body in brush not far from the campsite. A month later he'd thought he'd found the men who'd raped and killed her, and he'd felt something akin to elation at the prospect of killing them, been so ready to do it. But among their belongings he couldn't find her ring or any of the other things he needed as proof before pulling the trigger.

Long ago, he'd told Katherine about searching for Julie's kidnappers and what he'd felt when he found their camp, but you don't tell your second wife about your continuing dreams of your first. And he didn't have to tell Katherine about the empathy he felt with Jed Vandemere's father. She knew.

He'd brought Julie's body home to her parents and buried her where she'd grown up at the base of the Bitterroot Mountains. It had been a long time later, almost fifteen years, when he'd fallen for Katherine. Theirs was a soft, warm-rounded, gentle love, a comfortable easiness together. It wasn't a lesser thing, but different. When he'd gone to Africa with Julie he'd been so in love that the world felt completely open. That was youth and this was middle age and the two were different, even for those that liked to say they felt the same inside.

"Give me something I can call reassurance or tell me you can't," Katherine said.

"This guy seems to be carefully checking me out. He sent a couple of aggressive guys out on the last buy and called me today to apologize, to keep stringing it along. He wants to keep the money coming."

"What's his trip then?"

"I don't know."

"But not like Kline?"

"No."

Kline had been a drug smuggler, a contract killer, a career black marketeer who'd branched into abalone because they brought fifty dollars each and he could gather thousands of them. Breaking that ring had been violent.

"He's using guys he hires to do these buys with you?" she asked.

"He insulates himself."

"Someone must know him."

"That's what I'm betting, Kath."

Marquez turned up the mountain road and they began to climb away from the ocean. They could see the moon over the water, a long line of reflected light.

"You'll take him down," she said and smiled at her own use of those words. She lived a totally different urban life, running her two San Francisco coffee bars. Her friends called her Cappuccino Kathy. She laughed and recovered the earlier mood of the night.

"And I'm going to take you down when we get home," she said. "You're going down tonight."

12

Katherine and Maria were asleep when he climbed into his truck. A couple of deer bolted through the darkness down the slope into the brush and trees, and a few minutes later he was on the road, holding a coffee cup in one hand, adjusting the heat and defroster fan with the other. He liked the early mornings, the quiet chance to think. The conversation with Ungar yesterday disturbed him, was on his mind this morning. When he finished his coffee he talked with Shauf, listening closely to her report of the search for bait piles and her plan to return to the Crystal Basin.

"We've heard fresh reports of off-road vehicles at night and we're checking those areas today," she said. "Where are you?"

"On my way to Nyland's trailer park."

"You heard they kicked him loose, right?"

"Yeah, Kendall called me."

"Hey, he's our new best friend."

Marquez didn't want to get into a Kendall conversation this morning. "I'll call you after taking a look at Nyland's place."

Ducks lifted from the rice paddies along the Sacramento River flood plain as he crossed the causeway. He drove through Sacramento and then into the foothills and an hour later exited onto Six Mile Road, remembering Kendall's wry "There should be a road sign for peace officers that reads 5.7 miles to the Nyland trailer overlook."

Marquez stopped short of the ridge, turning down a dirt track and following that until he could hide his truck. He walked back out the dirt road, smelling oak, pine, and brush, dry and waiting on rain. Near the ridge he cut left into the trees and found a place where he could see the meadow below. He saw the flat gray house foundations in the middle, the abandoned sales office on one end, a broad deck off it layered with brown pine needles. On the far end were three aluminum-skinned trailers, one of which Kendall had told him Nyland lived in. The trailer with the propane tank. Nyland's Toyota and an older blue Ford F-150 were parked nearby. A hound sat on the Toyota hood.

Nyland's trailer had a window like an opaque eye facing the meadow, the interior hidden from Marquez's binoculars by curtains, iron stairs running down from the trailer door to the dry meadow grass. Behind that one and up the slope were two other trailers, these resting on cinder blocks. The door of the second was padlocked, and the last trailer, the one bordering the trees, missing its door. He watched a dog hop out and guessed the dogs slept there.

He brought the glasses back to the Ford pickup, jotted down its license plate. Nyland had a pretty good setup out here, a lot of wooded country and no one around to question anything he did. He could skin a bear on one of the slab foundations, and no one would be the wiser.

Before Marquez had reached the highway he'd learned the blue Ford F-150 was registered to Sophie Broussard. He drove back into Placerville and passing the Waffle House saw Petroni's Fish and Game truck. He doubled back and pulled in alongside it.

Petroni was in a booth wearing a neatly creased uniform though it was Sunday morning.

"Saw your truck when I drove past and couldn't pass up the chance to talk to you."

Petroni's look was morose, distant, but he gestured. "Have a seat."

After Marquez had slid into the booth and ordered scrambled eggs and coffee, Petroni volunteered, "I've got a special meeting at the sheriff's office this morning. I'm meeting Kendall and his partner in fifteen minutes."

"What do you have left to say to him?"

"Nothing he doesn't already know."

"Then maybe today will end it. I just came from Nyland's place. There's a Ford pickup parked out there that's registered to Sophie."

"He owes her money, and he's supposed to fix her truck to pay her off. She says that's the only way she'll get paid. She's been driving the car of the people she's house-sitting for, but supposedly he's got it fixed now. What does Sophie have to do with you?"

"Nyland tried to run me off the road the other night."

"Then maybe your cover is still good."

Petroni started to slide out of the booth, saying, "I'm late."

"Do you want me to come along?"

"Why would I?"

"It might help to have another wildlife officer in the room."

The offer was about more than helping Petroni out, and of course, Petroni knew that. Marquez wanted to know more about Kendall's investigation, felt he needed to know.

"No, thanks."

Petroni walked out of the Waffle House ahead of him, got in the truck without looking back, then stopped and lowered his window as he came alongside Marquez.

"About a year ago word got back to Kendall I'd told the sheriff he ought to fire him. This is his payback."

"Wouldn't hurt to have me there."

Petroni stared hard before nodding.

13

After parking outside the sheriff's office Marquez walked over to a small black Mercedes and looked through the windows, confirming what he'd already assumed. Bell's wife's car. In the slot next to it was a state car, an old Crown Vic with a soft black leatherbound book on the passenger seat, a Bible belonging to Charlotte Floyd, one of the department's two internal affairs officers. He doubted Petroni knew that either she or Bell would be here.

Inside, Marquez asked where the meeting was, and they held him there until Kendall came out. "This is complicated enough already," Kendall said. "You don't need to be here."

"We had breakfast together. He asked me to come."

"Right."

They stood close to each other, Marquez looking down in his eyes. He could feel Kendall debating whether he could trade it for something later. Kendall pointed. "If, and only if, you don't say a word."

The room held a long, scarred linoleum table and metal folding chairs. Hawse adjusted a video camera resting on a tripod in the corner of the room. A small tape recorder stood on end like a gravestone miniature in the middle of the table, Floyd and Bell sat next to each other on the right-hand side, next to them chairs for Hawse and Kendall, and across the table, Petroni sitting, with his palms on the table top, a faint sheen of sweat on his forehead.

"Lieutenant Marquez," Kendall said, "take the chair at the end of the table."

Marquez looked from Petroni to Charlotte Floyd, smelled the perfume she favored and watched her jaw tighten as she acknowledged him, remembered how her hands had trembled as she'd leafed through pages of her Bible to prove him wrong when he'd questioned the accuracy of her quote from Ecclesiastes. She'd been right about the quote but wrong about him.

In a quiet voice Kendall explained his problem. He hoped the meeting would be brief, the confusion quickly cleared up. He paid Petroni a compliment as the area warden around here that everyone knew on sight, adding, "It's Sunday morning, all of us have better things to do. My partner here has a football game he doesn't want to miss."

No one so much as smiled. Petroni's eyes found a spot high on the wall behind Bell's head, his face set as he waited for Kendall to finish listening to himself talk.

"Put bluntly, we have overwhelming evidence Warden Petroni lied to us and impeded a murder investigation."

Kendall flipped through notes sequentially recapping interviews and misleading statements. He addressed Petroni directly for the first time.

"Do you understand that we're going to ask some questions this morning that may later be incriminating?"

"Yes."

"You can request that a lawyer be present—"

"I've been in law enforcement twenty-two years, Kendall."

Kendall listed the individuals in the room as the videotape started. He asked Petroni if he was uncomfortable with the format or felt coerced. Petroni looked across the table at Bell, as if for support, though at breakfast he'd referred to him as "No Balls Bell," said he was the worst he'd ever worked under, an administrative hire, a climber who'd never spent a single day in the field.

"Did you have any contact with Jed Vandemere in June or July of this year?" Kendall asked.

"Yes."

"Are you aware that you've previously answered 'no' multiple times to the same question?"

"I ran into him in the Crystal Basin several times in the early summer."

Petroni had brought in his logbook. He opened it and they waited, watching him slowly flip the pages.

"Union Valley Reservoir is where I first talked to him. I also saw him at Ice House Lake, Loon and Barrett Lakes."

"Do you remember me asking you if you'd met with Jed Vandemere at Barrett Lake?"

"Yes."

"So are you saying you previously lied to me?"

"Yes," and it came out easily, as if it were normal in the course of a day that he'd lie to Kendall, or that anyone in their right mind would. Marquez read quiet satisfaction on Kendall's face, caught the gleam in his eyes, victory over a liar after all the denials. Kendall repeated the dates, reconfirming chronologically the times and places of Petroni's meetings. Forty-five minutes later Kendall flipped the cassette in the recorder and asked if anyone wanted to take a break. No one did.

"Let's go to early August," Kendall said. "Did you see him on the first of August?"

"August third."

"Where?"

"Ice House Resort. He'd approached me once before about gunshots he'd heard at night. He was concerned they were shots fired by poachers, and we talked about that. I investigated and didn't find anything to go on, but I asked him to keep an eye out."

"Did you like him?"

Petroni frowned at the question, said, "I didn't like or dislike him. He was a college kid with a big imagination. He wanted to find something. There were men in and out of Barrett that he was sure were poachers, but when I questioned him he didn't have anything I could work with."

"People he thought were poaching bear?"

Petroni forced a big false grin, said, "I think that's what we're talking about."

"Do you have dates on all your conversations with him regarding poachers?"

"You're welcome to copy my log."

Bell nodded approval, and Hawse slid his chair back, got heavily to his feet. He took the log and left the room.

"You were on a first-name basis with Jed Vandemere?"

"I barely knew him."

"How many times over the summer would you say you talked with him?"

"I don't know."

"Make a guess."

"Ten."

"Are they all in your log?"

"I don't know."

"Did you ever speak with him outside the Crystal Basin area?"

"Yes."

"And where were those conversations?"

"In Placerville."

"Do you remember denying you ever saw or talked to him in Placerville?"

"It really doesn't matter."

That got a stir out of the room, a shifting, but nothing from Kendall. He was cool with that. There was no hurry, no place left for Petroni to run.

"Did he say anything to you about arguing with bear hunters?"

"No."

"Are you certain?"

"Look, Kendall, I heard the same story you did, so don't make it sound like you're trying to discover something." Petroni's voice hardened. "You talked to March Baylor, the same as I did. Bear hunters were out running their hounds, and Vandemere followed them. They got angry when he honked his horn and messed with them teaching their dogs. March was there, that's what he told me, and I know for a fact that's what he told you."

"When did this incident take place?"

"End of the first week of August, and I tried to find Vandemere after I heard about it, but I couldn't find him. I thought he'd left the basin."

Kendall turned to Bell and explained, "Baylor is an old coot, a hunter who's been here forever. He knows everybody." He turned back toward Petroni, then paused purposefully before asking his next question.

"Are you saying you lied to me because you thought I'd heard the story somewhere else already?"

"I'm saying I know for a fact you'd already talked to March Baylor. You didn't need me. You'd already heard the story."

"So it was okay to lie?"

Petroni stared at Bell, said, "Goddamn you, Kendall."

Kendall pushed his chair back. He got slowly to his feet and walked to the empty end of the table as if contemplating something and unaffected by Petroni's emotion.

"Let's get something clear," Kendall said, "because we're straying from it. You're not a suspect in a murder investigation. You're not even, what is that horseshit phrase the Feds use, 'a person of interest.' In fact, we could shorten this interview if you'd just tell us why you lied to me. I know there's a good reason. I'm going to find out what it is."

Petroni lifted a hand from the table, glanced at Marquez, and shook his head. Kendall walked back to his chair.

"Was it because of Sophie?"

Petroni hesitated a long time before nodding.

"I'm sorry, warden, we need a verbal response."

"Yes, it was."

"You wanted to keep her out of it?"

"I know how you operate."

"Is that why you wanted to minimize her involvement?"

"I knew you were after me."

"You didn't want me questioning her about Jed Vandemere because you think it's personal between you and me?"

Petroni didn't answer and Kendall didn't press him, saying instead, "What I'm going to ask next may make you uncomfortable." He paused. "Did Vandemere take an interest in your girlfriend?"

Petroni was slow to answer. He stared hard at Kendall, said, "Not one she wanted. He came on to her but she didn't have any interest."

"Because she was already going out with you?"

"Because she wasn't interested."

"Did he harass her?"

"In a way."

"Threaten her?"

"No."

"Stalk her?"

"No."

"Did she ask you to do something about him?"

"She asked me to talk to him."

"Did you?"

"I did."

"What did you say to him?"

"I told him she was frightened by the way he wouldn't leave her alone."

"Did you warn him not to go near her?"

"Not really."

"Does that mean you didn't warn him, or that you did?"

"It means what I just told you. I asked him to leave her alone."

"Not show up where she works?"

"Yes."

"What did you tell him would happen if he showed up there?"

"I don't remember."

"Try."

Petroni said nothing.

"Did Sophie stay with you last night?"

"No."

"Do you know where we could find her this morning?"

"She'll be at work later."

"Do you know where she stayed last night?"

"No."

"All right, let me ask something else, and please understand I have to ask this, so don't be offended. We've talked to people who think the attraction between her and Jed Vandemere was mutual. Is it possible she told you one thing and felt another?"

"You don't know her, Kendall. You think you do, but you don't." Marquez, watching Petroni's face as he said that, no longer doubted that Petroni loved her. "She made the mistake of telling the Vandemere kid that she worked at the Creekview Saloon in Placerville. After that he wouldn't leave her alone. She couldn't kick him out, and she didn't want to lose her job by making it an issue with the manager. She and her manager have had problems anyway. She asked me to talk to him in early August, so I did, but there was nothing too personal about it and the conversation was friendly. I never threatened him." He frowned. "Why would I?"

"Because he was in love with your girlfriend."

"You don't know that."

"No, we're not going to find it in your log, are we?"

It was the first sarcastic comment Kendall had made, and Marquez knew Kendall wished he could pull it back.

"You know," Petroni said, "I fell in love with a younger woman and my wife is divorcing me. I've made a mess of my personal life, but you don't have the right, you've got the mouth, but you don't have the right to say what you're saying."

Kendall raised a palm to stop Petroni's retort. "How did Vandemere answer when you told him to back off Sophie?"

Petroni seemed to turn inward. When he spoke his voice was leaden.

"He waited for her after work the next night. He was standing near her truck."

"When was that?"

"She'll know the date."

"How did he respond to you?"

"Said it was none of my business."

"Did you tell him she was your girlfriend?"

"He already knew."

"How did he know?"

"I don't know and I never saw him again."

Questioning went on another hour. Kendall made a show of thanking him for coming in, and then it was over. Petroni walked out without a glance at anyone. Marquez was the last out. He watched Charlotte back out of her slot and drive away, then stood talking to Bell.

"How much of this did you know about?" Bell asked.

"I knew about the problems with his marriage, and Kendall came to Sacramento looking for a way to get Bill to talk to him about Vandemere."

"The day he came to see you?" Bell asked. "He didn't say a word to me about it."

"He's doing it his way."

"I'm sure the union will file a complaint on Petroni's behalf and provide a defense, but I'm suspending him while this is investigated. There's nothing that can excuse what he's done, and it's very, very disturbing to me. He has intentionally obstructed a murder investigation."

Marquez could easily picture one idea any homicide detective would tease out after this interview—a handsome grad student comes after Petroni's new young girlfriend, and Petroni tells him to back off. The grad student tells Petroni he'll go out with her if he wants, and not only that, she wants him too. The warden becomes enraged. Already on edge because of his divorce, he loses it and goes hunting. He knows about Vandemere's problem with the bear hunters so he uses a bear rifle. Marquez looked at Bell's sober face. It wasn't that much of a leap.

"Is he involved yet in your operation?" Bell asked.

"No."

Bell got in his car, lowered the window, and added, "I don't want your team to have any contact whatsoever with him until this is resolved."

Marquez nodded, then watched him drive away.

14

After Bell left, Marquez drove to the team's rented office in town, walked from there a quarter mile to the Sierra Guides office, sandwiched between brick buildings along an alley. Through dusty windows he saw two desks and a sitting arrangement, couch and chairs grouped around a bearskin rug, a coffee table, with hunting magazines resting on top. Mounted on the walls were the heads of a rhino, a water buffalo, a lion, and a grizzly. He read the office hours in white script on the glass door. Closed Friday–Monday. "Gone Hunting," a sign announced.

Most California hunting guide businesses were small, the enterprises of hunters trying to marry what they loved doing with making a living, which was hard to do. Bear hunting was tied to a lottery system, and a hunter couldn't know whether he'd win a tag in a given year or not, so a guide who specialized in bear couldn't count on repeat business. Occasionally, guides turned out to be fronts for poachers, not often, but it did happen. With

Nyland working here it made sense to learn everything they could about the ownership.

Roberts had found new information on the listed business owner, a Joe Durham—gossip she'd gotten after calling one of the numbers on Durham's website and asking for a reference. According to a former client, Durham's main income was a coalition of timber industry companies seeking better logging access in the Sierra Nevada. Durham lobbied for them. He was very knowledgeable about forest management and U.S. government policies and, from what she'd gathered, a switch-hitter on environmental issues. It just depended on who held the checkbook. The former client knew Durham from working with him at the state capitol, and that relationship evolved into a weekend boar hunt along the central coastal mountains. Marquez called Roberts as he walked away from the alley. They picked up the earlier conversation, Roberts relating what she'd learned from Durham's former client.

"Nyland was on that hunt," Roberts said. "They called him Durham's right-hand man, the guy in the field, made it sound like Nyland did the real guiding and for Durham the guide business is more of a vanity."

"Or a cover."

"Sure."

"Durham represents timber?"

"Yeah, can you believe that?" She laughed. It threw a new twist at the SOU cover story, pretending to do business in an area this guy might know too much about.

"Keep digging."

Marquez sat at his desk in the TreeSearch office and worked the phone, computer, and fax. He'd started an "around the world" on both Nyland and Durham, checking for any criminal history. He drove down to the sheriff's office and read the file on Nyland— a first confrontation with police at age eighteen, a second three months later, a month in jail, questioning in a burglary, guns stolen, Nyland a suspect in a drug case, charges dropped, then an incident where he'd boxed in a cop in a parking spot, locked his truck, and went into a shop to buy coffee, trapping the car of an officer he'd gone to high school with and later calling it a practical joke. The officer had consequently been unable to respond to an emergency call, and Nyland did five months and service work for that. There was bad beating of a man outside a bar that left the victim blind in one eye, though witnesses testified that Nyland had only defended himself, witnesses who were Nyland's friends. Got off on that one too. Then the Tuolumne road rage incident and another where he'd tailed a Mariposa cop, a young woman, for days until undercover officers finally arrested him. He'd never given an explanation. He hadn't been arrested since until the Creekview confrontation with Petroni.

Marquez read the file, then drove back to the TreeSearch office, ate lunch in front of the computer, looking over Durham's website. He talked to Roberts again later in the afternoon, and she listed the arsenal of guns registered in Durham's name, including seven hunting rifles, one of which was a .30-30 Winchester.

Later that afternoon he met with Brad Alvarez, having decided Alvarez would be the best on the team to meet with Durham. They roughed out what he'd say, that he had a bear tag and wanted a guided hunt to increase his chances of bagging a bear, that he was looking for the right guide outfit.

"Think I need to shave?" Alvarez asked.

"You could always clean it up a little bit." Watched him smile. "But don't overdo it. They're selling you, you're not selling them."

Alvarez had cut his wiry hair short and lost his black goatee. Put an oily Mackinaw on him now and he'd be the guy who'd come out to the house, climb up a tree, and top it for you. He knew guns, hunting, the woods. He was a confident liar, and cover stories came easily to him, a fact he attributed to being smaller than average and growing up in a tough neighborhood.

"If you can avoid talking about TreeSearch all the better," Marquez said, "because this might be one guy who knows how to check up on government grants."

Alvarez studied the driver's license photo of Durham. It was a hard-to-read face, composed, serious to the point of severe, a left cheek that looked like it had been caved in once. He touched the face in the photo.

"I've got a friend who got hit with a baseball bat. It crushed his cheekbone and he didn't get it fixed correctly so now one nostril runs all the time. His wife left him because she got tired of it."

"Come on."

"I'm not kidding. He used to take antihistamines, but he drives a UPS truck for a living and the stuff he'd take would make him fall asleep. I'm not saying he and his wife didn't have other problems."

Marquez glanced at the license info again. Durham's birthday was in a week. He'd be fifty-three. Somewhere Roberts had gotten the idea he'd only been in the state for five years. If so, he'd done well for himself in that time, and except for the damaged cheekbone he looked like a banker type.

"There's a website," Marquez said, as Alvarez settled in front of the laptop.

"Let me check my email, and then I'll take a look."

When Alvarez clicked onto the Sierra Guides site Marquez stood over his shoulder, though he'd already studied it. "About Us," "Hunting Tours," "Home," and three or four other icons, each with a particular blandness, description, and pictures but nothing really there. A photo of Nyland standing over a big buck. No photo of Durham.

They fleshed out more details of Alvarez's cover story. Alvarez worked for TreeSearch, was hired in Vancouver where he was from and had just been reassigned here. He liked Placerville okay, mostly liked that you didn't have to drive far out of town to get into open country. He would trash-talk TreeSearch a little, let them know he was his own man, then take the conversation back to hunting. Tell them some of his hunting stories. In his wallet he had a photo of himself with a bear, a poaching kill the SOU had handled.

He would say he'd hunted with his dad, mostly boar and deer hunting, not all of it legal, then got into bear on his own later in Canada where there wasn't a lot of enforcement looking over your shoulder. Wasn't much here anymore either, he'd heard, budget cuts and all. It was pretty much the honor system, or open season, depending how you looked at it. At the right moment, if it came, if Durham or Nyland picked up on the implied, Alvarez would let slip that he was willing to pay to bend the rules if that's what it took to get a bear. Let them know he'd done that before, but not say where, even if pressed, letting them know he'd keep a confidence.

After they'd worked it out Alvarez headed back to the Crystal Basin to hook up with Shauf and the rest of the SOU. Marquez took a chair and phoned Matt Fong to see if he'd heard anything more on the computer hacking. Matt groused good-naturedly about his desk job, how he was getting soft and missed being with the team, though they both knew he was much happier being able to see his family every night, and the promotion had meant a lot to him. Marquez liked him, was glad he'd made captain, and hoped he would continue up the ladder. He would make a good chief. He listened as Fong downplayed the FBI's progress.

"John, it won't go that much farther. There's no easy way to track where they hacked in. What'll happen are new firewalls, but we aren't going to find out who got in. What I hear is that it was someone smart enough not to leave tracks back to his door."

"I want to float another idea with you," Marquez said. "You and I were at those legislative hearings in March. I'm wondering if the leak came from someone there. You know, worked its way from a committee to someone on the outside, a friend, a business associate." Or a lobbyist, he might have added but didn't want to yet.

"Not likely," Fong said.

"Mull it over anyway."

"I think about this every minute of the day."

Fong had a terrific memory and might be able to identify more of the people who'd been there. Now, as he hung up with Fong, someone knocked. Marquez walked over and opened the door to Kendall's face.

"I'm seeing more of you than anyone," Marquez said. "Come on in and sit anywhere you want. Sorry we're light on furniture."

He didn't particularly like Kendall's showing up. Anything more Kendall had to say today could probably have been done via phone, and Kendall knew they worried about their cover being jeopardized.

"I'm sorry about today, sorry I've had to come after Petroni." Kendall adjusted one of their flea market chairs and sat down. "Sophie doesn't corroborate his story. She says she was attracted to Vandemere and went swimming with him a few times at Loon Lake. Petroni caught them cavorting there."

"Is cavorting your word or hers?"

"Her exact words were cruder, and I guess Petroni just happened to be patrolling the area, or maybe he put his undercover experience to work and followed her. She didn't say it exactly, but it doesn't sound like she was fully clothed. When Petroni found out he got very angry, went to Vandemere, and threatened to haul him in on a bogus violation."

"What would that be?"

"You tell me, a four-inch fish, maybe, I don't know your business. According to her, Petroni routinely uses his badge to throw his weight around."

"Are you here to road test a theory?" *Here to see if I can knock holes in it before you take on Petroni.* "Petroni didn't kill Vandemere."

"Naw, of course not. Wardens don't kill geology students, and they don't take bribes or make up violations. Jealous boyfriends kill, not wardens."

"You're running too fast with this."

"You never know how they're going to go. The last case I worked I got burned on because I moved too slowly. This was a B and E of a cabin outside of Pollock Pines early this summer. The perps turned out to be gangbangers up visiting for the day from Sacramento, which is what they do nowadays. They go for a day in the country and visit remote cabins. Unfortunately, the owner was home when they broke in. They didn't realize it because he'd loaned his car to his son for the day. I'm talking about four shit-bags in a lowered Honda. The DA let them plea-bargain to manslaughter because I didn't have enough. I didn't lean on them hard enough early enough. They claimed it was an accidental death, they were only there to rob him. Truth is, they beat him to death with the tire iron they'd pried the front door open with. If I find who killed Vandemere, there won't be a manslaughter plea. "

"Good."

"There's a phone call I want to make with you. Can I buy you a cup of coffee?"

"You're not walking me to lunch again, are you?"

"No."

They walked up the street past the courthouse, then crossed to the old soda works that had become a coffeehouse with art hanging from the walls. In the rear of the building were rooms carved out of rock and a door that led to a mine shaft. They chatted about the building as they waited for the coffees. Kendall said that he was into California history and that the gold rush was still the single most significant economic event in the history of the country. Marquez wondered how the Great Depression weighed in, but left it alone. Then they carried their coffees across the street and found a place to sit.

"I've got another bear hunter for you to talk to," Kendall said.

"What's his name?"

"Brandt. Know him?"

"No."

"He wears a piece of dried bear heart on a leather thong around his neck, says it gives him power in bed with his girlfriend. He's pointed me toward other hunters, houndsmen, as you people call them. He's also suspected of being an accomplice on another case up here involving a theft, so he wants to stay on my good side. Right now, he's waiting on my call. I told him you're an associate and I'm going to put you on the line. What he's told me is that he and other unnamed people know of someone who makes monthly payments to a warden up here. They meet out some dirt road in the Crystal Basin, warden gets paid and afterwards stays out of certain areas for a period of time. I don't have a warden's name yet, but how many wardens are there, how many possibilities? The warden is stepping the rate up lately, and Brandt's been hearing the whining."

"Is the word out that you're looking for dirt?"

"I'm sure it is and I'm sure they're lining up to fuck with Petroni's life, but the punch line for you is he told me this unnamed warden warned these hunters to be watching for an undercover team."

"When did he tell you that?"

"A couple of days ago."

Marquez sipped the coffee, thinking about Kendall's motives, then said, "Okay, make the call," and watched him punch in the numbers, listened as Kendall told Brandt he was going to put another investigator, a colleague on the line. Marquez took the phone, and Brandt said, "I already told Detective Kendall I'm getting this from a friend who works in the business."

"You hunt legitimate?"

"Yes, sir, I don't have any problem with the rules."

"Let's talk about your friend who's giving you the information."

"Yes, sir."

"What business is he in?"

"Mostly he's a lookout, but he helps some with skinning and cleaning too."

"He's working for poachers."

"I guess so, but I'm not involved in any of that, sir."

"I understand." Marquez drew a quiet breath, looked at Kendall before speaking again, then said, "We called Fish and Game and they don't have any undercover team."

"All I know is supposedly the warden said there was one in the area and to watch out 'cause they're not under his control."

"What's this warden look like?"

"He's the regular warden."

"Petroni?"

"I guess, but I'm just saying I heard it was him. Don't go telling Petroni I said it." Then Brandt added, "Detective Kendall has got to stick to our deal."

Marquez handed the phone back to Kendall and listened to Kendall lie to Brandt about what he was doing to help clear him on the other case. He winked at Marquez, then hung up.

"You're a class act," Marquez said.

"Well, I owe it all to my clientele. They bring out the best in me." He patted Marquez's knee and then stood, saying, "I don't think Petroni killed anyone, but he may be dirty. Keep that to yourself, and I'll be in touch."

15

At dawn the next day Nyland drove to the rear lot of a bakery in Placerville and went in through a screen door. When he came back out a tall skinny baker trailed him and helped hump burlap bags across the lot to Nyland's truck. Bags that were likely full of day-old bread. Nyland cinched a tarp down before getting something from his glove compartment for the baker.

Alvarez, who had the best angle, called it out. "Looks like a bag of dope."

Whatever it was, the baker pocketed it, lingered, raced a cigarette, shifting like a crane from one foot to the other as Nyland talked. Their breath clouded the air in front of them. A few minutes later Nyland got into his truck and backed out.

The bread wasn't going to a homeless shelter. This time of year black bear instinctually eased away from protein and turned to a high-carbohydrate diet to accelerate the accumulation of fat for hibernation. Right around now, bread made good bait.

Nyland left the bakery and drove to a health club on the east side of town. He disappeared into a locker room at the rear of the building, then they watched him work out, pumping iron, running on a treadmill for half an hour. Marquez and Shauf were parked well down the street, talking as they waited for Nyland to move again. The rising sun brightened the inside of the truck cab, illuminating Shauf's face, and looking at her Marquez doubted she'd slept much last night. She talked about her sister.

"She told me she'd give anything to feel normal for a whole day. They're talking to her about experimental therapies."

"What do the kids know?"

"Just that mommy is sick."

"How old are they again?"

"Three and six."

"How are you doing?"

"Terrible."

They watched Nyland reappear on the sidewalk in a T-shirt and jeans, his face still red-tinged, hair wet. He loitered in the sun, talked on his cell phone, and a couple minutes later Sophie drove around the corner in her Ford pickup. She pulled up in front of the club but remained in the truck, and they figured Nyland planned to finish the conversation before getting in with her. That would leave the bread and Nyland's truck here, a precautionary move on Nyland's part. He would come back when he was ready to feed the bait piles.

But he didn't get in her truck. Instead, Sophie got out and came around onto the sidewalk in front of him. He held his hand up, shook his head in a not now gesture, then moved away from the club windows. She followed, and they heard fragments of her voice and saw her lash out, sending the phone flying. It blew apart on the sidewalk, battery skittering into the gutter. Shauf laughed as Nyland scrambled to gather the pieces. When he couldn't put the phone together he threw it down on the sidewalk and turned to her. It was easy to read: "You fucking bitch!"

"Makes me homesick," Cairo said over the radio, but the way Sophie had gone after him was eerie and the rest of the team was quiet. Sophie ran back to her truck, and Nyland hammered the roof with his fist before she pulled away.

"Petroni's heartthrob," Shauf said softly.

Nyland stayed in town all day, and at dusk Bobby Broussard joined him. They were playing pool in a second-story billiards hall when Marquez dropped Shauf at her van. Nyland and Bobby walked down to the Creekview Saloon and drank, and at 10:00 Nyland left the Creekview and drove out Highway 49 toward Georgetown, a two-lane winding road. Marquez sent Cairo in an old blue Ford van to catch him. Cairo drove the battered van up on Nyland's tail, hit the brights, and tapped his horn for Nyland to pull over to the shoulder so he could pass.

Of course, they knew he wouldn't, had counted on him not to, and Cairo tailgated him until he turned down the road to the Broussard property. Five minutes later Marquez followed, driving to the spot across the valley that they'd used in the past for surveilling the Broussard property. He drove lights-out up a badly rutted dirt road to a clearing where he could see back across the valley. He lowered his window, breathed the cold night air, and waited.

The Broussard property was a piece of cleared land that backed up against brushy terrain too steep for wild pig. A winding dirt road carved by a Caterpillar blade cut through a stand of pines and rose to the main house where Troy had raised his family. Behind the house Troy and his sons had chainsawed a clearing in the woods, and years ago they'd built a second structure that backed up against the steep slope but had never been finished. It still lacked electricity. A garden hose supplied water. The windows were covered with plastic. That was where Bobby lived, and Marquez could see him in the kitchen now with Nyland and Troy, Bobby hopping around like an insect drawn to the light.

There was a third building, a squat unpainted structure, a glorified shed partially hidden by brush, where the dogs slept in winter and where, mountain rumor had it, Sophie used to get locked up for days at a time as an adolescent.

Marquez remembered tracking Troy home years ago after a night hunt. Troy had taken three bears illegally, and Marquez had gotten here in time but lacked a warrant. While he'd stood guard over the house and waited for the warrant to arrive he'd watched Bobby and another cousin fill driveway ruts in the midday heat. They'd shoveled in dirt, watered it down, then compacted the soil by driving a jeep back and forth over the former ruts, drinking beer as they worked, a boom box hanging from the jeep's roll cage, playing loud rock and roll while Troy slept. The warrant had never arrived, and at dusk Marquez had left defeated.

At midnight the kitchen door swung open. Nyland and Bobby Broussard walked out, stood in the darkness near Nyland's truck, Bobby fidgeting, moving with nervous energy in and out of the light, his gawky movements made garish by the larger shadows he cast against the house. A few minutes later Troy joined them, headlights came on, and three trucks wound down the driveway and started toward Placerville, Nyland in the lead, Bobby a half mile back, Troy trailing.

Nyland went through Placerville and got on Highway 50 eastbound, Bobby not far behind, Troy well back, limping up the steep grade past Apple Hill, riding the slow lane, the headlights on his old truck no brighter than Halloween pumpkins, shoulders hunched as he gripped the wheel. Nyland drove past Pollock Pines and dropped toward the river basin, Bobby behind him, Roberts and Cairo trailing Bobby. When Nyland and Bobby crossed the concrete bridge and turned onto Crystal Basin Road, Cairo and Roberts hung back, then slowly followed.

But rather than cross over the ridge and drop toward the basin, Nyland parked on a shoulder before the road crested. Bobby pulled in behind him, and they killed their lights. Cairo and Roberts had the choice of continuing up and driving past them or parking on the shoulder well below.

"We're pulling over, pretending we've got a reason to be here, Lieutenant," Roberts said, and it was a questionable call, but Marquez didn't say anything.

They waited for Troy to arrive and thought he'd sweep the road from behind, guessing that he'd drive past Bobby and Nyland and become the lead vehicle as all three moved into the basin. Bobby would bring up the rear, taking Troy's place.

But it didn't happen that way. Instead, Troy pulled off the highway well before dropping to the river, three or four miles from where they were. He parked behind the shell of a long-abandoned diner and sat shielded from the highway, his lights off.

An hour passed before Nyland moved, retracing his route, leaving the basin road and crossing back over the American River. Somewhere between the river and where Marquez was parked, they lost him. Marquez assumed he was with Troy and decided their best move was to sit tight, so they waited, chattering to stay alert. Marquez backed his truck up among trees alongside the highway and drank from a Thermos of tea. He called Katherine, but she was sleepy and the conversation was short. Then Alvarez said he had something.

"There are lights up on the ridge way above you on your right."

"I don't see them, I don't have the angle," Marquez answered and saw only a dark, steep forested slope climbing to a ridge.

"That must be him," Alvarez said. "It's got to be him." For the next fifteen minutes they listened as Alvarez called out the progress of the lights. "Okay, they just went out."

Marquez looked at his watch, marked the time, and tried to put himself up on the ridge and in Nyland's head, getting out of the truck, in a hurry, dragging the burlap bags of bread. There'd been four bags, so maybe two trips. Awkward lugging those bags in the dark, and his boots would leave marks, the bags disrupting the duff under the trees. *We'll find your tracks tomorrow,* he thought, *and we'll find your bait pile.*

16

Nyland was up there long enough for Marquez to wonder if he had another way out, possibly a dirt road falling off the back of the ridge. But just before dawn headlights snaked down through the trees. Then Bobby Broussard's headlights came on, and he left the road shoulder where he'd sat all night. Nyland went past westbound, and Marquez cued his radio.

"Okay, he's off the slope and westbound in lane one at sixty-five, just passing Fresh Pond. Here comes S-2 right behind him, also lane one at sixty-five."

Marquez used the S-2 or suspect two designation for Troy, as they had through the night. Nyland was S-1, Bobby S-3. He called it out as Bobby went by a few minutes later.

Nyland exited at Six Mile Road, Troy and Bobby continuing to a restaurant in Placerville where Shauf reported Troy's getting wearily out of his truck, his fatigued face gray as granite in the early light. There was no reason to stay with them any longer and, with the exception of Alvarez, Marquez told the team to stand down, get some sleep, be ready to roll again later that day.

Alvarez met him across the river and up the canyon outside a restaurant in the small town of Kyburz. They bought coffee, a half dozen sugared donuts, and stood in cold wind near Marquez's truck, eating, talking, gulping coffee, letting the caffeine and sugar do their work. In Marquez's truck they drove up behind the abandoned diner and then along a potholed asphalt road until reaching a steel gate. Beyond the gate was a dirt track climbing into the forest. From tire tracks it looked like Nyland had driven up the steep slope and around the gate, and Marquez shifted into four-wheel drive and followed his tracks up and around pine stumps. They slid down to the thin track on the other side.

From there it was tough going, narrow and steep, forty-five minutes to get up onto the ridge. On top they stood outside the truck, zipping their coats against the cold early wind. Eastward, peaks rose above the dark green of forested canyons, and on the highway side, sounds of traffic carried up the slope. They could see into the Crystal Basin but were having trouble finding Nyland's tracks. They saw where he'd parked yet they hadn't found his trail. Alvarez hiked one direction, Marquez the other.

Walking north and a little bit down the lee side, Marquez found the semblance of a trail, followed that and found scuff marks, old bear scat, and boot prints. He dropped down the slope into a small clearing and got Alvarez on the radio.

"I'm looking at a three-sided wood shack built against an outcrop. It's got a new chain on the door. We'll need a shovel, a pry bar, a hammer, and two of the groundhog cameras."

Marquez checked out the shack while he waited. The plank siding had long ago weathered white. A door built of the same planks held a shiny chrome padlock and chain that looked new.

Marquez looked that over and then called Roberts, woke her, and asked her to start trying to find out who had the lease on this land. He wanted her to try to get around needing a warrant to go into the shack. He walked the perimeter and found bear tracks down alongside the creek drainage beyond the clearing.

"Looks like your house," Alvarez said, as he walked down into the clearing.

"Yeah, it might be sixty, seventy years old. Loggers or maybe a hunter's shack or someone living off the land. I'm building that addition this winter, and I'll need your help for a day or two."

"I can still swing a hammer. I worked summers on a framing crew when I was in junior college."

"Show me, I've been hearing about it for years."

When Alvarez laughed, Marquez smiled, and maybe they were punchy from the long night or maybe it was knowing they were close to finding something. He touched one of the square-headed old bolts and looked at the door's hinges, figured out the easiest way to get in, then decided to wait for Roberts to call back. They followed bear tracks down into the brush, decided to look for the bait pile first, and about a quarter mile below the shack heard the unmistakable whoof of a bear warning them.

Before they could back up a large black bear rose from brush, and Marquez registered a slash of white fur on the chest as it snorted another warning. He watched the bear's ears as it dropped to four legs again, watched to see if the ears flattened, knowing they were probably safe if the ears stayed up. The bear turned away, its coat rippling fluidly as it moved almost silently down through the trees, four hundred pounds or even bigger. It turned, looked back, its dark face visible well down the slope, then was gone.

"He's out of here," Marquez said. "Let's take a look."

Paper trash. The chewed remains of tin cans. Bits of Styrofoam, remnants of black plastic garbage bags. Alvarez held up a crust of bread. The bruin was missing a toe on his left rear, and there were other tracks, a second bear, an adolescent, and Marquez found tracks of two more adults. After looking it over they hiked back up to the shack, and the call came from Roberts.

"You're on Federal land leased to a lumber company," she said. "I got a hold of the judge at home. You're good to go. What's the situation there?"

"We found a bait pile. We don't know what's in the shack."

If the rusted screws and nails holding the hinges on came out easily enough, they could put everything back the way they found it, then bury the groundhog cameras and record anyone coming and going. Infrared beams on the cameras would trip with movement and start the film. Marquez messed around with the door hinges for a few minutes, then pried one loose, the nails groaning as they came out. He laid the nails on a rock. They would put it back together the same way.

Inside, it smelled heavily of rodents, chipmunks. There was a small table, a chair, a pine cabinet sitting on the floor, plank shelves nailed to the wall, blankets, a Coleman stove, white gas, an aluminum and canvas folding cot, three plates, two chipped mugs, an iron skillet, and cooking utensils. They found canned food, Vienna sausages, green beans, tuna fish. Marquez read the expiration dates, all fairly recent.

Alvarez bent and picked up an empty container, handed it to Marquez. "Freon."

"Petroni said something like that to me. He thinks Nyland is dialed in with meth cooks."

They searched for more proof that Nyland was cooking up here, but they didn't find it, though it was Marquez's guess the lab equipment wasn't far away. If they reported the Freon, they'd be leading the ATF or DEA up here, and he knew how that worked. Fish and Game would have to take a ticket and wait. He wasn't going to do that.

Alvarez climbed onto the table, checking a space above. The shack had a ledger board bolted to the outcrop that served as one wall. Roof rafters had been nailed to this ledger, and on one end of the shack a crude shelf was suspended from the rafters, a piece of plywood held in place by two-by-fours. He slid his hand along the dusty board, talking to Marquez as he did, feeling in the darkness for the wood ledger in back.

"I've got something," Alvarez said, then pulled down a package wrapped in canvas and tied with leather laces, handed it to Marquez, and hopped down. Marquez untied the laces, and the canvas unfolded slowly like a flower in morning sunlight. Then they were looking at a watch and ring, the ring gold with scroll-work, what looked like snakes encircling. The watch was a Seiko with a chrome band and showed the correct time and date. Marquez moved them around with a knife, didn't touch them.

"We'll videotape them and put them back," he said.

"Got to be stolen."

"I don't know what we've got here."

They put the hinges back on, buried the groundhog cameras, and started the jarring ride down. Thirty minutes later they bounced down the last rough stretch. Morning traffic raced by on the highway, and Marquez waited for a gap. They'd retied the laces and left the watch and ring in their hiding place. He dropped Alvarez at his truck. When Marquez got back on the highway he called Kendall.

"I'm going to steal your line," Marquez said. "I've got something to show you. Where are you?"

"In Placerville eating an early lunch."

"We found a bear bait pile and a hunter's shack we're pretty sure Nyland has been working out of. I've got a video we took that I want to run by you."

"What's on it?"

He told him, then listened to Kendall breathing.

"Can you take me up there?"

"Yes."

"I'm at the little yellow fast-food stand on the east side of town."

"See you in half an hour."

17

Kendall was sitting at a redwood picnic table facing the road, cleaning his fingers with paper napkins. No one else was at the food stand so Marquez brought the camcorder to the table and left Kendall with it. He ordered a black coffee and a hot dog, glancing at Kendall while squirting mustard and ketchup on the dog, then took a seat across the table. Kendall lay the camcorder down and pointed at the hot dog.

"You ever hear of a place called Charlie's Serious Chili Dogs?"

"In Rohnert Park?"

"Yeah, you know it?"

"Used to stop there all the time."

"So where's this hunting shack?"

"There's a dirt track running up to it near that abandoned diner along the highway." Marquez, knowing what he might set in motion here, wondered if his imagination was running away with him. "What do the watch and ring mean to you?"

Kendall didn't really answer until they were in the truck on their way.

"Vandemere owned a watch his parents believed was a Seiko. We searched the area where his body was found but didn't find it. Of course, his parents didn't know the model. They'd bought it on sale for cash at a shopping mall."

"You don't like Vandemere Sr. much, do you?"

"I don't like what he told the newspaper."

Marquez knew from talking to Petroni that in an interview in the *Mountain Democrat* Vandemere Sr. had been critical of the way the county had handled the search for his son. Petroni backed up the criticisms, said he knew for a fact that Kendall got tired of constant phone calls from Vandemere Sr. and would put him on hold until Vandemere hung up.

"How does bear baiting work?" Kendall asked, as they left the highway.

"You feed bears in a particular spot until they get accustomed to showing up there. Build a blind to shoot from and then wait for your bear."

"Lure them, then kill them when you're ready."

"Basically."

"Is there more to it?"

"No, that's it." Marquez slowed and eased off the shoulder. He pointed at the broken ribbon of asphalt ahead.

"I hate this off-road crap," Kendall said.

"You'll want to put your seatbelt on or we can walk, but it's about three miles and steep."

Kendall swore as they slid down the other side and bounced onto the dirt track. The ride up the ridge felt even rougher, and Marquez was unable to answer his ringing phone as he negotiated tight gaps in the trees. On top he saw it was Shauf that had called, decided he'd wait until it was easier to talk privately, and led Kendall out the ridge, then down through the trees.

"A Unabomber starter cabin," Kendall said, as they came into the clearing. He turned and added, "You know Nyland was on this ridge, but you can't place him at this shack."

"Yeah, we saw lights on the ridge and we knew he'd gone up here. There's some work still to match him to the shack and the bait pile, but we buried groundhog cameras. You and I are being recorded right now."

"Is that right? Well, I've got to tell you that later today I might have to bring crime scene techs up here."

"Take it slow, we've got a lot riding on this and our breaks don't come easy."

Marquez took the hinges off the door again, and Kendall pulled on latex gloves, treating the interior like it was a crime scene. As Kendall pulled the canvas packet down, Marquez reminded him that he and Alvarez had been all over in there.

"What aren't you telling me?" Marquez asked.

"This isn't our first look at Nyland. But anything we do, we'll do unobtrusively. Don't worry, Marquez, I'll be gentle."

"You and I could be headed to a problem."

"No, we're not. Look, you've been up all night, you're tired, and you're making more of what I'm saying than you need to. But don't forget this is a murder case first."

"You're telling me you've been looking at Nyland for Vandemere's murder."

"Yes."

Marquez walked outside, unsure how much of this he believed. If Nyland was a suspect, Kendall had been awful quiet about it. He stood outside thinking over the sequence of events, and when Kendall finished they put the door back on, did a search of the trees for any more evidence of drug manufacturing, then drove down.

"I want to look at something with you," Marquez said, as they got around the gate. He parked and got out, waited for Kendall, then pointed out where their tires had dug into the dry soil. "When he comes back he'll see this because he'll be watching for it. We've been up here twice today, and he'll notice those tracks. You can bet he put a lock on that shack because he knew somebody could be coming up. If a jeep or two goes up around the gate, that isn't going to bother him. Kids go four-wheeling. But if he starts seeing a lot of tire tracks, he'll get squirrelly and won't come back."

"We didn't need to get out of your truck for you to tell me that."

"If I'm hearing you correctly, the watch and ring don't mean much in the way of evidence yet. They might, but you're not sure. You're just hoping at this point. A bait pile he's going to feed regularly, so while you run DNA tests the only gamble is he'll reach up there and find the watch and ring missing and then back away, but meanwhile those groundhogs will film him and we'll both get what we need. It can work for us both that way, and he's likely to return in the next few days. Why don't you let the bears help you?"

Kendall smiled at the cheesiness of the idea that bears would help him. As they drove back to Placerville, Kendall reassured Marquez that his moves would be very calculated because he didn't want to tip his hand either. Yet his excitement was palpable. He couldn't wait to get out of the truck.

Marquez called Shauf after dropping Kendall at the food stand. He felt mixed about having taken Kendall up there, and he bounced it off Shauf, who had a predictable take on it.

"There's nothing we'll ever do that'll ever mean anything to him," she said. "He'll walk all over our operation if we let him."

Then she asked if he'd talked to Chief Bell in the last hour.

"No."

"A tip came in this morning that he's all excited about. He wants you to call him right away. He's been trying to reach you."

"What's the tip?"

A woman had called, talked to one of the dispatchers, and asked for Chief Bell. She'd told him she knew of an illegal bear hunt that would happen this week in the Placerville area and said the hunter would be someone well known.

"Bell is going to meet with her today," Shauf said.

"I'll call him when I get to the safehouse."

"He says he's been calling you."

Marquez would be at the safehouse in ten minutes, and he wanted to think more about how to work with Kendall before he got there. Last night he'd felt a rush of hope, felt the case moving again as they'd trailed Nyland, but that effort would be wasted if Kendall wasn't careful. Shauf was right about Kendall, and the idea that Kendall's moving too fast could wipe out what they had set up with the groundhogs left Marquez feeling low. He took the exit toward the safehouse and drove down the street under a white cold sky.

18

When Marquez walked into the safehouse Shauf was just hanging up the phone.

"That was Bell, says he hasn't heard from you."

"I left him a message as I pulled into the driveway."

"Then I must have been talking to him when you called. He's really wired up about this. He thinks this woman is for real."

"When's he going to meet her?"

"This afternoon. She works for a state senator."

"In Sacramento?"

"Yeah."

Marquez sat down on the couch, fatigue weighing on him. He unlaced his shoes as Shauf moved around too fast and close in front of him, talking, wearing a green fleece coat, a T-shirt, and jeans. He was tired enough to where he needed a little more space.

"The senator she works for is planning an illegal bear hunt," Shauf said. "Somewhere near here. Supposedly, this senator has always hunted big game. He spends his vacations doing guided hunts."

Marquez lay back on the couch, and Shauf's voice carried from the dining room table. The bear-hunting state senator would hold for a couple of hours. Besides, all tips sounded better than they were, three-quarters were just talk, let Bell go meet with her first. She could easily be a crackpot looking for CalTIP money.

The long night weighed in, and it seemed to Marquez that he'd lost some of the resilience he'd always been able to count on. He could remember going for a couple of days awake on a fast moving operation, but it didn't come as easy now and maybe that increased his desperation to make a difference, or maybe desperation was just a romantic word to make it seem more than it was. More like fear they weren't making enough of an impact. They hadn't gotten close to the bear farmer and were feeding him money. Shauf was still talking when he fell asleep.

He dreamed he was in Siskiyou County with his SOU team and they'd found a grizzly, an impossibility in California, where the last grizzly had been exterminated more than fifty years ago and lived only on the state flag. In the dream he swam in the Eel River alongside a giant silver-tipped male. His strokes kept pace with the bear, and the grizzly didn't turn to attack or seem to have any problem that he was nearby. Water rippled in smooth waves from the bear's shoulders, and he didn't know where they were going, but ahead he saw a line of men filing down on the left side of the riverbank. He watched them raise their rifles and aim. Bullets peppered the water around him, and dark weaving strands of blood trailed from the bear. The grizzly roared and bit at the air as one slug, then a second struck its head. It stopped swimming, its body rolled with the current as the riflemen packed their weapons and ascended a trail in single file, their job finished.

"You were making all kinds of noises in your sleep," Shauf said.

Marquez checked his watch, saw he'd slept four hours. He glanced out the window at the late afternoon and got heavily to his feet. He showered, changed clothes, drank coffee, ate a peanut butter sandwich while leaning against the cabinets in the kitchen.

"Turning into a strange day," Shauf said. "The Stockton police called while you were asleep. Dispatch put them through because whoever called from there said you'd called them."

That got Marquez's attention, awakened him more than the coffee. He turned and looked at her more closely.

"Yeah, I called a list of departments in the valley after I met with Kim Ungar. He told me his cousin had moved to the Central Valley. What did Stockton have to say?"

"They've arrested someone in a drug sting and found bear paws and what sounds like gallbladders in the trunk of a car."

"When?"

"Last night."

She handed him a scrap of paper with the Stockton vice cop's phone number. After he'd finished the sandwich he punched in the phone number and walked outside into the cooler air to talk. He connected to a smooth-talking vice cop named Steven Delano, who told him they were holding a man with the last name of Kim. Not every immigrant Korean family took on the Western habit of putting the first name ahead of the surname. Kim Ungar and this man with the last name of Kim could be from the same family, or it might even be Kim Ungar and he used both names. He listened quietly to Delano, mulling over the cousin conversations he'd had with Ungar. Delano said the Kim they were holding would probably make bail tomorrow.

"He's got the money for a top lawyer, so what's that tell you?" Delano asked but didn't wait for a reply. "If you want to drive down, we'll pull him out for another interview this afternoon."

"Will his lawyer let him talk?"

"I think I can get Kim to sit down with us."

"You've got other stuff on him."

"We're working on it."

"I can be there in an hour and a half. What's this Kim look like?"

"Black-haired. Tall. Thin. Runs with gangbangers up here."

"You've known him a while?"

"Oh, yeah, definitely, we've been trying to nail him. He comes complete with a street name. Tell you more about him when you get here. I've got another call holding I've got to get back to."

Marquez thought a second. It wasn't Kim Ungar out of San Francisco, who had a different build, stocky, a little above average height. Nor would Ungar run with gangbangers.

"I'm out the door when I hang up."

"Good enough."

He called Katherine on the drive to Stockton. She was behind the counter at her Union Street coffee bar, Presto, and mildly worried about a couple of calls Maria had answered at the house last night. She wanted his take.

"The caller ID read 'Unavailable,'" she said. "So it was probably some smart-ass working for a telemarketer. Or it could be one of Maria's friends messing with her."

"What got said?"

"A man asked her name and stayed on the line trying to get her to talk about herself. He asked her what she looked like, if she'd started dating yet. Told her she sounded cute. She's pretty sure the same guy called back about an hour later. She'll tell you about it."

"Where is she?"

"She went over to a friend's house after school." Marquez heard the light clattering of a cappuccino saucer and then the espresso machine running. "It's probably nothing, John."

"Which friend?"

"Bruce."

"I'll call her there."

"You can't."

"Why not?"

"This is the boy she has the crush on. She's over there with her friend Laura and if you call, you'll embarrass her." She added dryly, "This is her way of getting even with me for not letting her have a cell phone."

Marquez knew Maria had wanted a cell phone and Katherine had told her she would have to bring her chemistry grade up first and then find a way to pay for the phone. After that Maria started being difficult about taking calls from her mother when she was at a friend's house. Either Katherine would have to set her straight or he would, and he knew he'd been waiting for Katherine to do it.

"I think her imagination ran away with her, John. I don't think it's that big of a deal, so I'd wait to talk to her."

"Will you tell her I'll call her tonight?"

"We're not going to see you?"

"Doesn't look like it."

"Then I better tell you something else. She got a speeding ticket in Mill Valley yesterday."

"Great."

They'd been warned by their insurance broker to pay out of pocket for any fender bender that Maria got into in her first few years of driving. Insuring her and the old car they'd bought had been much more expensive than they'd expected and the bill had come with a second warning, if she got any moving violations, the insurance would jump.

"Forty-five in a twenty-five zone. I told her I was going to talk to you before we did anything."

"What's she saying?"

"Well, she figured out a good one. She claims she thought some guy was following her."

"I'll talk to her tonight. I want to hear about these phone calls."

"Where are you now?"

"Driving to Stockton to talk to a vice cop."

For a state agency like Fish and Game the phone companies charged up to a thousand dollars to check where a phone call came from. It didn't cost them anything like that to do the trace, but never kill a cash cow. The Feds, the FBI, had the money and the equipment to go real time on calls, but at this level, particularly with the home number where Marquez would need Bell's approval, the process was slower, the cost harder to justify. Still, there'd been the threat from their seller, and he could probably leverage that if there were more calls. He hung up with Katherine, saying he'd check back after 7:00. He took another call before reaching Stockton, this one from an upbeat Alvarez.

"We're on," Alvarez said. "I've got an appointment for tomorrow with Durham. Nyland returned my call, and he wouldn't be too hard to handle. He's eager to please. He wants the business."

"Wants to be a hunting guide?"

"Exactly. Suggested we meet for a beer and tried to tell me I didn't really need to meet with Durham, but I kept pushing for a meeting with the owner. Told me he runs all the hunting trips and Durham basically does the books and bankrolls the business. Durham doesn't like to meet with clients. He's busy with other work."

"How'd you leave it?"

"He wanted a couple of numbers to call me back on, not just a cell, so I gave him TreeSearch."

Bear season opened in just a few days, and Alvarez could legally take one bear. He'd told Nyland he wanted to be damn sure he bagged one, no matter what it took, and not a skinny or sick bear or some gawky yearling, but a fat bruin he could get good meat from and a rug. That's why he needed a guide who knew the area. He'd told Nyland he would pay extra freight if they guaranteed him a bear.

"How far did you push it?"

"Not over the line, but I sent the signals."

"Some of these guys tape their calls."

The line between entrapment and setting up a sting could be razor thin, and they needed to be very careful how they approached this guide business. But this was a good first step.

"Where you at?" Alvarez asked.

"In Stockton and about to go in and meet a vice cop. They busted someone on a drug rap who had bear parts in the trunk and the last name of Kim. I'll talk to you on the other side."

Marquez went in, met Delano, sizing him up as confident and serious, but not as hard-boiled as he'd tried to sound over the phone. Delano sketched a street history of Kim.

"Kim is affiliated with a Vietnamese gang that's branched into dealing drugs, mostly methamphetamine, which has put them up against the Hispanics who aren't wild about sharing that market. In fact, the Hispanics are in the process of consolidating."

"Kim is a hired gun?" Marquez asked.

"We're pretty sure he hooked up with the Vietnamese because he's willing to pull a trigger. Usually they keep to their own and when they don't there's a good reason."

"Really, a shooter."

"Of a kind. He's known as Nine-O, like nine millimeter with a zero on the end of it, and don't make any comments to him about it. All the good names like Fast Nine were already taken. The gang he works for used to specialize in carjackings and burglary. For break-in jobs they like to travel out of town. Their burglaries have included a number outside this jurisdiction. Two of them were arrested last month with property stolen from cabins in Kern County."

"They've had similar problems in El Dorado County."

"Everywhere up and down the Sierras."

Marquez told him now about the guns stolen and dogs poisoned in Placerville, suggested he call Kendall about that one. They talked about the similarities as they walked down the corridor to the interview room. No hunting rifles, but a shotgun and five or six handguns had been bagged when they busted Kim.

"You can go in alone with him or I'll go in with you, either way I should start you off with him," Delano said.

"Introduce me."

"I didn't tell you this over the phone, but Kim's got two strikes already, a drug and a robbery charge that he did time for separately, neither of which has anything to do with the Vietnamese gang. He made the career move to hit man when he realized he couldn't go down for a third strike." Delano tapped his forehead and smiled. "He's a thinker."

"Why's he willing to talk to me?"

"Probably trying to figure out what you've got on him, nothing more than that."

Marquez followed Delano into the interview box and didn't read any emotion in the eyes across the table, a studied flat blackness, a waiting this out, been here before look, and you cops are all pieces of shit.

"Nine-O, this gentleman is here about the bear parts in your trunk."

"Nothing to do with me," Nine-O said.

"We're looking for the car owner," Delano explained to Marquez. "Right now, it's open whether it's a stolen vehicle. It doesn't belong to Nine-O here. Maybe he stole it somewhere and it came with bear parts. You stealing cars out of the mountains again, Nine-O? Find the car in a campground somewhere you could take this officer back to?"

Nine-O shook his head, and Delano worked on him for a while before leaving as they'd prearranged. Delano said he'd be back in ten minutes.

"Where did the bear parts come from?" Marquez asked.

"Fuck if I know."

"I'm here because they told me you wanted to talk to me. Were they wrong?"

"Get them to drop this other shit and maybe I can find out something."

"You give me the people who are trading in bear, and I can probably make the bear trafficking charge disappear. I can't guarantee that, but otherwise, commercial trafficking is a felony. With two strikes down already you go up for life."

"Not for fucking bear paws."

"I'm not saying I think the law is fair." Marquez didn't. He thought the way the three-strikes law got blindly applied was immoral. "It'll make you the first man to get life in prison for killing a wild animal."

"Bagging a bear is no felony."

"This isn't killing a bear. Four gallbladders, the paws, that's trafficking, and that's a felony. I've got the code right here if you want to read it." Marquez started to reach for his wallet.

"Fuck your felony, man."

"Maybe you didn't know what was in the trunk and you were delivering it for someone."

"I don't hunt bear."

"Someone did."

"They planted all that shit."

"The police wouldn't know where to get bear paws."

"You want help, make it all go away."

"I'm only here about the bear."

"Talk to the man, he likes to deal." Nine-O looked at the mirror, spoke to it. "Make me an offer."

"You talk to your lawyer. I'll talk to the district attorney. Your lawyer can contact me through Delano, but after you're charged it's going to get a lot harder." Marquez stood up. "You don't know about the bear parts in the trunk and I didn't write the three-strikes law. It'll be a couple of days before we move on this, so you've got time and your lawyer can check out the statutes."

Marquez got up and left. He figured if Nine-O knew anything at all the three-strikes fear would sweat it out of him. And he had to know something. Delano walked out of the station with him, telling Marquez about a meth bust he was heading up tonight, SWAT team, the whole deal.

"This is a lab that can produce ten pounds at a time."

Marquez didn't share Delano's excitement but told him he used to be with the DEA. They had a conversation about the increase in meth traffic in California, and then probably out of politeness Delano asked about the SOU.

"Your Fish and Game team moves around a lot?"

"Yeah."

"You must see some of the mess these drug labs make."

"Sure, occasionally."

The cleanup was as bad as the trade, and Marquez's team had seen the waste products poured in creeks. To get a pound of meth you produced roughly five pounds of waste, hydriodic acid, lye, red phosphorus. He tried now to get Delano interested in the bear problem but didn't get the feeling he'd reached him, though he knew Delano would keep the heat on Nine-O.

On the drive back he took a call from Kendall, learned that the detective had already gone back up to the hunting shack with crime techs. As he laid the phone down Marquez knew that Kendall had screwed him. Like the vice cop, Kendall had only a vague curiosity about bear poaching. It wasn't on their radar screens, wasn't part of their world and never would be. Finding bear paws in a car trunk was a curiosity, a bait pile a quaint throwback to an America that didn't really exist anymore. Crimes against animals carried no weight when any other human crime was involved, and yet the justice system had produced a strange opportunity today. With two strikes against him Nine-O could only deal his way out. The lawyer hadn't been born who'd tell Nine-O he had nothing to worry about, so maybe something would come from Nine-O. If it did, it wouldn't surprise Marquez if it tied into what they had going.

19

The call came after he'd returned to the safehouse. He flipped open his cell phone and heard the now-familiar electronic whine, the pitch-altering adjustments their bear farmer made as he began to talk. You could buy a voice changer on the Internet for either a landline or a cell phone for as little as twenty bucks, but their seller had spent more. The audio expert who'd analyzed the recordings speculated that he had state-of-the-art equipment, near the quality a government spook might have.

Shauf slid Marquez a notepad and he looked at her, thinking that for a long time the best they could do was make a buy from him every six weeks to two months. But now he was very available and calling them. Marquez turned the notepad so everyone at the table could read.

He'd written, "Talking about bear farming. Wants to talk about it, could be our opening."

"I studied with the Chinese, but they haven't tried to improve their methods in a thousand years." There was a high-pitched whine, the voice changer shifting settings, and the flat mechanical voice started again. "The Chinese can't legally import and they aren't going to anytime soon. They think they're going to educate the world about their medicinal practices, but it isn't going to work like that. I've got bear bile products right here that are better than they're selling, and they're going to do nothing but run into problems with the UN geeks and the wildlife groups."

"My clients want pills, not powders, and they want to know the farms are sanitary. They want me to take a look," Marquez said. "I need a lot of pills. And I'd like to know who I'm doing business with."

"I answered questions about my business one time to a young woman who turned out to be with U.S. Fish and Wildlife. She'd told an associate of mine she was going to Utah on a vacation, a backpacking trip. She fell off a cliff near Zion. It took them months to find her."

"Were you there?"

"I hid her backpack between two rocks. You couldn't see it unless you were standing right over it. She caused me a problem in Idaho, and when I walked up the trail in Utah she knew what was going to happen. She begged and cried after I dragged her over to the edge. I can still hear her scream in my head."

"I'm buying for people that want to heal, so that makes a story like that hard to hear."

There was a long staticky pause, and Marquez had the sense their seller was debating.

"Who do you sell my product to?"

"Mostly to Koreans in LA and San Francisco. I had a wife who was Korean. She died of cancer, but her family deals in traditional medicines and I work with them. They're connected in the community and ship some of it home. They want more. They ask all the time for more."

"What was your wife's name?"

"I'm not going to give you any names."

"Then why do you ask so many questions?"

The line went dead and Marquez still gripped the phone, surprised at the abruptness and not sure what to make of it. He laid the phone down softly.

"He hung up," Marquez said, then looked at Roberts. She would help him track down this Utah story. He slid the pad to her and she made her own copy of what he'd written down. They went down a list of assignments, and Marquez recounted details of the phone conversation so he didn't forget them. An uneasiness stayed with him after they'd all left the table. He couldn't shake it.

A couple hours later he called home and talked with Maria about the speeding ticket. Her fingers clicked away on a keyboard, no doubt instant-messaging her friends. Lately, it was too much for her to have only one conversation. Even when he asked her to stop typing and stick with this conversation he heard her fingers lightly moving.

"We can talk now or later," he said.

"I already know I have to pay for the extra insurance and I'm really upset, okay. I don't want to talk about it. I'll baby-sit or get a job at Starbucks."

"You told your mom a man was following you."

"He was and I know no one believes me."

"Where were you?"

"Leaving town."

"Mill Valley?"

"Didn't Mom already tell you this?"

"I want to hear it from you. What did this man look like, what was he driving?"

"Because you and Mom think I'm making it up."

"I'm not saying that, Maria, I'm just asking what he looked like."

"I couldn't really see him."

"What was he driving?"

"Like a regular minivan, or something."

"A van that had side doors?"

"I don't know."

"Any idea of the model or make?"

"I knew you were going to interrogate me."

"Maria." His own exasperation showing. "I'm not challenging your story, just tell it to me."

"That's all there is."

"If you say it happened, that's good enough for me, but when I get home we're going to retrace the route you took. I want to see it."

"Because you don't believe me."

"No, because I want to think about and understand it."

He didn't believe or not believe her. She'd always been a very truthful kid, though in the past year or so she'd leaned more toward telling them what they wanted to hear. He asked now about the phone calls from the man who'd stayed on the line, and she was funny about them tonight, downplaying them, defensive, dismissing both the calls and his interest in them. Marquez told her he loved her, then said good-bye and sat for a while thinking it over.

Midmorning the next day Marquez drove out to Eli Smith's house with Shauf. They found him sitting on a small campstool near the front of his old truck. The right wheel was off, and Smith worked on an axle. His hands were black with grease as he showed them a crushed ball bearing, holding it in his palm as if it were a gold nugget.

"We were on our way down the highway and thought we'd stop in and see if you had anymore ideas on who killed your dogs. I just can't get that out of my head," Marquez said.

"I don't think I ever caught your name," Smith said.

"John Croft. Hell, I thought I gave you a card. We've got an office in town. The business is TreeSearch. We're only here on a government contract, though I like it so much I may move to Placerville."

Marquez fumbled in his coat and made sure he didn't find a card.

"We were just thinking about you and your dogs and we're in the area on a tree count. But I can see you're busy, we'll leave you alone. It's none of our business anyway, just thought we'd stop and see how you're doing."

"Y'all are here because you're interested in how I'm doing. Funny, the detective was back this morning too."

"Good. Has he figured out who did it?"

Marquez put on his best face but wasn't sure it was carrying, figured they'd back out of here. Then Smith surprised him.

"I owe five hundred dollars to a man for a hound I bought. She didn't never hunt worth a damn so I never paid him in full and he's been after me ever since. 'Bout a month ago he said he was going to even things up. I gave the detective his name this morning. He's the only one I can think of, but I don't have any proof."

Smith reached for a Pepsi can on his hood and drank. He wiped the soda pop that foamed off his chin and pointed toward his house.

"He knows where I keep the key."

"Why'd you wait to tell the police?"

"Because I'm not sure what else he'd do if he killed my dogs."

"Like come after you?"

"He's the type."

"What's his name?"

"I already gave it to the detective."

They left him standing by his truck and drove back to Placerville. Later that afternoon Marquez phoned Kendall from his truck while watching Alvarez shake hands with Nyland and Durham. Durham wore a flowered shirt, cleanly pressed khaki slacks, and brown leather shoes. His narrow face turned toward Alvarez. He'd crossed his legs after sitting down and folded his glasses, looked oddly prissy for a man with a hunting guide business. Nyland moved toward Alvarez, opened a leatherbound album, and showed photos of hunting trips.

"Eli Smith called me," Kendall said. "He wanted to know if you really are what I told him you were. Might not have been such a good idea to go back out and rattle his kennels."

"Did he give you a name of a friend that sold him a dog that wouldn't hunt?"

"No, he danced around it. Nothing has changed with him, and you ought to let me handle him. You don't do yourself any good questioning him as concerned citizens. He's not a fool."

"Let you handle it like you're handling our bear operation for us."

Kendall was quiet, then coughed. In the distance the mountains looked smoky and cumulus towered behind the highest peaks.

"You're short with me today, Marquez."

"You shouldn't have gone back up there so fast."

"I told you I wouldn't do it unless I had to."

"Why did you?"

"I can't go into this with you."

"Talk to you later." Marquez hung up.

20

Alvarez crawled under Nyland's truck and mag-
netically attached a GPS transponder and battery pack, then added
plastic ties before wiring the battery pack to the transponder. He
slid back out, dusted off his clothes, and Marquez gave Roberts the
signal. She headed upstairs to the pool hall, ordered a beer at the
wood-paneled bar, and hung out with a couple of biker types. Her
long legs, tight jeans, and brown hair falling loosely on her shoulders drew them, and she shot eight ball and cutthroat and laid her
money on the felt bumper to compete with a guy wearing a leather
vest over tattooed skin, nothing else. A strand of turquoise beads
circled his thick neck like a dog collar. She watched Nyland from
the corner of her eye, and when her phone rang she waved it at
the bikers, told them to shut up, said it was her old man and
nobody make any noise because she was supposed to be at home
making his dinner. They laughed as she moved to the windows
and talked with Marquez.

"Sophie is all over him. I mean, it's weird after what we saw earlier. They're at a pool table in the corner by themselves. Somebody should set Petroni straight."

"I think he knows it's over." Petroni had worse problems to deal with. He'd missed a meeting with internal affairs this afternoon and hadn't returned Bell's phone calls.

"I can tell you this," Roberts said, "if they're a couple that broke up you wouldn't know it, watching him slip his hands down the back of her pants."

"You've got a close eye on them."

"It's hard to miss."

Roberts ordered another bottle of Sierra Pale and shot three games with the bikers, letting one of them guide her through a more tricky shot as he leaned over her. When Nyland and Sophie got ready to leave, she left the bikers hanging and went down the stairs ahead of Nyland.

Sophie left her truck in town and rode with Nyland, who drove home to his trailer. Now the GPS showed his truck was stationary, parked out in the meadow, and Marquez doubted much more would happen tonight. Still, he drove out there, taking Alvarez with him, hiking through the trees across the ridge and then down to the rock outcrop. Nyland's trailer door was open. Light spilled onto the iron stairs, and they heard or felt a bass pulse of music. Then someone pulled the door shut and one of the lights went out.

The trailer was just a dull yellow glow now. And both he and Alvarez were tired. It was cold and late. It felt like the wind was trying to pick up, and he wasn't sure why he'd wanted to drive out here, maybe just to confirm Sophie was staying here, Sophie was with Nyland again. What would Petroni think if he was sitting here?

"Time to take off?" Alvarez asked.

"Pretty close."

Then they heard a scream, a sound that at first he thought was mountain lion, a sound like a child in pain. Marquez turned and scanned the dark slope behind them. It had seemed to come from somewhere up the slope.

"That wasn't a cat," Alvarez said.

"No, it wasn't, but maybe it's the wind picking up and two trees rubbing together in a funny way."

"Didn't seem like that either."

"The wind has come up."

"Yeah, and I'm freezing, but that was weird."

Now they heard it again, though different, farther away, lasting longer. Marquez thought he heard voices, people crying out, arguing, Below, the trailer door opened and a hound bayed as Sophie and Nyland came down into the meadow, lurching, laughing, staggering onto the road, drunker than when they'd gotten home. He wondered now if the odd sound might have been a distortion of the music Nyland played in his trailer, some trick of acoustics that had allowed fragments of sound to carry.

"That last almost sounded like voices," Alvarez said. "As though they were afraid and talking fast."

"Yeah.

Sophie carried blankets, and she and Nyland walked down the road running through the meadow. They stopped at the first of the abandoned foundations, spread the blanket on the moonlit concrete, and passed a bottle. Tiny fragments of their voices carried on the wind. They draped a blanket over their legs.

"Not my kind of picnic," Alvarez said. "Way too cold."

Then Nyland stood and moved out onto the slab. He took a stance and aimed. They heard the sharp hard pops and saw the muzzle flashes.

"Aiming toward the old sales office," Marquez said, and a faint sound of glass breaking carried on the wind. They heard Nyland's whoop. "I took a look at the building last time I was here. There were a couple of windows on that face that weren't broken yet."

"Job's done now."

Nyland went back to Sophie, and the bottle got passed again.

"Get drunk and shoot up something," Alvarez said. "Nothing has changed in a hundred years." He cleared his throat, voice much quieter now. "I swear those were voices we heard. That wasn't any music they were playing in the trailer."

Sophie stood, and Marquez saw that she had the gun. She pulled her clothes off with her free hand and held the gun on Nyland as he stripped and then lay on his back on the blanket.

"You seeing this, Lieutenant?"

"It's a game."

Sophie had a two-handed grip aimed at Nyland's head, and Marquez heard Alvarez mutter, "Yeah, my girlfriend and I play this one all the time."

The gray-white concrete slab was like a stage, and on the slope they became voyeurs as she straddled him, taking him with one hand and guiding him inside her, holding the gun to his head as she moved slowly with him in her, her free hand pushing down on his chest, her back arched, hair spread on her shoulders, breasts pale.

"Looks like they're still friends," Marquez said.

"She had Petroni fooled."

Petroni had himself fooled.

"Where's Petroni living now?" Alvarez asked. "He's not waiting at home for her, is he?"

"I don't know, but we're done here."

They hiked back up to the ridge and drove back to the safehouse. Alvarez went inside, and Marquez sat in the truck listening to music, a local station, old rock and roll songs, a lot of them thirty years or more old, songs written for times that had vanished. Lately, he'd been listening to some group he liked called Magnetic Fields, but he wondered if he would ever connect with modern music in the same way he had when he was young. He wondered if his beliefs about what he could get done running an undercover team were overblown and foolish. He lowered his window and reclined the seat, tried to make sense of the events of the past few days. He left the music on low, listening to the Doors' "LA Woman," and thought about Kendall's story of why he'd left LAPD and how vehemently Petroni contradicted it, how personal that was for Petroni. *The way Petroni was on me for a while.*

He thought of Brandt, the informant Kendall had let him talk to. Was there any chance Petroni was on the take? Of all things, that was hardest to imagine. With his eyes closed he thought of Sophie making love with Nyland and Sophie at the Creekview with Petroni. She was more than a woman alone, she was lost.

He fell asleep in the truck and slept the remaining hours of the night, waking with his cheeks numb from cold and his neck stiff. The night's dreams still lingered in him, and he looked at the house, lights out, team asleep. He could go in and make coffee, boil an egg, toast bread, and read the newspapers. Instead, he started the truck, backed out, and drove up an empty Main Street past the Liar's Bench, Placerville Hardware, the antique shops, and on toward the east side. He parked and went into the Waffle House; he wanted the light and other people. Maybe Petroni would show up. He read the newspapers and made notes to himself. Later, after he'd paid and was back outside, he called Petroni's cell phone.

"This is Sophie," a woman's voice said. "Billy's asleep."

"This is the friend who helped at the bar that night, the Creekview. I need to talk to him." *When had she driven there?*

"He's really tired. Can you call back later?"

"Sure, and if I don't reach him, will you tell him I called?"

Marquez drove up the highway to the Pollock Pines address where Petroni had been house-sitting with Sophie. The old orange Honda was out on the street with a layer of frost on it. Sophie's Ford pickup was there, her windshield clear of frost, heat still rising from the engine. He thought about parking and knocking on the door but didn't. Later he would wish he had.

21

At sunrise Marquez was up behind the old diner, studying the vehicle tracks the county had left, deep gouges where wide heavy vehicles had started the steep ascent. Kendall had bragged that they had made it look like a break-in when they'd torn the door from the hunting shack, claimed Nyland would read it as one of his buddies ripping him off. But whatever else Nyland was, he was also a hunter and his eye would read the multiple tracks, what looked more like a troop movement than a couple of guys in a four-wheel drive. Staring at it made him angry. He walked back to his truck, flipped open his phone, and got a groggy Kendall on the other end.

"Nyland will turn around when he sees this," Marquez said.

"Are you an expert on him now that you've known him a week?"

"What happened to reinterviewing Sophie and telling her Nyland's in the clear? You were going to give him a chance to come back up here."

"I already explained this and we did reinterview her. She wanted to talk about Petroni. She told me she's never been in love with him. He was a sugar daddy except the sugar went away when the ex-wife cut off the credit cards and froze the bank accounts—excuse me, the bank account. She was very candid with us, and I mean way too candid for church."

"Don't blow smoke at me this morning. You didn't do what you told me you would and it's cost us."

"Sophie's been with Nyland a long time and what I told you the other day about her being damaged goods is true. A woman hurt that way when she is young will never really be with anyone. They build an emotional inside they can never get over the top of. Self-esteem takes a permanent hit and the emotional circuitry never runs correctly afterwards. The old-timers on the force say she would run away as a kid and hide up there in the Crystal Basin because if she went into town the cops would drop her back at the house. It's why she hates law enforcement. That's why no one around here believed she really had anything going with Petroni."

"What does any of that have to do with you taking an army up to the hunting shack?"

"I'm getting to it. She also told us she and Petroni routinely went up to that shack during the early days of their relationship. The first blush of love among the empty Freon containers, going at it on the cot. She also said she told Petroni that Nyland used the shack for bear baiting. Which means Petroni has known about it and done nothing. He's probably seen the bait pile you showed me."

"I doubt it."

"I'm trying to tell you that Sophie has ridden around all those mountains with Petroni. I didn't bring up that hunting shack, she brought it up."

"Why'd she bring it up?"

"Listen, I gotta go, I'll talk to you later."

The disjointed conversation left Marquez agitated all morning, and he couldn't reach Petroni when he tried to get a hold of him. Shortly before noon he pulled the team together at the TreeSearch office. An hour later Alvarez went into a second meeting at Sierra Guides, where Durham explained that a guide such as Eric Nyland was billed on a daily basis, a thousand dollars a day plus expenses.

"That's the best I can do," Durham said, parsing his words, his voice dry, the words pinched. He wore a plaid shirt today, tucked into designer jeans, snakeskin boots and belt. The rate was extremely high for the area, and Alvarez didn't know how to react without offending him.

"We'll guarantee you a shot at a bear," Durham said. "You're a good shot, aren't you?"

"It's a lot of money for me."

"You may need someone cheaper."

"I was hoping to work it out with you."

"Those are our rates." Durham smiled. "You're from Mexico, you say. There's really not much bear down there, is there?"

"I grew up in the States."

"You know what I mean, I think."

Marquez knew what he meant. Durham meant to unsettle and possibly anger Alvarez. Durham suspected him and was going to kill the deal.

"No, what do you mean?" Alvarez asked.

"There's no cultural tradition of bear hunting or big game for you Mexican guys."

Alvarez got the picture out of his wallet, handed it over. "Taken in Vancouver. I shot the bear in the photo."

Durham barely glanced at the photo, handed it back.

"Let's talk about other costs," Alvarez said. "What are they?"

"Vehicle. Support. Dressing the meat."

"I don't have any problem with that, but I want to know I'm going get a bear. I know you can't guarantee it, but do you ever do any kind of enhanced hunt?"

Marquez winced as he heard that. Alvarez had sounded like he was going to recover and get the conversation on track and now he'd rushed into this. Durham folded his arms over his chest and stared hard this time.

"I've heard of enhanced penises," Durham said without any trace of humor. "But I don't know what an enhanced hunt would be. Some of our tight-eyed friends come in here and ask that question. I usually throw them out as soon as I hear it and the offer of extra money."

"I'm not asking for anything illegal."

"Then what do you want? You've already got a bear tag. What are you asking?"

"A longer trip, out farther where there are more bear." *Come on, Brad,* Marquez thought, *you're only getting in deeper.* He could see only part of Alvarez, his hand gesturing. "I don't know when I'll get a bear tag again. I did some hunting last fall in Ontario and got three bear. Wasn't an issue there, but that's different."

"Tell us again how you got into bear hunting."

"I've got a better idea, I'll meet you this afternoon and show you how Mexicans shoot. Where's a range?"

Nyland laughed, enjoying Alvarez's coming back at his boss. Durham forced a smile, said, "No offense, Mr. Gutierrez, but no thanks."

Alvarez came out a few minutes later. He looked shaken and angry, and Durham followed him out, called to him, walked down the sidewalk, and offered his hand. Marquez watched the effort Alvarez made at being friendly. He shook hands with Durham and walked toward Main Street, starting the route they'd planned past

Rexall Drugs and Pyramid Outfitters before crossing the street and going into Hidden Passage Books. Then Durham got in his car, and Marquez swung onto the highway behind him, talking to Alvarez as he drove.

"I've got him in view. He's on his way down the highway. Seemed like he got under your skin, but do you think he's onto us?"

"He was definitely taking a good look at me."

"Yeah, I could see that from where I was. We could hear him trying to rattle you."

"He didn't get to me, but do you think I overdid it?"

"You were fine."

"Where is he now?"

"I'd guess he's headed back to Sacramento. I'm turning around."

Marquez got off at the next overpass and started back toward Placerville. He was still thinking about Durham when he took a call from Petroni.

"I need to talk to you," Petroni said.

"What's up?"

"I've got to talk to you about this whole thing."

Twenty minutes later Marquez pulled into a 7-Eleven parking lot on the east side of Placerville.

22

Marquez parked in a corner of the lot and watched kids messing around on skateboards, jumping a cardboard box on the sidewalk, one kid going end over end into the street. A car swerved around him, and the driver hit the horn as the boy's friends laughed. Marquez returned a call to Katherine as he waited for Petroni. She'd managed to get to the cop who'd ticketed Maria for speeding. The cop hadn't seen anything suspicious, but he did remember Maria.

"He said he could have written her for a higher speed. She came flying out of town like she was taxiing down a runway."

"Is Maria sticking by her story?"

"She's rounded it out a little more."

"What do you think?"

"That she's telling the truth. Why don't I give you the officer's phone number?"

He copied that down and ten minutes later, when Petroni still hadn't showed, went into the store, bought a newspaper, a pre-packaged turkey sandwich, and a Calistoga juice that he took back to his truck. He peeled the wrapper off the plastic case and pulled the sandwich out. The lettuce was dark and crushed, the bread soggy, the turkey without any flavor, but he was hungry enough to eat half of it before giving up.

Petroni pulled up in the Honda. From its dusty sides and windows it looked as if he'd been off-road with the car. He had a few days' growth of dark beard and acted like a guy looking over his shoulder this afternoon. The smell of stale sweat came off him after he got in Marquez's truck and shut the door.

"Do you mind if we drive somewhere?"

Marquez drove the road out toward Mosquito Creek. He figured Mosquito would be empty and slow winding into the hills.

"Bell wants my badge."

"I almost lost mine five years ago when Charlotte Floyd came after me."

"Kendall's got some recidivist shithead to say I'm on the take. I talked to the union rep and she told me they're investigating me for taking bribes. I've never taken a bribe in my life."

"What are these bribes supposed to be for?"

"Charging extra fees to some hunters and agreeing to stay out of an area while a hunt is going on. Helping poachers, Marquez. Doesn't matter how many years I've got in or what I've done."

Marquez nodded, though somehow this felt staged. He waited to hear something that would confirm that feeling and listened to Petroni rant about Bell's using Fish and Game as a stepping-stone into state government, Bell's wife's having family money, Bell's living in a big house and having no idea what it's like being a warden. At lunch Bell walked down to the Capitol Club and exercised. At night he went to political fund-raisers, cocktail parties, or home where they had a chef that came in four days a week.

"He cares more about getting a reservation at a restaurant than he does about you or me," Petroni said.

Marquez didn't have an answer for any of it though they drove for miles. When he finally turned his truck around, he was still unsure why Petroni had called him. Petroni had friends, family in the valley, people he could talk to. But now, Petroni spoke to him directly.

"You don't owe me anything, the opposite, actually. But I need your help with Kendall."

"Kendall?"

"He'll listen to you."

"I wish he would."

"About a year ago I found Kendall parked down a dirt road in the Crystal Basin with a thirteen-year-old runaway he was supposed to be transporting. She was in the front seat with him, bent over his lap. Kendall saw me coming, and she denied it when they questioned her, but I know what was going on. I told the sheriff the next day that he ought to fire him."

"What happened with it?"

"They dropped it."

"Was that when you and Kendall first had problems?"

"No, it started over something else a couple of years before."

"You want my opinion?" He wasn't sure Petroni did but was going to give it to him anyway. "Go in and defend yourself. You made a mistake in judgment with the Vandemere deal, so get it over with and ride out the suspension. It's not the end of the world. These other accusations you're going have to get aggressive about, go after the affidavits."

"It's too late."

"Only if you want it to be."

"I've got a friend with a cabin up at Wright's Lake. I'm moving up there until I get things figured out, and I've got a cousin with a good roofing business and he's shorthanded."

"You'd fall off a roof in half an hour if your knees didn't give out first. You're a game warden."

"He needs someone to help bid work and drive around and make sure the jobs get done right."

"Bill, you're a game warden. No one up here knows the area like you do. No one in the department knows bear the way you do."

"Jesus Christ, Kendall and his partner followed me last Sunday afternoon, then tried to tell me I'd killed the Vandemere kid. I'm getting out of my car around dusk, and they appear out of nowhere, tell me they've talked to Sophie and they learned some new things. They took me in and tried to get me to confess. They said Sophie had talked about how I told her I'd killed Vandemere. They drove me back down to the sheriff's office, and we were in there for hours. He's not going to stop until he gets me behind bars."

"Did she say that?"

"No, it was all to try to get me to confess. That's how far this thing has gone."

"Kendall told you he made it up."

"Inferred it from something she'd said, or bullshit like that. I know you're talking to him. Tell him if he backs off I'll quit the department. Bell's going to find a way to get me fired anyway, and I've got to make some money that Stella can't get her hands on. The state will just garnish my salary. Stella's got the credit cards and the bank accounts frozen. I have a $1.88 in my checking account. $1.88, Marquez, and I'm forty-seven. I'm not that far from living out at a campsite."

"Where are you at with Stella?"

"She only talks through her attorney."

As they drove back into Placerville, Marquez stopped at an ATM. He pulled three hundred dollars and handed it to Petroni when he got back in the truck, trying to make the gesture small, no more than handing over a newspaper. Petroni held the money but didn't pocket it. Tiny beads of sweat showed on his forehead, and his left hand alternately balled into a fist and released. His face was as pale as it had been during the Sunday interview.

"I've got seventeen years in."

"Then don't quit."

Petroni opened the door and got out. As the door swung shut, Marquez saw the money he'd pulled from the ATM lying on the seat. He lowered his window.

"Take it, Bill."

"I don't know when I'd get it back to you. Besides, I've got money, it's just not mine. That's something I'm going to show you. Today's just not the right day, after all."

"What's that mean?"

Marquez held out the money again, but Petroni wouldn't take it. He got in his Honda and backed out, almost hitting a car before pulling away.

23

Not long after dropping Petroni off, Marquez took an unexpected call from his old friend, former SOU member Sue Petersen. Her voice was as clean and clear as the dark blue sky over the mountains and carried him away from the Petroni conversation. She'd retired from the SOU team and from the department, but for a lot of years they had worked together and there'd never been anybody before or after he'd liked working with as much. They chatted and he sketched out the operation they were on, some of the frustration and difficulties, in part, perhaps, because she might have an idea or see into it a way he didn't.

But that was only hope. Sue was away from this life and laughingly told him she'd gotten back into surveillance work lately herself, trying to catch a contractor who'd done some work on her house but not finished what he'd promised to do. Hearing the light roll of her laughter was like being there with her and he hung up, smiling.

Two hours later Alvarez called and said Nyland had just called his cell and suggested having a drink together at the Creekview that night.

"I told him I'd call him back."

"How do you feel about it?"

"I'm okay with it."

Alvarez sounded confident and they decided he would go. They'd wire him up and Alvarez would buy all the drinks, tell Nyland next time around was his buy.

When Marquez hung up with Alvarez he drove to meet Shauf and Roberts. He climbed the winding Crystal Basin Road, then broke from that onto Weber Mill Road, a dirt road cut into the canyon face high above the highway and river. About a mile down Weber Mill, they were waiting for him. He read their upbeat expressions as he slowed to a stop, Roberts with her hands jammed in the pockets of her coat, hair floating off her shoulders in the wind, and Shauf in a T-shirt, oblivious to the ridges of goose bumps along her arms, her solid face loosened with pleasure.

Driving along Weber Mill, Shauf had spotted a sun-faded Budweiser can sitting on the whitened stump of a pine tree maybe twenty yards below the road. Roberts hit the brakes, and Shauf hiked down the steep slope to the beer can. When she picked it up she found it was filled with sand and then started looking around, guessing the can had been left as a bait pile marker. Sometimes it would be a strip of cloth tied to a limb or a slash in the bark of a tree.

"I saw it sitting on the stump and thought about Nyland making all those beer runs to 7-Eleven before driving home at night." She turned. "Do you want to walk down there?"

Roberts stayed behind to watch the road. They might have to hustle back up the slope if she spotted someone, but they could clear the area before anyone drove up. Shauf had found a path of sorts, and they followed that down through dry grass and brush. It was slick and steep and then the brush was chest high, and through the trees Marquez could see the highway and the white-water of the river running shallow in October. He heard a truck downshifting, each gear shift carrying easily in the steep canyon. They wouldn't tell anyone about this bait pile. He thought about where they would bury cameras as they got closer, and he saw the makeshift blind. Shauf pointed out a route at least one bear took coming up through the alder and gooseberry.

"We found tracks of four different bears."

The bait-pile smells were rotted fish and the winey vinegar of old apples. From debris and paper trash and bear scat, he saw enough of everything that it told him whoever serviced this bait pile had been at it a while.

"Waiting for bear season to open," he speculated. "Three days from now no one will notice the rifle fire."

Shauf pointed to a shirt and an old leather boot, meaning who-ever kept this bait pile was trying to familiarize bears with human smell.

"So I was thinking one camera here," she said, and Marquez looked up the slope to where they'd walked past a fallen oak and the trench dug behind it where the hunter would wait.

"Yeah, that seems right," he said.

They hiked back up the steep slope to the road and drove on farther down Weber Mill, winding along, tracing ravines and folds, driving through stands of pine, darker there, and then out across the open face until the dirt road hooked up with the second paved access road climbing from the highway east of Kyburz.

"Melinda is going to make the run down to Sacramento to get more cameras," Shauf said. "Then we'll bury them later this after-noon."

After Roberts drove off, Shauf lingered and Marquez leaned back in the open passenger window of her van to talk to her. Her question was simple. "Did Petroni screw up?"

"I don't know."

"The rumor is bribes. One of the dispatchers down at the Region IV office asked me about it."

"It's out?"

"Big time."

"Kendall is passing on rumors, but he's getting them from more than one spot."

"I wouldn't trust Kendall to park my car, so that doesn't go far with me. Have any of these people come in and signed anything?"

"I don't think so, but he put me on the phone with one of them."

"No kidding?"

"A man who said he'd heard about a warden who was getting paid to be scarce and had warned about an undercover team working in the area."

"When was this?"

"A few days ago."

"How come you haven't said anything?"

"I'm not sure I believe it."

She was quiet, then said, "Coming from Kendall, I don't either, but that's worrisome."

"Yeah, it is. I'll see Bell this afternoon about the tip on the politico hunt and if there's a chance to talk about Petroni with him, I'll ask what's new. I know Kendall is talking to him."

"Think he'll tell you anything?"

"He might. Do you want to get a cup of coffee before I take off?"

They bought a couple of lattes in Pollock Pines and sat in her van. Two hours later Marquez was in Sacramento sitting across the desk as Bell cheerfully told of the second meeting he'd just had with the senator's assistant.

"Her name is Dianne," Bell said. "Or that's the name we're going to use. She gave me a copy of a travel itinerary for the senator, bookings that she did for him. When she asked if he had a permit, a bear tag, he told her he didn't need one. So she did her own research and found out you do need one."

"What made her do the research?"

"Said it was just curiosity about how it all works with bear hunting. Then she started thinking about it and got upset. Someone I met at a fund-raiser gave her my card."

"What fund-raiser was that, chief?"

"I don't know. But does it matter?"

Bell drummed on his desk as he described her certainty and his own confidence that she was telling the truth. He envisioned the publicity that might come from the case and dismissed the idea that they'd be accused of targeting this senator for political reasons, not entirely dismissing it but explaining he would handle that part. He leaned to slide Marquez a printout of the senator's itinerary, dates and times over a three-day period.

Marquez stared at the dates. They would hardly have time to get ready, and they had their hands full already.

"I'll get you more wardens. We'll transfer people in," Bell said.

The itinerary showed Senator Sweeney staying at a South Lake Tahoe casino the first night and the next day coming down from Tahoe to a refurbished boutique hotel in Placerville called the Lexington. Marquez knew the hotel, checked the dates again, saw Sweeney had reserved at the Lexington the night before opening day of bear season.

"I'm not even certain your team should know his name," Bell said. "This could leak very easily." He stared earnestly. "It'll be a bombshell if we bust him. We could see CNN coverage."

"If this assistant is correct and he does take a bear illegally and we arrest him, her name will come out. Does she know that?" Marquez asked.

"It won't come from us."

"We probably should tell her."

If Bell heard that, he didn't give any sign. He started talking about Sweeney, where he'd come from, how he'd gotten elected.

Sweeney still owned a car dealership in Bakersfield, was partnered with a former sports figure, baseball or football player, Bell couldn't remember which. But Marquez knew Sweeney's face, had driven past a billboard on Highway 99, Sweeney, the guy who'd grand-standed by suing the governor over the budget, smiling down at the highway. A short guy with a big head, a lot of hair and attitude.

"Why does he want to risk hunting without a bear tag?"

"He thinks he's above the law."

Every intuition said it wasn't that simple, not with a guy who had so much to lose. Marquez knew Bell was waiting for him to show more enthusiasm, mildly frustrated that he hadn't. But he didn't feel any enthusiasm and wondered if it wouldn't be better to take this Sweeney aside and tell him he just got lucky; they were too busy to set up, bust him, and take down his political career. See you next time. He could also visualize the shit storm after they busted this guy, and, Bell must see it as well. But Bell pressed the point now, his voice uncharacteristically emotional.

"She's doing this because she cares and it offends her that he'd take a bear without a permit. And, yes, because I know you're wondering, she's got other issues with him, but I told her those wouldn't go any farther than me. He's going bear hunting and the question is whether we'll be ready in time." Bell tapped his desk again and said, "I've never asked you how you vote, but I have to ask here if it affects your approach to this."

"What political party I vote?"

"Yes."

"I vote for the candidate I like, not the party. If you're asking about my hesitation, I'm just wondering if we can take this on right now and whether we know enough."

"This will go national, Lieutenant. If you want to throw a big-ger shadow with your team, this is the biggest chance you've ever had. If he takes a bear and we take him down, that makes a dra-matic statement about poaching and about our prosecution of the game laws, about the priority we put on saving wildlife. I'm amazed I have to convince you. This is the most significant opportunity to come across my desk in a long time, if ever."

"Taking down a state senator."

"Showing no one is above the game laws. It's about integrity in times that want integrity."

"What's the name of the guide Sweeney is meeting at the hotel?" Marquez asked.

"She doesn't know. She only booked the travel."

"I think you ought to go see him, chief, and tell him not to go bear hunting. Tell him we've been looking closely at the different guide services operating out of that part of the Sierras, and we have a problem with a few of them that he could get caught up in. We're spread thin, and I'd rather keep our focus on what brought us into the area in the first place."

"We're going forward with it, Lieutenant. Figure out what help you need and call me by 5:00 this afternoon."

"Then I'd like to ask Chief Keeler if he's willing to help. We can use him under the retired annuitants program."

"Why would he want to do that?" Bell looked past Marquez, speaking to the wall or the problems he saw with letting Keeler get involved. "There are other wardens we can bring in."

"We'll need them too."

"What would ex-chief Keeler do?"

"Camp at Ice House Lake and scout for us. It's as simple as driving a road and then being there when we need him to check somebody out. When they see a white-haired older man they don't get suspicious."

"Let me think about that one." But Bell looked like he already had. "Call me at 5:00."

24

Marquez never made the 5:00 call to Bell. Cairo slow-cooked pumpkin soup in a Crock-Pot he said was perfect for long surveillances, and Marquez ate an early dinner at the safehouse with the team. They toasted the bait-pile find with a Zinfandel that Roberts had brought from home. She had the wine interest and every now and then would bring something to the table. Good as the wine was, Marquez drank next to nothing. After dinner he passed out copies of Sweeney's itinerary, briefed them on the meeting with Bell. The team had the same questions he'd had about the reliability of the information and how they would manage everything if they heard from their seller while they were trying to track Sweeney.

"Tonight's the only night we'll refer to Sweeney by name," Marquez said. "So we'll need a name. And nothing political. We're going as far away from politics as we can get."

"Call him 'Unlucky,'" Cairo said.

That got a couple of laughs, and there was still an air of disbelief in the room. They all needed to absorb the idea, then see some proof Sweeney intended to follow this itinerary. Still, it wasn't the first time they'd been short-noticed with a tip that had proved out, so if the poacher turned out to be a state senator they'd make the adjustment, and Marquez could feel the change already starting. He listened to the joking names they came up with as monikers, names that didn't show any respect for the intensity of scrutiny that could come their way. The moniker needed to be benign, unprejudiced, and dispassionate.

Marquez's cell rang and it was Bell. Bell didn't say anything about his failing to call at 5:00 and after Marquez walked outside and took a seat on one of the cold lawn chairs, they talked over his concern that busting Sweeney would tip their bear farmer an undercover team was in the area. They talked about ex-chief Keeler, and Bell okayed using him, if Keeler was amenable.

When Marquez hung up and walked back inside he saw that another bottle of wine had been opened. It was good to see the team relax. He went to a back bedroom, slept a couple of hours, then drank a cup of black tea and got ready to leave at 10:30. While he'd been asleep Nyland had called Alvarez and postponed having a drink until tomorrow. Alvarez was in Placerville and watching the GPS readout from Nyland's truck.

"Looks like he's heading home," Alvarez said.

"What about Sophie?"

"At work. She's behind the bar."

"I'm going by to talk to her."

"I'll keep track of Nyland. Call me on the other side."

When Marquez got to the Creekview he found it fairly empty. No music tonight. A few people drinking, young guys mostly. There were two bartenders, and he took a seat on Sophie's side of the horseshoe. He was sure she recognized him, though she didn't say anything when he ordered a beer. She slid a paper napkin in front of him, put the glass down on it. He watched her draw another beer off tap, her face softer, more feminine in this light.

"You're Billy's friend," she said, coming over now. "You broke up the fight that night."

"Yeah, how's he doing?"

"I don't know."

"No one I talk to knows anything tonight."

"You broke up the fight. Then Billy and I broke up."

"That's too bad."

"It was the morning you called."

She had her hair pinned up tonight, a diamond stud in her right earlobe. She leaned toward him, her face level with his.

"Since you're his friend, I'll tell you that Billy and I were definitely not meant for each other. More than just age difference because I happen to like older men."

"Did he move out?"

"In about twenty minutes."

"Know where he went?"

"He said he might camp at a lake for a couple of weeks, someplace he goes to fish."

"Late in the season for fishing."

"I can't think of anything more boring to do anyway."

"You don't fish."

"I eat them but I don't chase them around."

He watched her eyes drift toward another customer. She didn't want to hear anything more about Petroni. She didn't want to talk about him.

He watched her take drink orders from two young men, asking for an ID from one of them, then looking at his face not his ID. She gave them their drinks and flirted with them after bringing their change. Now she came back and leaned over the bar again close enough to where he could see gold flecks in her brown irises.

"How's your beer?" she asked.

"It's good."

"Cold enough."

"Plenty cold."

"Always filling."

"Always."

"That's what I like."

There was the beer commercial, tastes great, always filling, or something like that, but that wasn't what she was talking about. Sophie wore a tight black sweater and when she leaned on the bar the sweater pulled up and the curve of her upper hip showed. He could feel sexuality radiate off her. He took a drink of beer, leaned back, and gave her a little space.

"So did you come in to talk to me?" she asked.

"I came in looking for Bill. I know he's going through a hard time with the divorce."

"Is that why you're here?"

Marquez shrugged.

"Do you want to know why Billy and I broke up?"

"If you want to tell me."

"He got real angry because I slept with someone else this summer." She watched him intently. "Did you read about the guy who got murdered?"

"You're kidding."

"No, he just disappeared in August."

"Jed something."

"Vandemere."

"You had an affair with him."

She laughed. "They don't call it that around here. Anyway, now I'm sort of back with my old boyfriend."

"Sort of?"

"Let's just say he wants to get back together." She smiled and made a quick hand gesture toward the other two men at the bar. "But I'm done with all these guys." She reached and touched his hand, her fingers long and cool, one finger touching his wedding ring. "I've got to get these people at the end of the bar another drink. Do you want another one?"

"I've got to go meet a friend."

"Then come back and see me sometime soon."

"I will."

When he got outside he pulled his phone from his coat. It had started vibrating in the bar and he saw there'd been three calls from Alvarez, called him back now.

"Show time," Alvarez said. "He picked up some restaurant scraps behind that Italian place below town. Bobby Broussard's Chevy is about a half mile behind him and they just went into the basin. Where are you?"

"On my way to you."

"See you here."

25

Then it was a lot of the same game again, Nyland driving through the Crystal Basin and Bobby trailing behind, Nyland making multiple stops, thirty-two by Marquez's count, and Bobby reversing directions, roaring back down the road toward them, a fighter pilot in a beater pickup hoping to surprise the enemy. They dodged Bobby and kept track of Nyland's GPS coordinates. Whenever Nyland stopped they marked the coordinates and clocked the time. Gradually, he worked his way toward the lip of the basin, then instead of dropping down the steep road to the highway, he turned left onto Weber Mill Road.

"He just turned onto Shauf's road," was how Alvarez called it from his truck.

Nyland made three stops along Weber Mill, including one right above Shauf's bait pile before driving home. Bobby continued down the highway toward Placerville, and Marquez followed Nyland out Six Mile Road, hustled out the ridge, and saw him back up to the second trailer, tailgate down, headlights shining into meadow weeds. If they were able to find bait piles at any of the GPS coordinates they'd marked tonight, then they would have enough for a search warrant. They would get into that trailer as well as the main one. The second must be where he stored equipment.

After Nyland coasted his truck back down to the flat meadow, Marquez started to leave, then stopped as Nyland walked back to the second trailer. He continued on up past the third trailer and disappeared into the woods. A chained hound bayed, and Marquez talked on and off with Alvarez while he waited for Nyland to reappear. They speculated that he had a storage area somewhere in the woods he'd just walked into. Marquez looked down on the long oval meadow, the slab house foundations where they'd watched Sophie and Nyland, the faint aluminum luminosity of the trailers, and then from the direction Nyland had disappeared Marquez saw flickering that looked like firelight. It vanished as tall trees along the meadow moved with the wind, showed once more and burned for thirty minutes before winking out abruptly. And still Nyland didn't reappear. He waited another half hour, and when nothing more happened he climbed through the trees back to his truck and drove to the safehouse.

The next morning as Marquez was having coffee he tried to make sense of it. They had a case building against Nyland for bear baiting, one that included Bobby Broussard and, very likely, Troy before it was over. But the disparate pieces, Sophie's role, the watch and ring, the firelight, the strange triangle Petroni was in or had been in, Marquez couldn't fit these things into a framework. He was turning the pieces in his head when Kendall called.

"Do you know where Petroni is this morning?" Kendall asked.

"No."

"When did you last see him?"

"Yesterday afternoon. What's happened?"

"I'm in Georgetown."

"You're at Petroni's house."

"I am, and you'd better come here," Kendall said. "Stella Petroni has been murdered. A neighbor found her body this morning. I'll tell them to let you through the tape."

Images came, nothing coherent, Marquez asked, "Killed at the house?"

"Stabbed. Beaten. Kicked." It was a different voice than he'd heard Kendall use before, no undertow of bellicosity or wheedling edge.

"When?"

"Let's talk here."

When Marquez turned onto Petroni's street he saw the coroner's van and a small crowd of neighbors who looked like mostly retirees, standing together, shock plain on their faces. They watched him walk up. Stella's car was out front, Petroni's Fish and Game truck in the garage. Marquez knew a number of calls had been made requesting that Petroni turn in his truck. Bell had authorized it impounded and towed but must have assumed Stella wouldn't allow him to hide it here. Marquez's guess was that Stella had gone along with it, that they'd come together on the issue of Petroni's fighting his suspension because his state salary was the only source of income. Marquez lifted his badge when he got close to the first cop. Then Kendall walked out onto the porch, waved him up.

He followed Kendall in, past crime tape near the front door and a blood splatter that had reached up on the wallpaper and soaked into the side of an upholstered chair.

"We found a bloody axe handle," Kendall said. "Neighbors tell us she was cautious about who she opened the door for, but we think she was attacked first out here. She may have turned and run, made it as far as the kitchen." Marquez remembered Stella's sliding the curtains, taking a look at him before opening up. "The phone was on the floor of the kitchen. She may have had it in her hand," Kendall said, then stopped and turned to look at him. "Let's say she recognized who it was and opened the door. Or her assailant had a key and she came out when she heard the door open. She gets struck but makes it back to the kitchen before he overtakes her."

Kendall led him to the kitchen where Stella lay on her side on the floor, her face tipped up toward the ceiling.

"You see the boot prints," Kendall said. "The killer stood over her, not to one side but over her, straddling her after she was down. Like chopping firewood, bringing the axe handle down on her head."

Marquez made himself draw a breath. The bone structure of Stella's face had been crushed.

"See what he was doing?" Kendall asked.

"Erasing her identity."

"I wish I had a partner like you. You're right, he was taking away her face."

Blood was everywhere. They couldn't step into the kitchen. On the upswing the axe handle had lined the walls with splatters. Her nightgown was hiked up past midthigh, raising the question of rape. Kendall's reason for showing him this was obvious, though Marquez didn't accept it.

A neighbor walking his dog before dawn, a retired gentleman in his seventies, ex-cop, said he'd shone his flashlight at the house, seen the front door open, and become suspicious. He'd seen blood on the floor when he'd looked inside the house, and when Stella didn't answer his calls he'd tied his dog's leash to a porch post and gone in to investigate. When he found her he called 911 from his cell. He hadn't touched her, hadn't seen a need to check for a pulse.

"This neighbor told me that Stella has always been afraid someone would break in and rob her. He's like you, he can't picture the statistically likely assailant. Where in Placerville did you last see Bill Petroni?"

"At 7-Eleven." Marquez gave the time of day, a shorthand account of what they'd talked about. "He's upset about his suspension and the bribe accusations. He's angry at you. He said you'd passed on rumors to Bell so you could turn the heat up on him, even though you knew the accusations were false."

"Then maybe I'm next. What was he driving?"

"The Honda."

"Did you know this truck was here?"

"No."

"He didn't tell you he was storing it here?"

Marquez let the second question slide off him. He watched a TV van roll in and pointed at it.

"I don't want to be on their tape. Let's take this conversation somewhere else."

They walked down the road to where Kendall had parked and got in the sedan.

"What did he want to talk with you about?" Kendall asked.

"You, for one thing. He feels like he's being framed. He wants to know if you have any signed statements from anyone claiming he took bribes."

"The answer is no, I don't have anything signed, not with Brandt, the man you talked to, and not with anyone else either."

Marquez took a deep breath, the images in his head those of Stella on the floor, the odd tilt of her neck, the hinge of her jaw torn loose. He'd known Stella in a lighthearted way when he'd been friends with Bill, been invited here when Petroni and Stella had bought the house, and remembered her loving to dance. He looked at Kendall, admiring the discipline, finding that to like about the detective, Kendall's doggedness.

"Did you expect Petroni to call yesterday?" Kendall asked.

"No, it surprised me."

"He called your cell?"

"You want the time he called?"

"Yeah."

"I'll get it."

"I hope I don't have to explain our interest in his whereabouts this morning. Who's the friend he was going to meet?"

"He didn't give a name."

"What else did he talk about?"

"Going into the roofing business. There's a cousin with a roofing business and I don't know the name of it but the wardens who work with him probably do. That cousin might know where Bill is today."

"He talked about money problems?"

"A little bit."

"And?"

"He wouldn't take a loan from me."

"How'd he show his anger toward Stella?"

"He didn't."

"You're the perfect alibi, Marquez. You're the go-to guy for this situation. You're credible and you're not going to cover for him. But underneath it all you back him because you're that type of guy. If he can show us that he was with you and then with this other unnamed friend later in the afternoon, and if she died yesterday afternoon, and it was somewhere around then, he's got a step up on us, and I know you don't believe a word of what I'm saying. It's inconceivable to you, I can see it on your face, but I'm betting he used you yesterday."

"You said the neighbor noticed the open door this morning."

"It was probably open since yesterday."

"Stella is in on the kitchen floor, the door's open all night, and no other neighbors noticed?"

"The porch light was off. There are six neighbors on the street, two weren't home last night, one is bedridden. None of the others walked or drove down to the end of the street until the gentleman this morning with his dog."

"That's not what I'm getting at."

"I know what you're getting at. You're wondering why the killer would leave the door open, and there are several possible answers, one obvious being that after following her into the house, the killer may not have wanted to be seen going out the front again, may have been afraid someone would recognize him." Kendall's eyes narrowed. "What's he take home a month after taxes?"

"Not enough."

"Not for both alimony and a life, and believe me I know the feeling. He's trapped and there's no way out as long as she's got her hooks in his regular check. He did the math and it didn't add up." He paused. "How much did you offer to loan him?"

"Just a few hundred but he didn't ask for it, and that stays between us. I don't want it coming back over the table in Petroni's face. I pulled the money out of an ATM to loan it, but he never asked me to and wouldn't take it. He left it on the seat."

"Don't protect him, Marquez. Try to keep an open mind."

"How open is yours?"

"I try to treat all homicides more or less the same." He added quietly, "Before I heard about bribes I heard some other stuff I'd call unsavory, Petroni demanding additional fees from some of these bear hunters, that kind of thing. Not a lot of money, but twenty, thirty dollars a pop, and in cash from scraggly-ass locals he knew wouldn't go to the police. He had a hard-on for some of them, so he made them hurt. And I wasn't born yesterday, Marquez. I know three-quarters of these guys are more than happy to see a warden go down, and they don't care how it happens as long as the warden's life gets messed up. I'd heard all these stories before we had that Sunday roundtable with your chief and the internal affairs officer. I cut Petroni that break, but in the back of my head I kept asking myself why lie to me over trying to get Vandemere to quit harassing her. I couldn't make that work so we decided to take another look at him and decided to see how he'd react to these accounts that he was on the take. I let him listen to one of the tapes, and he started getting loud. Telling me how he was going to sue me and the county and ruin me personally for slandering him. I had to get a couple of deputies to come into the room. He was running right on the edge and I think he crossed over yesterday."

A sheriff's deputy walked down the road toward them now, an officer young enough to still have acne. He looked both earnest and shocked, approached at a brisk walk, his eyes on Kendall in the driver's seat.

"Looks like they need me up there," Kendall said and unlatched his door. He turned to Marquez before getting out. "I know you're shocked, but I can also tell that you've seen your share of killings before. I know when somebody has. Is that from your DEA time?"

"Yeah."

"And now you're in wildlife." Kendall pointed at the young officer walking toward them. "Petroni needs to come in before we turn these kids loose to apprehend him along one of these roads somewhere. If he calls you again, tell him he's got to come in immediately, and if I was Petroni I wouldn't make any assumptions about what his years in law enforcement will do to protect him."

"What's that mean?"

"It means he's wanted for questioning in connection with a murder."

26

When Marquez left Kendall he drove to Wright's Lake in the Crystal Basin and slowly cruised the lake road looking for Petroni's orange Honda. Half an hour later he called Kendall.

"I'm at Wright's because he told me he might borrow a friend's cabin out here. Didn't say he would, said he might."

"You should have told me."

"I'll check it out first."

Marquez walked the rocky shoreline, aware that he was visible to anyone in a cabin along this side of the lake. He talked to Alvarez, then Roberts, telling both to stay focused on preparations for Sweeney's hunt and checking the sites Nyland had stopped at last night. But it was useless. Stella's murder and the hunt for Petroni swept everything else away.

"I'm less than five miles from you," Roberts said. "I'll drive there and help you."

"Run out to Dark Lake first and have a look there and across from the wilderness lot."

Marquez hung up with her and kept turning over a thought that he didn't want to hold, that Kendall was right, Petroni had lied and there wasn't any friend's cabin. Petroni had used him as an alibi, nothing more, a final fuck you to a friendship lost many years ago.

He picked his way around granite boulders at the water's edge and looked at a dark brown cabin with two open windows facing the lake. He climbed stairs up to a weathered deck, knocked on a door, and when no one answered leaned through one of the open windows and called hello. A gear bag sat on the floor near an old sofa, a worn green Army duffel bag. He knocked harder.

"Anyone home?"

He stepped away from the window and walked to the railing facing the lake, didn't see anyone on the shoreline or boats, and walked back to the window, stepped through into the cold shade inside. When he leaned over the duffel bag he saw the initials WP written on it in black marker. Without debating the right or wrong of trespassing, he unzipped it. Under a couple of folded T-shirts was a DFG uniform belt and shirt, everything neatly packed, and he remembered Petroni's talking about his father, the Army major, what it had been like growing up a military brat.

He zipped it shut again and checked two bedrooms and a bath. The rooms were empty, in the bedrooms metal springs showing on cots, everything covered, protected from rodents. He went into the kitchen and saw that the refrigerator was on. Inside was a head of lettuce and a deli bag. So Petroni was staying here or planned to, though it didn't look like he'd slept here yet. *Dropped the bag, opened the windows to air the place out, then took off? Or he'd planted the story with me and staged this.*

Marquez took a final walk through the cabin before going back outside. He didn't feel any impulse to call Kendall yet, wanted to think it out a little further, running through possible reasons why Petroni might leave his gear. *May have gone with the roofers for the day. Riding around with his cousin learning how to bid roofs. But if that was the case Petroni would hear about the murder over the radio. He'd have contacted the police by now. Dropped the gear and went where, then?*

Marquez took a last look around before walking back to his truck. As he got there his phone rang and it had to be Kendall or Roberts who was somewhere nearby. He expected to find out that Petroni had been located. But when he picked it up the screen read "Unavailable," and as he answered he heard the tonal beep of a voice changer initiating.

"Your business in Placerville," the toneless voice said. "Who's your contract with?"

Marquez adjusted to his surprise at their seller's calling. His team had a phone number and a name at the Department of Energy ready to back up their story. But still, the cover story was weak. Anyone intent on knowing could find out what public contracts and grants the DOE had let.

"It's with the DOE, but why are you asking. You checking up on my business?" Marquez opened the door of his truck, got in, and flipped through a notebook. "We're part of a study gathering information on global warming, in our case looking at particular tree species for evidence of change. Call this number, ask for Bob Phillips. Tell him John Croft said he should tell you anything you want to know."

There was silence now and then another adjusting of the machine, the cell phone their seller was on no doubt working off a counterfeit or stolen chip as he had previously done. *He's too close to your operation,* Marquez thought, as the silence continued. *Bell's right, Shauf's right, I've pushed this too far. Shut the office down and pull the team. You're trying too hard to make it work with this guy, and he's prowling around you because he's suspicious. Pack up and move out of the safehouse and come back at him a different way. He's not calling to sell anything today. We're not hunting him anymore, he's hunting us.*

"I have the galls you bought. Do you want them?"

"If you dip them in chocolate."

He heard laughter, a strange "Hack, hack, hack," through the machine. Marquez had thrown the answer back as a flip comment, but dipped in chocolate was a way smugglers sometimes disguised galls, trying to make them look like figs that had been coated.

"I can drop them at your business or meet you."

"I won't be around the business for the next few days, so maybe we'll have to meet."

"I'll call you very soon."

Marquez drove away from Wright's Lake. He phoned Kendall when he got out to the highway and told him what he'd found.

"I'm on my way to you," Marquez said. "I'll take you there."

Kendall was in the garage with Hawse and two other detectives when Marquez walked up. They'd pulled the contents of Petroni's truck and spread them on plastic on the concrete walk leading up to the house. Marquez saw the satisfaction on Hawse's heavy face and knew they'd found something.

"I'm talking to you only because Petroni came to you and maybe you'll help us find him," Kendall said. "There are threatening messages from Petroni on her answering machine. He was angry about her cutting off the credit cards. Her lawyer just told us she saved them for a judge to hear. They aren't apologies. They're not the voice of a man trying to get back together with his wife."

"He put the blame on himself yesterday."

"Sure, and she paid the ultimate price. Let me show you what we found in the truck."

They had photos, shots taken of Sophie Broussard and a young man who it took Marquez only a moment to recognize. Behind them was a lake, and from the gold light reflecting off the water he knew it was taken near sunset. Sophie wore a black thong swim-suit. Her tan skin glistened with beads of water and suntan oil. Vandemere's left hand cupped her ass as their hips pressed together.

"What lake, Marquez?"

"I'd guess Loon."

"That's what one of the officers here said." He shook the evidence bag with the photos. "Buried in his truck."

Vandemere was tanned, lean, looked fit. Sophie's long legs were as tall as his. Her hair was longer than it was now and wet and dark on her shoulders.

"Taken with a digital camera and printed off on ordinary paper. We're going into the house where he was staying with Sophie as soon as we get a warrant signed, and that's going to be soon. Can you give me a job-related reason he'd be driving around with these photos?"

"Not offhand."

Marquez led Kendall and a couple of county cruisers to Wright's Lake. He showed them the cabin, the duffel bag visible through the window.

"I'll need a warrant to go inside," Kendall said, "and I'm going to write down that you stopped by to visit because he told you he was staying out here. You with me on that?" He didn't wait for an answer. "How'd you know it was that cabin?"

"I saw open windows."

"He wanted you to find it."

When Marquez left, Kendall was giving instructions to a county cop to park his unit out of view and wait.

"Officially, Petroni's wanted for questioning," Marquez told Alvarez as he reached the highway and started for Placerville. "Unofficially, he's wanted for murder, and Kendall still thinks I know where he is. There's a chance he'll try to have someone follow me, so take a look behind me as I come into town."

"Got you covered."

Half an hour later in a surprised but clear voice, and after Marquez had made several turns on Placerville streets, Alvarez confirmed a car more or less staying with him, not aggressively, but
there.

"I'm not sure it's a cop."

"What kind of car?"

"White TransAm."

"I need gas, I'll stop for it now. Let's see what he does."

Marquez pulled into a Shell station. He caught just a glimpse
of the car as he got out.

27

"What do you think?" Alvarez asked.

"Sit tight, and I'm going to kill a few minutes here before getting on the highway."

Marquez paid for the gas, bought a newspaper, a bag of roasted almonds, and coffee, then walked slowly back to his truck and tried Petroni's cell phone after getting into the cab. No answer. Tried it again and left a message this time. He drank a little of the coffee and pulled onto the highway westbound toward Sacramento, nerves humming, Alvarez following five minutes later.

Where the road flattened before Sacramento the car showed up again, hanging well behind Marquez but staying with him, and he still thought it might be Kendall putting a tail on him. He slowed as he entered Sacramento city limits, and Alvarez closed the gap, got the plates, ran registration, and the name Marion Stuart came back.

Alvarez read off 141 Valero. "Recognize that, Lieutenant?"

"Durham's home address."

"You got it."

"Is that him at the wheel?"

"It's hard to tell. The driver is slouched down and I can't read him well enough from here. Looks like him but I can't say for sure. Do you want me to get closer?"

"Yeah, try to get a look."

Alvarez never got the chance. The TransAm dropped down the Tenth Street exit into Sacramento, and they decided not to chase him. Marquez continued past Sacramento, crossed the causeway, drove through Davis, and Alvarez broke off.

"I'll go back through Sacramento and check Durham's house for the TransAm," Alvarez said. "I'll call you from there."

"Run the name Marion Stuart every way you can. I'm headed to Keeler's."

"I'll call if I learn something."

Five miles outside Davis, Marquez turned down the long driveway that ran through an almond orchard to ex-chief Keeler's house. He saw the unused decaying barn first, then the greenhouse where Keeler spent his days with orchids. Sally, the spaniel, charged out to meet him. The kitchen door was open, Keeler sitting at his table, fingernails dark from working the greenhouse soil, wearing an old sweater and pants that hung too loosely on him now. The room smelled of cigar smoke, and Marquez saw the stub lying on the table.

At the retirement party held here in the spring, Keeler and his wife of forty years, Clara, stood holding hands like a teenage couple, before raising their champagne glasses in a toast to the friends gathered in the yard. He'd given such a soft-spoken sentimental speech that the officers used to his gruffness and sharp temper had joked about it for days afterward. He and Clara were going to travel the national parks. He'd do a lot of fishing and they'd see the country together, which they hadn't done since their honeymoon. He pointed at a greenhouse he was restoring, and when he said he was going to grow orchids and win competitions the crowd laughed, Keeler, the flower grower. Smoke from pork ribs barbecuing had drifted across the gathering. White almond blossoms swirled and drifted onto the patio as the party continued into the dusk. Two weeks later Clara complained of a pain in her abdomen, lay down on their living room couch, and died of a burst aneurism.

"Bill Petroni's wife has been murdered," Marquez said, taking a chair at the table. "They're looking for Bill to question him."

He told Keeler about Stella's murder, then took the call from Alvarez confirming the TransAm was parked up near Durham's house. He asked Alvarez to get a hold of Roberts, let her know what had happened, tell her he wanted to focus on Durham's background. Then to Keeler he described his last meeting with Petroni and the Sunday morning at the sheriff's office where Bell and Charlotte Floyd had been present. Keeler listened and got awkwardly to his feet, a hip bothering him. He went to the refrigerator.

"That's very, very sad about Stella," he said, and pulled two Coors cans. "I know it's early for a beer." Keeler handed him a can. "And no one can find Bill this morning?"

"I looked for him. The county is looking hard."

"He was here with Stella at our retirement party," Keeler said. "I remember them dancing, but you're saying he was already with this other woman."

"Chief, I really don't know what's going on with his life. He doesn't seem to be going out with the younger woman anymore."

"Is he part of your operation?"

"The truth is I haven't had much communication with Petroni."

Keeler took a drink of beer, looked through the open door at the sunlight on the yard, and asked, "What is it I can do to help you?"

Marquez told him what they had going on, including Sweeney. They came to the question of whether Keeler was willing to drive his camper up to Ice House Lake.

"I haven't gone anywhere in it," Keeler said.

"Maybe it's time. It's cold in the morning, clear, most of the people gone."

Keeler's eyes crinkled with dry humor. "Like going on vacation?"

"I trust you, chief, and I'm in a situation I'm not sure about."

"All right, let me think it over today."

Marquez talked with Bell as he drove into Mill Valley. There'd been phone calls from several TV stations and newspapers about Petroni. There'd been several calls from Kendall. The department was preparing a statement along the line of being very saddened by the murder and wishing the best for the family. No comment would be made on Petroni's status, though his suspension and the fact police sought him for questioning were already in the news.

They talked about Sweeney, who, if he stuck to his itinerary, would leave for Tahoe tonight. Bell wanted to know they were ready, and he listened quietly, asking an occasional question. Two wardens in the Tahoe area would assist. Another they'd worked with before and liked the style of would drive up tonight from Kern County. Marquez told the chief he had visited Ed Keeler and was now in the Bay Area and wouldn't return to the mountains until later tonight. He didn't tell Bell about the TransAm, was still mulling that over. They discussed the latest call from the bear farmer, the offer to drop off the galls.

Marquez didn't hang up with Bell until after he'd parked in Mill Valley. He watched Maria walk toward him, jeans low on her hips, belly exposed. She'd talked with Katherine months ago about piercing her navel, and Katherine had told her absolutely no. Her walk now, though teenage awkward, was that of a young woman. They were nearing the point where they could still advise her and exert influence, but not so easily control her. *Nor should we*, he thought. She smiled at him as she got in the truck.

"Hey," she said. "How long are you here?"

"I've got one other stop in the Bay Area and then I'll head back up. We've got a lot of action right now. Tell me about this new call you got while we drive."

"Okay, well, this guy called last night and had a kind of a twangy voice. He wanted you."

"Twangy like an accent from somewhere."

"More like he was pretending to be."

"What else?"

"About his voice?"

"Anything that comes to mind."

"That was all he said. Mom blew it all out of proportion."

"I thought she was going to field all the unknown calls."

"My friend was calling back. I thought it was him. If I had a cell phone, then none of this would be a problem. We wouldn't even be having this conversation."

"We're going to get you one today."

"Really?"

"This afternoon."

"No way!"

"But your mom is only willing if you stop talking about piercing your navel or anything else, like your nose."

"I would never pierce my nose."

"Well, you can think about whether you want to agree to those conditions while we check out where this guy followed you."

They drove to the street where she'd first noticed the minivan behind her. Retracing the route she remembered more about the caller with the southern accent.

"He didn't want to leave his phone number, and he called me 'little girl.' What a freak! He said he was your hunting friend."

"My hunting friend?"

"Right."

This morning Marquez had talked with Katherine about pulling Maria out of school to go visit her grandmother for a week. Katherine would also move out of the Mount Tam house and stay in San Francisco with her best friend. It was giving into the fear and worry, but Kath said she'd rather do it this way, though it was obvious now that she hadn't talked to Maria yet. And there was nothing that said a week would make a difference, but if they were going to take precautions, now was the time. He'd called Matt Fong and suggested he do the same, and he'd had the same conversation with his team. The phone call Maria had fielded last night had only reinforced that feeling.

As he drove the route Maria had taken through Mill Valley he remembered two men in a dark blue Chevy Suburban driving slowly down a residential street in Phoenix twelve years ago. They'd bounced two wheels up on the sidewalk and run over an eight-year-old boy on his bicycle, then backed up over his skull, dropped back down onto the street, and slowly drove away. The slow drive away was meant to convey power, not the killing. The killing of the boy was the lesson, the slow drive said they weren't worried about the justice system. Cartels had no problem going after families of law enforcement officers.

"I was watching the guy following me like you taught me to do, but I got scared," Maria said. "I know you and Mom don't believe me. I know it sounds like the perfect story."

"It doesn't sound perfect to me."

"Are you being sarcastic?"

"No."

She showed him where the cop had pulled her over and how she'd turned and watched the other car go by. She craned her neck looking behind, and he pictured the cop's description of her crying as he'd told her he was going to give her a ticket. Marquez doubted she'd been very focused on the vehicle following or that it had been anywhere nearby at the point the cop walked up, but he felt she was telling the truth about thinking she was being followed.

"How would you feel about missing a week or so of school and going down to stay with your grandmother?"

"Missing school would suck."

"Let's go get a cell phone for you."

She picked out an inexpensive phone, and they went through the deal of signing up for a phone plan, the salesman talking as though they were buying a house. She got to choose her phone number from a list, and Marquez had no doubt she'd go over her monthly limit, or plan, as the phone company called it. The "plan" was to take all your money. As they left the store, Maria high on her new phone, he took the conversation back to visiting her grandmother and how unsure he was about the suspect they were trying to find. He tried to give her the information in a balanced way.

"What, like I drive down to Grandma's?"

"Your Mom would ride with you."

"This is insane."

He turned and looked at her. "Yeah, you're right, Maria, this is insane. But I think it's what we've got to do."

He dropped her at her car in the center of town and wished he could drive up the mountain behind her. That he had to worry about her safety stirred a much deeper anger inside, and he drove away with that. When he reached the freeway he called an old friend at U.S. Fish and Wildlife. Though they'd already talked to Fish and Wildlife about Durham, he asked a favor, asked her to check again to see if there was anything anywhere in their system with Durham's name on it, and also the name Marion Stuart.

Pulling Maria from school might be an overreaction. He held the phone in his hand, second-guessing himself, debating calling Katherine and changing plans. Instead, he punched in Vandemere Sr.'s number. When he answered, Marquez told him he'd be in Orinda in forty minutes.

28

Marquez hadn't been in the town of Orinda in a long time, but it didn't seem much different. He followed a residential street into hills surrounding a golf course, drove past tennis courts and a country club, then around a small lake where the slopes above the driveways were grown over with ivy. The Vandemeres', a three-story Spanish-style stucco house, had a black iron gate left open this afternoon to let him in. A tall white-haired man came out, walked over, and offered his hand as Marquez got out of the truck.

"Pete Vandemere," he said.

Marquez liked the man immediately but couldn't have said why. Upstairs in Jed's room he looked at the posters on the walls, a lacrosse trophy, framed photographs, the things in the room that bore some stamp of Jed's personality, though Pete told him Jed hadn't lived at home for five years. Pete had wanted him to see the room, perhaps to get a sense of his son. Now he led him down to a room where a TV played. A young girl got up from the couch and clicked the TV off as soon as they came in.

"My daughter," Pete said, after she'd left. "She's the one who has had the hardest time of all. We still find her in his room asleep on the floor some mornings. She idolized him."

Marquez sat in a stuffed chair and read the emails of Jed's that Pete had printed for him. He felt Pete watching him and read two that were just bantering with a college friend, then one that started with "I've met a girl named Sophie that I like a lot. She knows every trail up here and has been showing me places." He read on, then looked up at Pete's eyes. "Does Kendall have copies of these?"

"I gave him copies the day I filled out the missing persons report. He asked for more recently. I think he lost the others."

There were several emails mentioning bear poachers, a reference to high school, the Bear Initiative he'd worked on, one to his dad, suggesting he might be in the area poachers were working and had talked to the local warden about it.

"He went up to support the Bear Initiative in Idaho when he was in high school. Saved all his money and rode a bus up there but came home a little disillusioned, didn't feel like he'd really accomplished anything but spent all his money. I told the detective this the first time we met."

"He mentioned it to me."

"I didn't know he wrote it down. Didn't seem like he wanted to listen at all when we first reported Jed missing, and I know all kinds of people go missing. But he didn't acknowledge that we knew our son, and, of course, it was in the wilderness area, not his territory."

"But it's his case now."

"It is, and it wouldn't have made any difference." His voice quavered. "My son was already gone."

"I'm very sorry."

Pete raised a hand, didn't say anything, then, "I'm not doing well with this." He picked up a manila envelope off his desk. "These are copies for you. All the emails he sent this past summer. He was an enthusiastic young man, had a great life ahead of him." He looked up and stopped talking about his son. "Do you know this Sophie Broussard?" he asked.

"I know who she is and I've met her. Has Detective Kendall talked to you about her?"

"No, he won't talk to us about the case. He says he'll keep us apprised of real progress. Well, you should know this, he got angry with me because I tried to do my own investigating when I didn't feel anything was happening. I asked the wrong questions too early, before Jed's body was found."

"Did you talk to Sophie?"

"Yes, I talked to her and another young man named Eric Nyland. He was quite helpful and she was unfriendly. She works at a bar in Placerville and wasn't the person I expected at all." He paused, studying Marquez's eyes. "The detective has told me not to speak to anyone about this, but I'm going to tell you. She told me she had a short fling with my son and it didn't mean anything to her, said she could barely remember his name."

"When did you have that conversation with her?"

"In late August. That's hardly three weeks after that email in your hand where he's talking about what they're doing together. So you can imagine the things that have gone through my head. I know from emails that he met her in June and the relationship went on longer than she claimed. Jed wouldn't lie about something like that, or anything else. Whether she wanted to shock me or cover something up, I don't know."

Marquez nodded in sympathy at Vandemere's frustration that this woman his son had been so enthusiastic about was so cold to him. The date of the last email was August 6 and in all this, what Kendall hadn't told him, what he learned now, was that Jed Vandemere's birthday was August 7 and it was understood that he was going to call his parents.

"In the last few years have you talked to him on his birthday?"

"Always on his birthday, but forgetting us, he knew Caitlin would be waiting for the phone to ring."

"Was that Caitlin who left as we came in?"

"Yes." Vandemere was quiet a moment. "Caitlin had made him a card and a present. There's no way he would have missed that call and no doubt in my mind that he was killed in that twenty-four-hour period."

"He mentions seeing two men at the end of July that were looking around his campsite—"

"I know the email you mean."

"He doesn't describe the men in the email. Did he ever mention them over the phone?"

"Yes, but he never gave a physical description, just that they were acting funny. Oh, he did say one was an older man."

"Did he ever meet Sophie's family?"

"He told me she wanted nothing to do with them. So I don't think so. Why do you ask?"

"Sophie's father did time for trafficking in bear products."

"Detective Kendall never told us that."

"He may not have known, and it doesn't necessarily mean anything."

Marquez said good-bye, thanked him, and promised to pass on anything he learned. He saw Caitlin in the window as he drove away. On the road east he told Alvarez he'd be back in time to help cover Sweeney. During the ride back to Placerville he reread several of the emails. He thought about Nyland's pretending sympathy when Vandemere talked to him.

Marquez arrived in Placerville a little after 4:00, just before Sweeney left Sacramento. If Sweeney stuck with his itinerary he'd continue up the highway fifty miles beyond Placerville to the South Lake Tahoe casino where he'd spend the night.

When the budgets were larger, Marquez's team had been ten wardens, twice what it was today. With ten undercover officers it was much easier to follow a suspect over this kind of distance. A larger team could spread out, float ahead and behind, but with only five it was more of a hopscotch and handoff game. Sweeney's driver sat in the fast lane and rode the accelerator. Most of the SOU was strung out along the highway ahead of Sweeney. They communicated using their four-digit call numbers, calling out just the last two numbers for ID. They'd assigned a number to Sweeney as well—the number twenty-one because his first destination was a casino and their informant had told Bell that Sweeney was a big blackjack player. It was also, Marquez had decided, a number that most juries might associate with good luck, one that a defense attorney would have trouble twisting into a politically malicious symbol.

Sweeney's car rolled through successive green lights as the highway cut through Placerville. Marquez picked him up there, reading nothing through the tinted windows of the black car as it passed. He called out each exit sign Sweeney's vehicle passed. Then it was beyond Placerville and starting the long climb.

"In number one at seventy-five," he said, giving the lane number and speed. A few minutes later, "Passing Apple Hill, still lane one at seventy."

Near Pollock Pines, he saw its headlights come on, relayed that on. Sweeney's car moved steadily up the highway and everything was calm enough that he made a quick call to Katherine to check on her and Maria. He knew they'd left the Bay Area about the same time Sweeney left Sacramento, heading south to Katherine's mother's house outside Bishop in the Owens Valley.

"We're on Highway 5 almost down to the cutoff to Yosemite." Her voice was light, enjoying her time with Maria despite the reason for the trip. "She's driven the speed limit the whole way," Kath added, and he chuckled. "She wants to drive the whole way. Here, I'll hold the phone to her ear."

"Hi, Dad."

"Hey, Maria."

"So what are you doing?"

"Checking out a tip. How's the drive?"

"It's empty out here. I'm listening to music. Mom fell asleep right away."

"Maybe it's your music."

"Very funny."

Up ahead, Sweeney's car changed lanes, and Marquez knew he'd have to hang up.

"When you get tired you hand the wheel to your mom, okay?"

"What if she's asleep?"

He smiled, said good-bye, and then relayed Sweeney's position ahead to Roberts, who had the next leg. Roberts started ahead of Pollock Pines—running a reverse point, watching Sweeney's car in her rearview mirror. She continued up the river canyon ahead of Sweeney's car as Marquez trailed and then broke off, heading toward Wright's Lake, winding out through forest and meadow, driving past a county cruiser hiding near Chimney Flats, knowing that Petroni would spot the cruiser just as easily.

Kendall was in Petroni's Wright's Lake cabin with Hawse. They'd separated Petroni's belongings, spread them out on the couch and floor.

"What are you looking for?" Marquez asked.

"A key to a storage unit," Kendall said.

"Who told you to look for it?"

"The dark angel," Hawse said. "Sophie."

"She ever been to it?"

Neither answered that, but Kendall elaborated. Sophie was pretty sure that's where most of his belongings had gone after he'd moved out of Georgetown. Though they hadn't found the key, they had found his logbook and were puzzling over Petroni's leaving it here. Or maybe not puzzling, possibly baiting him?

"What do you make of him leaving it here?" Kendall asked.

"He may really believe his career is over."

"There are all kinds of names in it. We found a name that he's entered twice very recently. Did he say anything to you about Howell Road?"

"No."

"Take a look."

Kendall handed the log over. "Howell Road," was written in pencil, underlined, and near it was written "Johengen."

"We found it here too," Kendall said, showing him the inside cover of a paperback book they'd spotted "Johengen" written in as they'd opened it. It was finding it in the paperback that provoked their interest.

"So who's Johengen?" Hawse asked, his round face a moon of innocence.

Marquez stared at Petroni's handwriting, thinking about it. He had nothing to offer, though all of his team knew Howell Road.

"A bear hunter, a poacher, someone Petroni had a beef with, a friend he might be staying with?" Hawse prompted, then smiled at his next idea. "Yet another girlfriend? So far we can't find a Johengen who lives on Howell."

"I get it, Hawse, but I don't know of a Johengen."

Howell was a long road that ran forever out into backcountry. Once you got out a few miles it turned rural real fast. Some of the marginal people Petroni complained about had set up shop out there. Could be that he'd seen something out there and was paying attention to it. Marquez flipped through other pages of the log.

"Nothing clicks for you?" Kendall asked.

"No, though I'd bet Johengen's is out Howell Road."

Petroni had his own code for noting things. He'd written another entry that had a capital J and the note "needs looking at."

They talked about that, and Kendall gestured around the cabin, said that they were in touch with the owner and that it was as Petroni had claimed. The owner was a friend and had loaned Petroni the cabin for as long as he needed it. In the light of the single pale bulb overhead the cabin looked particularly spartan, the walls with pine paneling, cold in the October twilight.

"Have you eaten?" Kendall asked.

"Not yet," Marquez said.

"Why don't we grab a bite and talk a little more. Let's see if we can get around our recent snag."

"We've got a surveillance running, but I'll meet you for an hour."

On the drive to Pollock Pines to have dinner with Kendall and Hawse, Marquez checked with his team. Cairo had the last leg. He called out Sweeney's position coming into South Lake Tahoe. The black car was just pulling up to the casino.

"I may play a little blackjack," Cairo said.

"If you lose your money, don't lose him."

"I'm lucky at the tables, Lieutenant."

"Talk to you in a couple of hours."

Kendall and Hawse ordered hamburgers, onion rings, beer, Hawse making the remark it wasn't going to do much for his diet. Marquez picked at the night's special, turkey meatloaf with mashed potatoes, a mistake that brought a little humor to Kendall's eyes.

"I need to understand why Petroni called you," Kendall said. "The very first time we interviewed him after Vandemere's remains were found, Petroni said I should be talking to you and your team, not him. He was disparaging when I asked who you were, said they'd drummed you out of the DEA after you were the only survivor on an undercover operation and the DEA was no longer sure which side you were on. Then through connections you got a job at Fish and Game."

"The first part of that is true, but not the second, and either way, Petroni got that story from me."

"How many died on this DEA operation?"

"Eight, but five of those were Mexican nationals and at the time the DEA wasn't counting Mexicans."

"You're bitter."

"I lost some good friends."

"So why did he confide in you? Why did he bring you to his Sunday confession?"

"I volunteered he might want me there. He said no at first."

Kendall took a pull of beer, his face serious as he closed his eyes with the bottle tipped. When he put the bottle down he said, "Petroni's name has come up too much."

"And you think I know more about that."

"You knew about Wright's Lake, but I don't know why he told you. Petroni is the type of guy who's always up against the whole world. Everyone is always backstabbing and screwing him. He's always getting fucked by a superior. Right now, it's your Chief Bell. He's the type of guy it happens to all life long and from the way he talked, you did it to him also. So why come to you unless it fits into a bigger plan, a way to get even, for instance."

"I don't have the answer."

"You've asked yourself?"

"Sure."

"He's turning to you in his time of need when everything is on the line."

"Let's hear your theory."

"All right. He's taking bribes and learns your team is in the area and starts worrying you're going to find out. And by the way, I've got testimony from more than Brandt."

"If the other is Bobby Broussard, you can throw it out."

That surprised Kendall. He put his beer down.

"What's the matter with Bobby Broussard?"

"I've seen him perjure himself."

"I still think it all fits. Sophie is tied in with Nyland, Nyland is tied in with poaching, and Petroni suddenly has new financial demands. He knows the bear population is relatively stable, and he can let these guys take a few. I'm saying he's got a financial need, there's a conduit through Sophie to make an offer, and he crosses the line."

"As long as I've known him he's been proud to be a game warden."

"Right, and he was an Eagle Scout too, so were some of those Enron guys, weren't they? But let me finish. You're up here with your team and he doesn't want anything to do with you, but in order to keep track of your whereabouts he's got to weave you in. So lately, he's started to make contact and feed you information."

"He didn't make contact all summer. We barely spoke."

"This theory has a few gaps, but hear me out. Stella figures out that he's got more money than he should have. She lived with him a long time and she knows the money. She senses something is wrong, confronts him, and maybe even tells her lawyer to start threatening him and he panics."

"How much money are you talking about?"

"You tell me."

"It's not going to be big money unless some guide is passing it on to a client. Maybe a grand a month otherwise."

"That could be the margin of difference."

"It's a big step for a warden."

"Big step for any cop."

"I can't see Petroni doing that."

"Right, and deep down he's actually a really good guy who talks shit about everybody because he has an insecure streak we should all forgive him for. Walks like a duck, talks like a duck. We've got people talking bribes and Petroni evasive about who he's talked to and when. I don't like the way it feels, and I'll throw another one at you—Jed Vandemere figured it out, saw Petroni involved in something."

"Then he wouldn't be the guy I knew."

"Marquez," and Kendall's frustration surfaced, "Petroni doesn't have anything good to say about you."

Marquez pushed back from the table. They left it that they'd talk tomorrow or as soon as either knew anything. Then as Marquez walked out he saw Troy Broussard's truck parked near Kendall's sedan. A cigarette glowed in the darkness behind the windshield, and Bobby, sitting in the passenger seat, called "Hey, you," as Marquez walked past. Though he knew he shouldn't, he veered toward them.

"They're going to put him down like a dog when they find him," Bobby said. "We're calling everyone to help hunt him down. Detective has asked our help finding him."

Troy turned to face Marquez more directly. "Don't you think we know you, you sonofabitch?"

"Who is it you think I am?"

Troy started his engine and touched his forehead. "A man kills his wife like that deserves a bullet right here."

Marquez watched their lights disappear down the road and found his hands were shaking as he got in his truck. He sat for several minutes before picking up the phone, checking with Cairo again, then Shauf. Cairo reported Sweeney was downstairs at the casino and happily gambling. Shauf had watched Nyland load restaurant waste and scraps at the back door of a Chinese restaurant.

"Looks like egg rolls at the bait piles tonight."

"Is he alone?"

"He is and he's worked hard to lose anyone tailing him, but it's hard outrunning a satellite."

"Give him plenty of room tonight."

"We will."

Near midnight he called Katherine, and Maria answered, saying Mom was asleep and she was on Highway 395, it was beautiful and she wasn't tired at all.

"The clouds are really white in the moonlight and I can see these tall mountains off to my right. I guess I got driving from you, because I feel fine."

"Those mountains off to your right are the ones John Muir called the Range of Light. We'll hike up there together someday. You okay taking it in from there?"

"I'm fine, Dad."

"I'm sorry about this, Maria, sorry we're doing this to you. I know it's hard on you."

"I already have a C in chemistry and I'm going to miss an English test."

"At least you'll get to see your grandmother."

"Grandma isn't going to take the SATs for me."

"How's your cell phone working?"

"I'm talking to you on it."

"Call me when you get there, okay?"

"Okay."

"I love you."

He heard her quiet "I love you too," and then hung up.

29

The next morning he heard from the Stockton vice
cop, Delano. The bust had gone splendidly, yielded four pounds of
crystal meth and six suspects. They'd also found more bear paws.

"We're starting to wonder if we're going to run into a live
bear." Delano laughed and said, "I can fax info on the guys we
busted. I should also tell you the local warden here, Ann Knight, is
on her way in. She says she knows you."

Marquez gave him the fax number at the TreeSearch office. He
knew and liked Ann Knight and was glad to hear it was her. "How
many paws?" he asked.

"Sixteen in two coolers in a refrigerator in a garage, but they're
in bad shape. We also recovered two rifles from the garage and
a vehicle there has an address up your direction."

"What's the name on registration?"

"Edward Broussard."

"He goes by Bobby Broussard up here. He was in the Crystal Basin last night."

"What's that, another meth lab?"

"Different crystal, it's a wilderness area. He was feeding bear bait piles with someone we're watching."

"We'd like him to explain what his car is doing in Stockton."

"I can lead you to him." Marquez paused a moment before committing to more, yet felt the first bubble of excitement. "Tell me about the rifles."

"A .30-06 and a Winchester .30-30, numbers filed on both."

"Have you called Kendall?"

"Just talked to him."

"Do you want me to do anything about Bobby?"

"I already called Detective Kendall. I'm waiting to hear back from him."

"You're going to ask Kendall to bring him in for you?"

"I already did."

"Will you ask Ann Knight to call me when she gets there?"

Half an hour later Knight called. She reported that the actual paw count was seventeen, about half from yearling bears, four from cubs, the rest adult. They were in poor shape, not salable, and it was Marquez's guess that the sales pipeline had been interrupted by some event, possibly the earlier arrest of Nine-O. Knight would photograph the paws and bring them to Sacramento. He could get a look at them there, if he wanted. He told her about the two rifles, what he'd said to Delano about them, and added that he'd call her if anything came of that.

He checked in with Cairo as he drove out Six Mile Road. Sweeney had left the casino and gone to a lakefront estate near Tahoma on the west shore.

"I'm parked where I can see over the fence," Cairo said. "It's one of these multimillion-dollar houses on the water. There's an oiled redwood gate in front, and his car is inside in the courtyard. People are getting here. It must be a lunch deal."

"Does Sweeney still have a driver?"

"Yeah, the driver is with the car, standing outside it talking on his cell." He heard Cairo yawn. "What's going on down there?"

"I'm on the ridge above Nyland's trailer waiting for Shauf to get here. We're going to check out the firelight I saw the other night. I'll call you on the other side of that."

Below, the dry meadow was yellow-brown. He saw a couple of Walker hounds on long chains, the chains silvery in sunlight. He heard Shauf approaching and figured they'd need twenty minutes to cross the slope and drop down near the last trailer. When they did, the chained hounds started barking and a third leaped out of the doorless trailer and charged upslope. Marquez sat down on a rock, coaxed the dog over, and quieted her. Then the hound followed them but only as far as the last trailer. They picked up a trail and followed it along the rim of a reed-filled depression, what might have been a shallow lake a hundred years ago. A quarter mile later, after it ended in a small clearing, Marquez looked back up at the ridge where they'd started and knew they were roughly in the right spot.

"There's your fire pit out in the middle," Shauf said.

It was built of concentric circles of stones fitted tightly together like a woven basket of rock set into the ground. Capping it was a circular iron plate that had an eye ring that a stick or something could be slipped through to lift it off.

"There was firelight and then it winked out. This explains it. Look over there."

Shauf walked over to a neatly cut stack of split pine kindling and a jug she said smelled like kerosene. Marquez found a stick and stirred the ashes, met resistance, and stuck his hand in. He pulled out fragments of bottle glass, fused and melted, a blackened metal button, then a piece of bone, short and thick, like a piece of femur, one end crushed and broken. He put the heavy cap back on and studied the bone fragment again before handing it to Shauf. He walked the rest of the small clearing, checking out the stacked wood, rusted axe, gallon container of kerosene. He tried his phone and couldn't get a signal.

"I can't tell what it's from," Shauf said.

"Looks to me like it could be human."

"It's old."

"Yeah." It was quite dark, mineralized. "We'll bag it and take it."

They walked back, and Marquez again quieted the hound. He looked in the trailer with the missing door, saw folded horse blankets, and heard another dog growl from the shadows. There didn't seem to be anything else there, and they hiked back up to the ridge.

In Placerville at their office the fax from Delano had come through, and Marquez read the rap sheets on the men arrested last night. None of the names caught his eye, but he called Kendall and left a message listing the names and asking Kendall to flip through Petroni's logbook and call him back if he found any matches.

Marquez didn't hear back from Kendall all afternoon, and Sweeney began to move in their direction. Within an hour he was less than forty miles from Placerville. Then they watched him drive into town and stop in front of the Hangtown Grille on Main Street. Both Sweeney and the driver went inside, and a third man showed up minutes later and joined them at a table. Alvarez walked past.

"Sweeney is eating a steak," he said. "I don't recognize the third man, but the steak looks like a sirloin and it's making me hungry."

When they'd finished dinner it was dark, streetlights were on, and Sweeney and his friend, a middle-aged man, walked down the sidewalk while the driver drove to the hotel and carried the bags in ahead of them. After Sweeney had checked into the Lexington the team moved into positions around it. They watched him get into an elevator with his luggage, a bellhop, and the friend. A couple of hours later a green Land Cruiser with Nyland at the wheel drove past the hotel entrance and parked on a side street. Nyland walked back wearing a down parka, canvas pants, and boots. He paused in the lobby, looking uncomfortable and stiff in his new clothes. The gel in his short hair gleamed under the lobby lights.

"Here's the hunting guide," Marquez said.

"And maybe that's why Durham followed you," Shauf theorized. "He knew this hunt was coming and was jumpy about it. It's got to be Durham who set this up. He's the lobbyist. He must know Sweeney. But what's he doing this for? He's got a nice house, must be a decent job consulting and lobbying. The money he makes guiding a hunt can't be worth it."

"He likes being the game hunter, and maybe he's our bear farmer."

Marquez watched Nyland nervously appraise the lobby, then move toward the bar.

"Nyland looks like a Ken doll," Shauf said. "Ken goes hunting."

"He wants this," Marquez said.

"What do you mean?"

"The guide business, crooked or not, he's invested himself in it."

"He belongs in jail."

"He may get there tonight."

Roberts slipped into the Lexington, went to the bar, took a place in the shadows, and ordered a drink but didn't touch it until Sweeney and his friend walked in. Nyland got to his feet, came around and introduced himself, and everyone shook hands, Nyland acting as though Sweeney were some sort of celebrity.

As the others took a table in the bar Durham's car rolled up to the hotel entrance. Marquez watched him hand the keys to his Cadillac to a teenage valet.

"Head honcho coming in," Marquez said, as Durham strode through the lobby. Unlike the others, he wore a sport coat and slacks. "Not making the ride tonight," Marquez said, wondering again if Durham was their bear farmer.

Drinks got ordered, and Marquez could see Sweeney was here to relax and cut loose. He smiled easily and seemed perfectly comfortable with the situation. He obviously knew Durham, and only Nyland looked out of place. Marquez kept his focus on Durham. From the way Durham had talked to Alvarez, it was clear he prided himself on his other big game exploits. There were photos from Africa, Canada, South America, and Siberia on the walls of Sierra Guides. Sweeney's presence proved the guide business dovetailed with lobbying work, but it was still a long step from there to trafficking bear parts or farming.

Marquez checked Nyland again, a guy uncomfortable in his own skin, something eating at him tonight. *Maybe he doesn't think he'll be able to deliver a bear, or maybe he's thinking about us.* Nyland's eyes kept darting toward Durham, who ignored him and entertained the others with a story, gesturing with his hands, smiling, a complete about-face from the grim guy who'd grilled Alvarez.

Then, Marquez saw Sophie walking down the sidewalk toward the hotel in a dress so tight it showed all the lines of her legs and cupped her breasts. She crossed the lobby and entered the bar. Sweeney and Durham got to their feet. Sweeney kissed her on the cheek, and she sat down next to Durham, not Nyland.

There was another quick round, a final before Nyland, Sweeney, and Sweeney's companion stood. Durham shook Sweeney's hand, though he didn't stand, more the handshake of two equals, one leaving now. The trio moved to the hotel door, and Marquez caught Nyland's glance back as Durham covered Sophie's hand with his own. As the others stepped out into the cold fall air and went to Nyland's Land Cruiser, Durham urged her to slide closer.

30

Rumors of Troy's abusing Sophie had followed her since grade school, and Marquez knew there'd been at least one incident where an elementary school teacher's concern had caused the police to pull Troy in for questioning. She'd been eleven years old when that happened, nine when her mother died. There'd been talk at the time of placing her in foster care, but eventually she had come home and the only thing society's temporary concern had achieved was to mark her and separate her from her friends.

Petroni had grown up in Placerville. He'd known Sophie since she'd been a young girl. He'd known all the Broussards, the stories told about them, their poor southern rural roots and culture of living off the land. Even here in the mountains where many people cobbled together a living through a willingness to work a variety of jobs, the Broussards' poverty emanated from them like an odor.

Petroni had tried to explain his attraction to her when Marquez had driven with him through the hills behind Placerville. He'd talked of seeing her as a young girl walking through town in the same clothes she'd worn the previous several years, her sweaters hiking up her forearms as she grew tall, thin, and lanky. He'd described driving out Highway 49 in his first Fish and Game truck and feeling sad for her as she'd walked the shoulder of the winding two-lane highway, alone in a place where she shouldn't have been. Petroni told him that she wasn't really Troy's daughter, but rather the daughter of his wife's sister who'd died in an accident.

Marquez could understand the feeling of being worth less than everyone else, what it felt like inside. It was easy to remember an older girl telling him when he was seven that he was a throwaway. His parents, unable to deal with raising two children, caught up in the importance of their own lives, had elevated their struggles against drug and alcohol dependency to a level that subsumed any real responsibility for raising him or his sister, Dara. The final abandonment came when their mother dropped them at their paternal grandparents, a temporary solution that was just supposed to last as long as it took her to get it together.

He'd pieced together enough about Sophie Broussard's life to know that no luck like that had ever come her way. When she'd finally escaped home she'd ended up with Nyland, and now she was back with him, but as she'd admitted at the Creekview, not really with him. From what Marquez had seen in the Lexington bar tonight, he knew she wasn't with anyone.

While Nyland was inside the Lexington, his Land Cruiser had gotten equipped with an option the rental company didn't offer, twenty-four-hour tracking, the team's last GPS transponder. They had his position, knew he'd just turned onto the access road to the Crystal Basin Wilderness. A few minutes later he broke from the paved road onto Weber Mill, and Marquez realized there wasn't going to be any cat and mouse or doubling back.

"What do you think?" Shauf asked, slowing to a stop along Crystal Basin Road.

"This is it. It's the bait pile you found or another like it along Weber Mill. It's a quick and dirty hunt, the big guy doesn't want to waste time."

"Not just using the road to cut through."

"No, I think he rented the Land Cruiser for cover, and I'm guessing Sweeney doesn't want to do the hijinks, doesn't want to sit out all night somewhere cold, and asked for the nearest easiest bear to shoot. It could be part of Nyland's nervousness, he knows we're out here and wanted to take Sweeney deeper into the woods."

Marquez called the pilot of the DFG spotter plane. She was south of them and approaching with lookdown infrared equipment. Ten minutes later the pilot confirmed that there was a stationary heat signal where GPS showed the Land Cruiser had stopped. As the team moved into the Crystal Basin, drifting one vehicle in, then the next, a van, an old pickup, a car, Marquez decided that he and Alvarez would work their way down the steep slope, keeping to the trees and brush, and the rest of the team would cover either entrance to Weber Mill Road.

He alerted the wardens they'd called in for help, then took a cheerful call from ex-chief Keeler who said he was in his camper with his dog and on the road nearing Placerville. He had a campsite reserved at Ice House Lake.

"We're watching a suspect now who looks like he's about to hunt."

"Then I'm too late."

"This isn't the one I need your help with."

By the time Marquez moved down with Alvarez there was a moon rising above the ridge across the canyon. Pale light washed the dirt road below, and they made out Bobby Broussard's truck parked near Nyland's Land Cruiser and a second truck near the southern entrance to the road. When Marquez talked with Shauf she reported that Troy Broussard had just passed her position and driven on, slowly climbing toward the lip of the basin.

It grew colder and the moon rose over the river canyon. Voices no longer drifted up from down the slope. Bobby walked the road, standing almost directly below them, glancing upslope as he smoked, farted, moved back to his truck. He squatted there, talked briefly on his CB radio, then started up the road in the other direction.

When that happened, Marquez tapped Alvarez and they scrambled down, crouched as they ran across the road, and dropped into trees. Lying beneath trees on the downslope below the dirt road, they worked over to a group of oaks, belly-crawling through brush, avoiding the gray-white light reflecting off the open slope of dry grass.

Marquez pulled himself forward with his elbows, eased down a little closer, though he heard their voices. Low murmurs and a long silence. The hunting blind was no more than a hundred feet below. He turned, let Alvarez know this was it, they were good. They could record from here.

An hour passed and then a downwind started, and that's what was needed, heavier air to push the bait pile scents toward the river bottom where a bear could pick up the smells. Bears used the river like a highway at night. Marquez worked a cramp in his thigh, heard faint murmurs from below, then brush breaking and a low growl. With night goggles Marquez read one, then a second bear at the bait pile.

Now came a flicker of laser scopes, gunshots, sharp hard echoes dying quickly, the moaning cries of a wounded bear thrashing, breaking through brush, and Nyland's voice, clear and authoritative, giving directions, going after the wounded one, calling out that the other was down. Spotter lights came on. Nyland led them down, Sweeney and friend trailing well back.

"I got him," Alvarez whispered. "I got Sweeney shooting. He got the bear that's down. His friend wounded the other."

They heard Nyland's sharp warning to the men to stay back, saw his light sweep through the brush below the bait pile, heard a sharp crack of a rifle shot. The moaning stopped. The voices of Sweeney and his friend, their excitement, the adrenaline release, carried up the slope as they reached the bait pile. Alvarez lifted the camcorder and recorded Sweeney's putting another bullet in the bear lying there.

"You ready?" Marquez asked, and as Alvarez nodded, Marquez radioed Shauf to bring the other wardens up, to get ready.

"Bobby's coming your way with an ice chest," she said.

"Okay, we see him."

Bobby Broussard went past them, half sliding on the dry grass, carrying a cooler. Below, Nyland skinned the bear at the bait pile. They heard Sweeney giving Nyland advice and watched as the gallbladder was removed, dropped in the cooler, the hide cut off and folded. Bobby was given the bloody task of humping it back up while Nyland went to skin the other bear.

"Bring everyone in," Marquez told Shauf.

Bobby brought the first skin to the road and went back for the other as Nyland started up with the cooler. Marquez and Alvarez climbed back up the slope, waiting near the lip of the road as Nyland crested it.

Sweeney and his friend wouldn't be a problem. Nyland was the one to watch. Sweeney and friend stood catching their breath at the road's edge, moonlight on their faces, looking down at where they'd hunted, savoring the moment, while Nyland and Bobby loaded the vehicles, bloody hides going in Bobby's rig, Nyland in a hurry to leave. Sweeney play-punched his friend on the shoulder, talking loudly to him, made brave by the excitement of the kill.

"Did you see that bear drop?"

"Aw, come on, you had to put another one in him."

"Big damn bruin, isn't he?"

"He's big all right."

"He's the biggest goddamned bruin I've ever seen in this state."

"I've seen bigger in the backyard at my cabin."

"The hell you have."

They both laughed, and Nyland walked over. His parka was bloody and nothing the other men wanted to be too near.

"Guess I need to wash up," Nyland said, and Marquez gave the signal. A powerful halogen light shone on Nyland's face, and voices rose, calling out, "Fish and Game! Fish and Game! No one move!"

The uniform wardens closed in, Marquez and Alvarez coming over the road lip with their masks on. Cairo stepped out from behind Bobby's pickup, gun drawn, and the uniform wardens already had Nyland and Bobby lying down, faces turned toward the darkness, getting Mirandized. Nyland got cuffed and loaded into one of the warden trucks.

Then from the other end of Weber Mill, a mile or more away, a horn honked a warning and Shauf chuckled, said, "A little late," assuming it was one of the guys standing guard trying to warn Nyland. Then, just as he got his rights read to him, Sweeney, who'd said nothing and been docile, jerked free of the warden holding him and vaulted over the road lip, tumbling as he landed on the steep grassy slope. Flashlight beams tracked him and he looked comic, except that as he arrested the slide he ignored the called warnings to stop and soon disappeared downhill into darkness.

"He must have a phone on him," Marquez said. "Heading for the highway. Let's get everyone except his friend out of here."

They watched the wardens back out with Nyland and Bobby Broussard, and when they were gone Marquez walked across and questioned Sweeney's companion.

"What's your friend's name?" Marquez asked.

"I'm not going to give any information, officer. I'm sorry."

"At least give me a first name so we can talk to him. He's making a dangerous mistake."

"Are you threatening him with violence?"

"No, sir, we're going to try to talk him off the slope with a bullhorn unless you think you can do that. If he's still there at daylight, we'll get a helicopter and dogs. That'll bring the media, so you're not doing him any favors by holding his name and you might be putting him in danger. Is he armed?"

"I don't know."

"Do me one better than that."

"There's no way he'd shoot at you."

Marquez looked away from him now. He looked past the man down the dirt road and saw Shauf walking toward them. She carried the cooler that Bobby had brought up. Her hands were bloody, and she showed Sweeney's friend two bloody gallbladders in plastic bags laid out on ice. Marquez fished one of the bags out and held it up close to the man's face.

"Your friend has run from a felony arrest."

"What are you talking about?" Now he put it together. "That's the goddamned guide who cut those out. As a matter of fact, we didn't shoot anything. The guide shot the damned bear. He's the one with the tag."

"There's no tag."

From behind him, Alvarez added, "We videotaped you."

"Maybe I took a shot but I didn't hit anything, and my friend didn't have time to shoot."

"We have videotape and audio of him bragging about your kill."

"You people are too heavy-handed." He stared at Marquez, showing a little steel now. "You could ruin your career. You're making a mistake you don't understand."

"You're not helping your friend." Marquez turned his back on the man and said quietly to Shauf, "I'll go get him. He's not armed."

He checked his watch. There were still four hours before dawn, but Sweeney might not have gone any farther than the bait pile or where they'd skinned the second bear. If Sweeney was there, Marquez figured he could talk him up. He touched Shauf on the shoulder.

"Get the documentation done, then pull out." He turned to Sweeney's friend again, asked, "What do you do for a living?"

"I'm a lawyer and I promise you if anything illegal was done here, it's the guide who's the problem."

"Your friend ran from an arrest. You're a lawyer, you know what that means and you probably understand he's not going to escape. It makes a lot of sense to give me his name before I go looking for him."

"He didn't do anything wrong."

"Are you his personal lawyer?"

"Yes."

"Then when I find him I'll tell him he needs a new one."

31

The bait area reeked with the smells of rotting fish and chicken. Marquez shone the light on the skinned carcass, then knelt near bear tracks, making his presence known by moving the light around. It was important that Sweeney saw him coming. Not that he expected a problem but still didn't want to frighten him. He turned and spoke toward the dark trees and brush below.

"If you're here and you're listening, you want to give yourself up. Come on up and we'll forget you ran. You can ride in with me."

After waiting a couple of minutes Marquez moved down the slope and tried it again. He found the second bear, saw Nyland had done a rushed job skinning it.

"If you hear me, give me a yell and we'll talk."

His flashlight beam skimmed broken grass, followed it across the slope, and he radioed Shauf before starting across the slope.

"I think I see the direction he ran. How are you doing up there?"

"The lawyer is still threatening us, but he's about to take the ride to the county jail." Marquez had the feeling the lawyer could hear her talking. "I'm about to drop down to the bait pile. Any luck yet?"

"No."

She said the county had set up a perimeter to catch Sweeney and Marquez saw the police flashers below. Sweeney must see them too, but Marquez also knew they wouldn't be able to hold the county along the shoulder of Highway 50 indefinitely, at least not this kind of presence. He read the long strides Sweeney had made without light, running as though afraid for his life. He followed the tracks across to a stand of oaks, listening for movement, knowing Sweeney saw flashlight. Under the trees it was easy to track him. Sweeney had gone steeply downhill, heels gashing the soil, then cutting sideways. *He must have rested here in the trees.*

Several of the county cruisers parked on the highway shoulder below pulled away, sirens sounding as they accelerated. Marquez's phone rang. It was Roberts below with the county officers.

"There's been a car accident," she said. "That's why you're seeing cruisers pulling away."

"How many left?"

"Three."

"I'm on his tracks. See if you can get the county to reposition farther up the road. That's the way he's moving."

"Okay."

Marquez followed faint marks and climbed, thinking now that Sweeney had a problem with one leg, was limping, dragging the bad leg uphill, trying to stay under the cover of trees and work across and up, moving parallel to the highway. He heard noise ahead, brush snapping, knew it was Sweeney. Then his flashlight beam caught movement, Sweeney's coat. He let Shauf know, and she began to bring everyone around, rotating the perimeter like a baseball infield moving for a particular hitter.

Marquez closed on him, the light steady on Sweeney's back, then his face, no real hurry, giving him time to come to terms with the inevitable and give himself up. A call came from Roberts.

"They're telling me there's a dark green Blazer that just made its third pass on the highway," Roberts said. "That could be his ride. I'd bet he's been on the phone."

"All right, I'm going to try to talk him down again. He's not far above me and he's hurt."

Marquez lifted his badge as he walked up the slope to where Sweeney waited next to an oak. He held the badge so Sweeney could read it.

"I'm going to ask you to put your hands on that tree and not do anything sudden. You're under arrest."

"My ankle is hurt."

"We'll get you down to the highway."

Marquez quietly gave him his rights and arrested him, though Sweeney all but begged him not to. Because of the steep slope and Sweeney's sprained ankle, Marquez didn't handcuff him and led him down slowly as Cairo and two deputies hiked up to meet them. Marquez turned to Sweeney.

"That's a Fish and Game officer coming up to meet us, but I want to ask you before we get out, how you hooked up with this guide outfit."

Sweeney's response was clipped. He'd gone from pleading to angry. "My assistant hired them. Talk to her."

"What's her name?"

"Janet Engle. She told me the hunt was completely legitimate." He added sarcastically, "Why don't you arrest her? She's a nice woman. Maybe you'll get your picture in the newspaper before I get your budget canceled."

"Why'd you run away?"

Marquez paused, gripped Sweeney's arm to steady him, waited for an explanation that didn't come. He looked down at a Blazer

that had pulled in near Roberts and still hesitated, waited for
Sweeney to explain. Below, the driver was out and talking to Shauf.

"I didn't shoot anything," Sweeney said.

"We'll look over the videotape together and you can tell me
who's who."

"Do you know who I am?"

"You can tell me any time you want."

"You're going to be very sorry. You're going to throw away
your career."

"That's what your friend kept saying. It's getting old."

Marquez watched Sweeney loaded into the back of a county
cruiser, then phoned Bell and briefed him as he stood looking
down the slope.

"He took it hard. He called us a paramilitary organization that
it would shock California taxpayers to know they were supporting.
They may claim we didn't identify ourselves or inform them of
their rights. He says he's going to put us out of business and he'll
personally make sure not a dime gets through on next year's
budget."

"He might have to stand in line to do that. No one knows
where next year's money is coming from. Did it get rough?"

"He hurt himself when he ran."

"But you didn't struggle with him?"

Marquez drew a slow breath, looked at lights on the highway.

"No, sir."

He left it with Bell that they'd immediately get warrants to
search Sierra Guides and Nyland's trailer park. Marquez could
send the warrant application from his laptop this morning. They'd
be racing the bondsman and Nyland's posting bail, but the local
judges were baby boomers who were generally cooperative on
commercial poaching, and as charges were filed this morning they
ought to be able to hold him through arraignment. He told Bell

he'd call him again after the booking and then drove toward the sheriff's office at sunrise.

Kendall and Hawse were waiting when he got there. "You're up early, gentlemen," Marquez said.

"We heard about the excitement. Your hard-charging Stockton friend, Delano, is also coming up early. He's got to be in court later and promised to buy us breakfast if we met him here." Kendall's eyes lit with wary humor. "Don't worry, Marquez, I'm still not getting any sleep. Hawse is going for coffee. You want any?"

"Sure, I've got to type a warrant app."

Kendall smiled. "Arrests make happy times. We're hoping some of that rubs off on us." He leaned conspiratorially, ran a hand over his new short hair. "We're making a little bet about what the headline will be. Twenty bucks whoever is closest on Sweeney. You want in?"

"I haven't got a guess yet."

"Here's mine: 'Sweeney Running from Office.'"

"Too long, too long," Hawse said, his big frame shaking, tears dribbling down his cheeks as he laughed.

Marquez was grateful for the coffee. He booted up the laptop and filled out the warrant application, knowing if he didn't he'd fade away into exhaustion. He thought about Petroni's story of finding Kendall parked down a dirt road with a runaway he was supposed to be transporting. He couldn't look at him this morning without wondering about it.

He'd hoped to question Sweeney and his lawyer, but as expected, neither was willing to talk. They'd post bail later in the morning, a lawyer was already here and making noise. The county would continue to hold Nyland, who'd made threats to a law enforcement officer on the way in. Charges against him wouldn't file until later in the afternoon. Marquez's team would go through the impounded rented Land Cruiser this morning, and after the warrant app was processed he'd try to get a judge to sign. Now he walked out with Kendall, took him to his truck, and handed him a Ziploc bag with the fragment of bone.

"We found it in a fire pit back behind Nyland's place."

"And you've been driving around with it?"

"I knew it was old. Take a look at the mineral in it."

Kendall flipped the bag over, looked at the dark bone from the other side. "You'll have to show me today."

When Marquez described the fire pit more carefully, Kendall told him a story about the meadow and what he called a crackpot local theory that the real estate development out there had been doomed from the start because the meadow was haunted. There'd been rumors that during excavation for the foundations they'd dug up bones.

"Years ago there was a confrontation between Native Americans and gold miners who'd staked a claim to the area. I think they were Miwoks. Didn't I already tell you this story? The gold miners panicked, started shooting, and killed six or seven. Buried them out there without telling anyone, and it didn't come out for years. After the miners died in freak accidents in that area, the local bright lights decided the area was haunted. More like the economy up here is what's haunted. Recession took that real estate project down." He held the bag up. "We'll check it out. I agree it's old and as you know bone doesn't last long if it isn't protected, so I don't think we're looking at Native American bones."

"Different question for you—where's Petroni's log?"

"I've got it."

"Can I see it?"

"Delano is here, can it wait? Don't you want to see these guns?"

Delano got the guns from his trunk. The silver inlay, the scrollwork, Kendall read aloud from Smith's description of the stolen rifles.

"These are probably Smith's," Kendall said. "We'll have to get him in here today."

"Problem is I can't turn them over today," Delano answered.

Delano chewed on gum and stared back at Kendall. His black hair was slicked back and he wore a leather jacket and jeans. He looked like Hollywood next to Marquez, Kendall, and Hawse. The detectives started trying to work out a plan, and Marquez got the logbook from Kendall, then left them. He went through the logbook and found the name Mark Ellison with a question mark after it. There was also a license plate number. He copied that down, talked to Roberts, and they ran Ellison's name and came up with nothing.

Later in the morning Marquez rode out in Delano's car to the Broussard place. He took Delano to the lot his team used for surveillance and pointed out the tar-paper-wrapped A-frame in the back of the lot where Bobby and another one of the cousins lived. It impressed Marquez that Delano still wanted to see where to find Bobby later, though he was very easy to locate this morning in the county jail.

Delano dropped him back in Placerville and half an hour later Marquez checked into the Gold Nugget Motel, into a stuffy room smelling like dusty carpet and oiled plastic. He'd backed the team away from the safehouse and spread everybody out. He opened a window, let the cold fall air in, laid his cell phone on the bed where it would wake him up. He wanted to take a shower but didn't, called Katherine instead and was talking to her, the phone still in his hand when he fell asleep.

32

"I'm ready to meet you," the mechanical voice rasped. Marquez cleared his throat and sat up. "I'm going to take you to one of my farms. You'll meet me, leave your car, and wear a hood until we get there."

"I get claustrophobic." He stalled. "You're going to take me to a farm?"

"Yes."

"How long will I have the hood on?"

"A couple of hours."

"I'm not good with the hood, but, yeah, okay, I'll do it."

Silence now, a mechanical whine, a television or radio playing in the background on their seller's end, the noise coming from it distorted by the voice changer. Marquez felt adrenaline start in him. He checked his watch, saw it was nearly 3:00 in the afternoon.

"Leave Placerville and go east on Highway 50 at 5:30 today. I'll direct you to where we'll meet."

"I drive out of Placerville at 5:30?"

Their seller hung up, and Marquez had two thoughts. One that he'd do it, and two, there wasn't much time, just over two hours before he was supposed to drive up the highway past Placerville. Before that he'd have to drive to Folsom to the Region IV office and pick up the show car. He left the motel room and called Alvarez, Cairo, Roberts, and Shauf as he made the thirty-minute run down to Folsom. The car was where they'd left it on the gravel lot and he parked, switched into it, and took a call from Chief Bell as he drove away.

"We're going to drop charges against Sweeney and his lawyer," Bell said without any preamble. "The district attorney has heard their side and requested that we do that."

"That was fast."

"The state police interviewed our tipster and believe there's a chance she misled us and Sweeney. Sweeney thought he had a bear tag and another of his staff backs that up. Our tipster told Sweeney and this other staff member that she'd acquired one for him. She'd been working on setting this hunt up for him for a while. Had him sign the bear permit application, the whole thing, and set it up with Durham, who's been in and out of their office on lobbying business for years. The kicker is she'd had an affair with Sweeney and was angry he broke it off. This staffer backs Sweeney's story that our tipster plotted it as revenge."

"How do they know what's what?"

"One of them knows about the affair. That in itself is enough."

"Sure, the same staffer that came to pick him up. Are we really going along with this?"

"I want you to know I'm fighting it."

"Did you know she was sleeping with Sweeney?"

"She'd told me they'd had a short relationship and that it might come up, but that it meant little and had nothing to do with this."

"Sweeney never asked to see a bear tag?"

"He'd known Durham for years, trusted him, Durham always talking about hunting. And the DA sees problems."

"So he's blaming Durham too?"

"Yes, he is."

"Okay, if he's innocent why did he run?"

"He told the state police he realized he'd been set up and panicked. It gets worse, Lieutenant, and I'm sorry for what's happened here. This one is all my mistake. We're being asked for an apology to offset political damage we've done to Sweeney."

"Apologize for what?"

"They're claiming their rights were violated, the bust mishandled."

"Who's claiming that?"

"The lawyer."

Listening to Bell, Marquez could tell he hadn't argued very hard the other way. Bell hadn't backed them up when it mattered. The arrest was going to be labeled a misunderstanding and the going official story that Sweeney had been deceived by a dishonest hunting guide who'd be prosecuted to the full extent of the law. Nyland's prior brushes with the law had been released to the media, and they were already doing a number on him. Sierra Guides would have its license suspended today, and Fish and Game would support Sweeney's contention he'd been deceived. In return, nothing would be said by Sweeney's office about an aggressive, politically ambitious assistant chief being manipulated by a jilted girlfriend. Bell was very frank in describing the threats that had been made toward him. He sounded both humbled and defeated.

"That's what you'll read in the newspapers tomorrow," Bell said.

The speed of it surprised Marquez, but why should it? Hadn't spin doctors only gotten faster and more skilled? *Better get off the phone before you say something you regret. Call your team and stay with what you're doing. Forget about Sweeney,* though it was his belief that each time an individual with access to power was able to get around the law it left a tiny tear in the fabric of society. He believed in a ripple effect, that however well these events were hidden they eventually touched everyone.

"I'm sorry," Bell said.

"Chief, I got a phone call a little over an hour ago from our seller. He claims he'll take me to a bear farm tonight and is calling back at 5:30 to direct me to where I drop my car. The team is already rolling. I drop my car, ride with him, and we'll arrest him at the bear farm. We've asked for county backup. We're going to take him down tonight."

"Called when?"

"A little over an hour ago."

"Who on your team has had any sleep?"

"Everyone."

"You have?"

They talked it out now, Marquez giving the details of the call, how he wanted the takedown to happen. Couldn't risk the drive with the hood so the bust would go down almost immediately.

"He'll meet me someplace he can watch. All the buys have been in canyons at dusk where he can monitor any traffic coming in, so I doubt I'll be able to get people in position to do it as I walk up, but as soon as we start driving."

"You could end up a hostage. That's very risky."

"It'll be hard and fast when it happens. We'll be overmanned and do it right at first contact if we can. If I see him parked, see his face, then we're there, no hood."

After he hung up he checked in with the team again and then watched the minutes count down. When he drove through Placerville his phone rang, the seller's voice crackling, "Continue east on the highway."

He drove a steady sixty miles, the phone sitting where he could reach it easily.

33

Marquez dropped into the river canyon and then climbed toward Kyburz. He drove past Shauf sitting in her van off the road shoulder. They'd made the first buy from their bear farmer in June in the Tahoe Basin. The southernmost buy was near the Fourth Recess on the eastern slope, and the northernmost near Eagle Lake off Interstate 80. They'd pushed pins into a map and stood around guessing at his home base location God knows how many times. Marquez had a full tank of gas, his team had him in view, but he really had no idea where he'd be directed now. Then the next call came.

"Turn onto the Wright's Lake Road."

"There was a Fish and Game bust up that way last night. It was all over the news. We don't want to meet anywhere near there."

"Turn left onto the dirt road near the top."

"Go up the road to Wright's Lake and turn left before the crest?"

"Yes."

That left turn marked the other end of Weber Mill Road. After he hung up, Marquez called Shauf.

"This isn't right," he said. "He's setting me up to drive down Weber Mill."

He turned off the highway, climbed the narrow steep road through the trees, Shauf's voice coming through the earpiece. Where Weber Mill Road reached the asphalt he stopped, the car poised there, looking down and across the canyon face at Weber Mill winding through the ravines. It felt like the car sat on a knife's edge, rear tires still on the paved road, dusk coming, no rational reason why their bear farmer would bring him here unless he knew who he was.

"Do you see any vehicles?" she asked.

"No."

"We're on the move and should be able to see the rest of Weber Mill soon."

His other cell rang, and she heard it too. "I'm going to take it," he said. "Here we go."

"Drive down the road and you'll see a van."

Marquez repeated for Shauf, "Okay, I'll look for a van. How far do I go?"

No answer, line going dead. Marquez laid his gun on the passenger seat and covered it. He started down the dirt road and the car rattled. He lowered his window, unlocked the doors, undid his safety belt, and drove with his lights off.

"Was that him at Tahoe," Shauf asked, "the man with the rifle on the slope?"

"You may be right."

"We can't miss tonight."

"Wait for my signal."

"You okay with this?"

"If we get him I'm fine with it."

He was maybe a mile from where the takedown had been last night. He slowed, rounded another fold in the slope, didn't like any of the thoughts going through his head. He came around another turn and saw a white van parked up ahead a quarter mile this side of where the bust had been. The phone rang.

"Park fifty yards behind the van, walk to it, and get in the passenger side. There's a bag on the floor. Put it over your head and pull the string tight around your neck. Sit in the passenger seat and wait for me. If you've got a weapon on you, leave it in your car."

"I'm here because I want to heal people. You don't have anything to worry about."

This time Marquez didn't wait for him to hang up; he hung up first and got a hold of Shauf with his remaining seconds.

"We're in the basin," Shauf said, "but we're not seeing a vehicle yet."

"It's this side of the bust about a quarter mile."

"Roger that." She called back seconds later. "We've got it."

"A white Ford van. I'm to get out, walk up to it, and wait inside with a hood over my head. I'll do that, but you've got to take him down as he approaches. I think he's up the slope in the trees above me. He could drive in, could be on foot, could be another dirt bike deal."

Or he's already in the van and waiting and there's no hood to put on. It's Durham. No one had been able to locate Durham since the bust. An auto-reply on his email said he was out of town. So did a voice mail message.

"I'm going to park in the next thirty seconds."

He decided to do a three-point turn and park facing the other way in case he needed to get away fast. He turned the car around and was slowing to a stop when he heard a loud pop that startled him. He saw the dashboard hole, heard the echo, and jerked the wheel, sliding the car nose toward the uphill embankment, as a second bullet shattered the window behind him. He heard Shauf screaming, "Get out, get down!"

The car plowed into the embankment as he rolled out, hitting the ground hard, a third shot punching through the open driver's door. He heard the whine of the bullet passing and rolled, scrambled behind the car trunk, and around to the other side, heart pounding, still not certain he was out of the line of fire. But it had to have come from above, from up the slope, so the gunman might be running through the trees right now, trying to set up for another shot on this side. *Get down the embankment, into the brush down where you were last night. Go, go, don't lay here, too risky*, and felt the seconds clicking by. He glanced around for his phone, saw it not far away, and crawled to it. His gun was in the car.

Now he looked at the slope above and decided he'd go up there instead of across the road and down the steep slope. He slid out, scrambled up the embankment, keeping trees between himself and the upslope. He stayed low under brush and got his phone out.

"I'm out, I'm okay, but I don't know where the shooter is. I'm on the slope east of the car."

"We think he just left on a motorcycle. There's a report of a man at high speed on a BMW bike racing into the basin. He passed a ranger going the other way. We'd called her for backup and she was on her way here. We're trying to seal the basin. We've called everybody there is to call."

Marquez assimilated what she'd just told him. A ranger had seen someone racing a motorcycle. That didn't mean enough. He could be on the slope above still.

"Don't come near here yet."

"We're going to get you out of there."

"Do all these deputies know he shot at me?"

"Everyone knows."

"Any chance they can get a helicopter?"

"They're trying."

She reported back ten minutes later. The motorcycle rider still hadn't been accounted for, but county cruisers were at every access to the basin. He saw police vehicles, lights flashing, come up the access road. Marquez waited another half hour, then walked over and got in the Taurus. The engine was still running. He backed up and heard dirt fall off the front grill as he drove out, lights off, his heart still going too fast, talking to Shauf.

"There's another report on the bike, not a BMW anymore."

"What is it now?"

"Dirt bike. Possibly a Honda."

"Sounds right, and he'll go off-road."

Marquez drove down to the highway, parked near the cruisers there, then inspected the bullet holes in his car, put his index finger through the hole in the driver's door. That one hadn't missed his head by much. All of the shots had been close and he saw it now, what was supposed to have happened, either getting picked off as he walked up to the pickup or after sliding the bag over his head, the shooter blowing his skull apart. When he'd turned around the shooter may have decided he was leaving.

Shauf pulled up and they searched the area above Weber Mill before dropping back down to the van. A county crime unit drove down Weber Mill and parked, two crime techs getting out, saying they had some confidence that if the suspect spent any time inside the van they'd find DNA or prints. But other than checking the outside handles and door frame for prints, nothing would happen out here. Only one usable print was found, that near the gas cap, and then the van was towed. In the passenger well was a black sack, the hood.

Twenty-two vehicles were stopped leaving the basin, none were allowed in. The county and the SOU checked each driver and searched well into the night, but the motorcycle rider was gone.

34

The next morning a light rain was falling in Placerville as Marquez waited for the county records office to open. No shell casings had been recovered, but a ballistics expert who worked with topo maps and computer modeling thought that as early as this morning he could narrow the area the shots must have come from. There was nothing the SOU could do to help with that work, so Marquez moved them in other directions.

Shauf and Roberts waited on the ridge above Nyland's trailers. When Marquez left here he'd join them. They had a search warrant for Nyland's trailers and were only waiting until Sophie went into work, didn't want her present when they went through things. Nyland's arraignment was on the docket for 1:00 this afternoon and that was another reason to go in this morning. They expected him to be released.

Along with the Sacramento police, Alvarez and Cairo had knocked on Durham's door late last night and talked to a live-in maid who'd told them the owner was out of town for several days. She reiterated what she'd said to police yesterday, that she didn't know where he was, he never told her where he was going. They didn't have a warrant in place yet for his house, they had asked for one and it was questionable whether they'd get it, though they did get a warrant for Sierra Guides. It was Marquez's plan to search Sierra Guides later today.

He drank coffee and read the *San Francisco Chronicle*'s account of Sweeney's adventure as he waited. Kendall had missed his headline, but the *Chronicle* caught it perfectly. "Fish and Game Does Catch and Release with State Senator Sweeney." It was a page A4 article, not many inches and with little detail. The arrest had already turned into a nonevent, the writer treating the bust as though it were a bizarre incident Sweeney had stumbled into via well-meaning friends, who according to a spokesman had made all the arrangements for the hunt. No mention was made of the SOU, and Sweeney only made the cryptic statement that he was not a hunter but that there were many hunters in his district and good land management should accommodate the interests of all citizens. The hunting guide would be arraigned today and could face felony charges if convicted of commercial trafficking in bear parts, but it didn't say anything about why he'd be charged with that. There was no mention of the gallbladders. It concluded with the sentence that poaching a bear in California was a misdemeanor with a maximum fine of one thousand dollars and up to six months in jail, and it noted that the California bear population was thought to be stable at roughly twenty-five thousand black bear but that bear species in general were pressured globally.

When the records office opened he wasn't sure he was in the right place, but the diminutive white-haired woman across the counter looked like she knew her way around. Her hearing was bad, and he wrote the name on a piece of the newspaper, handed it to her, then watched her evaluate the request.

"On Howell Road," he said, and her eyes pondered him. Then she gave him the answer without needing to retrieve any files.

"I remember the Johengens. They were Swedish and had family in Minnesota or Wisconsin. He was a very intelligent man and nice mannered. He trained as an engineer in Stockholm, and I remember he always wore a hat."

She described a felt hat now and seemed to want some explanation of why he was asking, as if perhaps he was prying into her privacy, not the name Johengen. He was close to showing her a badge but prodded her instead.

"Did they live on Howell Road?" he asked.

"For many years. They had a Christmas tree farm and grew apples. I don't think they called it a farm though. I seem to remember it was Johengen's Ranch. They had a wooden sign he'd carved. He was a very capable man until he got sick. Just a minute."

She went into a back room, was gone twenty minutes, and then came back out with an address on Howell.

"If it was me, I'd look for the rows of trees."

"Thank you."

As he left he checked with Roberts and Shauf, told them he was on his way to them, and Roberts reported that Sophie had left and that Alvarez had followed her to Placerville, saw her park and go into work at the Creekview. Alvarez was on his way back for the search of the trailers.

"I think we're good to go," Roberts said.

When Marquez arrived they popped the door on Nyland's trailer and cut the chain on the second one. Two hounds were locked in the main trailer, and they got them outside and clipped them onto long chains attached to a cedar tree. Marquez petted both, kneeling with them for a few minutes before going back up the iron steps.

Inside, the air was thick with the smell of dogs. A TV was the focal point in the tiny common space, sitting on the short kitchen

counter, facing the table. Marquez worked his way through cloth-
ing and belongings back in the bedroom, looking for anything that
might help build a bear-poaching case, and Shauf went up to the
second trailer to start searching there.

They hadn't been inside the main trailer long when Alvarez
called. "We've got company."

"Sophie's back?"

"No, it looks like Kendall, Hawse, and two or three cruisers."

Marquez walked forward, looked through the window, and
saw the vehicles crossing the meadow, Kendall and Hawse leading
in a county SUV.

"How do you want to handle this?" Alvarez asked.

"Keep going until we know otherwise."

Alvarez had finished with the little kitchen and hadn't found
anything, was flipping through magazines on the table now. A
checkbook would help, a record of Nyland's banking.

"Gentlemen," Marquez said, when Kendall and Hawse clanged
up the iron steps to the door. He took a look at their faces and
guessed correctly they didn't have a warrant to search the trailer.

"We came out to look at that fire pit you found the bone in, but
why don't you invite us into the trailer?" Kendall said. "It is a piece
of femur though very old. We'll have a warrant for the trailers by
afternoon and if I'd known you were here, I would've asked you
not to come in ahead of us." Kendall studied Marquez's face, shook
his head. "If I were you, Marquez, I'd be sitting in a bar counting
my fingers and toes."

"I'm okay."

"Are you?"

"I'd like to find Durham."

"We're doing what we can. You know Nyland will be out
today."

"Yeah."

They looked at each other, not saying anything, the moment awkward. Kendall didn't want them here, and they weren't leaving without a search. Marquez asked about the piece of femur, though he could tell Kendall already had some sort of explanation.

"It's very old, and it may explain vandalism and grave robbing in the old cemetery in Placerville. They've had a problem with it for a couple of years."

"Not someone Nyland murdered."

"Would I be asking you to invite me in?"

Kendall and Hawse followed him back to the tiny bedroom. Hawse picked up a pair of Sophie's panties and started moving them along, walking them across the room as though Sophie were in them.

"Like to see that," he said, and Kendall jumped him.

"Cut it out or wait outside," Kendall said.

"Hey, I was just making a joke."

"Make it outside."

"Christ, what's the matter with you today?"

Hawse left, muttering to himself, and Kendall asked without touching it, "What's this skull?"

"Bobcat."

The bobcat skull was very white, probably bleached, and sat on a little polished wood stand with an iron spike running up through where the brain had been. The spike tilted the skull so that the eye sockets stared straight forward. Near it was a necklace of claws strung on a silver chain and a photo in a gold gilt frame of a smiling Sophie naked and sitting on a horse. From the background, it might have been taken here in the meadow. There was also a black-and-white photo of a man in a much smaller frame. He looked enough like Sophie that Marquez wondered if that was her biological father.

There were hunting rifles and two handguns that Marquez bagged and tagged. In a drawer he found a razor-sharp hunting knife beneath Sophie's folded clothes and a small jewelry box that held maybe fifteen human teeth, three with gold crowns.

"Now, that starts my spine crawling," Kendall said.

And still Marquez had found nothing salient to their case. They were asking for Nyland's phone records as well as those of Sierra Guides, trying to ride the momentum of the bust, but phone records could be harder to get. Some judges were reluctant. He found a diaphragm with a happy face drawn on it and then looked at the teeth again and re-examined the knife. He touched the edge of the blade and cut through the latex glove.

"What are you doing with the teeth, Marquez?"

"I'll bag them if you want, but it's going to be hard to argue they have anything to do with bear poaching."

"We'll have our warrant this afternoon, but he may get out first. Bag 'em now, if you don't mind."

Marquez turned at the order, studied Kendall, realizing the detective had hid his true feelings about finding Fish and Game here. He'd hid his anger and frustration so he could get inside. Marquez bagged the teeth though, and they moved back out into the little living space. When they took the cushions off the seats built around a table bolted to the floor they found more stor-age. In those compartments were boxes of ammunition, including .30-caliber shells. These got loaded into Shauf's van and they would go to DOJ. Kendall wrote down the box numbers and photographed them.

In the second trailer were stacks of bear hides and a work-bench area where Nyland stored his power tools, a Skilsaw, a cord-less Makita drill, a white five-gallon plastic bucket with a carpenter's nail bags in it, a router and power planer, and then among the hand tools on the bench, Marquez pointed out a couple of surgical saws. There wasn't enough here for someone in the hunting guide business.

"He's storing equipment somewhere else," Marquez said. "Out at the Broussards', maybe."

Now he walked Kendall out the trail to the little meadow with the fire pit. They lifted the iron lid off, and Kendall knelt and began sifting through the ashes as Marquez showed Hawse what else they'd found out here. Kerosene. Firewood stacked near a tree. Marquez could see the detectives planned to be here a while, and he let Kendall know he was leaving.

"Marquez," Kendall called to him. "You're not going to want to hear this, but we're looking at the possibility Petroni took the shots at you."

"He'd aim at you first."

"What if your bear farmer is Petroni? What did you tell me you've paid for bile products so far? Thousands, right? And you're telling me there's a lot of money in this. That's real motive for a guy starved for cash and in a position to set up shop. Maybe that's what Stella knew about."

"You still don't have any idea of where's he's gone, do you?"

"Doesn't matter where," Kendall said. "Mexico, wherever, we'll bring him home. Do you know someplace in the mountains he'd go to hide?"

"No."

"Did you think anymore about what I threw at you the other night?"

Kendall kept talking and Marquez stood in the dry grass twenty feet from him but only half listening, his head buzzing, their bear farmer's voice and the shots still loud in his head.

"Petroni would have good reason to use a voice changer. Think about it," Kendall called, as Marquez turned and walked away.

After driving away from the meadow, Marquez took another call, this one unexpected but initially hopeful. It was Ungar.

"Hey, did you make that bust with the politician?"

"No, those were uniform wardens."

"I figured it was you for sure, and there were a couple of other busts in Stockton."

"How do you know about Stockton?"

"My cousin called and told me he lost a shipment of bear paw that was supposed to go to LA."

"Those were his?"

"So you know about them?"

"Yeah, we got notified. We hear about everything."

"I talked to him about your offer."

"What he'd say?"

"He wants to go for it but wants me to set it up."

"He must really trust you."

"I started feeling lousy after you were here last, thinking about what you're doing humping through the woods and driving around and not getting paid much."

"Don't let it get you down."

"You kind of pissed me off early this summer and I haven't shown you the right respect since. I mean, what I'm saying about my cousin, that's true, I don't want him going down. His life is messed up enough. He owes for the bear product that didn't deliver in Stockton, the stuff the police got. He's afraid it'll get him killed."

"Who'll kill him?"

"The man he's delivering for."

"Delivering where in LA?"

"I'll get it all for you. He'll come in and give you names, but we've got to work it all out first. I want to make a deal where he gives you what he knows and he gets immunity."

Marquez looked at the road ahead and drove and was quiet a moment.

"He's tied in with the guys in Placerville," Ungar said. "He knows who you're looking for. He knows the guy behind it all, the guy doing the bears in cages."

"Okay, get one piece of that from him, one piece that I can check out and we'll make it happen."

"I've got it."

"You've got it now? Let's hear it."

There was a long pause, Ungar drawing it out and anticipation flooding into Marquez. He knew Ungar had been up here several times. They'd always known Ungar knew more; the question was how much.

"It's not the type of guy you'd expect."

"You've already got a name."

"This guy is like me, he's got a successful business. He works out of Sacramento."

"Lives there?"

"That's right."

Durham. Has to be Durham.

"I need a name."

"Hey, I know, but not until we meet and you've got the deal done on your side. Then I want to meet you alone."

"Let me see what I can do, I'll call you back."

"When?"

"Soon." Marquez knew he could say yes right now, but something restrained him. "I've got to talk to my chief and the DA. I need more of what your cousin has been involved in. You told me before that all he did was deliver, but now you're saying he owes money. I need to know how involved he is before I can negotiate something. They're not going to approve anything without knowing first who they're dealing with."

"I'm giving you a way to get to the man you're after."

"Call your cousin, call me back." Marquez hung up.

35

Marquez took a call from Keeler, who was at his campsite at Ice House Lake. Keeler was so certain of who he'd seen that Marquez drove there next. He called Bell on the way, got it going in case there was a deal to be made with Ungar.

"Why's he coming forward now?" Bell asked. "Is it this Stockton bust?"

"I talked to Delano, the vice cop handling it, they don't have any leads, and they don't have anyone of Korean descent in custody or as a suspect."

"We're supposed to get this cousin immunity though we don't even know what he's done yet?"

"That's what he's asking for."

"And he's already leading you to Durham."

"Yeah, he's feeding us Durham."

"And you think he knows Durham?"

"All I know is he called the morning after someone shot at me."

He stayed on the line with Bell until driving up to Ice House and finding Keeler's camper. Bell said he'd find out what kind of deal could be offered, and they agreed to ask for more help in trying to locate Durham. They'd also try to re-establish surveillance on Ungar.

Marquez walked up to the camper, his mind still on Durham and Ungar. He'd given Keeler photos of all possible suspects, as well as photos of the Broussards and others Marquez believed might be suppliers. Then Keeler called this morning and said Ungar had visited him.

"Pull up a chair," Keeler said, and Marquez unfolded one of the lawn chairs leaning against the camper. Keeler was sitting alongside a portable grill cooking sausages and red peppers that spattered juices into the flame.

Marquez held out another photo of Ungar. "You sure it was him?"

"It was him. He sat just about where you are. I first noticed him when he was down by the water. I didn't know where he'd come from, thought he'd hiked in. He came over and said he admired my grill, asked where I'd bought it, and said he was thinking of getting one. Asked me if I was alone up here and if he could bum a glass of water off me and started talking about the camper, how he might get one of these. I got him a Coke instead of water, and when he asked what I did before retiring, it clicked."

"Did you tell him you're retired?"

"Yes."

Marquez tapped the photo. "He was a reporting party, then an informant for us. He called me this morning saying he can give us the name of the man we're looking for." He stared at Keeler as he tried to put it together. "How'd you register for the campground, chief?"

"Online. You can do that now. I thought about that myself."

"He is a computer guy. He's skilled that way. Do you think he knew you recognized him?"

"I don't think so. I told him I like to come up here in the fall and that my wife died recently and tried to lead him a different direction. I wasn't sure what he wanted at first. Truth is, he made me nervous, particularly after I recognized him."

"Yeah, I don't like it at all. Maybe we'd better move you to a different lake and not register. Or back you away."

"You tell me."

"It doesn't feel right. Let's get you out of here. Did you get a look at his vehicle?"

"No, he hiked out to the road again. Very polite, thanking me, and then I got the photos you gave and called you."

Marquez watched the chief's hand tremble as he moved food from the grill to paper plates. He watched Keeler stick a cigar back in his mouth and knew the chief had liked being part of the operation and didn't really want to leave. They ate, still talking about Ungar, and he could feel a kind of loneliness coming off Keeler as he agreed that he should leave.

"Chief, do you want to take a ride with me this morning first?"

"Where are we going?"

"I've got a place to check out."

After they got in Marquez's truck Keeler asked about the shooting, saying, "When you worked under me I never came to any conclusions, but let me ask you something, how much have you ever talked to anyone about your first wife's murder or your DEA team getting wiped out? I'm talking about what they call survivor's guilt."

"I got help after Clara died. It hasn't made it any easier, but it has helped me understand. Maybe deep down you don't think it's fair that you're alive and Julie isn't."

It surprised him that Keeler knew or remembered her name. "Are you telling me I have a death wish?"

"That's a loser's hand and you're anything but a loser."

"This connects with me getting shot at?"

"You had more than a few close calls."

Marquez took the exit for Howell Road and felt the change under his tires a few miles later. The conversation had returned to Ungar, but he was still surprised at Keeler's comments about him. The road dropped into a creek canyon thick with oak, bay, and willow, then climbed through trees and followed a long meadow. Where it wrapped the meadow was a barn with a big Nazi flag tacked on one side and four or five motorcycles up in front of the house. Smoke curled from the chimney of the house. A bald man sitting on the porch studied them as they drove by.

Marquez explained why they were looking for the remains of the Johengen tree farm, and they were out far enough now to pass only an occasional house and mailbox. At the last one he stopped, backed up, and read the number before continuing on, and then, following the advice of the woman in records, he watched the hills for rows of second-growth fir and pine. When he spotted lines of trees too uniform to occur naturally, he turned up a dirt road and drove a third of a mile up to a dilapidated, moss-covered wooden gate.

There was no address, and the gate had been chained and padlocked with a new bright chrome lock. If Petroni saw this, then he would have picked up on the new lock immediately. What it brought to mind was the lock on Nyland's hunting shack. Keep Out and No Trespassing signs were posted, and a barbed wire fence ran up into the trees. He looked up, following the line of barbed wire as it climbed the steep slope.

"Doesn't look like they want visitors," Keeler said.

"I'll go knock."

Marquez climbed over the gate and walked down to the bend in the driveway. He could see an old farmhouse with a red asphalt roof that in several places was missing shingles. There was a barn off to one side of a clearing and what looked like an old apple orchard beyond it. Willow trees and thick brush grew alongside a creek on one side of the orchard, and he guessed that was the property line. A cottonwood drooped over the farmhouse, and then behind the property, rising with the slope, were rows of trees, many well over twenty feet tall. He didn't see any cars, stepped onto the rotted porch, and knocked on the back door.

The door glass rattled, but no one came to answer. He looked at the sheets tacked over the windows and the mud wasps' nests overhead in the eaves and rapped the door again, though just for show. No one was here. He walked across to the barn, shoes sticking in the mud from the earlier rain, and he found the barn doors chained shut. He walked down one side of the barn and then back out into the cleared bare space between house and barn and scanned the orchard and hills before going back up the driveway to his truck.

"Your phone rang," Keeler said.

He'd missed a call from Roberts. She kept her voice neutral when he called back, but there was no need to hide her excitement.

"Bingo," Roberts said. "Durham had a game park in Michigan years ago, registered as the Marion Stuart Corporation. He got shut down for illegally buying lion cubs and had a list of other offenses. I talked to a game warden there who said Durham's ranch had some of the worst conditions he'd ever seen. Crowded cages. No water. He raised monkeys he sold to zoos and labs, and they tried to bring a case against him for that. He sold out and moved after that."

"What happened to the case against him?"

"He paid fines and agreed to close down. When he moved to California he picked up a second name and ID."

"He's living with two names?"

"That's what it's looking like. This Michigan deal was in 1992. I talked to another guy in U.S. Fish and Wildlife who connected with the name Marion Stuart. He thinks Stuart left the country for several years. They'd heard he was shipping animals out of Taiwan. Someone in their department was down there and saw him at an animal market." She paused. "Think he'll show up for Nyland's arraignment?"

"No, and let me tell you what happened with Ungar this morning." He gave her that and added, "I'll meet you and Shauf at Sierra Guides in half an hour."

He drove back to Placerville with Keeler. Though they had a warrant, Marquez had made the decision to delay going into Durham's hunting guide business. Shauf and Roberts had staked out the office this morning, hoping he'd show up there to retrieve records. But they'd also made contact with the landlady, and she was here to meet them and unlock the doors. The landlady was standing with Roberts when Marquez and Keeler drove up, a white-haired woman wearing a royal blue running suit with a Nike emblem. Keeler took over, talking to her outside as the team started searching.

One desk had a file drawer full of maps of the area and photos of other hunts. Marquez found a shot of Durham as a young man, posing over a lion, looking lean and intense, one hand tightly gripping his rifle. There were more photos but little in the way of paper. Roberts settled down in front of the computer, booted up, and began to try to get through the passwords. When she couldn't, she announced they'd want to take the computer with them. That was all they took, though in Nyland's desk they'd found a business card holder with the name of a gun shop in South San Francisco, a location that got Marquez's interest, and he copied down the address and phone.

He gave Keeler a ride back to Ice House, and shortly before noon Marquez was back in Placerville in a judge's chambers. The judge knew Petroni enough to be concerned and asked Marquez what he knew about Petroni's situation, what did he think? The judge was the first human being outside of Keeler who seemed concerned about Petroni. Marquez told him what he knew and then a few minutes later watched quietly from a side door as Nyland pled not guilty to all charges.

After leaving the courthouse he talked with Katherine from his truck. Kath was driving and almost back to San Francisco. She sounded more philosophical about Maria's missing school. Her mom, Lillian, had been a high school teacher and would help Maria with chemistry. She was also an avid outdoorswoman and planned to take her hiking to lakes below the Inconsolable Mountains. They were going to Lake Sabrina today, so whether they'd overreacted or not, there was at least the silver lining of Maria's spending time she wouldn't otherwise have had with her grandmother. Tomorrow they'd drive up to the bristlecone park ten thousand feet up in the White Mountains, and Lillian would show Maria the oldest living trees on earth. Years ago, on Maria's tenth birthday, Lillian had taught her how to shoot a rifle, taking Maria up a dry canyon behind the house with a handful of Coke cans. They planned to do more of that as well.

"Give Maria a call," Katherine said. "She needs to hear from you."

"I'll call her."

"Did I tell you the building permit got approved? They left a message. I told Maria, she's very excited."

"That's great."

Contemplating that build was like thinking about another world, but that was the world Katherine was trying to keep his head in, and he knew it was lucky they'd been approved.

When he hung up with her he tried to reach Maria on her cell phone, and when that didn't work left a message on the answering machine at Lillian's house. Then, driving away from the court-house he took a call from Kendall.

"I hear Nyland made bail but you've taken away his wheels."

"We impounded his truck. One of the lookouts was driving it that night."

Marquez didn't say they'd moved the transponder to Sophie's truck, didn't feel like he owed Kendall that. Alvarez had done it after she'd driven into Placerville and parked.

"He's going to be angry when they kick him loose," Kendall said. "He'll act out."

"That's the way we read it too."

Marquez had talked it over with the team that day and believed Nyland's reaction could be violent when he learned what they'd impounded. The charges, the equipment he was unlikely to ever get back, the loss of guide license, and the possible loss of the right to ever hunt again could easily set him off. They would have to assume their identities were known by Nyland and be very care-ful following him, yet at the same time the route to Durham most likely was through him.

"Did you think about what I said earlier about Petroni?" Kendall asked.

"Yeah, and I don't see it."

"You don't see or you don't want to see it?"

"Both." Marquez took a breath, debated, said, "I found the place on Howell Road Petroni had made notes about. Johengen's was a Christmas tree farm and apple orchard. Johengen died twenty years ago, and his wife is in a nursing home with Alzheimer's. A lawyer manages a living will. I was out there this morning."

"Tell me how to get there."

Marquez gave him directions, then parked his truck on the east side of town and waited for Shauf. They rode out to Eli Smith's house and found him sick with the flu and sweating when he answered the door. A half-full bottle of NyQuil sat on his kitchen table, and the heat was turned way up, windows closed. Coming from the cold outside air, it was hard to breathe in the house. Marquez showed Smith a badge, let him adjust to that before suggesting he be careful with his answers.

"We're about to make more bear poaching arrests."

"I don't do any illegal hunting."

"All you have to do is be truthful."

"All I did was get ripped off."

Marquez waited until Smith looked up at him again, face pale, body shaking with chills.

"Bobby Broussard gave us your name, but let's go back a couple of steps and talk about the guns you reported stolen."

"I told the detective I loaned them out. A man can loan his guns out to whoever he wants."

"No one loans prize guns to just anybody." It was why he'd loaned them that Marquez wanted. "Who'd you loan your guns to?"

"A friend I hunt with. His girlfriend came by and picked them up a couple weeks ago. He wanted to borrow them, and she brought them back to me the day before they were stolen."

After Delano had confirmed the rifles were registered to Smith, they'd asked that he not inform Smith yet. Delano had no problem sitting on the information, and Kendall didn't care about it because neither gun matched his Vandemere bullet.

"Did Nyland keep your guns because you owed him money?"

Smith flinched at the sound of Nyland's name.

"She brought them back."

"The guns have been found."

Smith looked down again. *Probably was promised by Nyland that they wouldn't be sold or found by anyone.*

"How much were your dogs insured for?" Marquez asked.

"What?"

"We know they were insured, same as the guns," Shauf said. "We know you contacted the insurance company the same day you found them, and they contacted the police and asked for a report."

Smith nodded, his eyes on Marquez. Marquez measured him, then taking a gamble, asked, "How much money did you owe Nyland?" He watched Smith string it together now, tying it to last night and making the assumption that Bobby had told them. The connection showed just for a fraction of a second in his eyes, and then he was slow to answer. He reached for the bottle of NyQuil and chugged a big swallow.

"Five grand," Smith said.

"And you didn't have a way to pay it."

"I've been working it off with the guide company."

"Sierra Guides."

"Yes, sir."

"We were there today and we saw your name in the records, but they haven't done many guided hunts. You could say business has been slow, or you could call the business a shell." Marquez reached over and tapped one of the survivalist magazines. "You know all about conspiracies, Eli. If we sit Sophie down and swear her in, is she going to testify she brought the guns back? What do you think? How far do you think she'd lie for Nyland now? Is she going to testify in court that she brought the guns back to you?"

"She did and they were here."

"How much were the dogs insured for?"

"I loved my dogs. I wouldn't do something like that."

Marquez waited and Shauf shifted in her chair, stared hard at Smith.

"Ten grand," Smith said.

"They pay out?"

"They're still investigating."

"Who came up with the idea?"

"What idea?" He looked baffled. He shook his head as though that would make it all go away. But nothing would ever make it go away.

"You owed Nyland five thousand," Marquez said.

"I've been working it off."

"Did Nyland get the guns as a down payment? Sold them cheap, filed the number so it would look like they'd been stolen? Not wanting to mess up your insurance claim, expecting to be paid from it. I'm pretty sure he sold them for what he could get, and it was on you to come up with the rest of the five thousand."

Was Sophie set to get part of the money? Marquez remembered Petroni's saying Nyland owed her money and that's why he was fixing her truck. *Maybe she took part in the scheme because of that. Had Smith poisoned his own dogs? If not him, who else? Neither Nyland nor Sophie would have had a reason to come out here that night.*

"I loved my dogs," Smith repeated, and Marquez didn't even want to know how he'd balled up hamburger meat and walked out and fed them. He wanted to know something else though.

"This is the last question I'm going to ask you."

Smith had started to cry and his head was bowed.

"Whose idea was it?"

Smith didn't answer and his head swayed slowly from side to side. Shauf got up and had to leave. She moved to the door and left it open as she walked out. Then as the air hit him Smith looked up, his eyes teary.

"Hers."

"Sophie's?"

He nodded and tears streaked his cheeks. He covered his face, and Marquez left him there at the table.

As they got in the van and drove away, Shauf asked, "Why is it that a scuzz like him will live to be ninety?" She didn't say, didn't have to, and my sister will die.

36

Sophie hurried out of work early and picked up Nyland after he posted bail. Marquez watched her lean over from the driver's seat, wrap her arms tight around his neck, and kiss him hard while the lawyer stood impatiently outside Nyland's window. From the courthouse they drove straight to a bar in Pollock Pines, and with the GPS unit in place it was unnecessary to follow closely. Marquez and Roberts hung back, waited, and it was almost two hours later in dusty gold late afternoon light that Nyland and Sophie walked side by side across the parking lot to her pickup. As Nyland looked around, Marquez spoke to Roberts.

"He knows he's not alone, but let's hope he leads us to Durham."

When Sophie's pickup pulled away Marquez parked alongside Roberts. She had a laptop balanced on the edge her passenger seat and read the progress of the GPS unit on Sophie's pickup. The readout put them at a rest stop up the road.

"Alcohol," Roberts said. "Maybe she needs to use the rest room."

But they were there too long, and at the half-hour mark Marquez decided he'd drive by and make sure they hadn't switched vehicles or, worst case, been picked up by Durham. He drove up there, didn't see the pickup, and phoned Roberts.

"The readout is coming from there still," she said, and Marquez cruised back past again, checked for anyone positioned to watch the rest stop, then brought Roberts up. Took them another hour to determine that the twenty-thousand-dollar GPS unit had been dropped in one of the chemical toilets. Frustration boiled up in him. It was his mistake. They could have stayed with them and shouldn't have lost Nyland, shouldn't have lost their best lead to Durham.

Nyland and Sophie could have driven any direction. Marquez checked out Six Mile Road and drove through Placerville and Pollock Pines, past the place Sophie was house-sitting before finally giving up. Roberts drove down to the Sacramento safehouse, and Marquez returned to the room at the Gold Nugget in Placerville. He talked a long time to Kath and left another message for Maria on her grandmother's answering machine. He went into town and picked up half a roast chicken, some string beans, and potatoes. After he ate, he checked Nyland's trailers again and drove back to Placerville, sat in the Creekview, drank a beer, and asked the bartender if he'd seen Sophie that night. He was still at the Creekview when Kendall called and he let it ring, then phoned Kendall back after he was outside in the cold wind.

"We lost Nyland," Marquez said. "Are you tracking him?"

"No."

"Petroni turn up?"

"No, but I got the report back on Stella Petroni today. Her face was kicked in after she was on the floor of the kitchen. Repeatedly kicked. Over and Over. Probably with steel-toed boots of the same type we found in Petroni's duffel bag. I remember a murder in LA where a young Latina was killed by her ex-boyfriend. He stabbed her one hundred fourteen times in the abdomen. I'll tell you what's going to happen. He's going to hike out of the woods somewhere with a big sad question mark on his face about what's happened to his lovely Stella. He didn't need any money from you that afternoon because he already had a plan."

"I don't need this tonight. Why don't you tell it to your girlfriend or Hawse?"

When Marquez hung up he drove back to the motel. It was 10:30. He couldn't understand Kendall hammering at the same theme without any more evidence unless it was personal. *Or maybe he does have more and still thinks I know where Petroni is, trying to get under my skin.* The thought only aggravated him more. He tried turning on the TV, couldn't begin to watch it or sit in the small room. He left the motel and drove back to the rest stop where the transponder was lost, cruised slowly past there, and drove into the Crystal Basin, parked near the edge of Weber Mill, and after ten minutes sitting there, drove up to Big Top, where he had a broad view of the basin. He looked out at the flat, near-oily blackness of Union Valley Reservoir and the dark forests beyond. Whoever had shot at him escaped into the basin. Late that afternoon, Durham had communicated with Fish and Game via his lawyer. At the appropriate time Durham would make himself available for questioning, but because he hadn't been charged with anything he'd pick the date and time. His lawyer made it clear that his client broke no laws, did nothing wrong. In a written statement the lawyer faxed, Durham denied any involvement in poaching and pointed to his long-standing record with Ducks Unlimited and other organizations. If his young partner in Placerville had broken the law, then Durham was willing to voluntarily shut down Sierra Guides. He'd be the first to agree the business should be closed down and the appropriate fines paid. The lawyer reported Durham was willing to pay double the maximum penalty, up to two thousand dollars a bear, to make restitution, a total of four thousand dollars.

Marquez thought of taking Maria out of school, hurting her college chances, Katherine's making the best of a guest bedroom in the house an old college friend rented from her, and for what? A system that let Sweeney walk and would slap Durham's wrists before turning to thank him for his cooperation. He couldn't get around it tonight the way he usually could. He left Big Top and drove the dark forested roads past Union Valley, heading out the back route, then stopping on the graveled road near the bar where the Broussards drank.

As soon as he pulled into the parking lot he knew he should leave. Instead, he took a place standing alone at the bar and was ignored by the bartender, a smirking pimply-faced kid, basking in the approval of the men gathered at the far end. Troy Broussard was there, wearing a dirty canvas jacket and standing with his back to him, a whiskey in his right hand, holding court. Alongside Troy a stout man with a black beard stood and glowered at Marquez.

The bartender finally came down, sloppily opened a beer bottle, and slid it over. Marquez laid a bill down and drank, his throat tickling with the cold wash of beer. *Have a beer and leave. There are no answers here tonight, no value in confronting Troy. Fall back, take it to another day. Durham isn't here. Let it go.*

But instead, he ordered another beer and looked at the bearded man, nodded in a way that said, stare somewhere else, you malevolent fuck. He watched the bartender bring his change and toss it down, a coin rolling and falling, and the bearded man started toward him.

"Troy says you're with Fish and Game."

"He does all the thinking around here. What'll happen when he dies?"

"Last night we had a couple of niggers come in here and now you."

"Shove it up your ass."

The man backhanded the beer, and the bottle blew foam as it went end over end and bounced hard on the floor. A big hand gripped Marquez's shirt.

"Get the fuck out of here."

But the words came from a great distance and the roaring in his ears was like breakers rolling in. The man's face haloed with red light, and Marquez felt a hard blow to his shoulder, a stinging blow at his chin that knocked him back and stunned him. Then he stepped forward and drove his fist through, felt chin hair mat against his knuckles and the man's head snap back. Hit him again and the man staggered, his fist deep into soft gut. When the man fell Marquez stood over him, catching his breath, waiting to see if anyone else moved. Then he walked out.

He didn't see anyone pull out behind him. But a set of headlights sat behind him now, hung there past Georgetown, and shadowed him as he drove through Placerville toward the motel. *Let them come,* he thought, *let them try.*

37

A gentle knock on the motel door woke him and he listened without moving. Another knock, soft, insistent, and Marquez rolled to his feet, the bed creaking as he stood. He eased the curtain back and saw Sophie Broussard standing under the pale yellow corridor light. The dark hood of a sweatshirt surrounded her face. She turned toward the window, her eyes meeting his. He opened the door.

"I have to talk to you," she said.

"How'd you find me?"

"I followed you."

"I didn't see your truck."

"I hid it. I was waiting for Eric to show up."

"You didn't want him to know you were there?"

"I was thinking about killing him."

Her eyes were shiny and unreadable. He tried to guess at why she was here.

"Can I come in?"

He stepped aside, shut the door, and she took a seat on the corner of bed. He smelled tequila and lilac. Her fingers turned like worms in her lap.

"Look," she said, and slid her hood back. Her left eye was swollen nearly shut, the white of the eye crimson, the bruising a purple-green darkness around the eye. "Eric thinks I'm helping you and that's how you found the bait pile and busted the hunt. He says he's going to kill you. He really flipped out because you took his truck and guns."

"Where is he now?"

"He's gone." She touched her eye and winced.

"Let me have a look in the light." He guided her over and looked at the bad eye. "You need a doctor."

"I can't afford a doctor."

"A blow like this can detach the retina. It ought to be looked at. I can drive you to the clinic."

He remembered Eli Smith sobbing, saying it was Sophie's idea to poison his dogs. She was much brighter than Smith and probably knew the insurance claim would never be collected. She pointed up at the overhead light.

"Can we turn that off?"

Marquez turned on the nightstand light and turned off the overhead. Drinking tequila might have blunted the pain but she had to hurt. He went to the coffeemaker and offered again to take her to a clinic. He asked again where she thought Eric was tonight and didn't get an answer.

"Coffee?" he asked.

"I'd rather have something to drink."

"I don't have anything."

"Don't you want me to talk?" Said that almost coyly, if that was possible after being beaten as she had.

"Were you really thinking of killing him?"

"He's lucky he didn't show up there. What do you want to know about? Ask me anything you want."

"Are you here to get even?"

"Seems like you'd want me to talk."

"Okay, tell me about Durham."

"He likes to sleep with me and I pretend to like him. He loaned Eric money so Eric could be a partner, and all Eric has done since is work to pay it back."

"So why sleep with him."

"He's taking off part of the debt. That shocks you, doesn't it? Well, I don't really care."

"You're doing it for the guy who just beat you?"

The smell of coffee battled the other odors now. He washed a cup, asked when Durham had entered their lives.

"Eric met him at a gun swap in Reno. You know what he told Eric after he got arrested this time?"

"What?"

"He said the partnership is over if the charges stick and he'll want the money he put up for Eric's truck and some of his guns."

"Even though he was in on it."

"See you know everything already."

"I don't know anything."

"That's right, I forgot, that's what you said when you came into the Creekview that night, that you don't know anything."

"Did I put it like that?"

"No, you pretended."

"So my cover has been blown for a while."

"Well, yeah."

Marquez poured coffee, showing little reaction. He offered her a cup.

"Durham also told Eric that if he did everything right he would take care of him afterwards. They'd start all over again somewhere else."

"What's 'doing everything right' mean?"

"Leaving him out of it."

"Will Eric do that?"

"I don't really care what happens."

He caught her looking at him, studying him as he poured more coffee, an almost feral look of cunning, assessing him, and he realized despite everything she might be here to try to get Nyland's truck freed. The idea blew him away, but it was possible Nyland had sent her. The only thing he'd heard so far that he didn't doubt was that his cover was blown.

"Does Durham ever hunt?" he asked.

"Haven't you seen all his big boy photos?"

"Does he hunt now?"

"He's not even a good shot."

"How good a shot is Eric?"

"Very good."

"Durham's lawyer contacted us. He's working another angle, wants to help us prosecute Eric. It'll get Eric away from you for a long time, but do you think we can trust Durham?"

"Did a lawyer really call?"

"This afternoon."

"I knew it."

He let her think about that and asked, "Where would I find Durham tonight?"

"I don't know where he stays when he's here. Some old run-down place is what Eric told me."

"You've never been there?"

"When I meet him it's at a motel or his office." She touched her eye. "Eric is talking about killing one of you, taking you out in the woods somewhere and gutting you, field dressing you and leaving you hanging from a tree. He talks about it with Troy. I really am warning you."

"Has he ever killed anyone?"

"Now we're getting really heavy and I need a drink. Do you think the night manager has a bottle? Can we go wake him up?"

"I don't think we should."

"We could go somewhere."

"Will it help you remember?"

"Maybe. One time Durham put his finger on my eye, right on my eye, not the eyelid, and he said he'd killed a man once and felt the life go out of him through his eyes. He said he could feel the energy and it made him kind of high. He told Eric it made him stronger, and now Eric does these bullshit ritual things like burning bones. He has a fire pit and he gets old bones. It's all supposed to make him stronger so he's a better hunter. He drinks blood. He drank some of my blood once." The one eye stared. "If he killed you, he'd probably drink some of your blood."

Marquez smiled, couldn't help himself. He had a lot of images of Nyland but none as a vampire. Neither did he believe her, though there was something chilling in her account of Durham's touching her eye. That had the ring of truth. He decided to give the Durham questions a rest for a moment and come back to them.

"No one has seen Bill Petroni," he said.

"I'm sorry if I hurt Billy, but he was the one who wanted to keep it going. I'm not really sorry about his wife though. She came into the Creekview looking for me, and it was pretty raw. She wanted to blame me for her marriage so I told her she could have him back."

"Where do you think Petroni is?"

"Everybody is asking me and people are blaming me, but Billy was freaked out over the money and because of the detective. He probably just split."

"Did he ever say anything that made you think he might hurt her?"

"He was real angry because she was screwing him out of his money. She was trying to take his house."

Car lights swept into the motel lot, and he heard an engine outside the window. He motioned to her to stay out of view and pulled the curtain back after she went into the bathroom. He saw Kendall and Hawse get out of the car, and opened the door before they could knock.

"You're working late tonight," Marquez said to Kendall.

"You know how I like the early morning."

They looked past him at Sophie, who'd opened the bathroom door and was wrapped in a towel. She walked across the carpet to them and touched Marquez on the shoulder as she opened the towel. She was naked and there were welts along her lower back and side that she turned to show him.

"This is what Eric did to me today."

She kept her eyes on Marquez until Kendall cleared his throat.

"Okay, Sophie, cover up," Kendall said, "and we'll take you down and get you checked, and we'd love to press charges against your boyfriend." When she went back into the bathroom, Kendall said, "I can't believe this."

38

"Let's not bullshit around," Kendall said, "you don't get home much." He stared at Marquez. "Was she here for sex?"

"No, after you drove up she went into the bathroom and stripped."

"You've got to be straight with me on this."

"That's what happened. She told me she followed me from a bar."

"Sure, back to your motel."

"I didn't invite her. She tailed me."

"And you're going to tell me she's so good at surveillance you didn't notice?"

"I knew someone was following."

Kendall shook his head, hid his disbelief by looking at his car, where Hawse was helping Sophie into the backseat.

"You let her follow you here?"

"Believe whatever you want."

"About an hour ago she left a message with a 911 dispatcher that she knew the whereabouts of a gun used to kill somebody in the Crystal Basin. She gave her name and told the dispatcher I'd want to know and to wake me up."

"Nyland beat her up pretty good. She's angry."

"The dispatcher tried to keep her on the line but she said she'd call back. She called back two hours and thirteen minutes later and gave this motel room, said she'd be here with you." Kendall opened his arms wide. "And here she is."

"She got here forty minutes ago, knocked on my door. I was in bed, went to the window, saw it was her, and let her in. She told me she wanted to talk."

"Knew you were Fish and Game."

"Yeah, my cover is blown." Marquez looked at the back of Sophie's head. She'd pulled the sweatshirt hood up around her again. "She needs a doctor. She took a bad shot to her eye."

"We'll get her eye looked at."

"She wanted me to think she was worried about things Nyland might do to me or one of my team now that the word is out who we are."

"Like what?"

"Like kill one of us. I questioned her about Durham and Petroni and didn't get anything in particular that's news, other than she says she hates Durham. She didn't say anything about a rifle and we didn't finish our conversation before you drove up, but her ostensible reason for knocking on my door was to warn me that Nyland is looking for a chance to get even with the undercover Fish and Game officers who wrecked his life."

"You had a close call up there on Weber Mill. Maybe that was Nyland shooting at you. Maybe it's time to pull your team out of here." Kendall pointed at the back of the sedan. "What you're looking at in the back of that car is a rat deserting the ship. She knows the whole damn story, and she's in the process of switching sides, testing to see how far she can make that work."

"Could be."

Marquez walked back into the motel room. He got his toothbrush and razor out of the bathroom and threw them in his gear bag. He packed the rest of his clothes with Kendall standing at the door. As he zipped the bag, Kendall said, "You've been in two bar scrapes since I've known you." When Marquez didn't respond, Kendall asked, "Why did Sophie drive from the Crystal Basin Wilderness to a little bumfuck bar and then park outside and not go in?"

"After a beating maybe she didn't feel sociable, or maybe as she says, she was going to shoot Nyland."

Or she took some inner comfort from being near the lights and the people inside. He remembered fifteen cars and trucks, and maybe she'd pulled in among them and he hadn't noticed her truck because of the state he'd been in.

"Okay, so you're saying she followed you when you walked out. Recognized you and followed you, didn't know you were in there. That is, it was a coincidence."

"I'm not saying it was coincidence."

"We'll ask her."

Marquez picked up his bag. Kendall was still in the doorway.

"You know someone has followed you back here and you respond by going to bed. I haven't known you long, but that doesn't jibe. Where are you going now? Are you done here? Going home?"

"Soon."

Marquez woke the night clerk to check out and then ate breakfast at the Waffle House. Near dawn he called each of the team and told them to take the day off and clean their gear, get some rest. When he told that to Shauf she said she was already on her way to him. Her sister had gone down to the medical center at Stanford with her husband, and the kids were with the grandparents.

"I'll meet you in Placerville," she said.

While he waited a call came in from Kendall. "I felt like I owed you the call. Sophie was in a confessional mood. We took a drive with her out to the trailer park, and she led us to a rifle double-wrapped in plastic and hidden beneath the floorboards in the former sales office. We'll start running tests on it today. Nyland never exactly told her why but he showed it to her one night, wanted her to know it was there, and she got the impression he'd shot Vandemere with it. This was recent, after they got back together, kind of bragging to her. It's starting to unravel, Marquez. He told her why. She just isn't telling us yet, but it's eating at her. She may even have had a role in the killing."

"Who is the gun registered to?"

"Marion Stuart."

"Durham."

"He buys everything huntingwise that Nyland owns."

"Did Durham ever report a missing gun?"

"No, and if we asked him he'd say he'd didn't know it was missing, that it was a Sierra Guides gun in Nyland's possession. You can hear it, right?"

"Sure."

"Is Durham your man?"

"He's at least a piece of the puzzle."

"But you're done here, aren't you? You said your cover is blown, even Sophie knows who you are."

"It is blown."

"Things are about at the point where we take over. Think about it and I'll talk to you later."

39

Marquez pulled up alongside Shauf's van and she got out wearing sunglasses though the morning was cold and cloudy. Her face was ashen and she said little as they drove out Howell Road. When they passed the barn with the Nazi flag draped over the side she pointed at a skinhead standing near a motorcycle and he flipped her off. Shauf gave him the finger back. At Johengen's, Marquez parked near the gate.

"When Sophie was in my room last night she said Durham stays in some rundown place she's visited but couldn't find her way back to."

"She grew up here. She knows this road. If Durham sleeps out here, she's probably slept in his bed."

"Might have been her way of trying to communicate."

"Manipulate is the word you're looking for."

Marquez got out a flashlight, and they climbed over the gate and walked down around the driveway bend. He saw the peak of the house roof with its curled and decaying shingles and then Petroni's orange Honda parked in the flat area between the barn and the house. For a moment neither of them said anything or moved. He turned toward her.

"Why don't you hang here and I'll walk down and take a look first," Marquez said.

"Is Petroni staying here?"

"As in hiding out?"

"Yeah."

"Seems like he'd find someplace farther away."

Marquez watched the barn and house and everything as he walked toward the Honda. When he leaned over and looked through the windows he saw a large bloodstain covering most of the middle of the backseat. Rivulets had run down to the floor carpet. He waved Shauf forward, keeping his eye on the windows of the house as he dialed Kendall.

"I'm at Johengen's tree farm. Petroni's car is here. There's a large bloodstain in back. You'd better come on out."

"Don't touch—"

Marquez hung up and knocked on the farmhouse door. He stepped to the windows and tried to look past lacy yellowed curtains, waited, stepped away from the house, and went back to the Honda where Shauf stood now.

"Someone died in here," he said.

Two slow-moving flies reacted to his shadow and rose off the backseat. The plaid material of the old seats was torn in several places, and he saw an old mug lying in the passenger well, saw some paper scraps. He felt the heart go out of him and stood a long minute staring before backing away, making himself walk to the barn. It was chained shut, would take bolt cutters, and standing near the barn doors he caught a waft of something dead. He looked toward the orchard. The breeze blew from that direction, and with Shauf he walked out among the old apple trees. Another smell, the vinegary sharpness of decaying fruit, and then as the breeze strengthened again the decomp smell was stronger. His pulse bumped up, and he studied recent tire tracks in the orchard weeds. An odd pattern of crushed grass, something dragged out here.

He moved ahead of Shauf toward the thickening smell, the edge of the orchard where the embankment fell away, then spotted a carcass he feared was going to be Petroni, but it was a bear, recently skinned. A cloud of flies rose as he moved closer. He stooped and retrieved a piece of plastic tubing lying in the grass near the carcass. Studying the tubing, he put it together.

"We've got to get in the barn," he said. "We've got enough for a warrant. Why don't you call Roberts and ask her to get going on it while I talk to Bell?" He held up the plastic tube. "Tell her we found evidence of bear farming."

"Why do we need a warrant with the county on the way here? Kendall will open the barn."

"We may need it later."

He looked at the barn, knowing Petroni could be in there. Petroni obviously knew this place, had put it in his log. Now Marquez called Bell, but the chief didn't process it the same way.

Bell listened quietly, then asked, "Do you think he moved her in the car?"

"Stella?"

"Yes."

Marquez realized how far Bell had gone toward accepting the idea Petroni had killed his wife.

"She never left her kitchen," Marquez said. "They're bringing bolt cutters to get into the barn here, and I'm ready to go into the house but we've been asked to wait."

"Give me directions on how to get to you."

Marquez and Shauf walked back across the flat open parking area to the orchard. A line of police vehicles rolled down the driveway and crunched through a glaze of ice over thin puddles.

"Protecting his crime scene," Shauf said quietly.

Crime tape got strung and the front door of the house opened. Officers went in with guns drawn. Marquez wanted into the barn but all they could do was wait. Things moved carefully, yet steadily, and he picked up a new respect for Kendall, watching him direct traffic. Kendall quizzed them, went back to the Honda, and now came back to Marquez.

"Show me the bear carcass while they're dusting the chain on the barn for prints."

"What have you found in the house?"

"Someone has lived in the bedroom. It's relatively kept up compared to the rest. "

"No blood?"

"Nothing."

"Sophie told me about a rundown place Durham stays at."

"I haven't forgotten."

Marquez walked Kendall out to the bear, and Shauf cut through the grass toward them. She'd been on the phone to Roberts and wanted to talk away from Kendall. Marquez stepped aside with her while Kendall looked at the carcass.

"Melinda talked to the lawyer managing Johengen's widow's estate. He's had this place rented to the same man for five years, though the name isn't Durham, it's Marion Stuart."

"Sure."

"She's faxing Durham's driver's license photo to him. He'll call back as soon as he gets a look."

Marquez took a closer look at the orchard as he told Kendall they'd faxed a photo to an LA lawyer. He pointed out the tire tracks to Kendall, the other area of crushed grass, his idea that something had been dragged out here, possibly the bear whose carcass was on the embankment. They'd found the catheter, so that bear hadn't come up from the willows and creek.

Kendall nodded and said, "There are media people already out on Howell. One of the deputies saw a couple of them hiking up outside the fence, so they may have cameras on us right now. I know you're camera shy, but I don't want you to leave."

"We'd be the last to leave."

Kendall indicated the plastic tube Shauf held. "That's from the bear?"

"It was on the ground here near the carcass. A tube gets inserted surgically and the bile gets drained once or twice a day. We know Nyland hasn't been coming out here twice a day, but we don't know about Bobby Broussard or anyone else. It's time to open up the barn. What are you waiting on?"

"It's happening right now."

Kendall left them and walked back out to his group. Looking around at the lack of bear tracks or scat and at the swatch of crushed grass, Marquez saw an image that explained the crushed grass, the bear dragged out here in a cage towed by a truck. He watched Kendall and Hawse go around to the creek side of the house past the cottonwood. As he walked toward them to see where they were going he caught a glint of metal and saw an old piece of plywood blackened with age and staked down with metal concrete stakes, the cover to an old well.

He pushed the grass along the edge of the plywood away with his foot and studied the metal stakes. They were a type that got used to support form boards in concrete construction, something he'd paid attention to lately as he schemed the bedroom addition at home. The steel stakes had bright nicks on them. Hammered, pounded in recently, nothing else would explain the marks. The plywood was blackened with age, spongy when he stepped on it, crusted with mud, and the stakes were rusty except for the bright spots, and now, leaning over, he determined the nails driven through the holes in the stakes were relatively new also. They were neither galvanized, nor rusted yet.

Kendall came around the corner of the house, waved across to get Marquez's attention, and then pointed at the barn, meaning meet him there, they were opening the doors. Marquez studied the plywood cover more before walking across the clearing. The steel stakes had been driven in at an angle, and from the resistance to his pushing he could tell they'd been pounded in at least a couple of feet to pin the plywood down well. It would take some work to get them out, might require a shovel.

A county deputy cut the chain holding the barn doors shut and as they swung open pale light cut the darkness. They could make out the shape of the near things, but not much more. From somewhere in there came a low, deep animal growl.

"Jesus Christ," Kendall said, and the deputy who'd cut the chain pulled his gun, and stepped back.

Marquez put a hand on the deputy's shoulder, slowed the man's quick step back, saying, "It's in a cage. It's not running around in the barn."

"How do you know that?" Kendall asked.

"We've been looking for this location for months."

"Okay, Marquez, you come with me," Kendall said. "Everybody else stay back."

They clicked flashlights on, and Marquez swept the flashlight beam along each wall and across the dirt floor looking for evidence Petroni had been in here. Their lights reached toward the back where the growl came again, and he saw cages, knew the bear growling was in one of them. He counted seven empty cages and then one with an emaciated bear in it. The cages were set up over a metal trough that water flowed through into a drain.

Excrement, urine, loose food, would fall into the trough and the water carried it away. He turned to Kendall.

"I wondered if I heard water flowing the first time I came out here. Thought I heard it and didn't check."

Marquez shone his light around the cages and back at the bear. It didn't react at all to the light. Blind, or too long in the darkness, possibly. He moved the light from cage to cage, talking to the bear as it growled, trying impossibly to reassure it. The other cages were in varying states of cleanliness; a couple looked like they'd held bear until recently, and that told him they'd probably find more carcasses.

He moved on with Kendall. He would come back to the bear and would call after they'd checked the barn. They would get the bear out of here right away. His flashlight beam came to rest on a weird contraption that looked like a shower stall with strips of dangling plastic where the door ought to be.

"What the hell is that?" Kendall asked.

Marquez moved to it, saw that the strips of plastic were the same as in a supermarket to keep the cold in. When he moved the plastic and looked inside, he understood.

"A drying station for meat, for gall bladders."

"You're an encyclopedia for this shit."

There were a couple of gall bladders hanging, suspended in fine mesh bags, could be to keep the flies off them. The bear growled, and Marquez swung the light and saw tire tracks in the mud and a stack of deer hides and more pelts nailed to the wall along with dozens of antlers.

"Don't step anywhere near those tire tracks," Kendall said, and Marquez turned his flashlight on a line of mounted bears all in different poses on wooden pedestals, counted five stuffed, mounted black bears, and moved the light on.

"It could be Petroni was part of this," Kendall said.

"That's not Stella's blood in the backseat."

"You don't know whose it is."

Kendall's light searched the soft soil of the barn floor, and Marquez knew he was looking for a grave. Marquez did the same thing himself as he moved through the barn to the back to where the caged bear was. He shone the light on the other cages, brought it back to the growling bear again, saw the tube running from its abdomen, the poor quality of the undercoat, and wondered if they'd be able to save it.

"We're going to get you out of here," he said, and heard Kendall walking over.

"I've smelled some rough things in my life," Kendall said. "I don't see anything, but I'll get better lights. We'll take one walk through and then back out."

"That carcass in the orchard was a bear in a cage that got dragged out there. You'll want to take castings of those tire tracks as well."

"Dragged from here?"

"Yeah, then released, and the bear would have gone for the creek, the water and cover there. Must have been frightened and sick. It was shot as it started down the bank."

They heard the hoarse rattle of an old freezer compressor kicking on and spotted its pale white reflection at the very back of the barn. They'd walked past it the first time, too caught up in the drying station.

"Let's check it," Marquez said.

"What are bile products used for?"

"High blood pressure, coughs, gallstones, asthma. It's a cure-all. That bear in the orchard was killed as recently as yesterday, could have been after Nyland was released."

"Nyland got released and disappeared with Sophie," Kendall said. "Then she starts talking to us last night, and before that she tells you this Durham sleeps at some rundown farmhouse."

"She didn't say 'farmhouse.'" When Kendall stopped talking abruptly, Marquez said, "Finish the thought. Where do you see Petroni in this?"

"I don't see a happy ending."

"You think he's here somewhere." If they didn't find him in here, the search of the grounds would widen. Dogs would be brought in. "The plywood cover on the well should come off."

The freezer was big enough to hold just about anything and that was reason enough for silence. It had an ancient lock latch, and Kendall wanted to be the one to open it. He grunted as he lifted the heavy door and Marquez shone his light inside. A black bear's head looked back up at them, a webwork of ice crystals filling its open mouth, its eyes iced grape skins dully reflecting the light. Kendall let the top rest against the back wall, and they removed twenty-two frozen paws.

"At least there are no human body parts," Kendall said. "At least not that, but it looks like we found the headquarters you've been after."

They swept the barn with light again as they walked back. Kendall squinted in the sunlight as they came outside, and Marquez said, "There's an old well that needs to get looked at."

"Okay, show me."

40

They slowly dug the stakes out, no one saying much, and with a county deputy and Shauf on one side and Marquez and Kendall on the other, they lifted away the heavy plywood cover. Two sheets of three-quarter-inch plywood screwed together formed the cap, and as they lifted it away Marquez saw that fresh concrete had been poured around the rim to bed the plywood. It had formed a kind of seal that was broken now, and the odor flowing up from the well was horrific. He caught a finger where a screw poked through the plywood, and his blood dripped on the weeds as they maneuvered the cap over and put it down.

The odor, the release of gasses was gagging, and they fell back, had to give the well a few minutes to vent, Kendall going to his car to get something to dull the smell. Marquez covered his mouth, didn't breath, leaned over with a flashlight. Near the bottom, roughly thirty feet down, was dark fur. He moved the beam along the fur, then straightened, stepped back, and watched

Kendall take a look while thinking about what he'd just seen. Then they shined both lights in, Marquez talking.

"Here." Marquez moved the flashlight beam to a place where the hide met unevenly. "Looks like a bear hide but it's been sewed together."

Kendall turned to Hawse. "We'll need a backhoe." To Marquez, "How deep would you guess?"

"Thirty feet."

Kendall turned back to Hawse. "Tell the operator we need to get down at least twenty feet, maybe more. No, at twenty we can lower someone. Tell the operator we need a deep trench. He'll know what to bring."

"Might be easier to lower someone," Hawse said, and Marquez stepped away from their debate. He saw Bell working his way through the officers on the driveway, Bell handing over a card rather than showing a badge. Marquez raised a hand so Bell knew where he was. Three TV vans were parked out on Howell, and Bell had waded through volleys of questions from the media but didn't seem displeased about it. Marquez showed him the well, the carcass in the orchard, looked in the barn with him while they waited for a backhoe.

When the backhoe operator fired up his machine, diesel smoke plumed into the cool air, a curling black cloud rising against the white sky. The teeth of the hoe pulled at the concrete rim, lifted one edge, flipped and dragged it away from the well. It looked like a concrete donut lying there. The hoe repositioned and began to dig a trough, the bucket arm unfolding, teeth chattering as they scraped over stones. A pile of earth and loose rocks built alongside the backhoe, and a trench formed and deepened.

The operator worked steadily without looking long at any of those watching. Kendall stood with his hands on his hips, his eyes periodically surveying the overall scene, directing the work like a construction superintendent, while Marquez walked back out into the orchard and then looked in the house, the one bedroom painted, carpeted, much cleaner than the rest of the place. There was a dresser but no belongings in the drawers.

His gut tightened as they waited. He had trouble focusing on Bell's questions but brought him up to speed on the search for Durham and Nyland, told him that he'd had another call from Ungar, one he hadn't answered yet, and that it was Ungar who'd visited Keeler at Ice House.

When a Fish and Game truck arrived with a bear trap chained down in the bed there was more waiting to confirm that all plaster castings of tire impressions had been taken. They'd share castings with the county. When the crime techs finished, the DFG truck backed into the barn. Marquez figured they could coax the bear with food into the trap, but the warden had a plan of his own and more experience. He was also quick to say he doubted the bear could be saved, had lost too much of its undercoat.

"We're going to try anyway," Marquez said.

More diesel smoke plumed upward as the hoe engine pulled against a rock and reached a point where it couldn't dig any lower without risking a cave-in. The operator climbed down, shaking his head, saying he needed more shoring, more steel plate. Phone calls got made, and they waited for shoring to arrive, Kendall fuming because he'd made it clear how deep they needed to go before the operator came out.

Then a call came from Roberts. She'd heard from the lawyer for the Johengen estate. He'd looked at the faxed photo and recognized Durham's face.

"He's positive," she said. "Durham or Marion Stuart is three years into a five-year lease."

"The photo faxed through clear enough for him to be certain?" Marquez asked, knowing the faxed quality wasn't that good.

"Remembers Durham's bad cheek. He's sure. Said his checks are always on time. What's going on in the background behind you?"

"A backhoe digging out a well."

"What's that about?"

"Something down there, not sure what it is yet, but dead."

She was quiet a moment, moved back to Durham.

"Sac police will assist on a stakeout of Durham's house."

"Thank them for us."

"I did."

When he hung up he told Bell the lawyer had ID'd Durham, then watched a young deputy get lowered into the newly shored trench. He fumbled with a rope and after a couple of unsuccessful tries were made, vomited, and readjusted the rope and the harness they were trying to slide under it. Then the carcass began to slowly rise. The chain extending from the hoe arm to wrap around it pulled taut, and the hide with whatever was sewed inside bumped against the sides of the well as it rose. Kendall directed the hoe operator to a wide sheet of clear plastic and the operator placed it nearly in the center. The chain hooked to the ropes got unclipped, and the hoe arm swung clear.

Marquez moved in closer, trying to make sense of the stitching. He brushed away the arm of a deputy trying to hold him back. It appeared a bear hide had been sewed with fishing line. He knelt with Kendall, their knees on the plastic sheeting as they studied the rough stitching. Kendall cut through with a knife and opened a small section. He repositioned Hawse, who was videotaping, and backed Marquez up and took another look himself, then motioned Marquez forward while holding off Bell.

"There's a body inside the bear hide," Kendall said. "I'm going to open more of it and I want you to take a look at the face with me." He added, "If there is one."

The hide made a sucking ripping sound as it pulled apart, and Marquez could see hands and it was funny but he knew from the hands alone. He saw a gaping wound under the ribs and then Petroni's face as Kendall reached and lifted more of the hide. As he saw Bill's face anguish gripped him, a hard wave of sadness.

"I'm sorry," Kendall said very quietly, and then talking to himself, "and I really did think he killed his wife, may have, I still don't know. If not, someone tried to make it look like he did. Those were his boot prints in her blood in the house. We found brochures and asked the Mexican authorities to watch for the Honda. I was sure we'd find him in Mexico."

Marquez thought of a time when the SOU was new and he and Petroni each headed a team. He remembered in the first days after they'd met each other, driving along Highway 1 in a former drug dealer's car they'd bought off a police lot on their way to sell abalone to a black market dealer they planned to sting. They'd stopped for a beer afterward and met another guy in the bar who wanted in on the abalone action. The guy had insisted on buying their beer and they'd laughed about that later and it had seemed then that the new undercover units were going to make a real difference. All these years later and he found himself wondering if he was making a difference.

"We'll check to see if they threw anything else in the well," Kendall said. "We'll be out here a while, and I'll need to be able to get a hold of you. We will find who did this, Marquez. I promise you that."

Kendall's words meant little to him. Kendall had been looking hard for Petroni, and his theories were all upside down as near as Marquez could tell. How had Petroni gotten here? That was a question to get answered. He had another and turned to Kendall with it.

"Have you ever seen anything like this?"

Kendall seemed to consider the question. When he spoke it was quietly as though the conversation was strictly between them, though Hawse hung at his elbow.

"I've seen bodies discarded like trash. Rape-murders where the body is dumped on a road shoulder. This is what it reminds me of. Take the warden, wrap him in a bear skin, and throw him down a hole."

Marquez nodded agreement. "It's about bear and Petroni's role. If he was taking bribes and that was all going along as planned, why would this happen?"

"He asked for more money, got in an argument," Kendall offered.

"But kill him and a new warden gets assigned. This is a state-ment." Marquez down at Petroni again. "It's the man who threatened us and took the shots at me. This guy is buying from us so he can take our money so he can burn us, prove he's better than us, and he hates us so much he'll risk trying to make good on his threats."

Marquez looked away from Petroni's body, glancing at the barn as he tried to make sense of it. *Durham's leasing under a different name. If Petroni was taking bribes, was it for a different reason?* He remembered Petroni's comment that he had money but didn't. His thoughts came in a jumble, not connected yet. *Could bitterness over having a Michigan game park shut down cause something like this? Was it Nyland as Kendall speculated, evening the score with Petroni? Like gutting one of them, as Sophie had talked about in the motel room.*

Marquez stepped back, was quiet as he watched how they handled the body, electing to transport it still sewed into the hide, a final degradation. He waited until the county had finished searching the bottom of the well and then with Shauf drove Bell back to his car. In his rearview mirror as they drove away he saw Bell talking to one of the TV people.

Later, he sat with Shauf in Placerville and tried to fight off the shock, piece together their next moves. Everything they did at Johengen's would need to be coordinated through Kendall. He wanted to go back there as soon as possible, but they'd have to stay clear until the county finished. Tomorrow would be the earliest they'd be allowed back into the barn, so tomorrow they'd go back and catalog everything. They'd continue to focus on finding Nyland and Durham. He figured they'd start with Bobby Broussard today. That was his plan when he left Shauf. Then Maria called and everything changed.

41

"What does this man want?" he asked Maria.

"He's checking something in the back. There's like a right away, or whatever, a land thing that's in the back, only Grandma didn't know about it."

"He's back there now?"

"Yes."

"Where's your grandma?"

"She's with him. He asked Grandma if he could walk around the back of the property because they're putting in a line of new pipe or something like that. He has to check on some survey stakes. Does that seem right, Dad?"

"He's a surveyor?"

"He's working for somebody marking where they're going to put cable for TV in a trench, but it's weird. He's all sketchy and he's got like sunglasses on and a cap and trying hide his face. His coat is turned up."

Her voice was rushed. She paused, waited for him answer.

"Is it cold?"

"It's windy, so, yeah, it's cold. He could just have his coat turned up because it's cold, and there's a lot of cable getting installed everywhere. So I'm just being way paranoid?"

She told him a man in a dull yellow pickup with a surveying company logo on his truck had driven into the yard about twenty minutes ago. He'd sat in the truck for what Maria had thought was too long, then got out, knocked on the front door, and stared at Maria standing at the window, watching her while he talked with her grandmother. Her imagination had run with the threat they'd sent her down there to avoid, and Marquez knew he hadn't done enough to reassure her how safe she almost certainly was. But a cable company with a right-of-way at the rear of Lillian's property did seem odd and from what Maria was saying, Lillian had gone back there with him, so Lillian had questions too. The house was miles outside Bishop and backed up to the alluvial plain of the White Mountains, nothing but sagebrush behind it before the dry canyons of the Whites. Still, for the last couple of years the cable companies had been doing massive rollouts.

"He's back there now?"

"Yes. He like hung around the front door after Grandma said it was okay to go around back, but then he went back."

"Describe him again. Black, white, Asian, what is he?"

"I don't know. I can't see a lot of his face. Sort of official-talking like he's used to ordering people around."

"How tall is he?"

"Average, maybe a little taller. Sort of like average."

"What color hair?"

"I don't know." Marquez heard frustration, the edge of fear. "He's wearing a cap like I said. Grandma's in the garden watching him because we saw him looking at the house really closely when he walked back. The back door was open and he went over to it,

but when Grandma came out he pretended he wasn't doing anything. It creeped me out."

"And you can see the logo on his truck?"

"Not anymore. I can't read it from here. Should I walk out, get
the number, and call it to see if he's supposed to be here?"

"No, stay on the phone with me, but why don't you go back
there and describe him."

He heard her footsteps now as she walked back, and her
breath was rushed as she told him what she was seeing. Her voice
rose quickly.

"Omigod, omigod, he just knocked her down! He hit her, he's
dragging her."

Marquez reached for his other cell phone, punched 911, and
held the phone to one ear as he kept talking with her.

"Listen to me, Maria, do you know where Lillian keeps the
gun in her room?"

"Omigod."

He could barely keep his voice calm. "Go to her bedroom and
get the gun."

"He's dragging her toward the house."

"Stop looking out the window and go get the gun. Do you
remember how to slide the clip in?"

Her voice quavered. He thought he heard "Yes." He heard her
moving.

"Do you remember how to rack the slide?"

"I don't know."

She ran down the hallway and he kept talking to her, trying to
calm her as his own heart pounded. He spoke to a dispatcher as
the 911 call picked up. He gave the address outside Bishop and said
it was an emergency, an assailant, his daughter on the other line.
He heard Maria get the gun out, drop it, and told her to slow
down. He hung up with the 911 dispatcher.

"It won't fit."

"Turn the clip around and shove it in."

Now he heard it slide into place and then the banging of a door slamming open and a frightened sound from Maria.

"He's in the house," she whispered. "He's in the kitchen, he's in the kitchen."

"Take the safety off." She didn't answer. "Maria, is the safety off?"

"I can't find it."

"Along the side."

He heard her tremulous "Like it clicks up," and he knew her hands were shaking.

"That's right. Okay, you've got to listen to me and you've got to think. He wants you to panic and you have to think. Remember what Lillian taught you about two hands." She didn't answer. "Stay with me, Maria."

"Two hands," she repeated, and, "he's coming, he's coming down the hallway. I hear him on the stairs."

"Where are you?"

"In Grandma's bedroom."

"Then you can see down the hallway. Don't let him get past the other bedroom and don't let him see the gun until you're ready. Aim for his torso."

"He sees me, he sees me, he knows I'm on the phone," and Marquez heard the man order her to come out of the room. He must have seen her face.

"Put the phone down, two hands and aim for his torso. If he sees the gun and keeps coming, pull the trigger."

He heard a sharp noise that he knew was the phone being placed on the dresser near the door to Lillian's room, and his heart hammered as he heard fragments of a man's voice, soft tones, quiet, someone taking pleasure in this.

"I see you, sweetie. Come here, if you don't want her to get hurt even worse you'd better."

Marquez heard Maria's scream and then two booming shots and the man yelled and a third shot came a few seconds later. Then running, furniture getting knocked over, sounds coming from somewhere else in the house and he waited and couldn't breath. *Come on, Maria, pick up the phone, please, God, let her pick up the phone, let her be okay,* and then the phone scraped as someone fumbled with it. *Don't let it be him,* and it was Maria breathless, her voice quaking.

"I shot him."

"You hit him."

"He screamed and he ran out of the house, Dad. He got in his truck and drove away."

She started to sob uncontrollably and Marquez kept talking to her, asked her to check the driveway again while he dialed 911 again.

"I'm going to Grandma."

"Stay on the phone with me."

Then Maria was crying, asking him what to do because Lillian was lying on the kitchen floor and not moving.

"Is she breathing?"

"Yes, and I can feel her pulse."

"Okay, stay, lock all the doors. There are going to be Bishop police and maybe Highway Patrol on there way to you in a few minutes. Stay with me, but I'm going to use my other phone for a minute, okay."

"Grandma is starting to move."

"Talk to her."

"I hear sirens."

"Hang in there."

Marquez scrolled through to the Highway Patrol number he wanted and called, gave the location and description of the truck. If the man stayed on a highway, then they'd get him because it was all open country and not easy to hide in. When he spoke to

Maria again he could hear sirens clearly, then Maria went to get the officers. Marquez spoke with a groggy Lillian. She'd gotten to her feet and the paramedics made her lie down again.

"They're putting her in an ambulance," Maria said. "The officer wants to talk to you."

"Put him on."

Lillian had a pretty good lump on her head but didn't want to go to a hospital and was arguing with the paramedics, the cop said. He told Marquez there were a few blood splatters outside on the dirt, and Marquez told him briefly about the threats and who he thought they were looking for. He repeated Durham's name and the name Marion Stuart. He read off license plates for three vehicles registered to the Stuart name, none of which was a truck, but maybe he'd dump the truck and pick up his Mercedes.

"Do you know it's him?" the cop asked.

"No, I know he disappeared and we're looking for him, and it could have been his voice. But I'm not certain at all."

"We're going to take this young lady next to me back to the station with us. She's going to teach us how to keep our cool under fire."

"I'm headed your way but it'll take me five hours."

"Your daughter is safe with us."

There'd been no delay getting the word out on the truck, but it was open desert country and the few police available were spread out. Marquez told Maria he was on the way and then called Katherine and told her what had happened. The normally pacifist Katherine was quick.

"I hope he bleeds to death on the side of the road somewhere."

If it was Durham, how had he found his way to Bishop and did that mean he'd followed Katherine when she drove Maria down? Marquez drove hard as he tracked alongside the eastern side of the Sierras down to Bishop, on the phone to the different police municipalities along the route, and back and forth with the

CHP. He watched the traffic across the highway and when he dropped down on Mono Lake and was making the run into Lee Vining, he wheeled around and chased a truck that turned out to be a couple of middle-aged women.

The hospital wanted Lillian to stay overnight for observation, and Lillian argued against it, which didn't surprise Katherine. But Lillian had a concussion and was mildly disoriented, a bad headache, and the hospital prevailed. When Marquez arrived she was in a hospital bed, her face pale, several of her network of friends standing in the room joking with her.

"If he comes back it'll be his last mistake," Lillian said to Marquez. She looked at the photo of Durham that Marquez had and said that it might not be him. Then he drove to Lillian's house with Maria and she showed how she'd crouched and aimed. He studied where they'd taken dirt samples trying to recover enough of the blood splatters to get a DNA sample. When Maria said she knew she'd hit him she started crying, and Marquez put an arm around her shoulder and held her close. Later, as they were driving north heading home he handed her the picture of Durham and saw the same uncertainty in her face he'd seen in Lillian's.

"It could be him," she said.

He looked over at Maria's profile in the darkness, reached, and touched her. "I'm really proud of you."

"Do you really think he would he have killed us?"

What was the truest answer to give her? They couldn't know, of course, and he didn't want to leave her with nightmares, but she'd also stood her ground and had the poise when it mattered. She'd earned his permanent respect.

"I think he was there to do that, and you did the only thing you could and you did it well."

42

They had the choice of going home to Mount Tamalpais or to the small house in Bernal Heights in San Francisco that Katherine still owned and where she'd stayed last night with her best friend, Janet, who leased it from her. Bernal Heights was where Maria had lived her first eight years, and he wondered if there wouldn't be a certain comfort going there. Then he learned from Bell that state police were already en route to Mount Tam and would guard his house.

They got in near midnight, and Marquez talked to the state cops parked out on the street. He listened to what they had for a description and debated bringing Maria out to talk to them, then decided against it, doubted the wounded man would come here. He offered food and coffee, which the officers declined.

Katherine scrambled eggs, fried chicken-apple sausage, and they ate while Maria numbly told the story of what happened. Her hands trembled, and she said she was going to take a shower and call one of her friends who she knew would still be awake. She wanted to go to school tomorrow, insisted she'd drive herself. Listening closely to her, Marquez knew she'd be okay. Then just before going to bed she came back out and asked if he thought there was any chance the man would come here tonight. He shook his head, said no as he had several times during the long drive home, and wrapped an arm around her shoulders and held her. After Maria was in her room he talked more frankly with Katherine about the possibilities.

"How badly is he hurt?" she asked.

"He lost some blood outside on the gravel, and they think the way it was flung suggests his arm was hit."

"So it might not be a bad wound."

"Hard to say."

"But they did get samples?"

"Yeah, they'll be able to type it and compare DNA."

"Then if they catch him they can hold him."

"DNA results will take weeks to come back, and the case doesn't have the components that would bump it up the list. Lillian is okay, Maria is unhurt, so most likely they'd hold him as long they could, then set a very high bail while waiting for DNA results. I talked to Maria on the way home, and it's anybody's guess whether she'd have a shot at picking him out of a lineup. He came in the house with a mask on, and you can bet if caught he'll say he only meant to talk to Maria, not hurt her."

"But he's wounded."

"Yeah, he's wounded. Two slugs got pulled from the wood-work; the third hit him."

"How did he get away on those desert roads they can fly a plane along?"

"Probably by switching vehicles. My best guess is he followed you when you drove down, but that means he was here and may have had other plans the day you drove Maria away. He may have been casing this house."

Later, Marquez walked out the gravel drive and talked to the state cop. He felt agitated and worried, and though he believed tonight was safe, he felt uncomfortable. He walked the perimeter of the house, returned to the back deck, and locked the slider, something he rarely did. He showered with Katherine, felt her water-slicked skin against him, steam clouding around them, her dark hair wet, and then Katherine pressing against him, lips finding his with fear-driven urgency. Her hand slid down his abdomen, and he traced the curve of her spine and hip with his fingers, touched the smooth skin of her inner thigh as she reached to arouse him. He didn't know where the desire came from tonight, but when he lifted her, pressed her back against the tile and entered her, he thought of nothing else. She felt very light in his arms, and afterward she held him tighter still and wept.

Toward 4:00 in the morning he lay awake with a hand on the warm skin of her back and a tightness like a clenched fist in his chest. He listened to Katherine's quiet breathing, remembered the emotion in her face as Maria walked in the door tonight. He dozed, woke again, before dawn made coffee, and took a mug up to the state cop, who said the only thing he'd seen were deer and maybe a bear, though he asked Marquez not to tell anyone that last part. They'd never stop laughing at him.

"You're not crazy," Marquez answered. "The first black bear sighting in a hundred years in West Marin was this last spring. That bear is an adolescent and still around here somewhere. He got into garbage and then beehives in Green Gulch near Muir Beach, then showed up at the northern end of the Golden Gate Bridge near Kirby Cove. He may be on the mountain here some-where."

On the back deck he sat with his notes in front of him and talked to Shauf, Alvarez, Cairo, Roberts as a plan formed. When Katherine came out they sat in the cold dawn and he talked it over with her. He believed that if it was Durham who'd made the assault, the way he figured it, Durham had good reason to try to find Nyland next. He told Kath what he'd learned this morning.

"There's a report that Nyland was spotted in the Crystal Basin last night and that makes sense to me. I think he'll take to the woods. But he probably has a way to contact his partner, Durham, and some prearranged escape plan. I'm going back up there to try to find Nyland because I think he's the key to Durham."

She pushed her hair back behind her right ear, a nervous habit. "Say that again," she said, and he repeated, "Kath, I've got to go back up. I think Durham will try to get to Nyland. My team will be better at finding Nyland than the county if he's hiding in the wilderness."

"Hiding with a rifle and no future."

"As far as I know he hasn't been charged with anything yet."

"But you know he will be. Haven't you done enough already?"

He was still talking with Katherine when another call came in. A Mercedes registered to Marion Stuart had been found by the highway patrol near Mono Lake. That was between Lillian's house and the Placerville area. It strengthened the idea that Durham had been the assailant. When he hung up, he continued with Katherine.

"When we went through Nyland's trailer we found articles he'd clipped on the antiabortionist who evaded the FBI for so long down south, the guy that took to the woods. A lot of people with the police after them would be in a car a thousand miles away by now. But what we've got is a report phoned in early this morning that someone who looks like him is in the Crystal Basin. For me, that fits, and I've got to go back up there and try to help find him because I really do believe he's the key to locating Durham."

"I'd like to say I understand, but all I see is you taking risks."

Marquez didn't drive straight to the mountains. At 10:00 that morning he walked into Armand's Outdoor Sport Guns in South San Francisco. The small balding man behind the counter said he was the owner, and Marquez showed him photos of Durham and Nyland. Through his computer records the owner confirmed what they already knew, Durham had purchased two rifles here, both .30-30 Winchesters.

Marquez watched the owner rub a ring finger that looked swollen with arthritis. Then he let go of his finger and reached to touch Durham's photo.

"I do remember him. He's a very particular man."

"Was he with anybody?"

"Not this other young man you're showing me, but there was somebody with him."

"Can you remember anything about him?"

"No, he never came to the counter."

Marquez questioned him further, thanked him, and told him it was likely he'd hear from a Detective Kendall about the rifles Durham had purchased. He got as far as the door of the small shop and turned back, looked at the owner, owl-like behind the counter, the shop small enough where someone not at the glass counter would still be close enough to see.

"This man who was here with him, you saw him well enough to know he wasn't the other man in the photo, so you must remember something about him."

"I get all kinds of people in here."

"Young, old?"

"He could have been in his thirties."

"Was he standing where I am?"

Marquez knew the owner was trying to remember. The main lights were all behind the counter, and someone standing here wouldn't be as distinct.

"He wore a cap turned around the way they do now. I don't know if this is true but he may have had some Asian blood, or been from one of the islands, but I really don't know. I won't be able to identify him if that's what you're hoping. There's no chance," and Marquez heard more than lack of memory in the owner's emphatic voice. He knew the man had decided not to remember either way. He didn't want any part of ID'ing someone who was wanted. Now Marquez walked back to the counter.

"Look up another name for me, okay."

"What name?"

"Kim Ungar."

Marquez leaned over the counter so he could see the screen. Ungar's name came up as a gun purchaser. The same guns that showed in their file on him were listed here. Two handguns. Two Glocks. No rifles.

"Thanks," Marquez said. "I may have other questions. Do you have a card?"

He took the card and drove to Ungar's apartment complex, used his cell phone to call Ungar from the steps of the apartment. Ungar didn't answer his phone but did answer the buzzer when Marquez hit it.

"I'd like to come in and talk with you."

"Now is not a good time."

"Just a few questions."

"I have a guest, and the TV said there was a body of a warden found in a well and evidence of bear farming. I heard it again this morning. They're looking for the man who leased the property, so it sounds like you've found him."

"Is he the man?"

"You're the one that should know."

"I'm asking you."

"We haven't made our deal yet. You haven't made any offers and I can't talk right now. I want to meet you somewhere, but not here."

"The DA wants your cousin's name. They need to know he's not wanted for other crimes before they'll make the deal."

"I can't give you his name without a deal first."

"Can you give me the name of the man in Sacramento as a show of faith?"

"Let me think about that. I'll call you."

43

On the drive to the mountains he took a call from Kendall. "Rifling matches," Kendall said, referring to the gun Sophie led them to. "Or let's just say the turnings are similar enough."

"Anything on the gun?"

"Wiped clean with solvent."

"So now you really need her to come across with more."

"Yep."

"Has she ever seen the rifle?"

"She says no. Nyland only alluded to it." Kendall elongated the word *alluded* for emphasis and followed with his opinion that Sophie was systematically disassociating herself, the same point he'd made last time they talked. "We need a full confession from her and she's dancing around the edges. How's your daughter?"

"Shaken."

"Keep an eye on her today."

In the midafternoon Marquez hooked up with the team, and they trailed Bobby Broussard into the Crystal Basin, then to Carr's Grocery, a general store and bar that had survived decades in a remote pocket of the Crystal Basin by selling the forgotten pieces of equipment, food, fishing lures and bait, maps, and, of course, alcohol. Pine wainscoting in the bar had darkened over time, and the yellowed walls above it were decorated with hunting photos of bear and deer kills, old black-and-whites that had yellowed with smoke and time. Proud hunters gripping antlers or lifting the head of a black bear laid out in the back of a forties-era truck.

Fish and Game was tolerated here, even liked by some of the younger family members that ran the business, and yet, Marquez felt that the place carried the presence of those who resented restraint or laws regulating hunting and for whom the rules changed with opportunity. But then, it had been years since he'd had a drink in the bar.

Bobby Broussard was alone at a table in the corner, his eyes darting from Marquez to the doorway behind.

"It's legal to have a beer, isn't it?" Bobby asked, grasping at a toughness he couldn't own. "What are you people following me for?"

"I want to tell you what I think will happen to Nyland if we don't find him first."

"He ain't going to no prison because he didn't kill anybody."

"Cut the hick talk, Bobby, and listen for a minute. You don't want to become an accomplice and that's the way you're heading."

Bobby grinned and lifted his beer.

"Did I say something funny? You know, Petroni was found," Marquez said.

"The warden killed his wife and got what was coming."

"What did he do after that, Bobby, drive out Howell Road where you've been milking bears, wrap himself in a hide, sew it shut with fishing line, and throw himself in a well?"

"What are you trying to put on me?"

"You've helped with the bear farms."

"I don't know about any bear farms."

"Milking the bears puts you at Johengen's where Petroni's body was found. You can figure the rest out yourself."

"Sophie said you'd show up like this."

"There were thirty-two gallbladders in that barn, a lot of paws and hides. You'll be locked up a lot longer than Troy was and maybe for a lot longer than that if you get named in a murder warrant. They've played you because they don't think you're bright enough to know the difference." He paused a beat. "Nyland is going down. So is Durham, but you don't have to let them take you down with them." Marquez got his phone out. "I'll let you listen to the voice mail I got driving up here. You've talked to Detective Kendall, you know him, don't you?"

Bobby shrugged, took a pull of the beer like nothing he'd heard interested him. He smirked as Marquez called up the voice mail message and replayed it, pressing the phone to Bobby's greasy ear. Kendall was talking about the murder warrant issued this morning. The county was going out to the public, maybe even as they sat here, warning that Nyland was armed and dangerous and wanted for questioning in the death of both Jed Vandemere and Bill Petroni.

Marquez pulled the phone back.

"When you kill a peace officer you get special circumstances. If you call Troy right now, I'll bet he'll tell you police have been out to the house this morning."

"They already been out."

"There might be a way out for you still, but Nyland is going down. He's in a lot of trouble, and Sophie is working with the detectives."

"She talks a lot of nonsense sometimes. They're meant to be together."

Marquez knew from the way Bobby delivered it, that last statement hadn't been his own. Maybe it was something Nyland had said to explain everything, but it sounded a lot like Troy talking.

"You're not hearing me, Sophie flipped, she's helping Kendall put the case together. She's feeding the detectives information because she doesn't want to go down with Nyland. She isn't going to keep him supplied. She might make you think she is, but she isn't and that leaves you holding the bag. If you can give me your exact routine at Johengen's farm, what you did out there and who directed you, then maybe I can help you. And I need to know where the other farms are. Where are the bears now?"

Bobby grinned like that was the funniest thing he'd ever heard, repeated it, "Where are the bears?" Then he stared and appropriate of nothing, said, "Supposed to snow tonight."

"Is Nyland here in the basin?"

"You're the one that doesn't know what's going on."

Bobby grinned again and Marquez left him in the bar. Half an hour later they watched him transfer two sport-type zip bags from Sophie Broussard's pickup truck. As Bobby pulled away and they got ready to follow, Marquez took a call from Kendall.

"Thought you were with your family," Kendall said. "You didn't say you were up here."

"We followed Bobby Broussard into the basin, and he just picked up a load of supplies from Sophie."

"She's cooperating with us. So is Broussard. Nyland is some-where in the Barrett Lake area and we've got people in there where the drop is going to happen, but let's hope it doesn't god-damn snow before we get him. All Bobby needs to do is drop the supplies and haul ass. We've got it from here, Marquez. This is ours now." Kendall waited a beat and then his voice hardened. "Are we clear on that?"

"Barrett Lake?"

"Don't even think about."

"You plan to arrest him when he picks up these supplies?"

"Yes."

"He'll see you coming."

"There's a SWAT team with a lot more training than you've got. You've got to stand aside now. I'll call you after we book him. I'm serious about this. This isn't even a conversation we should be having." Kendall hung up.

44

"We stepped into the middle of it and Kendall was doing his best to be nice," Marquez said after he'd pulled over with Shauf down the road.

"So what do you think?"

"If they catch Nyland picking up the supplies, we'll back off."

"Why not otherwise?"

"Because Nyland is the only reason I can think of for Durham to come back this direction rather than run."

He watched her mull that over. A thing he'd always liked about Shauf was that despite the tough persona she cultivated, she was a gentle human being at heart. She understood how to intimidate and create fear, but she didn't respect violence and didn't take any pleasure in it. Ninety percent of the people they chased were motivated by money. Some were brutal and dangerous if given an opportunity, but her mind didn't turn as readily as his did to the darker qualities of humanity.

He had no trouble picturing Durham taking risks to get to Nyland and meeting him at a prearranged rendezvous spot, perhaps a lonely spot on a dirt road in the Crystal Basin, a contingency plan made long ago. Durham might pull up in a pickup, Nyland step out from under the trees, glad to be rescued, thanking Durham and crawling under a tarp tied down over the pickup bed so he'd be hidden from view. He might lie on a dirty piece of foam as the truck bounced its way back to a paved road. Then he'd hear the reassuring hum of the tires on asphalt and believe he was safely away from the law.

But Durham had plenty to lose if Nyland was apprehended and then traded testimony against him for a lesser sentence. He might well hold the testimony that would put Durham in prison for life, so Marquez saw a different ending, Durham telling Nyland he needed to stay hidden until they reached a safe place, a remote cabin, for example, the spot where Nyland could hole up while the next plan was made. But what would that plan be and why would Durham want the liability and expense? There was a simpler way. It was a big step, but maybe not so big for Durham if he was the guy they suspected he was. Park somewhere a gunshot wouldn't matter, lower the pickup gate, and watch Nyland slide out from under the tarp, even help him. Then before he stood and straightened, two shots. The testimony Nyland could trade would end in a shallow grave.

Snow started while Marquez was on the phone to Katherine in the midafternoon. The conversation was laced with a bittersweet sadness, and they decided that she and Maria would stay at a hotel tonight because he wasn't going to come home. He told her Nyland had been found and he was going to do what he could to help bring him in.

"There's a jeep trail that runs five miles from the end of the paved road out to a lake named Barrett. He's near there and on the move. A SWAT team is on its way in and maybe they'll get him."

"Enough force and Nyland won't fight it," he said.

Marquez drove out past Wright's Lake and down to the entrance of the Barrett Jeep Trail. Shauf met him there, driving the jeep she'd picked up so she could get them off-road. Snow was falling in light grainy flecks that the wind swirled and tossed. Marquez stood with his hands in his coat pockets, snowflakes tickling his stubble of beard. The real storm was yet to hit, not forecast to for several more hours, but the sky was dark gray, the light already turning toward dusk. The radio was on, tuned to the band the SWAT team was using. Marquez listened to the back-and-forth as a helicopter backed away due to turbulence.

"Anything they do to catch Nyland is going to be on foot," Marquez said. "They just pulled their helicopter out."

"Where's he going to go in a snowstorm?"

"Wherever he'd planned to go if police showed up, but let's hope when we drive up they have him in custody."

Marquez stripped down and put a long-sleeved Thinsulite shirt, a Kevlar vest, then a fleece pullover and a Gore-Tex parka over that. The parka had a hood and drawstring to cover most of his face. He pulled on Thinsulite pants and thermal waterproofs over those, Gore-Tex boots, then packed gloves and additional clips for the Glock into his coat. He slipped the night goggles into a pocket and loaded almonds, chocolate bars, a hunk of cheese, juice, and water. He added a handful of aspirin, Advil, teabags, a small gas stove and canister, a survival blanket, Second Skin, extra socks, bouillon cubes because they always seemed to work for him. He packed bandages, compresses, a morphine shot. Bivouac sack and liner. GPS locator. He'd carry plenty of water. He had a radio and satellite cell phone. In an outside pocket he zipped in handcuffs.

They started up the rocky entrance to the trail, the jeep straining over the bigger boulders, tires slipping and then crawling forward. Then the road became dirt and much easier to drive. In a few places they had to climb over deadfall. They drove out of the

forest and across a meadow with the wind scouring the road
ahead, the sky a dark gray. Light would fade fast today. Twenty
minutes later they pulled up to the Barrett campsites and watched
the faces turn.

An officer stepping forward and already directing them to turn
their vehicle around.

"Let's go talk to them," Marquez said.

"Are you sure about this?"

"Not yet, let's see what they've got going."

"This storm is coming in."

"I'm carrying my locator. The satellite phone will work fine
and I'll hang a distance behind him." He turned to her. "But they
may have him or a good enough plan."

Marquez left the day pack in the jeep, and they went to find
Kendall among the officers mingling around the camping area. He
counted twelve vehicles and watched the SWAT commander stride
toward him.

"Why are you here?" the commander asked.

"Nyland's wanted for commercial trafficking in bear parts."

"That's the least of his problems," the commander said, and
the officers near him chuckled. "You don't need to worry."

"Have you got him?"

"We will."

"Where is he?"

"Up there. We've got his campsite secure." The commander
pointed to trees off to the left. "He was camped up behind them
and he must have heard us coming."

"It would be hard not to."

Now Kendall walked over and stepped into the conversation.
"Tell us where he's going to go, Marquez. He's worked his way
around the lake with a dog."

The SWAT commander moved closer to Marquez, pointed out
Nyland up on the ridge, handed Marquez binoculars. When he

focused those, Marquez moved along the loose granite behind the lake and saw Nyland climbing, the dog trailing just behind him and both of Nyland's hands in black gloves. If he had a weapon, it was a handgun. He wasn't carrying a rifle, but he was dressed for the weather and had a pack, same as Marquez had in the jeep. Nyland looked back down at the lake, but only briefly and then climbed again, his direction purposeful. Marquez lowered the glasses, looked across the gray water of the lake, the whitecaps, the dark gray rim of granite beyond. Snow flurries obscured the ridge and then it showed again.

"He's headed into Desolation Wilderness," Marquez said. "From there he has several exits if he stays on a trail, which he'll almost have to do in this storm. He can hike to Tahoe or Donner Lake, or even double back this direction, drop down to Wright's Lake via Rockbound. But you must be looking at trail maps."

Kendall nodded and Marquez realized his worst fear was true. They'd set up the bust planning to capture Nyland here with the helicopter giving them lookdown ability, and the weather screwed it up. The storm came in four hours early and they had to pull the helicopter. He looked from the ridge and the tiny figures of Nyland and the dog to Kendall's face.

"You didn't figure he'd walk away. You figured the storm would work to your advantage, but remember all that survivalist literature in the trailer. He wants to beat us this way. He's hiking out and I'm going after him."

Kendall shook his head, said, "No, you're not. The forecast is for three or four inches of snow and it's already starting. It's supposed to blow out tomorrow, but are you telling me he's going to walk through a storm in the Desolation Wilderness?"

"He's got night-vision equipment. So do I."

"What good is that going to be in a storm?'

"Not very good, but the trails are there."

"Crossing rock when you can't see ten feet ahead of you?"

"He's still running ahead of the storm, and a lot of the trail won't be hard to follow."

Kendall's frustration came through now. He'd expected to trap Nyland here and he had all the people to do it.

"You forget about Vandemere already? He can pick you off as you climb toward him. He doesn't have anything to lose."

"It's going to be dark soon."

"You're not going. You've got some sort of death wish."

Something hardened in Marquez when he heard that, but he wanted to keep it going with Kendall a while longer. He looked up at the rock where the first snow had melted as it landed. The rock was dark and wet, and clouds were low over the lake.

"I'm not going to let you lose him."

Kendall's retort was immediate. "And what if you're wrong and he's just up there making a last desperate circle and plans to shoot it out with us. What if he's waiting up on those rocks for someone to follow?"

"He's been talking to Bobby by cell phone, right? You've monitored those calls, so you know he's got a phone. My guess is he has a plan and he's made the call that sets up his ride out when he finishes the hike. He knows he's only got so much time to get away and he's got to take advantage of the storm. He also knows this isn't easy country to hide in, no matter how many survivalist magazines you read. It's open high rock, lakes, pine and fir, and you can dodge for a while but not forever. But he also knows the thing to do is surprise you with how far he can move through a storm. Then have someone waiting on the other end."

"You give him way too much credit. You go in there and there'll be Search and Rescue people looking for you tomorrow morning. You'll get lost if you don't get killed."

"Tell you what, Kendall, this is something I know a little bit about."

Marquez showed the GPS tracking device they'd gotten from the FBI on an abalone poaching operation. It could track him individually. He gave the Kendall the phone number for the satellite unit and a number for Shauf, though Kendall hadn't asked for anything.

"You're not going."

Marquez walked away from him and when the SWAT commander followed, he had a better conversation with that officer, pointed at the ridge, told him where he'd climb up, where the trail went through.

"If I lose him, I'll be hiking out the Eagle Lake Trail."

The commander frowned; he was a patient man and tried to get his point of view across.

"The detective is right," he said. "This suspect is likely to be desperate and unlikely to have any plan to hike away. He may reach that ridge and lay down on a rock and wait."

"He's carrying a pack."

"Are you from this area, warden?" the SWAT commander asked. "I mean do you live locally?"

"No."

"I do, and we may be in a whiteout in a couple of hours."

"I understand that."

"Storm blows through tonight, and we'll get a copter up with infrared lookdown and fly right over the trail you're talking about."

"He knows that and you and I know the wind will still be blowing tomorrow morning and a copter may not work."

"I'm trying to talk you out of risking your life."

"I appreciate that."

They could still see Nyland, but barely. Marquez pulled his pack on, looked at the SWAT commander again.

"You know our warden was murdered."

"Of course."

"If one of your SWAT team got murdered, would you watch the suspect walk away?"

"You're not hearing me."

"I am hearing you." He put a hand on the commander's shoulder. "I'll see you on the other side."

45

A steady snowfall began as he climbed the loose rock
behind Barrett, boots slipping, the wind flapping his coat hood like
a loose awning. Snow drove sideways as he crossed the ridge, and
it wasn't too late to turn around. He could drop back down to Barrett Lake and leave it to helicopters and dogs to try to find Nyland
in the next few days. He lost time now, searching for the trail that
really wasn't visible on the rock. He resorted to the topo, worked
his way to where the trail should be, and talked with Shauf. The
GPS locator could tell her where he was, and she could direct him.

He found the trail again, pulled the night goggles on, adjusted
his gloves, no longer worried about Nyland fixing laser gun sights
on him, no risk of that with this snowfall and twilight. The trail
dipped and descended, left the rock and became trough-shaped
after dark, curved like a chute ahead with the new snow layering it.
He spotted a footprint and adrenaline kicked in, then more boot
prints nearly filled with snow and he knew Nyland was somewhere

up ahead. He passed a wooden sign, Red Peaks Trail, crouched behind a rock, used his flashlight to study the map, drank water, ate, and made a call to Shauf. With the locator she confirmed he was on the correct trail.

"Any sign of him?"

"Footprints. I'm taking it slow, not trying to catch him, just keep track of him."

He signed off with her and started again, hiking in heavier snow but less wind. He'd gauged the whole hike across and through Desolation as eight hours and had been up here a couple. His hands and feet were cold, though everything else was fine. Cheeks a little numb. He squatted and checked marks on the trail, risked the flashlight again, and the marks didn't read as footprints. An hour later he made another call to Shauf and huddled under a granite shelf trying to warm up, telling Shauf he'd lost the footprints but figured he had no choice but to continue hiking across toward Tahoe. He fired the gas stove, let it boil a cup of water in the shelter of a rock cleft, wrapped bare hands around the flame, cleaned the goggles, and stared out into the storm again. *Where are you?*

When he started again he stumbled, kicking rocks newly covered by snow, losing the trail, losing time finding it again, using Shauf and the satellites to locate himself. The wind kept working the cold in, and each mile came hard. Then not long after midnight the snow lessened and there were breaks in the clouds, ragged tears, starlight on the new snow and darkness again. It became easier to keep the goggles operable. As he hiked toward Velma Lakes he knew either he had a break in the storm or it was ending, and he checked with Shauf, who was monitoring air traffic weather. She told him that Doppler radar showed the worst was over, which heartened him, took some of the leadenness out of his legs. He figured the expenditure of adrenaline and the cold gnawing away at him accounted for the unusual tiredness. He cleaned the goggles again and saw the outline of terrain farther ahead, saw no sign of Nyland.

At 1:30 he ate more of his food, the almonds, another candy bar, a slug of water. He sloughed ahead through snow drifted six inches deep in the low sections of trail. Anyone walking ahead would leave tracks, and periodically he stopped, leaned on a rock, and studied the terrain behind. He switched the Gore-Tex hood for a cap because he didn't like the way the fabric affected his hearing, the constant rustling.

Then he heard a hound bay and looked for a place to hide, left the trail and found rocks. He heard the hound again and with the wind couldn't place the direction, then realized it was from behind and that Nyland could be following his tracks, not knowing who he was. He crossed the trail, stepped among red firs growing closely together, stepping on patches of needles the snow hadn't reached, using the needles as stepping-stones to avoid leaving tracks. He pulled his gun and wrapped his other hand around the small flashlight.

With his belly against a rock he lay and waited, then heard Nyland quieting his dog, the hound whining and snuffling, Nyland hesitating, stopping on the trail, still not quite to where the trail passed below Marquez's position. The dog had picked up a scent. Now he heard Nyland's boots sloughing through the snow and the dog running ahead. He waited for Nyland to pass by and then got ready to come over the rock and slide down behind Nyland onto the trail. *Do it. It's not going to get any easier.* He drew a deep breath and went, clicked the flashlight on as he came down on the trail.

"Don't move! I've got a gun on you, Nyland. Don't move!"

But Nyland went into motion, spinning, and then coming at Marquez. Marquez had time to shoot him but didn't pull the trigger, and Nyland tackled him. Marquez lost his gun as he went down and the hound ripped at his pant leg. Nyland was strong, fighting hard, and was trying to get a gun out. He managed to pull it out and then it discharged, missing both of them.

Marquez struggled to get the gun Nyland held, pinning the arm that held it while Nyland clubbed at Marquez's head with his other hand. But now Marquez gripped the gun and twisted. Nyland's trigger finger was trapped, and it made a dry snapping noise as bone broke. The gun fell into snow and Nyland grunted in pain, tried to retrieve the gun, and Marquez brought an elbow down on his face, crushing the lens of his goggles. The next blow shattered Nyland's nose.

"Stop moving and lay still," Marquez said, gasping for breath, forcing the words out as he got ready to hit him again. Nyland surged, and Marquez had to hit him hard one more time, this last with the butt of Nyland's gun. He handcuffed him, the hound barking inches from his face. He searched Nyland for weapons, took yet another gun off him and a cell phone, he recovered his own gun and rested, holding the gun and flashlight beam on Nyland, deciding as he caught his breath how to do this, hike him out or wait for morning and help.

Nyland bled from the nose. The broken finger pointed sideways, and Marquez moved the flashlight back to his face.

"You're going to hike out, so suck it up. Unlike Petroni you're alive."

"I didn't kill fucking Petroni."

"You're a good man, Nyland, just misunderstood. You're going to walk ahead of me, but don't get up until I tell you to."

He went through Nyland's pack before placing it in the trail where it could easily be found in the morning.

"I can't see," Nyland said as Marquez got him to his feet.

"I'll shine a light through your legs. If you fall, stand up and start walking again. If you run, I'll shoot you."

Marquez had tied the thin rope he'd found in Nyland's pack to one of Nyland's ankles, figured if Nyland ran he'd bring him down by jerking his leg out from under him and dragging him. Keeping Nyland twenty feet ahead, they started walking, the thin rope sliding along the snow behind, the hound sticking near Nyland. A mile into it Nyland started playing games, staggering, pretending to trip, shuffling his boots through the snow, exaggerating his difficulty walking. Marquez said nothing to any of it. They moved slowly, but they moved, and sometime after daylight Marquez knew they'd reached the Eagle Lake Trail. An hour in he had Nyland stop and kneel on the trail while he called Shauf.

"I've got him. I'm walking him out."

"Okay, got your position, I'll notify everybody."

He hung up with her and listened to Nyland spit blood and mucus. He gave him some water, sat on a rock nearby and listened to the rhythm on his breathing, decided Nyland was fine to keep walking. But before telling him to get to his feet again he tweaked him.

"Who killed Petroni?"

"I don't know."

"Bullshit. Was it Durham?"

"I don't know. I hardly see Durham. I haven't seen him in three weeks."

"Who milks the caged bears?"

"I don't know anything about caged bears."

"Sophie has turned on you, but battered women can be like that. She led the detectives to where you hid the rifle in the sales office, and now they've got a murder warrant. She's turning state's witness. You're going to be the fall guy for Durham and whoever else."

"I don't want to hear your shit. Walk me out."

"Where were you headed? Is Durham waiting up ahead? If I was him and you could testify against me, I might be waiting up ahead. Of course, with all the police, I don't know. But I sure wouldn't want you to get a chance to plea-bargain."

They started down the trail again and nothing was said for another hour. When they took the next rest Marquez could tell Nyland was getting ready to try something, and then he asked for his night goggles back.

"You're doing okay without them."

"I can't move my hand."

"I've been looking at numbers on your cell phone." Marquez had relayed a list of them via text messaging and the satellite phone to Shauf. "Which one is Durham's?"

Nyland ignored him, then a little while later repeated that he hadn't killed anybody and didn't know about any rifle. His boots slogged through the snow ahead of Marquez, his voice stronger, saying he didn't "put Petroni in the teddy bear suit," but he wished he'd seen him.

"Sophie says you killed Vandemere for money. Who wanted him dead?"

"She's a lying bitch."

"If you want to hit back at her, start talking to me. You know Kendall isn't going to listen to you."

"Fuck off."

Near first light Marquez holstered his gun, figured Nyland was hurt and cold, tired, and didn't have much run left in him. Nyland was sluggish, exhausted, not quite the mountain man he figured himself for. He started to complain more about the pain in his hand.

"I can't take it any longer," he said. "My fingers are gone."

Marquez had slid a sock over the bad hand to prevent frostbite. He told Nyland to lie down in the snow. Nyland dropped to his knees, went face forward on the trail, and Marquez knelt and looked at the hand. It was badly swollen around the wrist and the fingers were bloodless, white. There was another six miles to go, a lot of it rocky and the steep downhill past Eagle Lake. Nyland's coat was multilayer, waterproof, ripstop, and Marquez got an idea.

"All right, don't move." With a knife Marquez leaned over and right in the small of the back he cut through the coat. "I'm going to uncuff you and if you move I'll do whatever I have to."

Marquez freed his wrists and then bunched the coat up and clicked the empty handcuff through the hole he'd cut. That would keep Nyland's good hand behind his back as long as he had the coat on. He told Nyland to keep the free hand, the bad hand, in his coat pocket, then got him to his feet and made sure the coat was zipped up tight before working the knife into the zipper at chest level and ruining it, so the only way he could get the coat off was over his head.

"If you can take me with one hand behind your back, now is your chance. Stay twenty feet ahead and don't take your bad hand out of your pocket."

"I wasn't there," Nyland said.

"Wasn't where?"

"I haven't been in the barn since we moved the bears to a place in Nevada that I didn't even know about before. I wasn't there when Petroni got it."

"Who was?"

"I don't know."

"How long has Durham been farming bears?"

"Durham doesn't know shit. It's the other guy."

"What other guy?"

"I don't know his name, a dark-haired guy." Nyland spit blood in the snow. "Fuck, man, my nose."

"Durham has a partner?"

"I don't know what their deal is."

"Where does this other guy live?"

"Look, I didn't kill Petroni."

"You killed Vandemere. Sophie took Kendall to the rifle." Marquez could see he finally hit home. Nyland stared at him without speaking. "Why Vandemere?"

"I didn't kill anybody. It was probably him, the guy who set up the farms."

"What's his name?"

"I don't know his name."

"Then you're nowhere. Where in Nevada are these bears?"

"On a ranch outside Minden. Troy drove the rest out there while I was locked up."

"Sophie says you bragged about killing Vandemere."

"She's fucked up."

"I need the bear farmer's name."

"Hey, man, he's way fucking smarter than you are."

"He must be, he hired you. Let's go."

They shuffled through the snow another mile before Nyland answered. When he did his voice was different, empty.

"Petroni was out there."

"Where?"

"In a cage at the place in Nevada, in one of the empty cages. It wasn't anything to do with me and I didn't see him. I wouldn't do shit like that even to that asshole."

"Stop walking, face me and say that again."

The wind felt colder and seem to blow down his spine as he listened to Nyland. He shone the light on his face.

"Petroni was in a cage?"

"For a couple of days. That's what I heard from Troy."

"Troy saw him."

"I don't know if he saw him."

"Sophie?"

"I think she did."

Marquez got up close to him, and Nyland ducked his head like he was going to get hit. "She told you as you made bail?"

"Yeah."

Nyland was silent after that. Dawn came. The dark blue line of Lake Tahoe showed in the distance when they started down the steep canyon and passed Eagle Lake. Marquez checked in with Shauf. A half mile later as they started down a long open slope, Kendall and three deputies came out of the trees well down the grade.

"Want to tell me anything else before they get here?"

"Maybe I knew he was in a cage, but I didn't see him and I wasn't there when he got done. It was the freak that did him."

"Why do you call him a freak?"

"Because he wouldn't ever let me see him."

Marquez took a guess now. "The freak paid you to do Vandemere. Vandemere saw him one day and questioned what he was doing. After that the freak wanted him killed."

"You're fucking crazy."

"Am I?" Marquez pointed at Kendall and the deputies crossing a snowfield, their guns drawn and their voices starting to carry up. "They plan to lay it all on you and you know Kendall, he'll do it. He'll make it work. If you know anything more that can help you, you've got to tell me now. I'm looking for the bear farmer, and if you're telling anything like the truth you need him found as badly as I do."

Nyland didn't answered, stayed focused on the approaching men.

"Where's this ranch, what's it look like?" Marquez asked.

"It's got some metal buildings way out in a field. There's a little Chinese dude that lives out there all the time, but I've only been there once. I didn't shoot Vandemere. I've been bear baiting, that's all."

"Maybe they put you up to shooting Vandemere. Durham and the other guy, the bear farmer. You could get a much lesser sentence for that, but they've got you for that one. You wiped the rifle with solvent but not well enough. DNA is like dandruff, falls everywhere, nothing you can do about it." Marquez paused. "And you know Kendall. If he doesn't have the evidence, he'll make it. This guy has a name, you've heard a name."

"We just call him Bearman."

"Who knows his name?"

"Durham knows fucking everything."

The hound surged forward and Marquez grabbed his collar before he could charge the officers. There wouldn't be but another sixty seconds to talk.

"What road is this ranch in Minden on?"

"Old something road. I don't have anything to do with the freak's bear thing. I wouldn't do that to an animal."

The dog lunged, and Marquez lost his hold. When that happened, Nyland jumped off the side of the trail, pulling the rope out of Marquez's hand as Marquez struggled to get a hold of the dog. Nyland stumbled, ran, his strides long on the steep slope, sloughing through snow toward trees below.

"Freeze, Nyland, freeze," Kendall yelled.

Then came a warning shot, but Nyland made it down into trees and there was a lot of yelling as the county officers spread out and went after him. It wouldn't take long to catch him, and Marquez tried to slow a deputy hustling down.

"Hey, hold up, he's hurt, he's unarmed, he's not going to get far. We can talk him out."

The man continued past him, and Marquez turned and yelled, "Kendall, slow it down."

A deputy called out, "I see him. He's moving down the creek."

Trying to get to his ride, Marquez thought. *Still thinks he can get there and it'll be okay.* Marquez heard more yelling as he hurried down. He heard the shot, and Nyland was on his back, one leg folded under him, bleeding out from a neck wound when Marquez arrived. Blood pulsed onto the snow. A deputy moved to try to save him but there was no point. He died within a few minutes.

The deputy who'd shot him pointed at a dry branch about an inch thick and two feet long that Nyland had picked up as a weapon. He moved over to show Kendall what had happened, explaining, his voice rushed.

"I didn't have a choice."

From behind, Marquez heard Kendall's voice. "It's okay, just back away from the body, Pete. We all heard you order him to stop."

Marquez slowly turned to look at Kendall, who was still talking to the deputy.

"You did what you had to," Kendall said, and then to Marquez, "I hope you've got all the answers because I sure don't. Why'd you let him run?"

46

The stick Nyland had charged the deputy with had flown out of his hand when he fell. Nyland's broken finger was coated in blood, the violence done to him, the bruising around the nose, bright stain melting new snow near his neck, made him appear the victim rather than the perpetrator. Nearby a snow-covered tree shook loose last night's drop, and Marquez moved away from Kendall and the other officers and in among the saplings. He saw the deadfall where Nyland had snapped off a stick. Running, dodging trees, was it just final desperation or did he have a place he was supposed to get to?

Marquez made his way back to Kendall, kicked the snow from his shoes, drank more water, retrieved his pack, and looked at Nyland's crumpled body again. He felt little compassion, more regret and anger.

"What do I need to know before you go?" Kendall asked, trying to hold to his detective role.

"He claimed there's a bear farm in Nevada just over the border in Minden. He said Petroni was kept there, then he got moved to Johengen's."

"How did he know all this?"

"Sophie told him and he acted like Troy has been there also. Claimed he was in jail when it all went down, named Durham and referred to another man as Durham's partner, called him 'Bearman' and 'the freak.' He told me Bearman was in charge of everything, even Durham."

"Do you believe anything you heard?"

"I think there's a bear farm or farms somewhere, and Nevada just might fit. And, yeah, there might be a Bearman."

"Where's Petroni fit in?"

"He didn't say, but I'm wondering how Petroni got to Nevada. Maybe they lured him there or maybe he found it on his own."

That was the thought Marquez had been having, hiking out the last mile, that Petroni got there on his own, which meant he was trying to find it. He related Nyland's story, a ranch with metal buildings and a lot of acreage near Minden, an illegal Chinese immigrant doing the daily work of caring for the bears.

"My team will search for this place in Nevada," Marquez said. "We have an agreement with Nevada wildlife. We'll make the call this morning. Nyland didn't say it, but it sounded like the bear out at the end of the orchard got shot because it was sick and the other bears got moved to another farm in Nevada."

"Everything while he was in jail, right? He didn't have a part in any of it."

Marquez didn't answer that yet, continued explaining. "We're sure from scat and food that there were other bears at Johengen's recently. They moved them somewhere. It makes sense the bears would have a permanent caretaker, and a Chinese immigrant with experience bear farming would be the right person."

"If Nyland was so innocent, why'd he take off running?"

"He was hiking out to meet a ride."

"He told you that?"

"No."

"We checked everything out there, including your people."

"What about the lake?"

"There are whitecaps, no one is on the lake."

"My team picked up on a boat in Emerald Bay. Nyland may have thought he was going to cross the road, drop down to the water, and take a boat ride out of here. That may have been what he had in mind."

The deputy who shot Nyland approached, and Marquez took the moment to step away and call Shauf. She was parked at the Emerald Bay Overlook. He heard emotion choking her voice and for a moment was afraid something had happened to one of the SOU.

"I just talked to my sister," she said. "She's turned down the option of more extensive chemo. She wants to talk about what kind of aunt I'll be to her children."

Her voice broke off, and Marquez looked back at Kendall and the assemblage of officers with their brightly lettered coats, talking about whatever. Waiting on the coroner. Two officers on horseback were riding up to retrieve Nyland's pack, and Marquez watched the horses climb into the trees. He heard Shauf sob and looked at Kendall and the deputy who'd shot Nyland. They were the only ones still focused on what had happened here.

"You'll be the best aunt there ever was," he said. He waited for her to catch herself, added, "I'm on my way out. Talking with Kendall about the boat right now."

"It's a Colbalt with blue trim." She drew a breath. "After sunrise there were a couple of boats that came into Emerald Bay and we figured them for photographer types trying to get a picture of the bay with the first snow on the mountains. But there was also a lone guy in a Colbalt who circled the island, then sat along the shore for a while. He stayed on this side in the shadow so we could never really get a good look at him. When the patrol units showed up he moved farther back and then took off back out the channel. We got the CF numbers and it's registered to an Ed Schultz who lives in Palo Alto. We're trying to get a hold of him."

"Where's the boat at?"

"Near Zephyr Cove, starting to work its way up the east shore, and it's rough out there, rougher still on the east shore."

"See you soon." He didn't hang up with her yet. "Carol, this isn't the same but I've got to say this to you. I had a wife I was so in love with once that after she was killed I didn't think I'd ever get over it. But what I've learned is that as long as you have memories, she's going to be with you forever." Part of that is true, he thought.

Kendall was coaching the deputy to remember Nyland charged him with a stick that could crush his skull. He broke from that and turned toward Marquez.

"I'm going to need a formal statement from you. A couple hours with you this afternoon."

"I'll call you."

Kendall nodded and as Marquez started to leave, started walking with him, leaving the deputy. Marquez knew what was coming. He stopped and watched Kendall gesture back toward the stick Nyland had brandished.

"The sheriff is an old pacifist. He'll want to know there was no other way with Nyland, so he may want to talk to you. But you saw it."

"I didn't see it, I heard the shot."

"You must have heard the deputy order him to stop."

"I heard Nyland yell."

"You didn't hear our deputy order him to stop?"

"No."

"All right, then, answer this for me," and Kendall pulled his hand back. "Why wasn't he handcuffed?"

"One wrist was clipped to his coat. I had him cuffed for most of the hike out, but his hand with the broken index finger had swollen so much I felt I had to take the cuff off that wrist so he'd have circulation and better balance for the steeper parts. His hand might have frozen."

"So you devised this deal where he was cuffed to his coat."

"That's right."

"With his hand hidden behind his back, the deputy thought he might have a rock or a knife. We didn't know you'd cuffed him."

"Did anybody hear me yelling while Nyland was running?"

"I heard you, but they were down here trying to find him."

They looked at each other, and Marquez knew there hadn't been much warning given. His guess was the deputy had shot him as soon as Nyland lifted the stick, and yet, what Kendall said about the hand hidden behind his back carried weight.

It didn't take long to hike out, and Shauf picked him up in the parking lot. He ate a ham sandwich, an apple, and drank coffee that Shauf had in a stainless Thermos. He felt better almost immediately and wished he could comfort Shauf more about her sister, but she seemed to want to focus on what was at hand.

Lake Tahoe is twenty-one miles long, twelve wide, with the state line separating California and Nevada running through the middle. If the boat worked its way very far up the east shore, Marquez knew it would be harder to track where the road climbed away from the shoreline. They could call for help and get a patrol boat out, but he was reluctant to call unless they had more to go on, and so far, the Colbalt pilot was just a guy who'd motored into Emerald Bay and was dogging through the waves to wherever he was headed back to. Then Alvarez called and said they'd gotten through to the boat owner, Schultz, a doctor in Atherton. Marquez shifted the coffee cup and listened.

"They have a condo they rent in Richardson Bay. It's leased right now to a man named Ben Karin. He's got permission to use the boat because he's thinking of buying it. Schultz bought a new one."

"This Karin leases their condo in Richardson Bay and docks the boat there?"

"That's right, and there's no boathouse. They pull it out in the winter and park it in a garage at the condo. It's one of those condo developments set up for boat owners. You know, with the big garage and heated just enough to keep things from freezing. Karin is a nature photographer doing a calendar on Lake Tahoe."

"So he's probably legit."

"Could easily be," Alvarez acknowledged. "But he's the one who caught our eye this morning. If he was there to get a good photo of the first snow on the mountains, seems like where he was didn't have that angle. "

Richardson Bay wasn't far south of there and with the lake as rough as it was, Karin wasn't out for a pleasure ride. But then, maybe he was testing the boat to see how it handled rougher water. Marquez turned to Shauf, asking Alvarez to hang on because Shauf had Roberts on the line.

"She's got him in sight still and says he's still getting pounded," Shauf said.

"He's going somewhere," Marquez said, and Alvarez told him now that the Schultzes had called the realtor who handles the lease. She was going to call back in a few minutes.

Half an hour later they met the realtor, a middle-aged woman in a baby blue parka and bright red lipstick, at the condo complex in Richardson Bay.

"I have another appointment soon," she said. "What's this all about anyway?"

"We don't know yet," Marquez said. "How well do you know the tenant?"

She pointed out the condo, a corner unit up a flight of stairs, and when they asked about boat storage, she pointed at the high garage doors. She'd done the original lease but hadn't seen Ben Karin in four months. She checked her watch again.

"Shall we go up and knock?" she asked, after no one answered the phone. "I have the owner's permission to go in."

"Hold for just a second," Marquez said. "We want to show you some photos."

Alvarez slowly flipped through six photos, including Durham's face, and she fingered Chief Bell, said he looks most like him only with very black hair.

Marquez touched Bell's photo and said, "We'd like to lock him up, but he's not the guy we're looking for today."

"I admit I've only seen him from a distance. Oh, well, this man's is too old anyway. Mr. Karin has a different build. He's bigger in the shoulders. He wrote on his application he was thirty years old, but we did everything by mail and he prepaid for a year." She added, "There's maid service that comes in once a week."

Shauf took a call from Roberts as Marquez went upstairs with the realtor. She knocked twice, unlocked the door, and called for Karin. Marquez followed her in and didn't see any personal belongings. While the realtor was talking he started looking around and in the bathroom found a wastebasket and in it wadded bloody bandages. He unfolded those, saw the quantity of blood, then flipped his phone open and called Roberts, told her to stick with him no matter what and they'd call for all the help they could get.

Marquez put the call out to all the locals and reached Kendall, who was close by on his way back to South Lake. Kendall drove up as they were trying to figure out how to get the garage door open. The realtor thought she had a key for the side door, but complained about it not being keyed the same as the main door, about people subletting their garage spaces when they weren't supposed to. She went to her car to get an extra set of keys.

Durham had staged out of here, Marquez thought. From here it was easy to drive over Echo Summit and down to the Placerville area. He had run the buys they'd done at the lake from here.

"Okay, I have it," the realtor said. "But now I'm late for my appointment."

When the garage door rose they were looking at Sophie's Ford pickup. No one said anything until Kendall muttered, "I'll be damned." Marquez walked in first and saw the truck was locked. Then a woman came out of a nearby condo and told Alvarez that the pickup had arrived a couple of hours ago with a dark-haired young woman driving, and that she'd left in another truck, a green one with a camper shell. She didn't know the make, but it was definitely a "snow car," a four-wheel drive.

"When did you see her last?" Marquez asked Kendall.

"Late yesterday afternoon. We had her with us to try to talk to Nyland."

Marquez looked inside the truck and then felt the hood. It was still warm. Judging from the cold in the garage it hadn't been a couple of hours, more like an hour, he thought. Then he put it together.

"She's Durham's ride. He's taking the boat somewhere, she's going to pick him up. He was supposed to get Nyland at Emerald Bay, and she would have picked up both of them."

"All right, I'm going to tell you all some things you need to know. Yesterday, Sophie gave me everything else we need to charge Nyland. We had someone from the DA's office there to assure her we'd work out a deal with her. What she explained is that she's been scared to come forward, but Nyland bragged to her he'd killed Petroni and sewn him into a bear skin. He told her all about it and that's when she called him stupid and he beat her. Nyland said he'd stabbed Petroni once for every time the warden had fucked with him. Sophie was shaking and crying and talking about the things he'd done to her, and now her truck is here."

Kendall turned to Marquez, a look of open surprise on his face. "I don't get it. On top of that, we had surveillance on her. She must have slipped away."

"Did Nyland kill Petroni?"

"Are you going to tell me you believe Nyland's story?"

"I'm asking you how reliable Sophie is. You wanted a confession from her that she knew how Vandemere got killed and you got it. You cut your deal with her and got your star witness, but now she's screwing everything up by fingering Nyland for Stella and Petroni as well. She's got answers for everything."

"How do you know about Stella Petroni?"

"I'm making a guess."

"Well, you're right. We recovered bloody clothes and boots that belonged to Petroni. They were there with the rifle in the old sales office. Nyland hadn't decided what to do with them yet."

"Nyland or somebody else."

Kendall nodded and Marquez saw he understood. "Sophie told us she took them from the place she and Petroni were house-sitting. She gave the clothes to Nyland. It was all part of a plan to frame Petroni."

"A plan like that is over Nyland's head, but I don't have to tell you that."

"She says Nyland wore those clothes to kill Stella. He told her about it later. He thought she'd enjoy hearing how he stomped her face because Stella had come into the Creekview earlier this summer and insulted Sophie, called her a whore."

"I'd bet he got paid to kill her, and I'll bet he got money to kill Vandemere."

"Then why is she here today?"

"With her I think it's hard to know, but if Durham is behind this, he might have good reasons to get rid of Nyland. Rescue him, then lose him out on the lake, put a bullet in him and push him overboard. She might be here for that."

"That's just more speculation."

"I know."

Kendall moved toward his car and the radio there. She had to be across the lake. The truck she was driving couldn't be that hard to find. But there was also something off here that the realtor had revealed. Ben Karin was likely another alias for Durham, yet the realtor was sure his build was different and his hair darker. He'd waved to her from the boat the day she'd come down to meet him. He'd worn sunglasses and talked to her from his cell phone, but he hadn't motored into shore despite assuring her he wanted to say hello. She'd said that it had hurt her feelings, which made her all the more likely to remember him.

Shauf touched his arm, "Ready?" Marquez glanced over at Kendall, saw his car was already rolling, and looked back at Shauf. "The realtor," he said. "She didn't describe Durham."

"But it's Durham in the boat. Melinda is certain."

"Who did it sound like the realtor was describing?"

"It was a pretty sketchy description. She never saw his face without sunglasses and it sounded like she was looking at his body. Besides, he was on a boat a hundred yards from her. How much could she have seen?"

"Who came to mind?"

"I don't know, didn't really match with anybody."

"But who did you think of?"

"You'll laugh."

"Try me."

"Ungar."

"It's him—we've got to get a call off to Nevada Wildlife."

"Then let's do it from the van."

47

"I've lost visual," Roberts said. "He moved in closer to the shoreline and I'm up here on this road." Her tone was plaintive. "Where's the plane? Where's the patrol boat?"

The patrol boat was on its way from the north shore. A spotter plane had just lifted off from Truckee Airport and would fly over the lake within the next few minutes. Police were on the alert all the way around the lake. Everyone who could be notified had been. Marquez focused binoculars on the mountains behind the north shore. He saw a black shape cross low and fast above them and relayed it onto Roberts.

"I see the spotter plane."

He watched it bank toward the lake, the outline of its wings sharper. He kept the binoculars up and heard Shauf working the radio, then the chatter of the pilot filled the van. Now Roberts directed the pilot and they heard his terse, "Lone male at the wheel of a boat running toward Glenbrook. Is that your man?"

Roberts's voice crackled on again. "Boat should be a Colbalt with blue trim."

"I'm taking it down lower," the pilot responded.

The patrol boat checked in. They had the boat in view and expected to intercept it at Glenbrook. Alvarez communicated with the Nevada Highway Patrol, who dropped toward Glenbrook. Marquez watched the plane come low across the water. He lowered the binos and turned to Alvarez.

"Is Nevada clear that her truck should be there and that this is an armed situation?"

"Very clear."

In the van they raced toward Glenbrook and the pilot confirmed blue trim, wasn't sure about the make of the boat, wasn't a boater, but definitely it was a lone male who'd reacted hard as the plane came in low. But who wouldn't, Marquez thought, with a plane diving on you.

"Can they catch him before he docks?" Marquez asked.

Before that was answered a Nevada highway officer reported a woman in a Chevy Blazer backing down the boat ramp. Alvarez glanced at Marquez, answered the previous question, saying, "They say it's going to be close."

There was too much radio chatter and back-and-forth to ask for a description of the woman. The patrol boat closed in and used a bullhorn. The patrol reported that the man had stopped short of the dock as ordered and they were boarding.

"All right," Alvarez said, and Marquez used his cell to try to reach Roberts.

It turned out the only thing the startled man would admit to was being late pulling his boat from the water. His blonde-haired wife was out of the Blazer now, and Marquez heard enough from the radio to know it was a fiasco.

"Wrong man," Roberts said, as he got through to her. "He must have put in somewhere farther north. I'm just getting to

Glenbrook. Do you want me to stay and deal with this or look for him north of here?"

"Keep searching. We'll ask the patrol boat to go up the coast and get Nevada to redirect the patrol."

But no agency likes a wild goose chase, in particular one based on loose information to begin with, and Marquez took over trying to communicate that they still needed help and that every minute mattered. He got the patrol boat to start north hugging the coast as best they could, though it meant skirting large shallow areas and working with binoculars, searching for a remote place he might have put in. Talk of the boat's capsizing started. They looked for a hull and reported waves of four feet, and on land the search widened for the green Chevy pickup with the camper shell. Reno police went alert, watched the road over Mount Rose.

About an hour later the boat was found beached between rocks along a remote stretch, partially covered with a camouflage tarp the wind was removing. In Shauf's van they drove toward it, and Marquez closed his eyes momentarily. He listened as the patrol reported their problem.

"We can't put in here, and we don't want to anchor too close to shore. Too many rocks."

GPS coordinates got relayed, and Shauf found a place on the road shoulder to park the van along the road above the lake. On the other side of the guardrail was forest dropping steeply toward the lake. The boat was down there. Roberts pulled up and then Cairo behind her.

"You're done hiking, Lieutenant," Cairo said. "We'll go down and check it out."

"He may be hiding in the woods," Marquez said. "Could be he panicked when he saw the plane and beached short of where he was supposed to meet her."

It was a different sort of predicament. Three of the team went down, Marquez leading, and they didn't find anything in the boat.

The hull had been damaged when the boat beached, and it wasn't going to be simple to extricate. They hiked back up and found what might be his tracks as he climbed toward the highway and his ride. Roberts started trying to line up a dog team. Nothing had been removed from the condo in Richardson Bay yet, but a piece of the bloody bandages could be taken from there to scent the dogs. One of the team would have to make a run over there, the realtor contacted and found, this stretch of highway secured, and yet, Marquez doubted they'd find anything.

Still, with the differing police agencies on the lookout for the pickup, there was little else to do. Marquez left Roberts in charge of the area search, and with Shauf and Cairo he conducted a sweep of the lake towns on the off chance they'd spot the pickup and Sophie. He talked to Kendall, who'd followed things as far as Glenbrook and since returned to his sheriff's office.

"Where are you taking it now?" Kendall asked.

"We'll start searching for this other bear farm."

"Are you going out there today?"

"We're on our way there now."

"It'll be dark in a couple of hours and more than likely, Nyland lied to you. This is what murder suspects do. They concoct fanciful stories that explain it all away."

"We saw other tracks in the barn. You took castings, what have you done with those?"

"Nothing yet."

"A truck big enough to move the bear cages was probably something like a Ryder rental."

"All right, we'll check the rentals. We'll run the list of names by them."

"What do you think about the idea Petroni's car was brought back to Johengen's in the same rented truck as a way to keep it from being spotted on the road?"

"Petroni in the backseat already dead?"

"Yeah."

Kendall grunted, didn't really respond.

"Either way, there were other bears," Marquez said. "One got shot and was probably sick, the others got moved. I'm going to take another run out to Johengen's tomorrow and look for what we missed."

"You were going to come in this afternoon and sit down with me."

"It'll have to wait."

Later, Marquez talked to Katherine from his truck cab, sitting outside a restaurant where Shauf and Alvarez waited inside. The initial search in Minden had turned up no obvious buildings, and they'd driven back to Placerville after dark. Roberts had reported that the dogs keyed on the scent of a piece of bloody bandage. Almost certainly, whoever's blood that was had been in the boat and hiked up to the road. The trail had ended there, and the dog handler eventually got nervous about his bloodhounds searching along the edge of the highway. They'd held traffic for a while, then concluded the man driving the boat had gotten picked up along the road shoulder.

"And now you think it's a different man?" Katherine asked.

"The informant that started us on this case."

"You're kidding."

"No, and we've got the same problem with our house. You and Maria are going to need to stay in the city."

"Then we're going to rent a hotel room and start using the construction money."

There was a mixed message in that, one he'd have to think about. When he hung up a wave of depression mixed with exhaustion swept over him. Ungar was Nyland's Bearman, but where was he? San Francisco police had gone to his apartment an hour ago and he wasn't there, and not only that, they said there weren't any computers anywhere inside, so he had to be moving one step ahead of them again. Marquez went in and ate with Shauf and Alvarez, registered Shauf's sober face and Alvarez's questioning look as he told them he wanted to make another search of the barn out at Johengen's before leaving for Nevada tomorrow morning.

Alvarez sopped chicken gravy with a piece of bread and kept his eyes on his plate. His silence told Marquez he thought they were just spinning their wheels going back to Johengen's. Marquez knew Shauf and Alvarez thought the right thing to do tomorrow was devote everything to searching for the Minden ranch. Alvarez's lean face betrayed another question, this one about Marquez's judgment.

"Tell you what, I'll go out there early alone and then we'll go over to Nevada midmorning," Marquez said.

48

Well before first light Marquez drove out Howell Road. A light rain was falling and the road ahead dark. At Johengen's the gate was open, but likely it was just someone with the county who'd forgotten to lock it. The dirt driveway was slick, and his headlights caught fluttering pieces of crime tape as he came around the bend. He saw where the backhoe operator had refilled the trench, soil humped and looking like a long grave. With the key Kendall had given him he unlocked the barn.

Inside, it felt another ten degrees colder, and the cold reached him. His body was still bone-tired from the hike and stiff from wrestling with Nyland. He located the light switch at the far end and lit the string of bulbs hanging from the rafters. A bat squeaked overhead and then the only sounds were the rain and wind, the big door creaking as the stronger gusts moved it. It was dank, the bear smell still strong. The barn had been cleared except for cages yet to be hauled away by Fish and Game. The stuffed and mounted bears, the contents of the freezer, were gone, the freezer no longer running. The drying station was gone, even the racks of antlers that had been on the walls. What was left were old rusted garden tools and the carcass of an ancient pickup sitting on jacks in a dark corner.

He stood a few minutes looking at the cages, then turned his attention to the tire tracks. He studied the whitened areas where plaster castings had been taken. Kendall was checking out the rental agencies and trying to come up with a tire match, and Marquez had his team working on that now as well. He followed tire tracks toward the cages, saw where the DFG truck that picked up the bear had parked. Then, beyond that point he spotted a faint divot in the earth that he guessed was where one skid had rested as the Honda was rolled off and out into the yard after Petroni's body had been dealt with. *That's when you loaded the cages. That's when you moved the bears to Nevada or wherever you moved them, and that's how Petroni's car got here with him in it.*

It would have taken at least two people and a way to winch the cages up into the truck. The truck was probably rented near where the other farm was. As it fell together he contemplated calling Kendall, then decided to think it over more first. He called Shauf and suggested she and Alvarez get some breakfast and he'd check one more thing in the barn, then they'd drive tandem over the mountains and into Nevada.

"Find anything?" she asked.

"Looking at the tire tracks. I'm going to check one more thing before leaving."

"What else are you going to do out there?"

"I had an idea last night that no one checked the rafters. There's a ladder in the barn. It won't take me long." Before she could ask, he added, "Because of the hunting shack."

There was a long wooden ladder, its round rungs worn smooth by years of boots. The ladder had two metal hooks that slipped over the bottom chord of the roof trusses. He slid the ladder along the barn wall, climbed up the sixteen feet, and used his flashlight, scanning the top plate where the roof trusses rested. It wouldn't take another fifteen minutes to cover the perimeter of the barn, and then they'd be on their way to Nevada.

A stronger gust blew rain in through the doors, and the big door swung shut with a loud noise. So far he'd found only cobwebs and bat guano, but now, as he climbed the ladder in the area above the empty cages, he shone the light on what looked like a rag or a towel. He had to climb down again and move the ladder before he was close enough to see it well. The towel was blood-stained. He climbed down and retrieved latex gloves from his truck. Peeling one corner of the towel, he saw a knife hilt and part of a bloody blade, then let the cloth fall and stood frozen on the ladder. Below were the bear cages, the dark floor of the barn, above the sound of the rain on the roof. In the pocket of his coat his cell rang as he tried to imagine the mind that put this here.

He came down off the ladder and lowered it, leaving the towel and knife up there. He had to throw his shoulder into the barn door to get it open. He called Shauf from the truck after he'd relocked the barn and was on the road.

"They've got her," she said. "I just called you. Or they've almost got her. She's in the Crystal Basin with a string of police cars behind her, doesn't seem to be trying to get away, doing kind of an OJ thing, driving slowly with the police behind her."

"Alone?"

"No, there's a man in the seat next to her."

Going home, he thought. *Going to where she'd always sought refuge.* He stayed on the line with Shauf, telling her about the knife as he turned onto the highway and pushed his speed past eighty, heading to the Crystal Basin. By the time he got there Sophie was trapped by police vehicles on a dirt road outside Yellowjacket

Camp. Durham had been identified as the passenger and was possibly wounded. He wasn't moving. Neither had responded to orders to get out of the truck, and a debate was underway about what to do next.

Marquez argued his way toward the front where Kendall was crouched down behind a police door. A marksman had moved into a position where he could shoot either Sophie or Durham, but he had just reported that Durham was either unconscious or dead. Kendall talked to Marquez with his eyes still on the pickup.

"She's armed. She showed us a handgun. Durham may be dead. They're saying it looks like his head is taped to the headrest."

"She killed him?"

"That's my guess."

Sophie sat straight-backed in the pickup. There was another bullhorn attempt to reach her, and her head didn't move.

"Anybody try walking up?" Marquez asked.

"She held a gun out the window and fired into the woods. She almost got herself shot."

"I've been out at Johengen's this morning. I was thinking about Nyland's hunting shack last night, the watch and ring. There's a ladder in the barn, and I worked along each wall checking the top of the wall between each truss. I found a bloodstained towel with a knife in it. It's out there sitting on top of the wall above the bear cages." Now Kendall took his eyes from the truck and looked at Marquez. "I left it and drove here from the barn."

"On the wall above the cages?"

"Yeah, and I also found a mark that could be one of the truck skids they rolled the Honda down." He didn't add that he thought they loaded the bear cages at the same time. *Let Kendall come to that on his own.* "How long has she been sitting there?"

"Forty minutes. Her father's on the way."

"Whose idea was that?"

"He volunteered and no one had a better one. Someone moni-toring the police band got a hold of him."

He listened as Kendall called for a county unit to block off and guard the entrance to Johengen's. Ten minutes, a bullhorn warned her, they were going to shoot her tires out and she still had time to get away from the truck. She didn't move, and a marksman shot her rear tires out. The pickup sagged, then Sophie's door swung open and she got out holding a rifle that must have been behind the passenger seat. She kept the barrel pointed at the road, though ordered by bullhorn to drop the weapon. Officers scrambled for better cover, but she didn't move.

"I'll go out there," Marquez said, because she stood paralyzed as though guarding the road from intruders. "Troy's the wrong guy, keep him back."

"You're a fucking nut," Kendall said and picked up a bullhorn. "This is Detective Kendall, Sophie. I understand your situation and want to help you. But you need to put the rifle down."

Instead, the rifle barrel rose slightly and Sophie stared in his direction. Officers near Marquez sighted on her, fingers on triggers.

"Do not lift the rifle any farther," Kendall ordered, and clicking the bullhorn off said, "Oh, fuck."

But it wasn't Kendall she was looking at. Troy was coming up from behind them. He passed Marquez, muttering, "Goddamn her," and with his booted pigeon-toed steps strode away from the deputy escorting him and toward her as though nothing could happen. "She's mine, I'll take care of it," was all he said and stopped only when she ordered him to a second time. The steel and anger in her voice carried to where they were, and Marquez heard weapons adjusted again.

Troy raised a hand perhaps to try to convince or reassure her, and maybe she saw the hand that had struck her as a child or maybe she knew the bullhorn promises were lies. Her gun rose abruptly and Marquez stood and yelled across the police line, "Don't shoot her." He yelled to Sophie, "Wait," and stepped out in front of the cruiser onto the road. He raised his hands shoulder high to show Sophie and turned back at the police vehicles and lights, calling, "Don't shoot her."

Her eyes were on Marquez, watching his slow advance toward where Troy stood frozen. "Sophie," Marquez said. "It won't make anything better. It won't change anything."

He thought he heard her say, "It's already over." Her eyes returned to Troy, and Marquez heard her say, "I should kill you, you bastard."

"Put the goddamn gun down," Troy said.

"Shut up!"

Her yell carried down through the police lines, the fierce anger in it unmistakable. Marquez saw it happening but before he could reach her she kicked the shoe off of one foot, dropped the rifle stock on the other foot, and put her mouth over the barrel. With the shoeless toe she found the trigger.

Blood and brain blew across the wet road.

49

When she crumpled Marquez went to her, but Troy, for reasons only he could explain, spat on the ground near his feet and walked back toward the police cruisers. A piece of skull with hair attached lay in the mud ten feet away, and Marquez gripped the arm of a deputy who simply didn't see it and almost stepped on it in the hurry to get to the truck. Marquez moved back to Sophie, knelt near her, curiously unsure of himself, stunned by what she'd done. He heard Kendall backing people off and asking him to get away from her body.

Marquez backed away, walked to the truck where Hawse and several others were cutting the duct tape wrapped around Durham's neck and the headrest. Someone called out "He's alive. We've got a pulse," and paramedics rushed forward. Marquez watched them extract him. He'd been gutshot. His shirt, coat, and pants were soaked with blood, a lot of it already dry and black.

Turning back to Sophie's body, he saw Kendall leaning over, pulling a handgun from her waist. He removed the clip, bagged the gun, and looked at Marquez. "Insane. All of this is insane. You tell me why she did that."

Because she couldn't face what came next. Because of the things she'd done and what she'd become, what there was no returning from. Because she'd probably showed Nyland where Vandemere was doing his research and may have been there when he was shot.

"I want to get them to check Durham's arms for wounds," Marquez said.

"He's just barely hanging on," Kendall said. "You know that's Vandemere's truck she's driving. They painted it, put different plates on it."

Marquez nodded. He'd figured it out a few minutes ago. He walked over to one of the paramedics, a husky bald man, leaned near him to say, "There may be another bullet wound on one of his arms."

Durham wore an expensive-looking down parka, North Face logo on it. The paramedics slit each arm down the inseam, cut his shirt off. There weren't any wounds on his arms, only the one shot to his lower abdomen.

One of them glanced up at Marquez, said, "You owe him a coat."

"Will he need it?"

They were pumping fluid into him, Durham ghostly, his face slack. Hard to believe he'd make it. Marquez watched as they started moving him, looked in the truck again, and then straightened as it started to rain. Sophie's body was getting photographed. Her hair glistened.

"She must have shot him before taping his head," Kendall said.

"He's got a good-sized lump on his temple."

"Doesn't matter, he isn't going to make it." Marquez saw Troy starting to drift back, heard Kendall mutter, "He looks like he knows something."

"Are you going to try to do anything out here with the truck?" Marquez asked.

"Not with the rain. We'll close it up and tow it in." Kendall nodded toward Sophie and asked, "Did you know that was coming?"

"No, but I have a sense of what she was missing inside."

"I'll tell you what Durham is missing inside, a couple of quarts of blood."

They both turned as Troy argued with a deputy, Troy trying to get through.

"You'll have to wait to see her, Mr. Broussard."

"I don't care about seeing her. I want to talk to him."

He'd looked their direction so Kendall walked over, said, "What is it?"

"Not you. Him."

Marquez walked over, and Troy spoke as though he'd rehearsed what he had to say.

"I don't care much for you or any of you people, but I know what you're after and I'll lead you out there. God didn't put bear on earth to be in cages."

"Where is it you're going to lead me?"

"Nevada."

"Give me an address."

Marquez wanted to phone ahead. He wanted to secure the area around the ranch, enlist the help of anybody they could get in Nevada.

"I know where it is, that's all."

Marquez and the team followed Troy's old truck down a long dry desert road outside Minden, Nevada. Well short of the ranch, Troy pulled over and parked. His truck canted steeply, two wheels in a dusty ditch. He lowered his window but didn't get out.

"Those buildings up ahead. He's there. That's his car and you'd better be damn careful."

"What's your role here, Troy?"

"If I had any part of it, would I bring you out here? Let's just say he's asked me to, but the law says I can't trap or hunt."

Marquez looked at him, thinking, *You did anyway, didn't you.* He looked out across the sage and tumbleweed and knew they'd never nail Troy for it. If there was any chance of that, Troy wouldn't have led them out here, and the question now was why had he. *Must see Bearman as a competitor or has some other grudge against him.*

From here it was roughly three-quarters of a mile to the house. He saw the car Troy meant but couldn't tell the make from here, amazing that Troy could. The nose of a car was visible around the back of the main building.

"The boy you killed up in the mountains brought me out here."

"Nyland?"

"Yes."

Funny, Nyland had said the opposite, but it could wait. Marquez glanced at Troy again, wondering if the old man was hoping they'd get killed approaching the buildings.

"Are there bears in those Quonset huts?"

"There are. Those aluminum buildings have bear in cages all lined up. I figure you and I are even now."

"Do you feel anything for her?"

"I lost my little girl a long time ago."

"And around town they say you know how you did it."

"Sophie was a born liar, no different than her mother."

Marquez watched him drive away and four Nevada police approach, dust roostering up behind them. He put on a flak jacket and briefed the Nevada officers on what he thought they were going to find. Another attempt was made to contact the ranch by phone

KIRK RUSSELL

and after that failed, someone spotted a man standing out in front of the house.

"That's Ungar," Marquez said, after lifting binoculars. "That's who we're looking for and he sees us." Ungar didn't move, stood frozen facing their direction. "He's not sure what to do now. I think we can drive down there."

Marquez rode in the lead vehicle. The Nevada officers took over as they parked near Ungar, asking Ungar if he was armed and Ungar shaking his head no, turning around, raising his arms so they could check him.

"I solved it for you," Ungar said as Marquez walked up.

"What did you solve?"

"What you're looking for is in those aluminum Quonset huts. My cousin called, gave this address, and I decided to check it out before calling you. There are twenty bears in there. I counted. There's a little Chinese man in feeding them. He doesn't speak a word of English. I was just about to drive somewhere my phone will work and call you. How'd you find this place?"

Marquez let Ungar walk with him to the Quonset huts. A crowd of officers flanked them, two Nevada wildlife officers close behind Ungar. Sunlight reflected brightly off metal roofs ahead, and yet, the day was cold, the rain over the mountains to the west approaching, wind blowing hard. He watched Ungar's black hair whip across his forehead, no cap this afternoon, no sunglasses, a shiny black leather coat. As they reached the first hut a small man in black baggy pants, black shirt, sandals, showed briefly at the door before retreating.

"What's his name?" Marquez asked Ungar.

"Han."

Marquez swung the door open, called to Han. He was maybe seventy, didn't seem to speak any English, spoke rapid Cantonese that Ungar responded to.

"I barely know any Chinese," Ungar said. "But I told him not to move, that you're the police."

"Don't say anything else to him."

Marquez left him with the state troopers and Nevada Wildlife, left him explaining how he'd helped California Fish and Game solve this case.

Marquez walked through the thick bear smells. It was so different from the cold sage-laden wind outside. The metal walls and roof creaked in the wind as he counted. Twenty, same as Ungar had claimed. Heavy stainless cages, thick, the same water trough system, same cages as Johengen's. He looked at each bear, the catheters, eyes staring at him, then walked back.

"Troy Broussard trap the young bears?" he asked Ungar, taking in his mocking expression, not getting any answer, just a blank face.

Ungar grinned, said, "Do you want to play this game again?"

Ungar turned and as an aside explained to one of the Nevada wildlife officers that he'd been under suspicion ever since coming forward to help.

"But why would I have anything to do with undercover wildlife officers if I was engaged in something like this."

To keep track of us, Marquez thought, *and because you're driven by hate so strong you have trouble controlling it. You found a like spirit in Durham. U.S. Fish and Wildlife shut Durham down in Michigan, and somehow you two found each other out here. Thing is, Durham didn't have quite your ambition and he also had another successful business life.*

"Do you know Joe Durham?" Marquez asked.

"No."

The Nevada wildlife officers began to question him. They'd take him in, start there. Before leaving here they'd ask him to remove his coat, check his arms for a wound. He'd have to provide the cousin's name, whereabouts.

Cairo and Roberts went back for camcorders, notebooks, what they needed to start documenting. The first thing was to find a legitimate way to hold Ungar more than overnight. Marquez listened to the wildlife officers start with Ungar again, their patience infinitely greater than his own, and he walked out and down to the second Quonset hut. No bears were inside, but the cages were set up, the trough, the systems in place. He looked around outside again, the desert, neighbors far away, plenty of room. When he walked back into the first building he heard one of the Nevada officers liken the Quonset hut to a hog farm, the most apt description yet.

After everything had been recorded, but before the bears were moved, Marquez walked the cages alone, looking at each bear again, counting the yearlings, eight of them. He walked farther into the hut, empty cages stacked in a dark corner, the smell of bear excrement thick down here, despite the roof fans whirring overhead. Then he saw what he'd missed, a cage with a crumpled blanket, what looked like a pet bowl with dried spaghetti strands. He smelled urine, heard Nyland talking in his head, knew it was true.

He brought the wildlife officers down. They called a detective, handed the phone to Marquez, and he related what Nyland had told him and gave the detective Kendall's phone number, said he'd wait here for him.

The SOU began documenting, and Marquez went to Ungar. They were getting ready to arrest him because he'd refused to produce a way to reach his cousin.

"I have nothing to do with this," Ungar repeated. "You're incompetent. You're fools. You're the same as he is." He indicated Marquez.

An officer moved in, and Ungar struggled against the handcuffing, fought three officers, but it was Marquez who reached over and gripped the bicep he'd seen Ungar favor. Lifted him by it and a cry of pain came out of Ungar. Cuffs went on, his coat got stripped, an officer explaining they wanted to make sure they hadn't hurt him. The bandage wrapping his right bicep was exposed.

"Is that a bullet wound?" Marquez asked.

"A hunting accident," Ungar said. "A kill I haven't finished yet."

"I don't think you ever will."

"Oh, you can bet I will," he said, as they walked him toward the door.

50

Nevada held Ungar while they tried to sort out the situation with the help of the California SOU. The ranch was owned by a Marion Stuart aka Durham, and Durham couldn't answer questions, might not ever be able to. He had yet to regain consciousness and according to doctors attending him, suffered an as yet undetermined degree of brain damage due to oxygen deprivation. One doctor suggested in private to Marquez that Durham's future, if he had one, was in a vegetative state in a nursing home. He was, the doctor added, perhaps unlucky to have been rescued.

Marquez returned home, asked Bell for a week's vacation, and worked on the case against Ungar from there. Without testimony from any of those directly involved it was particularly difficult, and they had yet to obtain a warrant to search Ungar's apartment. Nothing had been found in his car or on his person.

Alvarez and Shauf also requested a week off, and for the same reason, one Marquez had yet to inform Bell of. Then a call he'd waited two days for came from Kendall. His voice was hoarse, said he'd been battling a fever.

"The knife you found in the barn was used to kill Petroni. The fingerprints on it are Ungar's, but the DA doesn't like the chain of evidence. He's got a problem with you finding it alone after we'd already made two thorough searches of the barn. He sees a defense attorney tearing into us, you on the stand." He coughed and added, "They'd come after you personally."

"That's all right."

"That's what I say too." Kendall coughed again, apologized for having a cold, then said, "But you see the problem."

"Sure, but aren't there enough other pieces?"

"The problem is Ungar will claim he didn't do the actual killing. In fact, he didn't even know what the knife was. He saw the dried blood on it, picked it up, asked Durham or Nyland, and got told it was used on a bear. With those two out of the picture he's free to say whatever he wants."

"Any luck with Troy?"

"Sticking with a story that Nyland drove him and showed him the inside of the first Quonset hut on a day when no one else was out there. He just wanted him to know where it was and what the Bearman was doing."

"Why'd he want him to know?"

"He wouldn't say. What's your guess?"

"That Troy supplied some of the bears. Yearlings. Cubs."

"That's what I thought."

"Ungar needs to stay behind bars."

"I hear you. What's going to happen in Bishop with your daughter and her grandmother?"

"They showed Lillian photos and she can't pick him out. Her memory of the whole thing is still hazy. Maria is scheduled for a lineup tomorrow."

"But he wore a mask into the house?"

"Yeah. There was some blood recovered out front but it could be argued it was contaminated, and it'll be weeks if not months before it gets analyzed. If there's enough corroborative evidence, he may argue he came inside because Lillian had tripped and hurt herself. That he never meant any harm."

"Same problem I have."

"Basically."

"What's the judge like?"

"Law-and-order type, a ball breaker, or so they tell me. The hope is he'll set a high bail, or if we're lucky, continue to hold him pending DNA and blood results."

"Can your daughter pick him out of a lineup?"

"Based on what I've heard her say, I doubt it."

"Then it's like you said, hope for a high bail. You going to be there?"

"Yeah, I've taken some vacation time and so have a couple of others on my team. I'm also going to come see you. I've got an idea I want to run by you."

"Good. There are a couple of things I want to show you, including Sophie's journal."

"Kept a journal?"

"She did. She was a lonely woman. There's a few entries with Vandemere, one that got me thinking. I'll show it to you when I see you. Listen, before we hang up, will you tell me what you're planning?"

"I'll come see you tomorrow."

After Marquez hung up with Kendall he made some coffee and worked at the picnic table out on the deck. An hour or so later he heard the front door open, leaned around, and saw Kath was home.

"I took off work early," she said, paused, "to be with you, because if you remember we were never going to let this happen to us again." She straddled the picnic bench, sunlight on her face and bright on the ghost streak of white hair that ran from near her temple. "That's all I'm going to say."

They'd been separated, come close to divorce, and found their way back, done as much as they could to put it behind them. He closed the file, rested his coffee cup on it to keep the breeze from lifting it, and went inside with Katherine, talked with her for hours. Maria was staying at a friend's house tonight, and toward dusk they made love on the throw rug in the living room. Now he lay near her, the light fading through the windows as they talked about dropping down to town and getting some dinner. She turned toward him, and he took her in his arms and held her tight. She spoke to him with her voice pressed against his chest.

"You can't catch all of these guys," she said.

Later they did go down into town and ate, then came back up and sat outside under the stars with a couple of drinks. The next morning he drove to Placerville, met with Kendall out Howell Road, then drove south. He was in the courthouse at 10:00 the following morning as Judge Faribault set bail for Ungar. A collective murmur of approval went up from Lillian's friends when the amount was $250,000, but only Marquez and the team had anticipated that Ungar would make bail that day. They knew the money he'd been making, just didn't know where he kept it. They waited outside for him. With Alvarez's help Marquez had illegally attached a GPS unit to Ungar's car, and they watched now as Ungar walked out and scanned the parking lot and the street.

"Looking for us," Marquez said. "He knows."

They could hold their breath and hope, but it was up to Ungar. He walked to his car, got in, started south on the highway out of Bishop, went almost to Lone Pine before turning around and coming back. They watched the satellite readout as he did a number of backtracking moves on his drive north on 395. It took him nearly ten hours to get back to Placerville, though a straight drive would have put him there in five.

Shortly after 9:00 P.M., Marquez made another call to Kendall. "He just pulled into Placerville," he said. "He's buying gas."

"Christ, I hope you're right."

"You ready on your end?"

"Yeah, we're good to go."

Then it looked like Marquez was wrong. Ungar got back on the highway and headed westbound. It was Alvarez who voiced the fear tightening Marquez's gut.

"Lieutenant, he could be driving to your house."

Marquez hadn't yet answered when Ungar exited the highway again. He drove into a new mini-storage complex alongside the highway. They saw him punch in numbers and then an access gate swung open. They got the number of which unit he visited, but couldn't see inside.

"We thought Petroni had a unit there," Kendall said. "Sophie was sure he had one. That's the key we were looking for up at Wright's Lake."

Ungar was in the storage unit until after midnight. Then, his headlights came on. The car swung out of the lot and back onto the highway. He continued eastbound past Placerville.

Marquez heard the electric change in Shauf's and Alvarez's voices and felt it himself. He talked to Kendall, his voice tightening with urgency as Ungar's car slowly exited at Howell Road. A quarter mile beyond Johengen's barn he pulled off and parked in the trees.

"We've got him just beyond Johengen's," Marquez said.

"We've got him in view. He's sitting in the car."

"I'm starting down Howell."

It took Marquez twenty minutes to get within a mile. Near Johengen's the road ran straighter for a third of a mile, and he pulled over before then. He killed his lights, knew where he'd leave his truck and walk. Talked to Kendall again from his cell phone, told him Shauf and Alvarez had moved in from the other direction.

"He's out of the car," Kendall said, "getting something out of his trunk."

"He'll probably cross the creek and come through the orchard."

"Half an hour ago I was freezing my ass off. Now, I feel like I'm on fire. Let's just hope he's not headed somewhere else in the woods because he's got something buried. Hold on a second." When Kendall came back on, he said, "It might have been a shovel he got out of the trunk."

Marquez, Shauf, and Alvarez crossed the creek and came up alongside the old farmhouse, seeing it all, the orchard in moonlight, trees skeletal and bone-colored. Marquez saw Ungar first, pointed him out, a dark figure moving, almost floating through the grass. The Bearman. He crossed the orchard to the barn, then disappeared around the back, and they heard boards being pried off, nails wrenching. Light shone through gaps in the siding. A ladder banged against the barn wall, scraped as it slid up to the rafters, and then light climbed the wall, shone through cracks. Along the orchard perimeter the SOU and county officers moved into position.

Ungar descended the ladder, the flashlight marking his progress. He dragged the ladder back, and the groundhog cameras Marquez and Kendall had buried recorded it all.

They heard boards pounded back into place. When his flashlight went out they waited for him to show at the corner of the barn, but after a minute he still hadn't. Marquez heard Kendall's worried "Shit, please no." There was a chance he'd leave via a different route, climb into the rows of overgrown Christmas trees or come around the front face of the barn. He might even bury it up there and create new evidentiary problems.

Then they saw him leave the corner and start through the orchard, and they let him get out in the middle before lighting him up. He took two steps, froze, and abruptly threw the bundle holding the knife he'd retrieved. Marquez's flashlight caught the knife that had killed Petroni spinning through the air. It landed near the base of a gnarled apple tree, and Ungar made one dodging move to his left, dropped to his knees, calling, "I surrender, I surrender."

"Sonofabitch," Kendall said, "sonofabitch, we've got him."

51

The next morning Marquez drove to the mini-storage with Kendall. The manager got up from his couch and clicked off the TV when he saw Kendall's badge. He walked them down and unlocked the unit Ungar rented. Inside, they found a strange scene with candles and a rug and cushions, where it looked like he sat. There were cardboard boxes they started going through, Marquez taking two, Kendall two, both slipping on gloves first. Kendall lifted a black leather wallet, showed him Jed Vandemere's face on a California driver's license, and after Marquez had studied it, dropped it into an evidence bag.

"Must have had Nyland bring him the wallet," Kendall said.

"Nyland called him Bearman. I don't think he was lying when he said he'd never met him. Same with the pair we did the buys from. They'd never seen him face-to-face. They'd pick the bear parts or bile products up somewhere remote, and then get an envelope from a bartender somewhere later."

"What have we here?" Kendall said quietly, almost to himself. He lifted an ornate wooden box, something made of teak and other hardwoods. *For jewelry,* Marquez thought, and watched him open it, heard him say, "Marquez," knew from his tone it was important.

Resting on the velvet lining in the box was a California Fish and Game badge and even after all that had happened, seeing the badge affected Marquez. It turned him quiet and he worked through more of the boxes without saying anything. Crime techs arrived and Hawse. Marquez read through a journal of Ungar's, his ramblings, what he called essays.

"He's got tapes here," Kendall said. "I'll bet he recorded his conversations with you." He added, "I don't know if I told you last night, but we found a voice changer in his car."

Marquez read Ungar's tiny script, each letter made perfectly. Pages of writing, entries of things he'd done to people who'd crossed him. There were cases, some Marquez was familiar with, one, a poacher they'd busted last year, that Ungar noted, "Lost good supplier. Need to do something about them." He read Petroni's name, notes about Petroni's patrol habits, where he liked to eat, buy coffee, drink, then the line "S successful." A short sentence fragment after it, "Same old ursus," and further into the notes and ramblings saw it again. This time it jumped out at him as a simple code for SOU. *Ursus* was Latin for bear, and Ungar used "Same old ursus" after Petroni's name to indicate he thought Petroni was SOU. He read the name Mark Ellison, and it clicked that he'd read that in Petroni's log, said so to Kendall now.

"There's more than enough here," Kendall answered. "It's over. We can build the case."

"I remember this name from Petroni's log."

"You're thinking Petroni had some dealings with this Ellison?"

Marquez held up the journal he was reading so that Kendall could see it. "There's a lot written on Petroni in here. He followed

Petroni for months, wrote notes on his habits, where he ate, what he ate, meeting Sophie, Petroni and Sophie going up to the hunting shack. He must have shadowed him. Reads like he was sure Petroni was with the SOU."

"We think Petroni told Sophie he was."

"That's what she told you?"

"Yeah, and stuck by it. Maybe he missed being undercover."

Marquez read on about Mark Ellison, things written about selling gall to Mark Ellison. He looked through the rest of the box and another that had only clothes, and then Kendall suggested they back away and let the crime techs do their work. When Marquez stepped out of the unit he turned to Kendall.

"I'm going down to talk to the manager again," he said.

In the manager's office Marquez asked to see the list of everyone who rented here. The manager was a heavyset bearded fellow, from his tattoo, former Navy man. He pulled on his beard for a moment, then turned the computer screen so Marquez could scan the names.

"Where is unit 76 on the map?" Marquez asked.

"It's around back from the one you're looking in."

"Opposite side?"

"Yep."

Marquez read the name Mark Ellison again, made sure he'd read it correctly the first time. Now he looked at the map.

"Do you ever see this Mark Ellison?"

"I can't say I remember him."

"We need to open up that unit."

With Kendall and the manager, Marquez walked down the row of storage units, all with metal roll-up doors, cinder block faces, but simple sheetrocked partition walls inside separating the units. He didn't have to tell Kendall what he was thinking. Kendall was already there.

"It would account for him taking the bribes," Marquez said. "And explain some of the things he said to me."

The manager took hold of the chain and rolled the door of the unit up, the door rattling loudly. They turned the light on and as they saw the setup, Marquez knew Mark Ellison was Bill Petroni. He'd rented the unit exactly opposite Ungar's, and the manager explained how that was possible. This whole row hadn't rented out until early summer, some units were still empty. The complex was new and still gaining traction. He kept talking but neither Marquez nor Kendall was listening, Marquez studying a couple of fiber-optic lines that fed into the wall separating Ungar's unit from this one. He looked at the recording equipment and then at what else was in the unit.

Off to one side was a stack of belongings, not a lot of them, but what Petroni owned, what he'd had to store after the divorce. There was also a small metal storage box of a type Marquez had seen on construction sites. It was new, bought at a Home Depot, the tag still on it.

"That's going to have the bribe money it and everything else that relates to the case," Marquez said. "Petroni was onto Ungar and building a case on his own."

"Why didn't he tell you?"

"He wanted to make the case on his own."

"Wanted to show you up?"

"I don't know. Maybe. But it's here, look at this. Whatever he bought will be in that box, as well. Some of the bribe money might be in there, and the rest of it he probably used to make buys."

"What was going through his head, not telling anyone?"

"I don't know, but like you found out, the other wardens called him a real loner." Marquez thought about it and then wondered something else aloud. "Maybe he told Stella. Or maybe somebody got worried that he'd told Stella."

"Ungar knew and waited to deal with him, but he didn't know about this. He didn't know Petroni had this set up. It wouldn't still be recording if he did."

They could hear the equipment working, recording the crime techs on the other side of the wall. Neither of them spoke, thinking it out, then Kendall asked, "Have you ever heard of anything like this before?"

The only thing Marquez could relate it to was the drug world, where a drug cartel would sometimes keep selling to undercover officers just to take their money, not being worried about what came later. Ungar must have felt he could control the variables. Marquez talked it out with Kendall and knew it would be hours before the construction storage box was taken in and opened.

"How are you going to do this?" Marquez asked. "So far, he's saying he's not involved, right. Even after the knife last night. He's got a story for that too, doesn't he?"

"He did last night."

"Why don't you ask him if he wants to sit down with me this afternoon?"

"Why would he?"

"To try to beat me one last time. To brag about what he had going. He's that kind of guy and he's way into bear."

"He's up for murder one."

"Read his journal. Murder doesn't mean that much to him, but he saw himself getting rich selling bile products."

It was late that afternoon that Marquez's hunch was borne out. He walked into an interview box and sat down across from Ungar, who was shackled, wrists chained down to the ring.

"You had an incredible operation going," Marquez said. "Amazing what you set up out there in Nevada."

"Are you here to flatter me into telling you something? I had nothing to do with killing anyone."

"I'm a Gamer. Let's just talk about bear."

"The detectives think I'll say something to you?"

"I don't know what they think. I know they plan to charge you with murder, but that's not what I'm here about. I'd like to know how long you've been bear farming?"

Ungar couldn't stop himself. His eyes flickered over Marquez's face, something triumphant in them. "Almost four years."

"There must have been a vet involved."

"I put in all the catheters myself."

"You're good."

Ungar opened up a little, allowed he'd get the maximum sentence for trafficking in bear, but, "I'll be out in under two years, at the most three."

"You're probably right."

"Then I'll come visit you."

"And we'll talk some more." Ungar smiled, and Marquez said, "Let's talk some more today about the operation because I'm curious, and I'm not flattering you, you really had it going on. The things you invented are impressive."

They talked about the Nevada farm. Durham got a share of the profits, had owned animal operations himself, and knew the money to be made in bear bile and galls. Durham had been a good partner. The problem had been Nyland and the woman. Those were people that Durham had hired. The trough system Ungar had invented himself. He detailed how he'd figured out the systems and buying live bears, mostly cubs. His bile product sales were growing exponentially in Vancouver, San Francisco, particularly the San Jose area, and LA—LA was by far his best market. But he wouldn't say what he'd cleared, wouldn't talk about money.

"Why did Durham get involved?"

"I told him I'd make him rich."

"Did you?" Ungar looked away. "Was Petroni on the take?"

"Five hundred a month."

"To stay out of an area?"

"And provide information."

"And then you got it back from him with sales."

That was the first thing to fluster him and he couldn't hide it.

"What are you talking about?"

"Selling to Mark Ellison."

"I don't know any Mark Ellison."

Marquez wanted to say it all now, but Kendall would confront Ungar with hard evidence, the wooden box with Petroni's badge in it when they tried to get him to confess and bargain. Killing a law enforcement officer made Ungar eligible for the death penalty, but if he helped resolve the Vandemere and Stella Petroni murders, and gave a full confession on Petroni, it was likely the county DA would let him bargain for a life sentence. Ungar was a bright guy and thinking fast. The first edge of doubt was in his eyes. As Marquez got ready to go he had to leave Ungar with something.

"In the end, Petroni beat you," Marquez said. "He outsmarted you."

"He wasn't any brighter than you."

"He didn't have to be."

Marquez cut off what Ungar said next as he closed the door.

52

Ungar didn't go down as easily as Kendall had antici-
pated. At the arraignment for Petroni's murder he pled not guilty. It
was another two weeks before he fired his lawyer and made
the deal with the prosecutor, and even then never confessed to
Stella Petroni's murder, which Kendall now believed was an effort
to frame Petroni, taking advantage of the discord in Petroni's life.
Ungar did admit to paying Nyland ten thousand dollars to kill
Vandemere because the county wouldn't make the deal without
that confession, and evidence of the payment showed in his
records. The only explanation he'd give was that Vandemere had
pried into business that wasn't his.

A week later, Marquez stopped by the Placerville mini-storage
alone. He punched in the numbers, drove through the gate and
down to the unit Petroni had rented. It was empty now. There was
really nothing to see, but for some reason he wanted to stand in

the space and try to visualize what had motivated Petroni to keep his investigation to himself, how bitter he must have been, and yet, in here, checking the recording equipment, knowing he was building a significant case. It was remarkable he hadn't revealed it to try to save himself from being suspended.

Marquez looked at the holes Petroni had drilled in the shared wall, thought about him working in here. The storage unit was similar to some the SOU had rented in the past, and very similar to a unit his and Petroni's teams had shared a decade ago. He knew, despite all the talk otherwise, Petroni had never stopped thinking of himself as an undercover wildlife officer. He must have been waiting for the moment he'd call for backup and make the bust. He must have pictured the vindication, the feeling of taking down Durham, Ungar, Nyland, Sophie, Bobby and maybe Troy, all at once.

He had a conversation now with Petroni, one in his head, a conversation with the ghost of the guy he'd known. He let Petroni know how impressed he was that he'd pulled this off and said that he wished Petroni had taken a chance on opening up to him, that they could have worked together again.

Later that week Kendall, who'd been keeping him updated, said Ungar had unraveled another piece for them. He'd been behind another murder, the unsolved prior case that had drawn Kendall into the Crystal Basin murder of Vandemere. The watch and ring found in the hunting shack were taken from the earlier victim. Ungar had placed them on the shelf in the hunting shack.

"Why?" Marquez asked.

"Not completely clear whether it was part of some elaborate notion of framing Petroni or whether he was planting evidence that later would implicate Nyland. Several times he's talked about watching Petroni have sex with Sophie up at that shack, and I get the feeling it may have been part of setting up the framing of Petroni before killing Stella."

"But he's made his deal."

"Yeah, he'd have to want to tell us more. Listen, the real reason I called was we've got files off his computer there in the storage unit that you're going to want. A lot of names and contacts. I FedExed you a package with them. You ought to get it in the next day or so. And we've finally gotten through his passwords."

"Yeah, my chief told me."

"There are more files that will help you."

There was proof now that it was Ungar who'd hacked the DFG personnel files. He'd downloaded info on everyone working for Fish and Game. They'd also learned that he was something of a financial wizard, leveraging the $412,000 he'd made selling bile products into double that in value in real estate and stocks.

After the disks arrived Marquez and the team started working down the network Ungar had built. It was like peeling an onion and they would take it slowly, figure out how to build the cases with the help of U.S. Fish and Wildlife, as several of the connections were out of state. Locally, they had a list of people who sold his bile products, and Marquez set up another sit-down with Ungar. He tried to get more information from him by bringing up a competitor Ungar had referenced in computer files and writings.

Two guards and Kendall were in the room with Ungar, one guard chewing gum until Kendall stopped him. Ungar had lost better than ten pounds, leaving his face gaunt, the lines more pronounced. He'd paled, and he rubbed his thumb and index finger together continually.

"I don't want the guards in here," Ungar said. "Not you, either," he said to Kendall, and that wasn't any problem. Ungar was chained to the ring, wasn't going anywhere. The guards and Kendall left.

"You want me to bring this guy in Vancouver down."

"I'm asking for your help," Marquez said.

"You won't stop bile products from coming here. Can't stop people from using medicine they've used a thousand years or more. It's like smoking weed. The laws aren't going to even slow it down. Your side is losing everywhere."

"Not everywhere."

"You tell your daughter hello for me."

Marquez felt his breath catch in his throat. Despite corroborative DNA results and a case that was moving toward trial, Ungar had never admitted being in Bishop. He stared back at Ungar, asked him if he was admitting to being in Bishop. Ungar didn't make another sound, and later he told Kendall he wouldn't speak with any Fish and Game officers ever again.

In early December on a bright clear morning Marquez got a sad call from Shauf, her voice breaking before she could get it out, telling him her sister had died just after dawn. The following Tuesday with the rest of the SOU he attended a service for Debbie in Folsom, where the pastor spoke about the fragile preciousness of life, how we so often are unaware of our days passing, and how aware and close to God Debbie had become in her final days. Whether that was true or not, Marquez had no idea and sat silently in the pew. He saw the children standing near their father and Shauf grief-stricken and turned inward. He said good-bye to her in the parking lot and tried to make sure she understood he'd do whatever he could for her and the family. He knew her well enough to know he'd have to come find her, and he would.

On the drive home from Folsom he stopped to see Keeler and helped him transplant several orchids in the greenhouse. Later, as they drank a beer, Keeler asked, "How are you doing?"

"In what way?"

"With what's happened."

"If Petroni and I had talked at all, he'd still be here."

"He kept it from everyone, that's a choice he made, John."

They had another beer together before he headed home.

The following Saturday he started laying out the new addition with Maria. They were down along the corner of the house when Kendall called. Marquez walked back up to the deck, scraping mud off his shoes and sitting down at the picnic table, listening as Kendall sketched more details of Stella Petroni's murder, how he was going to make a case against Ungar after all. He believed he could prove Ungar had hired Nyland.

"Am I going to see you before Ungar's trial?" Kendall asked.

"I'll give you a call."

"I still owe you a lunch."

"I'm sure I'll be back that way."

Maria yelled up at him, and he told Kendall he'd call next time he was in town, though he knew he probably wouldn't. He laid the phone on the redwood table, came down off the deck and around to where they'd built batter boards and strung line to lay out the new foundation.

"What do we do now?" she asked, and he looked at her young face and the warm enthusiastic light in her eyes.

"We tape out and mark the piers. The drill rig comes Monday."

She held an end of the tape on the mark he'd pointed to, and Marquez smiled back at her, pulled the tape, dropping a stake where the center of each pier would go, a total of six. As he pounded them in Maria sprinkled flour around the stakes. Someone had told him it was an easy way to keep track of the stakes after the drilling started and dirt got tossed around.

"Did you hear," she asked, spilling flour on the hammer and his hand, "that same black bear was down near the Golden Gate Bridge again last night. Can you believe that a bear is almost to San Francisco? Wouldn't it be funny if he walked across the bridge?"

"He probably won't do that."

"I really like it. I mean, as long as he doesn't get into our house or something."

Marquez pounded in another stake and glanced up at her, very happy that they were starting this build together.

"I mean it's really cool," she said. "I like to think of him walking around here. Do you know what I mean, Dad?"

He glanced over at her. "Yeah, I think I do."

Acknowledgments

I'd like to thank Assistant Chief Nancy Foley, Lieutenant Kathy Ponting, and Assistant Chief of the South Coast Region, Mervin Hee, of California Fish and Game. The novel wouldn't have happened without their generosity and help. Thanks also to Greg Estes, Branch Russell, Lydia McIntosh, Adrian Muller, Jennifer Semon, Tim Stokes, John Buffington, Tony Broadbent, Paul Hansen, and Andrew Livengood. Barbara Peters for turning her keen eye to the early chapters. Jay Schaefer, thoughtful and gifted editor. Philip Spitzer, agent and friend. My family, daughters Kate and Olivia, and most of all, Judy. Finishing a first novel and getting published was exhilarating. Judy, finishing this second makes me remember a morning when we hiked for hours up through a long forested slope into sunlight, and finally could see how big the mountain really was. It's been possible to undertake this difficult business of trying to launch a career writing novels because of your belief in me. There are no words adequate to thank you.